THE GREAT GAME

Stuart Slade

Dedication

*This book is respectfully dedicated to the memory of
General Thomas Powers*

Acknowledgements

*The Great Game could not have been written without the very generous
help of a large number of people who contributed their time, input and
efforts into confirming the technical details of the story. Some of these
generous souls I know personally and we discussed the conduct and
probable results of the attacks described in this novel in depth. Others I
know only via the internet as the collective membership of "The Board"
yet their communal wisdom and vast store of knowledge, freely
contributed, has been truly irreplaceable.*

*I must also express a particular debt of gratitude to my wife Josefa for
without her kind forbearance, patient support and unstintingly generous
assistance, this novel would have remained nothing more than a vague
idea floating in the back of my mind.*

Caveat

*The Great Game is a work of fiction, set in an alternate universe. All the
characters appearing in this book are fictional and any resemblance to
any person, living or dead is purely coincidental. Although some names
of historical characters appear, they do not necessarily represent the
same people we know in our reality.*

Copyright Notice

Contents

Previous Books In This Series
Available From Lulu Press

The Big One	(1947)
Anvil of Necessity	(1948)
The Great Game	(1959)

Coming Shortly

Crusade	(1965)

Chapter One
Picking Sides

Carswell AFB. Primary Operating base, 305th Bomb Group

"Oh my God, she's beautiful. I think I've just met the woman I'm going to marry."

The subject of Captain Mike Kozlowski's sudden admiration was indeed beautiful. She was by the grass, sunning herself in the flattering glow of an early morning in Texas. Elegant, stylish, sleek, beautifully curved in all the right places. In the words of the prophets, she looked like the reason the riot started. For all her grace and allure, she looked almost demure in the sunshine but anybody who looked carefully could see the appearance was only superficial. Beneath the smooth skin she was feral, passionate, savage even. Her potential might be hidden now but it was still there for anybody with the eyes to see it. Life with this one was likely to be exciting. Nobody could claim to own her, but win her trust and she'd fight tooth and claw for her partner. Cross her and she'd go for the eyes with her nails. But, for all that, or perhaps because of it, she was breathtaking. There was no doubt about it, nor about the fact that Kozlowski was in love.

"I'm a nice girl."

The voice, drifting across in the humid air into Kozlowski's mind, matched the appearance, soft lilting, laden with a level of female hormones guaranteed to cause trouble anywhere, anytime.

"Captain Kozlowski, your attention PLEASE." It was General Declan, Commander of the 305th Bomb Group speaking. Kozlowski dragged his eyes away and focused on his new commanding officer. The General caught something in his eyes. "She was speaking to you wasn't she?" Kozlowski nodded. Declan turned to his aide. "Assign aircraft 57-0656 to Captain Mike Kozlowski Junior. What you going to call her Captain?"

Kozlowski stared at the RB-58C parked opposite. The name just popped into his mind. "She's *Marisol* Sir." Was it his imagination or did *Marisol* suddenly stand a little prouder, casting supercilious glances at her sisters, the other RB-58s that had yet to find their partners and be named? Imagination of course but...

He hadn't expected the B-58s. His heart had sunk when he'd heard he was to be assigned to the 305th Bomb Group operating out of Carswell AFB. Carswell meant a Convair group and that meant either the lumbering old B-36 or the mediocre B-60. He'd checked the Blue Book out and it had the 305th listed as an RB-36 group, due for re-equipment. That latter bit figured, the B-36 was painfully obsolete now, meat on the table for any of the new fighters entering service around the world. The old bombers were vanishing from the inventory as fast as their replacements could be built and the specialized versions were following them.

The RB-36 was next to go, the chances of one doing its job, of penetrating enemy airspace, mapping defenses, drawing their fangs and surviving were slight. The all-jet version of the B-36, the B-60, had never been modified to RB configuration, a tacit admission that it lacked the performance needed for the job. Some of the strategic reconnaissance wings had Boeing RB-52s but the 305th was a Convair Group.

With the B-36s almost gone and the RB-36s on their way out, that left only the GB-36s and their little Goblin fighters and the F-85 was almost as painfully obsolete as the B-36. So Kozlowski had resigned himself to flying B-60s at best and enduring the conventional bombing missions (hauling trash in SAC slang) to which they were mostly assigned.

Then they'd all seen the new bombers, lined up along the runway where they'd been towed over from the Convair factory opposite. The fabled B-58 Hustler. Capable of flying at twice the speed of sound. The first version, the B-58A had been a pure bomber. The Navy was taking delivery of those as part of its shore-based anti-shipping units, they called it the PB5Y-1. SAC had taken delivery of a few aircraft with uprated engines as the B-58B mostly for use as trainers. The ones here were the new production version, the RB-58C. The new mainstay of SACs strategic reconnaissance wings. Or that was the plan, anyway. And General Declan was about to tell them all about that.

"Gentlemen, for the last month the 305th has been a bomb group without aircraft. For most of that time, it has also been a group largely without personnel. This morning, the first of our new aircraft have arrived and now you are the first of their crews. Later, you will have your aircraft assigned to you however, before that I would like to speak a little about our mission. As you know, the 305th Bomb Group is being redesignated as a strategic reconnaissance unit. You may think that you will be flying bombers on the penetration mission. Nothing could be further from the truth. The RB-58C is the first of SACs new generation of strategic reconnaissance aircraft, tasked with opening a gaping hole in enemy defenses through which the load-carrying B-52s and B-60s can fly, You will have to master the roles of bomber, reconnaissance, electronic warfare and fighter aircraft. Perhaps all at once. You will have to be ready to go into enemy airspace, take on the best a desperate enemy can throw at you and destroy it.

"The task facing the 305th is not a simple one. We are the lead group in the conversion schedule. Following us will the 509th and 43rd Strategic Recon Groups. Our task is not made easier by an unmistakable fact. The B-58 is a hot ship, one that demands much from its pilot. Through varying causes, mostly pilot error, we have already lost seven in the test program. The Navy are having the same experience with their PB5Ys.

"The B-58 is a pilot's aircraft but an unforgiving one, once trouble starts it will multiply with frightening speed. It is a major leap forward in technology and many of the on-board systems need refining. In a very real sense, the B-58 is a work in progress. Bringing this new aircraft into operational service means we have much hard work to do. There is a six month training course to bring us all up to speed on our new aircraft. At the end of that we will have to qualify as the first of SACs new RB-58 strategic reconnaissance groups. This is not an option."

It wasn't an option indeed, the task facing the 305th was more urgent than any of the young pilots could realize. The truth was that SAC was facing a crisis. Its whole deterrent value, the whole rationale behind its effectiveness was its invincibility. SAC was invulnerable because people believed it was. Back in 1947, that had been true, during The Big One, the B-36s had cruised effortlessly over enemy defenses. That had left an impression everybody believed to this day. But, it was an impression that was already false and growing more so every day.

Every year that had passed had seen more fighters entering service, more missiles being built that could threaten the B-36. Every year had seen the vulnerability of the B-36 increase that much more, the chances of the aircraft getting through to its target decline. The introduction of the B-60 in 1954 had slowed the trend and the arrival of the B-52 two years after that had temporarily stopped it but now it was starting again. SAC was invulnerable because everybody thought it was. If SAC went to war and started losing large numbers of bombers, as it would if things remained the way they were, that perception would end. And the consequences of that happening were dire. In a very real sense, SAC was a bluff and the chance that somebody would call that bluff was increasing steadily.

The RB-58 was an answer to that problem. There was no way that the large, subsonic B-60 and B-52 could outclass the defenses the way the B-36 had done in its prime. There was a new bomber being designed that would outperform the defenses, the B-70 Valkyrie. and would take over their role. The problem was the B-70 was suffering from serious developmental problems with the metal alloys used and with the air feed to the engines. It would be eight or ten years before it entered service in numbers. So, until the B-70 was available, an interim solution was needed. An aircraft that could suppress defenses before the bombers arrived. The RB-58 was that aircraft. And it had to work. It didn't help matters that President LeMay disliked the aircraft and refused to regard it as anything more than an interim answer. Short range was his major criticism, "Fit only for bombing Canada," had been his most memorable comment. LeMay regarded a B-70 derivative, the RS-70, as the ultimate strategic reconnaissance aircraft but that lay even further in the future than its bomber sibling. So, despite his dislike, the RB-58 was it, for years to come.

"Gentlemen, we have much to learn indeed. We have twelve of our new aircraft here with more arriving over the next few days. The first eleven designated crews may go to the flight line and find their aircraft. Captain Kozlowski, introduce yourself to your new lady friend." That brought a laugh from the assembled pilots, most of whom were jealous of the fact that Kozlowski had already found his partner. Still, General Declan though, being the son of the Hero of Ploesti had its penalties as well as its privileges – and the kid had the good sense not to trade too heavily on the prestige the Kozlowski name carried in SAC.

How long this ceremony would continue was an open guess. The bean-counters and efficiency experts were already claiming that it made no sense to assign an aircraft to a specific pilot, that it would be more effective for the crews to take the first available aircraft on the flightline. They might be right, but it wouldn't happen in his group on his watch. And it wouldn't happen as long as General Dedmon commanded SAC. The parade broke up, one group moving towards the barracks and the O-club, a smaller group walking towards the aircraft parked on the flight line. Ahead of them, a single figure had given up the pretence at patience and was running towards *Marisol*.

President's Residence, New Delhi, India

"Her Excellency, the Ambassador-Plenipotentiary From The Kingdom of Thailand"

Sir Martyn Sharpe beamed with genuine pleasure. "Ambassador, it is good to see you again. Please take a seat. May I offer you a drink? We have some Johnny Walker Blue Label you may enjoy."

Sir Martyn poured a drink for his guest. He'd known the Ambassador for twelve years, ones that had treated her very kindly. There were a few laughter lines around the mouth, a few crows feet at the corners of the eyes, calluses on her trigger finger, but she could still be mistaken for a woman a decade or more younger. Yet in those years she had been at the center of the political maneuvering that had lead to the formation of the Triple Alliance and was now in the middle of the political maneuvering that accompanied the quiet battle for who dominated that alliance.

Perhaps battle was the wrong word, jockeying for position would be better. The three-cornered alliance between India, Australia and ASEAN was too important to be endangered by serious disagreement. There had been problems certainly, especially with Indonesia. The old Dutch East Indies had broken up. The core had remained a Moslem state but the easternmost islands around Timor, the Christian dominated ones, had become an Australian protectorate, a part of Australia's remarkable maritime 'empire'. Bali and a couple of smaller Hindu-dominated islands had become Indian protectorates. The diplomatic furore that had accompanied that split had strained the Triple Alliance badly.

Now, Sir Martyn thought it was time to rebuild the Triple Alliance and strengthen it. What was past was past and what was done was done. The future was ever more important. With the de-facto merger of Japan and China (some people were already calling it Chipan) settling down and becoming stronger, the dangers it presented made the penalties resulting from losing an argument within the Triple Alliance comparatively inconsequential.

The key was ASEAN, the Association of South East Asian Nations, another new creation and one for which the Ambassador had been largely responsible. The US had given the Philippines its independence in 1946 as it had promised and Indonesia had established its freedom from colonial rule in 1947, after The Big One. Thailand had been quick to form a regional grouping that expanded to include Malaya and equally quick to ensure its unobtrusive but absolute domination of that group. It was the standard pattern of the late 1940s and early 1950s, Thailand was using its strong economy and moral position as the one country in the area that had never been colonized to establish financial and political leadership. Combined with the prestige it had won by its defeat of France in 1940, it gave the country political punch far above its apparent weight. In effect, India, Australia and Thailand were equal partners in the Triple Alliance and their maneuverings had a certain good humor about them.

"To what do I owe the pleasure of this visit Madam?"

"Firstly, our new Prime Minister, General Sarit, wishes me to pay his respects to you and to the President. He also wishes me to assure you that our new government continues to hold the Indian Government in the highest regard and places the greatest importance on continuing – indeed strengthening - the Triple Alliance. And having dealt with the formalities, let us get down to business. We have a problem. Masanobu Tsuji is on the move again."

Sir Martyn cursed to himself. Colonel Masanobu Tsuji had caused serious trouble in the past and his machinations had been an unwanted complication in the days when India was trying to establish itself as an independent state. The Ambassador had been most helpful then and her presence here now suggested that the problems were genuine. "Allow me to refresh your glass Madam, I would like to call Sir Eric in to share this meeting if you have no objection?"

"None at all. This is indeed very fine Scotch."

Sir Eric entered almost as soon as Sir Martyn buzzed, he must have been waiting in the ante-room. He eyed the whisky bottle rather plaintively as he sat down.

"As you know, the integration of Japan and China is taking place with remarkable speed. It has happened before of course, China is successfully invaded, the invaders set up a new government and in a few short years are absorbed by the Chinese. It happened with the Mongols and the Manchus and now it happens with the Japanese. The supreme ruler of China may be the Japanese Emperor, but he rules by way of a Chinese communist government.

"Yet, the basic problem that Japan and China both face is the same. Shortage of raw materials. Oh China has them, in limited amounts at least, but recovering them and utilizing them is a task that requires investment and technology. They have neither. To secure easily accessible supplies they have two choices. One is to strike north against Russia. As you know, Russia is still weak after the Second World War and is still recovering the territory held by the German warlords. Their Siberian Provinces are plums for the picking, except for one thing. The Russians are American allies and an attack on them means Strategic Air Command will pay the attackers a call. The other option is to strike south. Against us. In this case us means both my country and against the Triple Alliance as a whole."

"But, Madam Ambassador, that would also surely bring down the Wrath of SAC upon their heads. The Americans have a simple view on the world. They like it peaceful. If it is not peaceful, they will make it so. I am told Germany is an exceptionally peaceful country these days."

"Indeed so. But the Chinese-Japanese do have an option." The Ambassador leaned forward and tapped Sir Martyn's map with a fingernail. "Here."

Sir Martyn looked at where her finger was pointing and suddenly grew very thoughtful. Sir Eric looked and winced.

"Precisely Sir Eric. Burma. Its status is, shall we say, ambiguous. Burma is a protectorate of India but its internal condition leaves much to be desired. Indeed, it could be described as anarchic. The central government holds authority but outside its remit, warlordism and banditry run rampant.

"I have information that Masanobu Tsuji is in Burma now, attempting to organize an insurgency against the existing government. If that was to succeed and detach Burma from India, then Burma could become -- re-aligned shall we say -- with the China/Japan block. That would drive a wedge right through the center of the Triple Alliance. It would give my country a very severe defensive problem, we would have hostile borders all around us. And for some reason the Japanese hold a grudge against us."

"Perhaps that has something to do with a destroyed infantry division and some foiled plans Madam. I do not think Colonel Tsuji enjoyed the experience of being outgeneraled so comprehensively. Especially by one so charming as your good self. The 1949 border incident was just icing on that particular cake."

The Ambassador nodded to accept the compliment. "Once Burma has fallen into the China/Japan sphere of influence, it will open many future possibilities for them. They could more against yourselves, exploiting the Moslem problem. Or against us, doing the same. Or against Malaysia and Indonesia with the same object in view. On the other hand, if Masanobu Tsuji's machinations were to fail, our own position would be consolidated and greatly strengthened."

"Madam Ambassador, your words and news of Colonel Tsuji's activities cause me much concern. I appreciate you bringing them to us. What are your thoughts on future actions?"

"Burma is an Indian protectorate, technically my country and its armed forces have no authority there. However, we are allies and it would be of great mutual benefit if we put some of our people in there to find out more on what is happening. We can do that better than you, there are close similarities between ourselves and out Burmese neighbors. Also, we have worrying information that Masanobu Tsuji may be attempting to infiltrate people into our Northern provinces from Burma. Obviously we would wish to carry out hot pursuit against such infiltrators. We should also speak to the Americans on this. Perhaps you could take this issue up with them?"

Sir Martyn nodded. The concept of Chipan linking up with the growing militancy of the Moslem states was disturbing. India already had problems with Moslem separatists in the North, determined to split away and form their own Pakistan. They'd launched attacks on the Hindus and Sikhs up there and the victims had retaliated in kind. The North splitting away wasn't going to happen, but the idea offered ground for external agitators to build on. At the moment infiltration from Chipan into India was hard, geography saw to that. But if Burma fell into the wrong hands, that defense would go away.

The Ambassador leaned back in her seat. The meeting had gone well. Masanobu Tsuji was a real threat and his apparent activity in Burma was a very real concern. And if dealing with that concern should result in Burma becoming detached from India and joining ASEAN, well, so much the better. There was always the question of Japanese-occupied Indo-China. Now that was a prize worth a little effort.

Carswell AFB. Primary Operating base, 305th Bomb Group

Captain Kozlowski made it to the top of the steps leading up beside *Marisol*. His two crew members Lieutenants Eddie Korrina and Xavier Dravar had caught him up and were at his heels all the way up. Korrina was the navigator/bombardier, he would occupy the seat behind Kozlowski, Dravar was the Defense Systems Operator and sat in the rear. They'd all assumed that the rest of the crew would be joining them at Carswell, well that was obviously wrong. They were it.

They were edging each other around as they looked into the crew stations. Each compartment had a separate canopy hinged at the rear for entry and exit. The compartmentalization prevented direct vision or physical contact between crewmembers during flight. The pilot had a windshield with six adjacent panels, plus one panel on each side of the canopy. This afforded excellent outside vision, and the pilot could see parts of the exterior of the aircraft as well as the engine nacelle inlets. The navigator/bombardier and the DSO only had small side windows. That solved another mystery, they'd all been measured at flight school and the largest had been washed out, sent to the B-52 and B-60 units. Now, they could see why. The RB-58C was cramped.

"Mind out sirs, the paint is fresh." Their Crew Chief's warning was timely. His people had already painted the Kozlowski's name under the pilot's canopy and were getting stencils out for the other two.

"Chief Gibson, who does the nose art around here?"

"That'll be Murray sir. He'll see you right. Twenty bucks be OK sir? Hey, Murray, get up here. Captain Kozlowski wants his nose art. Sir, *Marisol* is being towed into the hangar for her post-delivery checks first so he'll get straight on with it. There are a lot of classroom sessions before you need to fly her so she'll be ready for you." The Chief broke off as there was a clatter on the metal stairs. "You took your time Murray. Now listen to the Captain."

"Her name is *Marisol* Murray, can you do us a Spanish-looking lady?"

"Sure sir Let me think a little." Airman Murray got out a pad and soft pencils and started to sketch. After a couple of minutes, he frowned, tore off the leaf and started again. Meanwhile, Dravar was looking into his crew station at the rear of the flight deck. He had the defensive electronic countermeasures system to look after, an ALR-12 radar warner and an ALQ-16 radar repeater jammer that generated and transmitted deceptive angle and range information. As a last-ditch line of defense was the ALE-16 chaff dispensing system installed in each upper main gear fairing, with chaff being ejected through mechanically-actuated slots in the tops of each wing fairing. But, best of all, Dravar had the aircraft's only cannon, an M-61 20 millimeter gatling gun.

Ahead of him, Korrina was trying to make sense of the array of equipment in his position. It was dominated by the big display for the ASG-18 multi-mode radar. Using it, he could designate targets for the big GAR-9 missiles. Nuclear-tipped air-to-air missiles, they would give intercepting fighters something to think about. Then there were GAM-83B air to surface missiles, also nuclear-tipped, for eliminating surface to air missile positions. The nuclear missiles were held in the big belly pod. The upper half held fuel, the lower half, racks for eight primary and four secondary missiles. The primaries were the nuclear missiles of course, the mix of GAR-9 and GAM-83B could be varied as needed. The four secondary missiles were GAR-8 Sidewinders, if they ever needed those, things would be going wrong.

Then, outside the pod were shoulder mountings for ASM-10s, semi-recessed into the fuselage. That was another new system – a missile that homed in on the radar emissions of an enemy search or fire control site. The Navy had been developing this one and SAC had bought in on the concept. It had been part of a deal; the Navy had got the early B-58s, SAC had got the ASM-10 and some other missile programs the Navy was working on.

"What do you think of this sir?" Murray was holding his sketch pad out with a slightly nervous expression on his face. It was a picture of an obviously Hispanic woman, masses of curled black hair falling over her shoulders, with strongly arched eyebrows and prominent lips. A simple head-and shoulders picture, the face very slightly turned away. An expression of mixed affection and defiance in the eyes. The neckline was a simple white top.

"I was going to do the usual Esquire or Playboy cheesecake sir, that's what people mostly ask for. Tell you the truth sir we have stencils for those, its like painting by numbers. I started that but it seemed wrong. *Marisol* is special somehow sir, she deserves better. She's a lady sir, so I did this."

"Its beautiful Airman, thank you. Here." Kozlowski peeled off a twenty from his fold and gave it to Murray. Then, his attention returned to his new cockpit.

Behind him Gibson and Murray grinned at each other. Dumbcluck pilots fell for it every time. By the time they'd finished they would take this one for at least a fifty. As long as he didn't look too closely at the publicity shots of Jane Russell in The Outlaw…….

Life, Phong Nguyen thought, could not get much better than this. Sitting in the shade, drinking rice beer and eating some meatball soup. Flirting with the girls too, even though the Thai farm girls were a bit heavier-set than the Vietnamese women he had grown up with. But then, Thai girls and their families hadn't been robbed blind by the French for almost a century. Nor did they have to endure the Japanese who now occupied Vietnam and made the French look like saints.

The families here considered themselves to be poor and, Nguyen supposed, by international standards they were. Back-breakingly-poor. Even so, the villagers Nguyen had left behind in Vietnam could teach them something about poverty. Here, even if food was sometimes short, nobody starved. Here, the Government, such as it was up here, did try to help. Some aid with crops, some advice on fertilizer. But not too much for "Government ends at the Village Gates." The village ruled itself by way of its local headman. Even the local government, the Tambon, was a far-off thing. It collected the taxes, not too much and when times were really bad it "forgot" about them. When there was a disaster, it helped out, a little. The national government, far away in Bangkok, was even more remote. The villagers here had heard about it but that was all. They didn't care about the government and the government didn't care about them. That was fine for both sides. Benign neglect suited everybody.

But today was a little special, it was a year since Phong Nguyen had been sent to the village and this party was in his honor. Actually the village had decided it wanted to have a party and the anniversary was a convenient excuse. The girls had carefully put aside clean dresses to wear, the men had brewed up some rice beer and the loser in the cockfight the night before was now a primary ingredient in a chicken curry. Nguyen broke wind, winning grins of approval from the men around the beer jugs and refilled his cup. He really had to consider marrying one of the girls and settling down. His plan had always been to go back home when the French and Japanese were driven out but he was settling in here. He'd even been....

There was a stir of interest from the group around him. Two strangers were walking up the long path through the fields, towards the gates. Guarded interest, strangers could mean trouble. It had taken Nguyen six months to live down the title of "The Stranger" and that was with a letter from the King to the headman to help him. The government may be far away and disregarded but the King was loved, revered and unequivocally respected.

Strangers might just be passers though, on there way from there to over-there but they might mean trouble. A couple of years ago there had been trouble with strangers, a couple had come, offering well-paid jobs for the younger girls in "the city". Now, every so often girls did go and work in "the city" for a year or so and came back with some colorful stories and a lot of money. But the ones that went with the strangers had never been seen again. So strangers needed watching. But hospitality demanded they be welcomed, offered food, shade and drink. In exchange, some news of the outside world? A few good stories to entertain the listeners?

So the strangers were welcomed in, offered some rice beer and soup and seats in the shade. And they started to report the news of the outside world, some as far away as the central provinces and south of the country. Now, there was a legendary place, people down there didn't follow the teachings of the Wise Lord Buddha and didn't even eat pork. The strangers told stories of the riches of Bangkok, how the merchants there bought rice and teak from the peasants for a small proportion of their value and resold them at immense profits. How they had vast houses and kept slaves to satisfy their every desire. How the local Tambons collaborated with them and worked for the rich. How the King was the worst oppressor of them all, sucking the life out of the country to feed his own selfish pleasures. How the Army was used to kill any who opposed the rich. One of the strangers told how his sister had refused to "co-operate" with an Army officer. In revenge the officer had her raped to death then cut off her breasts and hung them from a tree.

But there was hope, the strangers said. A group of patriots were working to oppose the tyranny of the city and the rich. To take the country back for the Asian people who lived with it and throw off the shackles imposed by the evil Europeans and their

Triple Alliance. That was the real root of all evil, the strangers said, the Europeans and the Asian traitors who sold their countries out to them. If they were cast out and Asians stood together, then freedom and wealth would be for everybody.

Phong Nguyen listened to the speeches and stories with great interest. A generous two out of ten, he thought, if these fools had been his in the Old Days. And a really stern session before the self-criticism committee. They'd done everything wrong. They'd talked instead of listening. They'd poured out their propaganda without first learning what issues were really concerning the villagers. Who here cared if the merchants in the city were wealthy? They probably deserved it from accumulating merit in previous lives. And if they abused their good fortune in this life, woe and misfortune would be theirs in their next. And that ridiculous story about the army officer! There wasn't a girl in this or any other village who wouldn't "co-operate" if it meant a chance at catching a rich and influential husband.

No, the strangers, Nguyen stopped and corrected himself, the cadres for that is what they obviously were should have told harmless, believable stories while listening to what the villagers complained about. They should have told funny stories that made people laugh, about how foolish administrators got tricked by wise peasants, how rich arrogant people got cut down to size by shrewd workers. Then, when they came back, they could have stories that built on and amplified the real grievances the villagers had. Stories that people would have believed because the earlier ones had been true.

But, no, they'd ruined it and they'd been too self-absorbed to even notice how the atmosphere around them had changed. Nguyen had been worried when the strangers had attacked the King, that was a really good way to start something ugly, but the villagers had held their tempers. If the strangers had known their business, they would have praised the King but sadly added that sometimes his advisors mislead him. Whoever had trained these two had done so very badly. They'd read the books and read the words but they hadn't understood them. They'd read the theories of Mao but hadn't absorbed the realities and wisdom beneath them. That sounded like the Japanese.

Eventually, the two cadres left, probably to repeat their lamentable performance at the next village. "What should we do Khun Phong?" The village headman was now showing his worry and anger. It was happening again, strangers meant trouble.

"We should finish our party and forget those boring, ill-mannered barbarians who would spoil it. But first we should report their arrival here to the Tambon." That brought nods from everybody. Making a report would do no harm and if the other villages reported and they did not, questions might be asked. "And we should keep a watch out. Strangers mean trouble"

Again everybody nodded. Nguyen was pleased that he was accepted now, these were good people and he owed them. They'd taken him in even though there were centuries of rivalry between Thais and Vietnamese. Nguyen had tried to escape from Vietnam with his family when the Japanese occupation force had started to grind down hard. They'd fled through the jungle south and east, hoping to cross the Mekong and find refuge. But it was hard trip and evading the Japanese patrols was harder. His father and mother were suffering badly from lack of food and exhaustion. They were trying to persuade the others to leave them behind when soldiers found them.

At first Nguyen had thought they were Japanese and had almost cried with despair but they had green uniforms, not khaki and carried short, stubby rifles with long curved magazines, Russian-made AK-47s not the Arisakas the Japanese used. They were Thai troops, sent in to find escaping refugees and bring them to safety. They'd brought Nguyen's family out, treated their wounds and taken them to a refugee camp where they had been given food and shelter. Then, Nguyen had been interviewed by some Thai soldiers. When they'd found out who he was and what training he'd had, they were replaced by much more senior people, who had talked with him long into the night. Friendly talk with good beer and good food.

Then, one day, he and his family had been taken to a derelict farm in Cambodia. In the part the Thais called "the recovered provinces". Their guide had told them that French policies had caused the rural population to fall and many such farms were abandoned. But they were on good land, rich land. The farm could support a family that worked hard – and everybody knew the Vietnamese could work hard. If Nguyen's family wanted this farm, they could have it. They would have to stand on their own feet but they could work it and improve it. One day, when Vietnam was free again, they could chose, stay here or go back to their own farm in Vietnam. Do the former and they could keep the farm, choose to go back and the Government would pay them for the improvements they had made and give it to other refugees who needed a start. Then the guide had asked Phong Nguyen, "would you do something for us?"

"What?" he'd asked. The guide had explained the need for those with certain special skills to go to villages along the Burmese border, to help them defend themselves. Nguyen had those skills, would he go? The guide had hastily explained, this was not connected with the farm, his family could have that whether he decided to go or not. But his help was needed.

There hadn't been a question really, he couldn't say no. If the request had been a price for the farm he might have, but the farm had been a gift. One that had put him in a debt of honor, and such debts must be paid. So his family settled into the farm and started to rebuild it. His brothers and their wives put up a new house, other family members started to clear the land and plant crops. A European with a strange accent came one day and brought them a male buffalo and two females. 'A present from Oz' he'd described them. Oz, they'd found out, was Australia. A country far away, but one that was a good friend. Phong Nguyen had stayed for a few weeks, seen the start of the derelict farm getting back on its feet and then left for his new village. And that was how Phong Nguyen, once a Senior Political Cadre in the Viet Minh and a personal student of the great Vo Nguyen Giap, had become a chicken farmer in Ban Rom Phuoc and commander of the village's Tahan Pran militia unit.

Captain's Bridge, INS Hood, Mumbai

Captain Jim Ladone was proud of his ship. Old, she might be, and certainly she'd seen better days, but she was still *The*

Mighty 'Ood, once the pride of the Royal Navy and now flagship of the Indian Navy. For a ship forty years old, she wasn't in that bad condition. After the Great Escape back in 1942, she'd found her way to Singapore and then she'd been refitted and modernized. New anti-aircraft guns, radar, and a desperately needed machinery rebuild. Yet she still looked like the ship that had been the showpiece of the Royal Navy in the 1930s.

Even so, he knew her day was done. This was her last commission, even in the reduced role of training ship. Soon, she would be withdrawn from service and sent to the breakers like *Repulse* and *Renown* before her. There was little room for battleships in today's world and the crew needed to run *Hood* were assigned to the two ex-American Essex class carriers that had just been purchased.

Carriers ruled the sea now, but they didn't look the part. There, *Hood* still had them, her beautiful lines unsullied by the modernization work on her. But she wouldn't last ten minutes against air attack and Ladone knew it. Nor, in truth, was she really capable of taking on a Second World War battleship. Any of the American battleships could deal with her let alone the Japanese monsters. Ah well, to the task at hand. It was the annual Midshipmen's training cruise. Across the Pacific to Australia, port visits to Melbourne and Sydney, then over to San Diego and San Francisco, back across the Pacific to Pearl Harbor in Hawaii. Port visit to Thailand and then back home and the scrap yard.

India's burgeoning heavy industries needed the scrap steel so *The Mighty 'Ood* would have to go. Ladone ran his eyes down the manifest. Full load of 15 inch ammunition for his guns, they didn't really need that but a battleship without ammunition wasn't a real ship any more. Anyway, he had the last 15 inch guns in the world, might as well have some practice with them before they were silenced forever.

A world without battleships, that was something he'd never thought he'd see. When he'd joined the Royal Navy back in the 1920s, the lines of battleships stretched as far as the eye could see. Now they were all gone. The four Japanese Yamato class battleships, and four more Roma class in Italy, were the only ones other than *Hood* left in commission now. All the others had gone, the American Iowas were rusting in the reserve fleet, the rest were either museums or scrapped. The French ships scuttled in port, the German ships blasted out of the water at the Battle of the Orkneys.

That was a question that got asked at staff colleges these days – did the way the Americans destroyed the German fleet at the Orkneys act as an early indicator of the way they would later destroy Germany? Ladone shuddered slightly, the thought of The Big One made his skin crawl. An entire nation, wiped from the map. Much of the world looked on the Americans now as if they were a pack of savage guard dogs; one was grateful for their existence and the protection they provided but one didn't want to have them in the living room.

So, once *Hood* had finished fuelling and taking on supplies, she would be off on her last cruise. Then, Ladone would be going on to his next posting. A promotion and command of a cruiser squadron. Also ex-British ships, also getting old. One day, one day soon, India would be building her own major warships, her own cruisers and carriers.

Destroyers and submarines she was building already and impressive ships they were. Two of the destroyers were accompanying the Hood on this cruise. Big ships, well-found and mostly Indian-equipped. Eight 4.5 inch guns, in the new Mark VI twin mountings from Australia, and ten torpedo tubes. The torpedoes were weight and space holders, there was a new guided anti-ship missile being developed to replace them but it was a painfully long time coming. The catch was the new ships mostly had all-Indian crews, so opportunities for the British expatriates there were limited.

Still, in retrospect things had worked out well for India. What could have been a sudden and disastrous charge into independence had been slower and allowed an orderly transfer. Fortune had smiled as well, a few people who could have caused trouble had suffered accidents or died from natural causes at opportune moments. To stay with India had been the right decision, Ladone thought. Britain had only a tiny navy, the shattered countries of Europe had taken years to recover from the

Second World War and the Great Famine. Europe was inconsequential in the great scheme of things, having been the cockpit of world affairs for centuries, it was sliding into quiet obscurity as a backwater. And, given the hammering they had taken over the last twenty years, who could blame them? By staying in India, he had a good career, a great ship to command and a family a man should be proud of at home. Yes, he had made the right decision.

Flag Bridge, HIJMS Musashi, Kagoshima Bay, Japan.

Admiral Soriva snorted and tossed his readiness report file onto his desk. A battleship division! Who had heard of such a thing in the modern age? What was worse, the Imperial Navy had two of them. *Yamato* and *Musashi* in Division One. *Shinano* and *Kwanto* in Division Two. So they had the largest guns in the world and what was the importance of that? There were nuclear rounds for the guns in the magazines and who believed these ships would live long enough to get to use them? They'd be blown out of the water by airstrikes long before that.

The Triple Alliance had six aircraft carriers. Two Essex class the Indian Navy had bought from the Americans, the two the Australians had bought and two old British carriers the Australians had inherited from the Royal Navy. The Imperial Navy had twelve carriers but they carried fewer aircraft each than the Essex class. Still, if they could find a way of engaging the Indian and Australians separately, then things would go well.

Splitting apart the Triple Alliance. That was the primary target. It had to be. It was growing stronger all the time. Meanwhile, the China Incident was over but the Japanese Army was learning a lesson it should have considered earlier. Conquering China was one thing, ruling it was quite another. Simply ruling a country that big required a huge commitment of forces, and that was draining the resources of Japan.

The obvious answer was to recruit Chinese to enforce Japanese rule in China, but that had its own dangers. It seemed as if the Japanese who recruited the Chinese forces, themselves became more and more Chinese each year. Some of the Army officers in China had started quoting one of the Chinese warlords who had been hunted down and killed over the years. The warlord had written a little red book or something like that. It contained a few trite clichés and some mindless platitudes that were being quoted as if they were actually intelligent. Soriva shuddered. Who needed a little red book when Japan had Bushido?

And the China Incident was still draining Japan. That's why the Navy was in such poor shape. Powerful certainly, the second most powerful navy in the world, but there was a long gap between its capability and that of the first. The US Pacific fleet alone had 12 of their large CVBs with four even larger carriers coming. That didn't include the Essex class that were left, they were mostly in the Atlantic fleet now. And the Americans made no secret of their policy – if they went to war, nuclear weapons would be their first resort, not their last.

Anybody who looked at their forces could see they weren't joking. Over the last five years they'd completely re-organized their army into a new structure based around something they called the Pentomic Division. The Japanese Army people had laughed at it, called it small and weak and helpless. Pointed out how its five battlegroups were too small to fight on their own and the span of command too big for proper control. They'd spoken of how a Japanese division would crush a Pentomic with its superior will and dedication.

They'd missed what was staring them in the face. The Pentomic Division was structured to fight with nuclear weapons, so much so that it could *only* fight with nuclear weapons. And that meant that anybody who attacked a Pentomic Division would be struck by a nuclear counter-attack. One that would leave the country looking like Germany. Pentomic Divisions were a challenge. If one was in front of you, it was time to ask whether what one hoped to gain from a war was worth the total destruction of your country.

No, challenging the Americans was an act of insanity. Perhaps in 1940 or 1941 they might have managed it but not now. They could hurt America, there were submarines off the West Coast now with nuclear-tipped Ohkas, rocket powered and flown by brave volunteers who were the elite of the Japanese Navy. They could take out California's coastal cities. Perhaps. But the cost would be the annihilation of Japan and everybody in the Government knew it. Japan had to bide its time, absorb China and break up the Triple Alliance. One day, if that all went well, they could build up enough power to surpass America's overwhelming might. One day.

But now, he had a different task. The Army's God Of Operations, Colonel Masanobu Tsuji, had come up with a scheme to break up the Triple Alliance. He was one of those who had been entranced by the theories of that late and unlamented warlord. Quoted them all the time. He was proposing an operation to subvert Burma, to start an insurgency there and eliminate the government. The one he installed would demand "protection" and the Navy would put in a Special Naval Landing Force "to maintain order" and cover it with the guns of Soriva's two battleships. The threat of nuclear shells from their 18 inch guns would prevent the coup from being contested.

Once Burma was taken, Thailand could be isolated and destroyed, thus avenging the Army's defeat in 1949. Thailand was the economic bridge that linked the Triple Alliance and kept it together. Its destruction would leave the "Triple Alliance" two geographically isolated limbs that could be picked off at will.

That was the theory anyway. Like all the Army's plans it assumed the enemy were going to do just what the Army expected. Admiral Soriva was seaman enough to know that things never went according to plan. Still, that was in the lap of the gods. Now, he had to get his battleships ready for sea. There was an amphibious warfare group a carrier covering force, and a replenishment group as well. All of them parts of moving a battle fleet around. And it had to be done without annoying the Americans. The Army really had no idea what was involved in.

Chapter Two
Kick-Off

Road from Thafa to Houayxay, Laos

Colonel Toshimitsu Takatsu threw the papers across the back seat of his car. The fools were going to destroy everything, they seemed to have some sort of death wish. They would throw away everything Japan had spent two decades and millions of lives building, destroy it out of some blind hatred of everything European. These orders were perfect examples. Pointing out that other provinces were economizing on resources by taking comfort women for the Japanese garrison from the local population instead of importing them from Korea. Instructing other provinces to do the same. Were they determined to start a civil war – again? After just bringing one of them to an end? Taking women and forcing them to service the garrison would start one nicely.

If other things didn't first. Taxes for example. Other provinces were raising large sums for the Japanese treasury by squeezing the peasants until their bones squeaked. Oh, the tax rates weren't bad in themselves – but they were when the authorities demanded payment four, five or six years in advance. The peasant farmers were doing what they always did, they hid their crops and hid their livestock. Or, if that failed, they left.

By learning to defy the authorities in small ways, they were also learning to defy it in larger ones. Of course, what was happening up North was even worse. The idea had seemed so sensible. Instead of having the peasants in large numbers of small farms, each owned by a single family, consolidate them into large units run by the state. Much more efficient, it should increase production greatly. So why were the peasants resisting so hard? Last time Takatsu had heard, the death toll up there had reached over 150,000. And resistance was still continuing. Madness.

The local leader they had running things up there didn't help either. Nguyen Tat Thanh. A small-minded, stupid functionary with a thirst for personal glory and a total lack of moral backbone. He'd been a faithful servant of Stalin's communists and, when Russia had abandoned communism, transferred his allegiance to a communist warlord called Mao. When he'd been killed, Nguyen Tat Thanh had transferred his allegiance to the Japanese. Now he pranced around in Hanoi, wearing a Japanese uniform and proposing these mad ideas on how to reorganize the country. Poisonous insects like that were going to destroy everything. Bushido was supposed to stand for honor and virtue and moral courage, not fooling around with farms and abducting peasant girls.

He was doing things differently. He'd cut the taxes down to a level the peasants could live with. He'd thrown the "recruiters" out of the villages and towns and told them he'd slit their bellies if they showed their faces in his province again. Japanese soldiers who abused local people found themselves in deep trouble, assigned to the dirtiest, most degrading tasks, those who treated the locals fairly and honestly were promoted and honored. A sergeant caught extorting money from local merchants had been executed in public. The local population would never love the Japanese troops, but they didn't oppose them. Even though he was taxing them less as a proportion of their crops, he was bringing in more revenue. Why couldn't others do the same?

Because they were foolish and dishonest and corrupt. That was the truth of it. Because the Japanese Army wasn't what it had been and it had deserted the true traditions of Bushido. All the provincial governors cared about was extorting bribes, assembling a harem and scoring points with the high-ups so they could be assigned to new provinces with more bribes, more women, and more chances of advancement. They didn't care about their duty any more and weren't interested in advancing the cause of Imperial Rule. Instead, they looked only to themselves and their own ambitions. They had become Mandarins, not representatives of His Imperial Highness and were driving the local population to mutiny.

There was enough trouble brewing as it was. Oh, not in his province, the trouble hadn't spread here yet. There wasn't enough discontent to cause trouble and wouldn't be. Not as long as he could keep the Japanese rule as light as he could. But in other provinces, trouble was starting. Japanese soldiers would go out alone and not return, Or would be found dead, stabbed in brothels or strangled in back-alleys. Couldn't his brother officers see that abusing and exploiting the local population could only cause such things? But, even in this province, Takatsu made certain he had an escort whenever he traveled. There was an armored car in front and a truck with an infantry squad behind. Besides, he didn't travel outside his town that often, the roads weren't good enough, mostly just dirt tracks. He'd heard that Thailand was building blacktop roads near the border, well, more fool them. Spending money on roads that could be better spent on upgrading their army. Japan had scores to settle with Thailand.

The explosion tore all four back wheels off the armored car and sent the front half, complete with turret, bouncing across the road. All Takatsu could see was the billowing cloud of red dust boiling upwards with dark shadows inside. His car swerved to a halt as his driver avoided the gaping crater where the armored car had been. Takatsu was working on instinct, he was already bailing out of the back of his car when the truck behind slammed into it.

The crunching impact spun both vehicles around, throwing some of the infantrymen from the back. The rest started to jump out over the sides, the first dropping as a light crackle of rifle and machinegun fire started. Then there was the screaming sound of rockets. Three RPG-2s hit Takatsu's car turning it into a fireball. The Japanese infantry were seeking cover as machinegun bullets stitched into their truck. Some dived into the ditch beside the road, Takatsu screamed "No" but it was too late, a directional mine exploded and spewed metal fragments down the axis of the ditch. What seemed to be cover was really a deathtrap.

The survivors were firing back now, their rifles cracking as they sought out targets. It was ironic, the Japanese Army had converted from 6.5 millimeter to 7.7 millimeter rifle ammunition in 1939 and, less that a decade later, converted back again when the Japanese Army had finally adopted a self-loading rifle. Now his troops, or what was left of them were firing but Takatsu couldn't tell the difference between them and the ambushers. Both seemed the same, were the ambushers Japanese?

Whoever they were, they'd wiped his command out. The armored car crew were dead and their vehicle destroyed, not just destroyed but disintegrated. His driver was dead, he'd never made it out of Takatsu's staff car. Of the twelve infantrymen and the driver in the truck, some were around its wreckage, more blown to pieces in the ditch. Only three were left alive and even as he watched, one of them was killed. Takatsu drew his pistol, racked the mechanism and cursed as it went off. The Type 94 pistol had a design fault that made accidental discharges all too frequent. One light tap on the sear was all it took. Takatsu threw it away, absently noting that it had discharged again when it hit the road. Then he picked up one of the infantry rifles, previous owner having no further use for same. The Japanese Army was proud of its new battle rifle but in truth it was just a copy of the Russian SKS chambered for 6.5 millimeter and modified to give selective fire.

Takatsu knew that, he also knew it would make no difference what rifle he carried. The last of his escort had been killed and the ambushers were breaking cover and moving towards him. Professional to the last, he noted they were carrying old Model 38 rifles, bolt-action Arisakas. He lifted his own rifle up but saw one of the old Arisakas flash and he felt terribly weak. So weak, he couldn't stand any more and dropped down to his knees. The ambushers had drawn bolos now, the heavy jungle machetes with weighted blades. Why had they done this? Hadn't he tried to be a good governor? He never got an answer and the last thing he ever felt was the thumps as the bolos chopped into his body.

Carswell AFB. Primary Operating base, 305th Bomb Group

"Hey, Navy, what happened to your bird? Somebody drop a hangar door on it?" The strange Navy aircraft certainly looked that way, its wings were bent up, its tail bent down, the nose drooped, the rear was cranked up and it looked like it was bent in the middle. Even its coat of matt midnight blue didn't hide that fact that this was one ugly lady. There were a group of new Navy aircraft here; Convair had just delivered the last of the PB5Y-1s to the Navy and the dark blue bombers were waiting to be ferried over to Ford Naval Air Station in Hawaii. A few years earlier the Navy had experimented with a gray and white paint job but they'd gone back to dark blue now. Everybody approved, it just looked so much better. The odd-looking aircraft was going with them, part of its evaluation and test program.

"Hey, don't blame me, I drive a Phiver, that thing is just along for the ride." The Navy pilot appeared equally disgusted by the appearance of the strange aircraft. "Commander Paul Foreman, VPB-33 Batwings".

"Captain Kozlowski, 305th Strategic Recon Group. Sorry Sir, I thought you flew that --- uhhhh ---- airplane. A Fiver?"

"No problem, I used to fly Flivvers off *Gettysburg* but I screwed my back ejecting. It never got right again and the Navy transferred me to patrol bombers. Now I fly a PB5Y-1 Hustler."

"Hey whadya know? I fly the RB-58C version. Or will be soon, the 305th has only just re-equipped. We're still doing classroom. I got my bird though, her name is *Marisol*. How long you been flying them for?"

"About three months now. A little bit more than 30 flying hours. We've had a lot of problems getting them serviceable. The J79-GE-5s don't work so well, You're getting the GE-10s aren't you? We've got problems in the fuel system as well, the fuel sloshes around in the fuel tanks when we accelerate or slow down.

That causes stability problems. We've also had trouble with the afterburners, there's something wrong there that causes intermittent yawing at supersonic speeds. Watch landing, the Phiver comes in hot and hard. We've had problems with the wheel braking system causing tire failure at high gross weights or high taxiing speeds. The other problem we're having is the pod. Thing keeps coming loose on us. We've done high-altitude Mach two weapons release with gravity bombs and we're moving to a missile release as soon as Lockheed start deliveries. We heard the first one went crazy but the second and third shots worked."

"Sir, Can I stand you a couple of cold ones? One to cut the dust, one to wet the throat? I'd really like to know what you've learned flying these things?"

"Make it soda and you're on. I'm on alert and you know the rules. No smoking 24 hours before flying, no drinking within 50 feet of the aircraft. Don't know how much I can help you but I'll try. And forget the Sirs, my friends call me Flightcop. You don't want to know why, it's a sad story." Foreman shook his head sadly. "Man, that sure is one ugly looking aircraft."

Ugly or not, he would have loved to fly it. The Navy was re-equipping the carrier air groups; the fighter squadrons were replacing their old Cougars and Demons with the new F8U-2 Crusader and the fighter-bomber groups would be getting this new bird, the F4H-2. The heavy attack groups were already flying another big Douglas bomber, the A3D and a new supersonic bomber was being developed by North American. That was supposed to be really something. His back ruled out carrier operations though; his last flight from a carrier had been the escort mission over Paris twelve years earlier – the launch and recovery for that had put him in sick-bay for a week. Now, he was land-based maritime strike bombers only. Still the big birds had their compensations.

The new generations of carrier aircraft were changing the fleet in other ways as well. The old Gettysburg class, once the queens of the fleet were now barely large enough to handle the new aircraft. The CVB designation had been phased out, reflecting that. Now all the carriers were CVs again. The new ones were much bigger, 70,000 tons plus with four elevators and four catapults. Foreman hoped that they were better protected than the old Gettysburg class; he still remembered seeing the burning wreck of *Shiloh* rolling over and going down. The new carriers would be needed; the Japanese fleet was still out there and still powerful. Much weaker than the US Navy, that was certain, but the US Navy had to be everywhere, the Japanese only where they chose to be. They were strong enough to have local superiority at a given point of conflict until the US could concentrate its strength. That's where the Phivers came in; they could react fast and deliver their nuclear anti-ship missiles where they were needed. Hold the line until the carriers arrived.

Just what were the Japanese up to? Were they still the Japanese? That was a question people were seriously discussing now. Japan had "conquered" China for sure, but was Japan now being absorbed by its victim? A lot of people were arguing that was just what had happened, that Japan had conquered China only to become Chinese in the process. Those who believed in that already called the state "Chipan" and the name was catching on. One result had been that the Japanese had their attention focused on land for almost three decades now and they'd allowed their fleet to take second place. That could change. Meanwhile, the US Navy had other things to think about, the mess in Africa for example and the chaos in South America. President LeMay and SAC may believe that their bombers ruled the world but from the front lines, things looked very different.

The O-club was welcoming; this was a SAC base, not NORAD. SAC pilots still remembered that *Shiloh* had died to open the way for the B-36s in The Big One. Foreman started to think back over the hours he'd spent in his Phiver. What would this kid need to know about her?

Nike-Ajax Site SF-19, 78th Air Defense Battalion, San Francisco, California

"Enemy bombers and missiles inbound, enemy bombers and missiles inbound. Prepare to engage." It was the first in the series of events that preceded any missile launch. This was the warning sent by the Air Defense Command Post to the missile batteries along the imminent threat axis of an attack. Sirens were already blaring, sending personnel scurrying to their assigned battle stations. At the launching area, other groups of personnel were conducting last minute pre-firing checks and positioning the missiles on the launchers. NORAD had designed the missile sites with space-saving underground magazines capable of hosting 12 Ajax missiles. Now that the alert was in, an elevator lifted a missile to the surface in a horizontal position. Once above ground, the missile was pushed manually along a railing to a launcher placed parallel to the elevator.

As personnel readied the missiles, an incoming aircraft was picked up on a long-range acquisition radar. For the Nike Ajax system, this radar was known as LOPAR, an acronym for "Low-Power Acquisition Radar." When the target appeared on the scope, the battery commander flipped on his IFF system to determine if the target was friend or foe. No response, the inbound was hostile. The LOPAR operator transferred the hostile contact to a target-tracking radar (TTR) that determined the target's azimuth, elevation, and range, and then automatically provided that information to a computer for use in guiding the SAM-A-7 Ajax missile. Once energized, the guidance computer received a running account of the target's changing position.

Adjacent to the TTR, the missile-tracking radar (MTR) locked onto the missile selected to perform the intercept. Meanwhile. All the information was being distributed on the AN/FSG-l Missile Master systems. Missile Master was the first truly integrated command and control system featuring automatic data communications, processing, and display equipment. By eliminating voice communications, this Martin-built system allowed an area commander to use all his batteries to engage up to 24 different targets.

By now, the hostile aircraft was approaching the battery's engagement range and the battery commander launched the missile. After producing 59,000 pounds of thrust within 3 seconds to push the Ajax off the launch rail, the missile booster dropped away. Having ignited, the missile accelerated through the sound barrier. Once the missile was in the air, the MTR received continuous data on the missile's flight. In turn, by receiving updates from the TTR, the computer generated course correction information that was transmitted to guide the missile toward the target. At the predicted intercept point, the computer transmitted a burst signal that detonated the three high-explosive warheads. The missile and its target exploded in a brilliant flash of light.

In the Air Defense Command Post, a telephone rang. Major James, the battery commander picked it up "James, 19/78th here" listened for a few minutes and relaxed. "We got her guys, it was a drone fired from offshore. NORAD gives us a BZ for the shoot-down."

Major James felt the room relax. It was NORAD policy never to announce a drill until after it had been completed. And to get a Bravo-Zulu, 'job well done', for an intercept was rare. The battery had only received one before and that was for ground defense, not an intercept. James smiled fondly at the memory, it was one he treasured. Because of the small size of the Nike-Ajax batteries, the officer cadre all got to know one another pretty well. The batteries had a tradition, once a month of having a "dining-out" evening where the officers and their guests got suited up in full dress uniform and went through the whole dining-out ritual.

That evening, the officers and their guests had adjourned to the bar when the ground defense alert siren blew. That was an imperative, everyone had to get to their assigned foxholes throughout the area. The troops had loaded onto a couple of five-ton cargo trucks and made for the perimeter. Other units deployed accordingly and within seconds the infantry guard detail had started firing 81mm mortar illumination rounds. James remembered how those things could light up the landscape. A group of figures were trapped out in the open, quickly being surrounded by the infantry and military police detachments. After about a half hour to 45 minutes James and his men received the word to secure from the alert and return to the barracks.

It wasn't a drill, some "peace activists" had decided to break into the base with the aim of sabotaging equipment. They were lucky, the guards were authorized to use deadly force if the missiles were endangered. Instead, the "peace activists" had just been placed under arrest. James reflected fondly that there had been something incredibly stylish and satisfying about busting the ungodly while attired in full dress uniform. It had added a touch of class to the evening's alert.

Now the rest of the news. "NORAD also say that the battery will be going to Nevada for Red Sun in six months time. We will be there for a month for the big exercise, then we will be re-equipping with the new Hercules missile." That was a big step forward, Ajax had been a good first step but it was being outpaced by the development of new aircraft. The new Herc had much greater range and altitude capabilities and was equipped with a nuclear warhead. Left unsaid was another factor; converting to Herc meant the battery would also be getting ready to receive missiles with an anti-missile capability. Nobody, as far as James knew, deployed ICBMs yet but if they did, President LeMay wanted defenses in place waiting for them.

There was a major debate going on in defense circles now. The traditionalists favored continuing with their bomber forces, arguing that bombers were flexible, could evade and fight back against defenses and could be called back at any time right up to the final laydown. Their opponents, arguing for ballistic missiles, quoted the speed of reaction of missiles, their relatively low cost and their invulnerability to defenses.

James, at least, knew that the last claim was false. Missiles were, if anything, an easier target than bombers. They came in on a predictable course, at a known speed and their flight path could be projected easily. They were fast, that was certain, but nothing that guidance systems couldn't cope with. Even the Ajax missile had some capability against older ballistic missiles like the German A-4. Herc would have a lot of anti-missile capability and the dedicated anti-missile weapon, Zeus, more still.

The problem was political. The Republicans would have held the White House for 16 years by the next election. Two terms for President Dewey, one term for President Patton, one term for President LeMay. The Democrats had found the missile versus bomber issue a good tool with which to beat the existing administration over the head. The Democrat contender, John F Kennedy, had been briefed on what the real situation was and how vulnerable missiles really were to a well-planned defense, but he'd gone on with the anti-bomber propaganda barrage anyway.

The problem was he was young and charismatic. President LeMay had bilateral Bell's Palsy, a disease that had paralyzed his face in an aggressive-looking scowl. Television and radio were the new media for political campaigning and there, on television at least, President LeMay was doing badly. Fortunately, televisions were still in a minority of households and it was radio that people relied on for their news and opinions. Even so, the opinion polls had the candidates virtually even-pegging. Perhaps that would change when the radio debates between the President and challenger started in a few weeks time. Many people had had the experience of debating an issue with Curtis LeMay but few had come out of the exchanges having gained the upper hand. LeMay's meticulous staff work was a hard act to beat.

There was more to it than that of course, missiles and bombers were just one part of it. Over the last two Presidential terms, the Army had been cut back in favor of the Air Force and, to a much lesser extent, the Navy. In reality, the Army was now just a tripwire for the nuclear forces. American policy was "massive retaliation". Attack America or its allies and your country is wiped from the face of the earth. No ifs, no buts, no arguments, just a rain of nuclear weapons. America did not make war on its enemies, it simply destroyed them.

The sheer cost of running a modern army wasn't the only reason why the Army was being kept small and weak; a strong army could lead to commitments that were unnecessary or even dangerous. That was another aspect of existing American policy, war was a bad thing and shouldn't be fought at all, but if it was it should be ended as quickly as possibly by a massive application of force. Kennedy and his clique disagreed with that. They kept waffling about "limited force" and "flexible response". Part of their support were the "Peace Activists" who cried out for the abolition of nuclear forces and condemned the destruction of Germany.

As the horrors of what Nazi Germany had really stood for slowly receded into the past, their following picked up strength.

Their motto appeared to be that resisting evil was as evil as evil itself. They should go to the smoking hole where Germany had been and see where those ideas lead. LeMay's destruction of Germany had bought a decade of peace, disturbed only by a few minor clashes. Was that legacy to end?

As Major James watched missile battery 19/78 dropping back into its normal routine, he reflected that crises could take more forms than purely military ones.

Chapter Three
First Plays

First Class Cabin, Cloudliner "Apsaras" On Don Muang Final Approach

Landing was the part of the flight Sir Martyn Sharpe enjoyed most. From his seat on the upper deck he could watch the six pusher engines powering back while the flaps extended. There was something about the mechanism that extended the flaps that fascinated him. The Cloudliner was a great aircraft, the first of the really modern airliners but it was too slow. It was being phased out now, next year Air India was getting its new eight-jet Boeing 707s. They would cut hours off the flight to Bangkok. That was good for it was a trip he was making more often these days. But he really would miss the gentle comfort of the Cloudliner.

When the Americans had dismantled the Air Bridge after World War Two, many of the C-99s had been sold, in truth almost given, to civilian operators. With their huge cargo and passenger capacity they had revolutionized air travel. When he was a child, Sir Martyn had dreamed of, one day, traveling somewhere by air. The Cloudliner had made air travel so cheap it was now commonplace. The children on this flight seemed mightily unimpressed by the experience.

The other thing he liked about this part of a flight was the feeling of dropping in on the country below. Underneath his aircraft, he could see the green cross-work of fields, divided by hard-top roads and canals. Every year, a few more roads, a few less canals. Fewer long-tailed boats, more trucks and motor scooters. This was a familiar feature now, all three countries in the Triple Alliance were developing fast, industrializing as quickly as their infrastructure allowed. They were dropping quickly, he could see a child sitting on a buffalo wave at the aircraft and felt the wings rock slightly in acknowledgement. Then, he felt the thump as the wheels went down. They were passing over the airport perimeter and ....

The pilot was good as well, he'd settled the big bird down with no more than a gentle tap. The upper deck of the Cloudliner was high enough for him to get a good view over Don Muang airport. Far over to the right was the military sections, Sir Martyn could see the line of brand-new F-105B Thunderchief bombers parked over there. Sir Martyn knew that the USAF had changed the specs on the F-105, introducing an all-weather attack system but making the more-limited B-model obsolescent before it was delivered. The Thais had moved in and bought the entire B-model production run, over 75 aircraft, at a bargain-basement price. Obsolete for the USAF they may be but they were the best fighter-bombers in the region.

There were more new military aircraft around, he couldn't see them but he knew some of Thailand's new F-104As were on hotpad alert somewhere around here. They were a more controversial purchase, Sir Martyn's Indian Air Force advisor had hard things to say about the Starfighter. Sir Martyn envied the Royal Thai Air Force, India's air force was too large and its responsibilities too varied to allow them to adopt the same policy of quality over quantity. The RTAF was on its third generation of jets while the Indian Air Force still had some piston-engined aircraft in operational service. That was a thought, perhaps India could buy the F-84Fs the RTAF was withdrawing from service?

The front passenger exit was opening. In the old days, they'd have had to go down steps and walk across the concrete in order to enter the airport terminal. Now, there were big, bus-like vehicles that had an elevating passenger section. It would lift up, the passengers would enter and it would drop down before driving over to the terminal. It was rumored that the next thing in airport design would be a tunnel that extended to the aircraft from the terminal itself.

"Sir Martyn, Sir Eric?" A young Thai officer had entered from the service bus. "Please come with me." He lead them out into the bus and it dropped them quickly to ground level. There was a large white limousine waiting, as he got in, Sir Martyn saw the box-like passenger cabin lifting back up for the rest of the first class passengers. "The Ambassador has asked me to bring you straight to her office prior to taking you to your residence here. She apologizes for troubling you after your long flight but we have little time and much to do."

Sir Martyn looked out the window. When he had first come here, almost twelve years ago, the city had been a sleepy quiet place, shaded by trees and crisscrossed by canals. Now, the canals were being filled in to make way for roads and the trees were being cut down. There were small business and machine shops setting up all over. Banks too, the banking sector here was growing by leaps and bounds as the country became the clearing house for trade and financial dealings outside the China-Japan block.

There was a price being paid for progress, the character of the city was being lost, it was becoming like every other large city everywhere. The traffic was getting bad as well now, there were too many motor scooters, too many cars, too many trucks. But over there? Sir Martyn nudged Sir Eric and pointed. Across the road, an elephant was making its stately way down the street. Bangkok was still Bangkok.

The limousine pulled through the gates of a building and stopped. It was a large, square building built around a courtyard that still had trees and a small lake with a fountain. Their guide took them in and up in an elevator to the top floor. As they stepped out, The Ambassador was waiting for them. To his surprise, Sir Martyn saw she was wearing an Army uniform with a Colonel's rank insignia and a pistol strapped to one hip.

"Welcome, my friends. Thank you Captain, you may leave now. I will not be requiring you for the rest of the day. If you have no other duties, you are dismissed. Sir Martyn, Sir Eric, please come to my office."

The Ambassador lead them in to a large, airy office. From up here, the sound of traffic was muted and the air was cool. A large ceiling fan made for a pleasant current of air around the room. The Ambassador fixed drinks, Sir Martyn noting that she knew exactly what to serve and how, and settled down behind her desk . "Gentlemen, it appears that our original fears were correct. Over the last few weeks we have been gaining an improved picture of Masanobu Tsuji's movements and plans. The overall situation is a little less obscure than it was when we first met but there are still many holes to fill in.

"Firstly, we were correct in our hypothesis that we are seeing the start of a wide-spread attempt to begin insurgencies across this region. There are a number of factors playing into this, some of which may be beneficial to us, others present a serious danger. Burma is the primary arena for this offensive. The Japanese have been infiltrating large numbers of agitators, cadres the theorists call them, into the area. Some are Japanese military personnel who have been trained in insurgency theory, others are Burmese nationalists, or communists, or simply mercenaries.

"Whoever they are, they are moving around the villages, trying to stir up discord between the local people and the authorities. That effort is spilling over into our northern provinces. Some here claim that this may be an accident, they believe that the cadres, who are not very skilled, simply stray outside the area of operations. But the consensus is that a part of Masanobu Tsuji's plan is to start an insurgency here, to act as a diversion and prevent us acting against the developing insurgency in Burma.

"We have taken steps against this possibility already. As you know, there are large numbers of Vietnamese refugees seeking protection in our country. Many of these are Viet Minh veterans. As the refugees arrive in our territory, we are filtering out the most skilled and senior of the Viet Minh veterans and asking them to assist us by moving to villages in the insurgent-threatened areas. This is already working well, these are skilled insurgents themselves and they know what to look for and how to counter the activities."

"Can you trust them Ma'am?"

"Of course not Sir Eric. But we have set things up so that it is very much in their interests to co-operate with us. You see, there are more insurgencies developing around here than the obvious ones. We have had word, for example, that General Vo Nguyen Giap had founded a Vietnamese People's Liberation Army aimed at driving the Japanese out of Vietnam and Laos. We understand that they have much support and have already achieved some significant results. A few days ago a senior Japanese provincial administrator, Colonel Toshimitsu Takatsu, was assassinated. We believe that the VPLA may well have had a hand in that."

"I must admit Ma'am, we were puzzled by that attack. By all accounts Colonel Toshimitsu Takatsu was an enlightened and civilized man, a good and just administrator who had a genuine feel for the region and sympathy for the people. He seemed to be the least likely of targets." Even as he spoke, Sir Martyn got a sensation he hadn't felt since he was five years old and had publicly miss-spelled "cat" . The Ambassador and Sir Eric were exchanging glances and he could almost read the Ambassador's unspoken thought *He's your boy, Sir Eric. Don't blame me.* But when she spoke, the voice was as soft and polite as always.

"Sir Martyn, please remember this is an insurgency. One where the objective is to bring about a widespread and effective uprising of the people against the government. To do this the government must be hated and despised and the people must regard it as an oppressive enemy. You have one administrator who is a greedy, vicious, corrupt sadist who is antagonizing the people and driving them into our hands. You have another who is a humane and just man who does the best he can for the people he rules and has earned their respect. *Which one do you kill?*"

Sir Martyn nodded. Put that way, it made sense although he didn't like it. He got the distinct feeling he was entering a world he would rather not know existed.

"However, this is not the least of our problems. You are aware of the growing wealth in the Middle East and Arab world in general?"

Again, Sir Martyn nodded. Iran had been an oil producer for many years and Iraq had been so for almost as long. Now they were being joined by Saudi Arabia and the Gulf States. They had banded together in a cartel called the Organization of Petroleum Exporting Countries or OPEC. They were getting very rich selling oil to both Europe and to Chipan. That hadn't worried the Americans who ran their economy on their own supplies backed up by Siberian oil, but, it gave the OPEC countries a serious hold on Europe.

The problem was that the German occupation of Moslem areas in Southern Russia had radicalized much of the population there. That philosophy was seeping into the Arab world as a whole and had combined with the Wahhabite regime in Saudi to form a grouping that was militant, anti-western and wealthy. A bad combination. Then there was the Shi'ite groups centered around Iran. Perhaps it was fortunate that the two sects hated each other as much as they did.

"Much of that wealth is going to funding another insurgency, this time in your northern provinces. The demand for Pakistan is rearing its head again and there are strong signs that Masanobu Tsuji is behind that as well. There is, after all, much of common interest between the Middle Eastern states and Chipan. But there is something more, something we have not worked out yet. The Moslem insurgents in your Northern provinces, in our southern provinces and elsewhere are very poorly trained in insurgency techniques but extremely well trained in military tactics. That is a puzzle we need an answer to. Now gentlemen, before I take you to our briefing facilities for a more detailed discussion, one last word in private.

"Sir Martyn, I told you how insurgents always target the best and brightest administrators? And that you have an insurgency problem developing? Here, I do speak as a member of my government. Your services to your country and to your partners in the Triple Alliance have been valuable beyond calculation. That makes you a primary target for an assassin. Look to your life, Sir Martyn, we cannot afford to lose you."

Nellis AFB, Nevada. Primary Operating Base of 414th "Red Sun" Combat Training Squadron

In the eyes of many, Captain John Paul Martin was, despite his lowly rank, currently the most important officer in the USAF. Not because he was a Mustang who'd worked his passage up from the ranks and collected two kills with the tail guns of a B-36 on the way. It was because for the last five years he'd been the range officer of the United States Air Force Air Warfare Center more commonly known as Red Sun.

Martin couldn't help reflecting that he had the best duty assignment the Air Force could offer and anywhere after here would be downhill. It was his responsibility to maintain the elaborate instrumentation that covered the 7.9 million acre Nellis Range Complex – 2.9 million acres of which were severely classified. Civilians flying over the outer 5 million acres might, provided they were humble and penitent, get away with a vitriolic tongue lashing and loss of their pilot's license. Those who infringed on the inner 2.9 million acre part would, if they survived, face a diet of prison food for a long time.

The secrecy of the range had lead to speculation about what happened there. The woo-woo community had been rife with stories about space aliens and crashed spacecraft. Others claimed that secret aircraft of remarkable performance and astounding technology were being developed. The woo-woos were a problem so the Air Force had come up with an inspired solution; they'd set up a decoy area on the edge of the range and leaked that this was where the interesting things really happened. There'd been a competition over what to call it, Martin had won that with the entry "Area 51". It was a simple code, A=1, B=2 etc. Thus "Area 51" decoded to give "Area EA" – Enthusiast's Airshow.

Add a few discarded prototypes and mock-ups, deploy a few savage guard dogs and it kept the woo-woos happy for hours. Yet, the stories were closer to the truth than most people thought. Two remarkable new aircraft were being tested now, a long-range supersonic penetration fighter, the North American F-108 Rapier and the Lockheed F-112 Blackbird, a hypersonic home-defense interceptor. They wouldn't be ready for this year's Red Sun but the F-108 was due to make it for the 1960 exercises. Maximum speed: 1980 mph at 76,550 feet. Service ceiling 80,100 feet, things had come a long way since the early days.

Martin remembered he'd still been enlisted and a tail gunner back at the first exercise. Red Sun had been born as a result of what had been a virtual civil war inside the USAF. The tactical fighter groups had come back from Russia to find that Strategic Air Command with its nuclear-armed bombers was being treated as if they'd won the war single-handed. An attitude that SAC had done little to discourage. The fighter and attack groups found themselves overshadowed by the B-36s and the exploits of the Navy over France. First bitter at being "the forgotten Air Force" they'd become increasingly aggrieved and indignant. The fighter community had taken to claiming that they could have stopped The Big One – and it didn't take long before the more hot-headed were offering to shoot a B-36 down to prove the point.

Something had to be done and that something was Red Sun. The fighter groups had been instructed to send their best and brightest to Nellis AFB for a two-week exercise that would pit them against the B-36s of SAC. What had happened was completely unexpected. It had been assumed that the USAF fighter pilots would do at least as well as the Luftwaffe had managed a year earlier. After all, the American fighter pilots knew the bombers would be coming in high and the tactics they would use. Without that knowledge, the Germans had downed seven bombers and damaged another dozen.

When the exercises started the American pilots achieved – nothing. SAC had been studying the reports of The Big One as well and had spent a year defining its doctrines and tactics. The planned two weeks had stretched to four and then to six. Every day the B-36s had swarmed over the target area, serenely ignoring the fighters floundering around below them. The fighter pilots would go away, revise their tactics, modify their aircraft and try again – with equal lack of success. Below them. Observers watched and learned.

That was the secret of the Air Warfare Center, Red Sun was intended as a training exercise so that combat aircrews could train in the most realistic simulated war environment possible. Even the first Red Sun in 1948 hadn't been a competition between flying units, nor a duel between pilots. It had been a post-graduate university course in air defense technology and the lesson learned was simple. Air defense had failed completely, the United States was as vulnerable to high-altitude nuclear bombers as Germany had been a year earlier.

The lessons of the 1948 Red Sun had been compiled and circulated to strategists, tacticians, aircraft designers, anybody who could come up with answers. One answer had underlined how desperate the problem had been; since the B-36 was the only aircraft that could fly and fight comfortably at those high altitudes, the B-36 was assigned an air defense mission, to be executed by dropping nuclear devices on inbound enemy bombers.

Martin reflected that his last Red Sun before going away to become an officer in 1949 hadn't been any better. By then NORAD had been formed to integrate the defenses of the United States. It was loosely based on a German system called NAIADS that had failed to defeat The Big One. American investigators had liked the basic idea behind NAIADS but believed it had been executed badly. NAIADS had been a rigid, inflexible tree with information passing up and down a tightly defined hierarchy. NORAD, from its headquarters in Colorado, was the center of a flexible, multiply-redundant web by which information could flow around any damage caused by enemy action.

By 1949, the Air Warfare Center had changed as well. In the first Red Sun, the actions had been observed by spotters on the ground with binoculars. Over the year, they had been equipped with Contraves Kinetheodolites to precisely track the aircraft and record their maneuvers. The first radars had been installed and a series of lecture theaters had been built for debriefings. In doing so, a new science had been created called Range Instrumentation. A science that investigated the technology needed to measure and plot everything that happened over an area and reveal how it had happened.

Neither NORAD nor range instrumentation had helped much, not in 1949. Some of the fighters the defenses deployed had been stripped down and their engines boosted to develop more power at high altitudes. The modified F-72s and F-80s had managed to reach the B-36s that year but they had been staggering at the limits of their performance and the B-36s were in their element. As the summary at the end of the exercise had put it "The B-36s stopped ignoring the fighters and shot them down instead". If they'd been using real ammunition, Martin would have left *Texan Lady* an ace.

The glory days of the B-36 hadn't lasted of course. It had faded away slowly. By 1951 the first of the new jet interceptors, drawing on the experience of the earlier Red Sun exercises had arrived. The F-94 Starfire was a hasty modification of a twin-seat trainer version of the old F-80C, fitted with an afterburner, it could make it up to the B-36s and stay there to fight them. Not well, it lacked the firepower for that, but at least it could try. Then, in 1952, the Northrop F-89 had entered the exercise. Sluggish and with an appalling accident record, it had the firepower the F-94 lacked. One aircraft had the performance but not the firepower, the other the firepower but lacked the performance.

These new fighters, controlled by a thing called the "Air Defense Ground Environment", were the child of Red Sun but they were weak and sickly children. At the end of the 1952 exercise, the summary had stated proudly "after five years of hard work, technical innovation and unrelenting effort, our air defenses have now advanced to the point of being totally ineffective."

But, if 1952 had been disappointing, 1953 had seen a sudden change in the fortunes of the defenses. Two new fighters had joined the flightline at Nellis, the latest version of the F-94, the F-94C and the single-seat F-86D Sabredog. Both were able to fly and maneuver at the B-36 operational altitudes and, with their rocket batteries, had the firepower to do some real damage. The RB-36s were still out of reach but the loaded B-36s now had to fight to survive.

Something else was added to the equation as well, the first Ajax missiles had entered the exercise. Up to now, ground-based anti-aircraft weapons had been useless, ineffective against targets flying at over 36,000 feet. Ajax was effective against targets flying at up to 60,000 feet and that put even the RB-36 within reach. In 1953, for the first time, a combination of Ajax "firings" with attacks by the F-94C and the F-86D had managed to inflict significant "losses" on a B-36 attack.

Martin remembered that the ground gained had been lost during his first year at Red Sun. 1954 had seen the B-60, the all-jet version of the B-36 entering the exercises for the first time. About 80 mph faster and about 2,000 feet more service ceiling gave the B-60 the edge that the B-36 had lost. A year later the B-52 had made its first appearance. With over 630 mph maximum speed it marked an enormous advance over even the B-60. Yet that year, the first of the Century series fighters had arrived with their GAR-1 air-to-air missiles.

For the last five years, the B-60 and the B-52 on one side and the F-101, F-102 and F-104 on the other had been battling it out in the skies over Nevada. Electronic warfare faced off against missiles and radars. The old days when the bombers held an absolute technical advantage had gone but the fighters didn't have a decisive edge either. Now it was all down to tactics, technology and skill. And those were the things the forcing ground of Red Sun had been designed to develop.

Martin grinned. This year, two new Convair products were being deployed for the first time. As always, the best went first to Red Sun. SAC were sending their new RB-58C Hustlers and NORAD the F-106A Delta Dart. The 498th Fighter Interceptor Squadron based at Geiger AFB in Washington was going face to face with the 305th Strategic Recon Group fresh from conversion school at Carswell. This was going to be interesting. And, who knew? Perhaps he could talk one of the RB-

58C drivers into giving him a ride. At Red Sun all things were possible.

Baronial Hall, Walthersburg, New Schwabia

Field Marshal Walter Model, once known as "The Fuhrer's Fireman" and now Baron of New Schwabia listened carefully. It had been his imagination, or possibly distant thunder, but it wasn't artillery. Here in Walthersburg, the city once called Stalingrad, the border of New Schwabia was close enough, if there had been artillery fire, he'd have heard it. In some ways it was foolish for him to have his home so far forward but there was no choice. Walthersburg was the great industrial center of his state. Astrakhan gave him oil and Rostov a port but Walthersburg was his industrial backbone. Lose that and everything else would be lost.

He'd already been luckier than most. Of all the little states that had sprung up in occupied Russia after the Americans had destroyed Germany, his was the one that was most powerful. He had been left with the best troops, the better part of an Army group with Panzers and infantry and even an SS division. He'd been left with enough aircraft to make a reasonable air force and the ground he occupied contained the foundations of a modern state.

One by one, all the other German satrapies had been taken by the Russians but New Schwabia had been left until last. It had even grown a bit, absorbed some territory and refugees from the others. He'd also been lucky in position, he had the Black Sea guarding his left, the Caspian guarding his right and neutral Turkey guarding his rear. Only the Northern front was open and half of that was guarded by the Volga. When the Russians attacked, and it was a when, not an if, their front would be from Donetsk to Walthersburg. He'd stacked his defenses there and dug in. His army had spent twelve years digging in.

For all the digging, his army was still mobile, that was the wonder of it. His first crisis had been when the news of the American attack with their Hellburners had reached them. His troops were demoralized, most wanted to go home to see if their families had left. Some had and about half had made it back. Their message had been chilling. Nothing left, no families, nothing. The Americans destroyed everything.

His troops had faced reality. Now, New Schwabia was the only bit of Germany left anywhere in the world. The German soldiers had taken Russian wives (taken being the operative word, the women's consent had been neither sought nor desired) and built themselves new lives here. New Schwabia had become the perfect modern feudal state. Russian serfs, Wehrmacht Yeomanry, SS aristocracy and, over them all, Baron Walther Model.

That's when he'd faced his second crisis. Equipment. His German tanks and guns and aircraft had worn out in the end and there was little chance of getting replacements let alone developing new models to replace the obsolete designs. Then, a miracle had occurred. A miracle in the shape of a Japanese Colonel and an Iranian priest. Colonel Masanobu Tsuji and Ayatollah Ruhollah Khomeini. Negotiations were long and hard but in the end, a three-cornered deal had been struck.

The Islamic States bought modern arms, large quantities of them, from Chipan, paying for them with oil. They then sold those armaments to New Schwabia in exchange for Model training their soldiers. Soldiers from the Islamic States of the Middle East spent two years with the German colors now, learning to act like modern soldiers. Model grinned to himself. Act like was right, they weren't Germans and never would be but they were good enough.

Those meetings had been hard though. The Japanese had been reasonable enough, they had their own agenda and this was a part of it. Model could see that and negotiate accordingly. Khomeini had been more of a problem, he just wasn't a rational man. But common ground had been established; they both hated America, Khomeini for what America was, Model for what it had done. They'd shared another hatred as well, one that had cemented them together when Model had shown him films of his Einsatzgruppen making New Schwabia Judenfrei.

So now his Army had manpower and armor. His Air Force had aircraft. Now, when the Ivans came, he could fight. And, who knew? On a limited front with a mobile force he might even win. Better odds than he'd faced many times during the War. And better odds than facing Hellburners.

Chapter Four
Initial Gains

Ban Rom Phuoc, Thai-Burmese Border

The long dusty road into Ban Rom Phuoc was getting familiar now, just like the roads leading to a dozen more villages in the area. Well, perhaps not now. For some reason the Thai government was surfacing roads in the province with blacktop. Senior Cadre had reported that and it was puzzling headquarters. Blacktop held the heat and was uncomfortable to walk on in the noon sun. It didn't have the dust clouds of laterite of course but it seemed eliminating dust was a small benefit for such a great cost and effort. It didn't matter here-and-now though, this road was still laterite.

The Senior Cadre thought that this village was just about ready for the next step. He and his Junior Cadre assistant had made several visits, instructing the villagers in the evils and oppression of the Government, opening their eyes to how they were being exploited by the merchants and bankers, how the Europeans were responsible for their poverty and hardships. He'd told them all about how a new force was rising in Asia that would drive the Europeans away and the village could be lead into a new era of peace and prosperity.

He'd followed the book precisely, even though he couldn't agree with most of it. All this farce of walking from village to village, pretending to be traveling traders. Of treating the villagers as being equals. He was a Japanese Army officer, he should enter the village in style, impressing the farmers with his status and importance. How dare a bunch of uneducated farmers think they were his equals. He'd made his real status clear to his Junior Cadre from a very early point in the operation. Junior Cadre was a Burmese nationalist and now knew well where power and authority really lay.

Anyway, it didn't matter, this village was ready now. They'd have another consciousness-raising session this evening and stay overnight. Then, tomorrow evening, he would incite the masses into rising against the Headman they now saw as a tool of the Government and they would kill him and his family. The authorities would investigate but their investigation would prove little. In frustration, they would punish the villagers who would thus be driven into the hands of the revolution.

It was an inevitable sequence of events, clearly laid down in the books they had studied. Follow the manuals and it would go well, the first of his assigned villages would be won over to the side of Japan. By late evening, Senior Cadre was convinced that his judgment had been correct. Ban Rom Phuoc was ready to be radicalized. After the evening revolutionary consciousness session he'd told the villagers he and Junior Cadre would be staying the night. There had been a stir of unmistakable satisfaction at that. As he went to the hut the villagers kept for travelers who wished to stay overnight, Senior Cadre saw that the village was indeed ready.

Senior Cadre woke from a dream where he was suffocating – and realized it was no dream. Something had been thrown over his head, covering his face. Even as he struggled to wake properly, he felt a dreadful pain across his stomach, a blow, probably from a heavy bamboo stave. It was the first of many, raining down on his chest and stomach and legs. Some were flat blows from the length of the bamboo clubs, others were vicious short stabs where the staves were wielded as spears. Mixed in were kicks from feet, some hardened from waking barefoot, others softer.

From inside the muffling blanket, Senior Cadre could hear screams, his own and those of Junior Cadre. And more sounds of blows and kicks and the pants of those delivering them. Then he was dragged from the wooden bed and thrown to the floor, More blows, and his hands were tied in front of him, a bamboo staff rammed between his elbows and his back. He could feel himself being hauled through the hut door and hurled down the steps. The impact as he hit the ground at the bottom knocked what little breath was left out of his body.

Then the blanket was torn away and he could see again. The entire village was surrounding him, the scene lit by burning torches that gave a flickering orange glow to the scene. Some of the villagers were the local defense force, the Tahan Pran, in their black coveralls and carrying a mix of shotguns and muzzle-loading muskets. Others were the villager civilians, men, women and children who had gathered around the guest hut.

Senior Cadre saw Junior Cadre flying through the air to land with a dull crump beside him. Then, both were dragged to their knees to face the villagers surrounding them. Senior Cadre was bewildered, confused , this was a bad dream it couldn't be happening. He and Junior Cadre were supposed to be doing this to the Headman and his family, it was him and his wife and their children who were supposed to be kneeling here, bound and beaten, surrounded by an accusing crowd. Not him, he was Senior Cadre.

You poor fools, Phong Nguyen thought quietly to himself as he watched the two cadres being beaten and kicked into position. *You poor, poor fools. You had no idea did you? You were so swept up in your own arrogance, your own self-importance, you didn't see what was going on around you. You were so convinced you were following the book, you didn't see you were fighting the people who wrote that book.* He shook his head, a gesture that those around him mistook as anger at the injustices the strangers had committed but in reality was pity for two fools who were playing with things they didn't understand

and would now pay the price. But pity should never stand in the way of duty.

"These strangers are charged with committing serious crimes against the people of this village. Who here has accusations to make against them?"

There was silence for a minute then one of the young women stepped forward. Her name was Ai and she was a popular girl in the village, well liked for her friendliness and amiability. She pointed at the older of the two strangers kneeling in the dirt. "I accuse this one. He asked me to pleasure him and I agreed but he wanted to use me as a boy. When I refused he seized my breast and twisted it until I screamed. Look."

She opened her top, her breast had ugly and obviously fresh bruises on it. *Bless You My Child*, Phong Nguyen thought, memories of his time in a Catholic school resurfacing, that is one good start.

"And he hit me and threw me across the room. If two of our men hadn't come who knows what he would have done to me. Phong Nguyen noted that two of the men straightened slightly with pride. More of that later. Now he had his work to do.

"THIS ONE?" He roared with anger pointing at the older of the two men, the one he had no doubt was the Senior Cadre and almost certainly Japanese. "THIS ONE?"

His voice shook with simulated rage. "This is the one who on his first visit here told us how his sister had been raped and mutilated by our soldiers." It wasn't actually, it was the younger one who'd told that story but who cared? Truth had nothing to do with what was happening here tonight.

"He accused our brave soldiers, the soldiers who drove out the French from the Recovered Provinces and brought us the respect of the world, he accused *them* of raping and murdering his sister when all along it was he who does such terrible things." The crowd would remember that as the stranger confessing to raping his own sister, This was going well. Phong Nguyen spat on the ground in front on him. "Who else has accusations?"

An old farmer stepped forward and pointed at the younger stranger "That one took my best rice beer, the batch that I'd made for the wedding of Lat and Nod, drank a little and threw the rest away. And never even offered to pay for it." Phong Nguyen shook his head sadly "Your best rice beer you say, the finest in the province I'm told." That was a safe comment, every village knew the rice beer it brewed was unequaled in the province. "And never even offered to pay." A deep sigh and a shake of the head.

Nao stepped forward. An older woman, her husband had died of snake-bite in the fields four years ago, Since then, she'd rented the farm out and raised her family by doing odd work for others in the village.

"I did their laundry for them and they left without paying. Next time they came I reminded them and they called me a bloodsucking landlord." That caused a genuine surge of anger, what else could a widow do but rent out her farm? And Nao had never complained about her fortune but made the best of what life had given her. Her children were clean and polite and she never failed to make a generous donation to the monks.

"I heard them, we all heard them, insult our King."

Phong Nguyen didn't see who'd called that out but it was true, everybody knew it. Now, those holding the torches were banging the ends against the ground, making the shadows dance and sway in the night air. In the background somebody had started tapping on a drum, a bit melodramatic but, running a revolution was half theater, after all.

"They never made a donation to the monks!"

Another unrecognizable voice, this time a woman. And again true and everybody knew it. Watching the two cadres, Phong Nguyen could see that realization had sunk in, this was no dream, no game, they had been outfoxed and they were going to die. They were both looking desperately around for a way out, for

--

an escape for somebody to help them. It was pointless, they were already dead, they just hadn't stopped breathing yet.

Now the accusations were coming thick and fast. All the resentments, all the half-remembered injuries and wounds and insults of a lifetime were pouring out. In the atmosphere that was swirling around the village square, the two men kneeling in the middle were the focus of everything that had been bottled up and festered for years. By now, nobody could hear the individual allegations but it didn't matter. Few, if any, had anything to do with the two cadres in front of them.

It was a long-delayed release of frustration and anger poured out over a convenient target. Tomorrow, it would be remembered only as the two strangers being found guilty of all the things that had offended and insulted the villagers. After it had gone on long enough but before it began to ebb, Phong Nguyen raised his hand to stop the flood of charges. "Do we find these strangers guilty of their crimes against our village?" That was a loaded question of ever there was one – and even if it wasn't, the villagers could hardly turn around now and say no. The roar back was "YES". As if it could have been anything else.

Lin made what really was the best Chicken Pad Thai in the province. It truly was superb. She may not have been the most beautiful girl in the village but the other women had already glumly concluded that her Pad Thai gave her first choice of all the eligible men in this village and the ones in the surrounding areas.

Her secret was her butcher's knife. The girls from the village had once gone to the provincial capital, taking what little money their families could spare with them. Most of the girls had bought a new dress or jewelry but Lin had bought a superb Swedish carbon steel butcher's knife and sharpening stone. Her mother had beamed with pride at her daughter's foresight for now she could slice chicken so thinly the strips were transparent. Flash-fried in seasoned oil, they melted in the mouth, blending with the rest of the Pad Thai to make a dish fit for the Gods.

Now Lin had her knife in hand as she stood behind the older of the two strangers. When Phong Nguyen chopped his hand down, she grabbed the stranger's hair, pulled his head back and sliced the knife across his throat. The blade was so sharp that it slid through the flesh with hardly an effort. Lin carefully avoided the spine, she didn't want to knick the finely-honed edge of her precious knife on a bone. As the stranger's blood sprayed out, Phong Nguyen drew his Tokarev TT-33 pistol and shot the other cadre through the head. As he did so, he decided he would have to tell Vo Nguyen Giap that these tactics worked as well when you were defending things as they did when you were subverting them. That was an important lesson that should not be lost.

Then something happened which astonished him. The shock of seeing the killings they demanded, the villagers should have been stunned, filled with guilt and shame. Then, those feelings could be turned against those who the dead had represented. "See, it was their fault you were forced to do this."

But, here, now the people were proud of what had happened. They looked at the bodies with satisfaction. Looking at them, Phong Nguyen had an epiphany. In his years with the Viet Minh, he'd been attacking things, tonight he had been defending them. That was the difference, before the villagers had been attacking and destroying, tonight they had been defending and protecting. Guilt and shame went with destruction, pride and satisfaction with protection. The implications of that needed much thought. But first he had a message to send.

Next morning, Phong Nguyen was still sitting on the ground thinking over his discovery of the night before when the trucks arrived. He hurried over, he had to speak with the platoon commander and make some hurried changes to the script. That took a few minutes, by which time the villagers had assembled around them. Nervous and apprehensive but defiant. They'd defended their village hadn't they? And nobody could object to that could they? The Army Lieutenant got out of his truck and looked at the dead bodies. "What happened"

The Headman explained, now the accusations of the night before had become facts. At this point, the original script had called for the officer to break into a furious tirade lashing the villagers for taking the law into their own hands. Now, that had gone. Instead, he shook his head sadly and remarked how difficult it must have been for them to raise their hands against guests. But, the safety and security of the village had to come first and they'd had no choice. But now, the friends of these evil persons would be coming to take revenge. That brought them back to the script. Perhaps the Army could help. Would these be useful to you?

In the back of the trucks were crates, containing new Russian-made AK-47 rifles. The long war with Germany and the German warlords had made Russian infantry weapons the envy of the world – and the country's leading foreign currency earner. Most countries vastly preferred the AK-47 to the American M-1. The Lieutenant took one from its crate and gave it to the Headman. Phong Nguyen turned to the villagers.

"The Army has given us these fine rifles to help us protect our homes, our families, all that is ours. Who will join the Tahan Pran now?"

The first three to step forward were Ai and Nao and Lin. Women? Why not? There were women in the Regular Army and women had been some of the best soldiers in the Viet Minh. Besides, after last night's display of knife-work he was not going to upset Lin – and anyway, he liked her Chicken Pad Thai.

Come to think of it, she really was a very fine woman, she would make a good wife for a Viet Minh Senior Political Cadre. But, better yet, the men in the village were not going to stand back and let the women fight for them. They were already stepping forward, at this rate, the Tahan Pran would triple in size and their new automatic rifles would give them many times greater firepower yet.

The Army lieutenant was asking the Village Headman for permission to stay for a day or two so that his men could teach the villagers how to look after their new rifles. Meanwhile Phong Nguyen went over to Lin and started to show her how to use her new AK-47. As he did so, she nestled a little closer to him. The village women looked at each other significantly. The Vietnamese orphan they had taken in had gained much prestige and respect today, Lin had made herself a good catch.

Captain's Cabin, INS Rana, Melbourne Naval Base, Australia

It had been a hard cruise. *Rana* and her sister ship *Rajput* were brand new, fresh from the shipyard and carried a clutch of new systems, both Indian and imported. Integrating them had been a problem, getting some to work at all had been a worse one. Captain Kanali Dahm had written a scathing report on some of the dockyard work that had been done. It had been skimped, some of the welding was far sub-standard, and he had boiler problems. The good news was that his four twin 4.5 inch guns had worked perfectly and what firepower that gave him. 40 rounds per minute per barrel for 320 rounds per minute total. His torpedoes might be old but they were trusted and reliable. Other navies may have defective torpedoes but he could trust his.

Anchored across the way from the two destroyers was the flagship of the squadron, the battlecruiser INS *Hood*. During the destroyer's gunnery practice, she'd let fly with her main battery of 15 inch guns. Now that was firepower, accurate too. Captain Dahm had seen the big shells fall in a tight pattern around the selected target. He knew what would happen now that they had reached Melbourne and opened up for public visits tomorrow. There would be a line of people waiting to visit "*The Mighty 'Ood*" stretching far beyond the dockyard gates but his destroyer would be deserted.

This was good, because the only people who would be coming on board were his professional colleagues from the Australian Navy. And, of course, the members of the Naval Mafia who would come along to photograph his antennas. His crew had already been hard at work, applying a spot of strongers to his upperworks and hogging out the messdecks. He wanted his new command looking shipshape before his peers – and the naval press.

Mind you, port visits could be embarrassing sometimes. He'd been a sprog on the Old Renown when she visited London a few years back. Traditionally navies that traced their ancestry back to the Royal Navy had in common that the best hospitality onboard ship could be found in the Chief Stoker's Mess – but entry was by invitation only and a rare privilege. A minor British politician called Healey had been found hammering on the entry hatch to the CSM at 0300 demanding free beer. Avoiding a diplomatic incident there had taken deft footwork. Kanali Dahm had heard later that the same politician had attempted the same trick on an American ship and tried to force an entry into The Goat Locker – rumor had it that a Senior Chief had accused him of being a Democrat and thrown him over the side as a result.

That was another thing, he had to get the Ship's Poisoner to give the crew the usual lecture on how not to catch unspeakable diseases while on a run ashore. Not that they'd listen of course, this was a training cruise and the ships were full of cadets and trainees. That might explain some of the systems problems they'd had of course. A Jimmy Green and a new piece of electronics were a marriage made in hell. Come to think of it, that raised another problem. As always on a port visit, he had a pile of invitations for the crew.

There was something strange about them. "For parties of up to ten seamen at a time to visit the our brewery, sample our products and play the staff at cricket." Then there was this one. "To crew of INS *Rana*. Beach party, barbeque and a friendly game of cricket." And "Six Indian Sailors invited to piano recital and listen to the cricket". Was the entire Australian nation insanely devoted to cricket, did factory workers pour out from their machine shops on breaks to practice their batting and bowling? Even that didn't explain this one "Madame Sophie's House of Sin, visit us for an evening of strict discipline and cricket." Captain Dahm shook his head. Fortunately his Jimmy had arrived.

"Cricket, Number One? Is the entire Australian nation insanely devoted to cricket? We don't have enough sports equipment on board for a tenth of these invitations."

"Don't worry sir. The Harbormaster here believes that we are the ones who are all insanely devoted to cricket so he adds an invitation for cricket to every welcome message we get before he sends them over. The Yank cruiser out there got the same invitations with 'baseball invitations' added. Who knows what

French ships get. Perhaps it is better not to ask. Sir, that didn't sound right?"

There had been a dull thump, faint here in Dahm's cuddy but distinct nonetheless. There was a crash as the Sparker dived in. Captains differed in their approach but Dahm's was that if the message was urgent enough for a Sparker to risk a tongue-lashing, it was urgent enough to dispense with the formality of a knock. Almost simultaneously the "away fire and rescue parties" was sounding. "Sir, emergency sir, there had been an explosion on the *Hood*."

"Not her magazines?" The moment anybody mentioned a battlecruiser and explosion in the same phrase, people's minds went immediately to the magazines.

"No Sir At the Admiral's reception. No word on what happened but *Hood* is requesting all available assistance to handle casualties. *Rana* and *Rajput* are to go to full battle stations immediately and close down. Sir, messages come from Captain Ladone, no word from Admiral Singh. He asks you to attend him immediately once you have secured your ship."

There was a roar overhead, an American helicopter from the cruiser *Roanoke* lying offshore was heading for Hood. The Americans may be trigger-happy but they moved fast when they needed to. And that included helping their friends, Dahm thought. Right this moment, he would trade half his guns for a shipboard helicopter.

"You heard, Number One. Action stations now. Seal down. I'm going over to *Hood*." Outside sirens were sounding, from ships and from emergency vehicles on shore.

Quarterdeck, INS Hood

"Captain Dahm, thank you for getting here so quickly, and thank *Rana* for the speed of her response. God, what a mess."

That was an understatement. The quarterdeck looked like a butcher's shop that had been hit by a hurricane. Shattered wreckage and bits of bodies everywhere. Few recognizable. Captain Ladone shuddered, this was worse than a shell hit. "Don't touch anything, the bomb was packed with fragments, nails, bits of metal and there may be some sort of poison in it as well. We don't know if that's true or what it might be. The Docs say a couple of injured died even though they shouldn't have."

"What happened?" Dahm looked at the hideous carnage surrounding him. This was worse than anything he'd ever seen. He and Ladone ducked as one of the dark blue American helicopters lifted off, taking wounded to a shore hospital.

"The Admiral's Chief Steward wired himself with stolen explosives and blew himself up. Took a tray of drinks over to Admiral Singh and Prime Minister Locock and just blew up. They're gone, both of them. They must be around here somewhere, but, well you can see the mess. We've got at least forty dead, over a hundred injured. Its going to get worse, we've hardly begun to count yet"

He stopped while another American helicopter touched down to pick up casualties.

"The Steward was Iqbal, a Moslem. Been in the Navy for years. He left a note in his compartment. 'We Must Have Pakistan' it said. Kanali, you'd better be damned careful now."

More sirens and emergency vehicles arrived shoreside. The entire dockyard was a mass of ambulances, fire engines and police cars now, their lights giving a strange festive air to the disaster. While the political and military implications of the disaster started to sink home across the world, on the scarred and bloodstained quarterdeck of INS *Hood*, the medical teams worked frantically to save the wounded.

Wireless Road, Bangkok, Thailand

Even official limousines have problems sometimes. While Sir Martyn Sharpe and Sir Eric Haohoa relaxed in the back of their official limousine on their way to the Indian Residency on Wireless Road, their driver was trying to work their route through the evening rush-hour traffic. Once, this had been an easy task but no more. Increasing prosperity meant more private vehicles and that meant traffic jams.

Suddenly, their driver pulled into the side of the road. An army motorcycle had pulled in ahead of them and stopped. Now the rider, Army uniform but wearing a white helmet, scarf and gloves was walking back. Sir Eric noted he was keeping his hands in plain view and he had a terrible sense of unease. The soldier, from the Thai military police, an organization better known as "the White Mice" spoke with urgency.

"Your Excellencies, The Ambassador apologizes for the inconvenience and discourtesy but requests that you return immediately to Army Headquarters. The gravest of emergencies has arisen. My men and I will provide you with an escort through the traffic."

As he finished there was a howl that even drowned out the traffic, four F-104s went over the city on full military power, climbing hard. The other military police were stopping the traffic and making room for Sir Martyn's official limousine to turn. The F-104s were followed by a pair of the F-105s, straining for altitude with their wings loaded down with bombs. The officer gestured upwards. "You may see how serious the situation is, they even have got those working."

It was a grim and tense ride back through the city. Whatever it was that was happening, word was spreading. Crowds were gathering outside electronics shops selling the new televisions. Thailand had opened its first TV stations only the year before but the technology was catching on fast. The motorcycle outriders did a good job of clearing away traffic and they made it back to the Army headquarters in a few minutes.

Two M-41 tanks were sitting outside the building now and a General was running from one side of the courtyard to the other. If nothing else, that highlighted how serious the events in progress were. The Ambassador had already come to meet them. Now, she was carrying an AK-47 rifle slung over one shoulder.

"Sir Martyn, I am so terribly sorry have you heard the news?"

"No Ma'am, your men brought me straight back here."

"Very well, it came just a few minutes ago. Sir Gregory Locock has been assassinated. We have few details as yet but none that we have are good. It appears that he and other members of the Cabinet were attending an official reception on board the Indian battlecruiser *Hood* when a suicide bomber blew himself – and them – up. The dead and wounded are in hundreds. The hospitals in Melbourne are full. We have gone to full alert, you must have seen the aircraft taking off. Your President has done the same in India. We are setting up a communications link for you now. Our equipment here is much better than that at your Residency. Please come to our main conference room."

The room was full of senior officers, passing information around as it came in. Most were armed and many were wearing the green-and-black camouflaged uniforms the Army wore in combat zones. As the two guests entered they were seated at the main conference table with a young woman behind them. She started quietly translating as much of the meeting as she could, keeping the guests from feeling left out. Looking around, Sir Eric sensed the primary mood of the gathering was confusion, there was too much speculation, too little hard fact to base it on. Messages were coming in, casualty figures rising inexorably.

The Ambassador sat down with them, her rifle banging her hip as she did so. "The Deputy Prime Minister, Mr Joe Frye is taking over. He'll be on the line to us soon. Have you noticed the pattern in the casualties? The number of dead continues to rise but the number of wounded has started to fall. It seems though the most seriously wounded are dying at an unexpected rate. I think we will find that bomb was much more sophisticated than just a few sticks of explosive."

Suddenly every officer in the room jumped to attention. The new Australian Prime Minister had patched through on the secure communications link. The King had also been patched in and was speaking to Mr. Frye. It was the usual message of sympathy and condolence for a great loss but there was one surprising thing; the King stated that he was going to visit Australia in person for the funeral of Sir Gregory and the other victims of the bombing. Sir Eric could sense the wince that went around the room as the security implications of that were absorbed. Once the room had returned to normal he turned to the Ambassador.

"A very brave and wise decision if I may say so Ma'am. And a very far-sighted one for the whole of our Alliance. I think I see what we face now." The Ambassador raised an eyebrow. "I think I see Tsuji's plan now. This bombing, assassinating an immensely popular and effective Prime Minister on one of our warships, by one of our navy sailors, was intended to split Australia away from the Triple Alliance. It was intended to raise doubts as to the trustworthiness of India as an ally and concerns over the effectiveness of her armed forces.

"If there is any change in Australian policy as a result of this act, that will be a bonus, but the real target is the link between Australia and India. I think a further part of Masanobu Tsuji's plan was to distract and neutralize India by reviving the Pakistan issue. India has by far the largest armed forces in the Triple Alliance but a sustained insurgency in the northern provinces will stretch our resources badly. The insurgencies in your northern and southern provinces are intended to distract and neutralize you to give you internal problems that will prevent you mobilizing your forces.

"With all three partners in the Triple Alliance distracted by these problems, Chipan can move into Burma unopposed using the insurgency there as an excuse. By the time we get our act together and counter the move, it will be too late."

"A very fair assessment Sir Eric. One that, with some minor differences we agree. But I think it is a typical Japanese plan, it is very complicated and has many components. I think also there are parts of this plan that we are still missing. But it has the flaw all Japanese plans have, everything has to happen the way the planners intended and the other players have to fulfill their roles exactly according to the script. If all goes as planned and if everybody does as the planners expect then the results will be a great success. But we can see their plan and we are already countering the moves by doing the unexpected. His Majesty's visit is but one example. Tell me, Sir Eric, what do you do when you see a rabid dog?"

"Why shoot, the poor thing of course."

"No, Sir Eric, you capture it, with great care of course, and throw it into your enemy's house." Sir Eric saw the Ambassador's eyes and was reminded of the old saying *Stare into an abyss long enough and the abyss stares back.* "Sir Eric allow me to introduce you to our rabid dog."

The Ambassador lead him through the officers who'd gathered around a radio station that was broadcasting news of the catastrophe in Australia. She spoke quietly to one officer who turned around to greet him. Facing Sir Eric, wearing a Thai General's uniform with only a VPLA shoulder patch to distinguish it from the others in the room, was General Vo Nguyen Giap.

Krasny Kut, Southern Russia. Primary Headquarters, First Byelorussian Front

Everybody believes that secret weapons are weapons. Ask somebody to describe a new secret weapon and they will speak of a new gun perhaps or a new missile. Maybe a new tank or a new bomb. But, reflected Colonel-General Andrei Mikhailovich Taffkowski, sometimes secret weapons could be deadlier than any of those. The ones driving past him now were a superb example, an invention that had the potential to be deadlier than any gun or tank or missile. The long column of trucks were delivering Russia's new secret weapon to the troops as fast as the factories could churn them out.

Taffkowski maintained the stern, unyielding yet inspirational expression required of all Russian generals but inside he smiled to himself. America may have its big bombers, thank God it did have them, but Russia had its army. Much of it paid for by American dollars it was true the letters MSDAP were a wonderful thing. Mutual Self Defense Aid Program. A wonder indeed. America bought the weapons it approved from Russian companies and then gave them to the Russian Army. That was why the Russian nickname for the T-55 tank was the Washington – named for the face on the dollar bills that had paid for them. MSDAP had replaced the World War Two Three-Way Military Assistance Program and was providing those countries America smiled upon with military punch far above that they could have obtained otherwise.

MSDAP had proved to be an elegant solution to a whole set of serious problems. The Americans had changed the definition of war with The Big One. A country that went to war with America would be obliterated, nobody doubted that. But, there were other problems that were not in that category, regional problems, low-level problems that American nuclear bombers couldn't solve. So MSDAP armed American allies who would look after regional problems for her. It was easy to be an American ally, all you had to do was treat your civilian population decently , trade fairly with your partners and try to solve disputes with neighbors peacefully. The Americans didn't ask that you agreed with them or became like them. Just don't cause them trouble.

There were other benefits the MSDAP had brought to Russia and the other recipients. The equipment purchases pumped hard currency into the national economies, funding their recovery and the development of a new production base. In addition to strengthening the military forces of the country, they stabilized the economy and increased prosperity. That brought problems of its own of course, but the gains were worth the cost. For the Americans, it meant they didn't have to build things they didn't need.

If their own small Army didn't need them, their allies supplied each other with American dollars smoothing the way. Some of the purchases went to the American Army itself of course, the Americans used more Russian equipment than they liked to admit. All their biological warfare defense equipment for example. And now, Russia's new secret weapon. Andrei Mikhailovich Taffkowski had been present when the new equipment had been shown to the Americans. The head of the American purchasing commission, a Marine General called Krulak, had taken one look at the equipment. "I want them, they are mine, give them to me" had been his first words. He'd even offered to marry one.

The Americans had placed their orders for the new equipment but their own army and Marines would have to wait. There were more urgent priorities. The Russian Army had reached the end of its long road back from the grim days of 1942. Now, 17 years later, they were preparing to launch their assault on the last of the German occupiers who still sat on Russian land.

That was why his First Byelorussians were here and the First and Second Ukrainian Fronts and the First Khazak Front. They faced the survivors of Army Group South Ukraine under Field Marshal Walther Model. The problem was that the Germans were sitting behind some of the best natural defenses in the country. Andrei Mikhailovich Taffkowski knew that his right flank was blocked by the Black Sea, his left by the Caspian. The Assault was going to have to be head-on from the North and that was where his problem lay.

On paper, the front was almost 500 kilometers long, stretching from the Taganrogskiy Zaliv to the Volga Delta at Astrakhan. The catch was that half of that front was masked out by the River Volga itself and another large section was masked by the Tsimlyanskoye Vokh, a massive lake. In reality the ground for an offensive was packed into an 80 kilometer wide stretch east of the Tsimlyanskoye Vokh by Stalingrad and a 160 kilometer stretch south of the Tsimlyanskoye Vokh down by Novocherkassk.

The Germans were evil, not stupid. They could read a map and they knew where the attack was coming – and they'd had twelve years to stack their defenses. The problem was that lake. It split the two campaign areas so widely that they could not be mutually supporting. Hit both at once and the two thrusts would be bogged down in the defenses and the Germans would defeat them in detail. It was even worse because neither of those routes actually lead anywhere. The Southern route was sealed off by the

Don River after less than 40 kilometers, the Eastern one by the Volga-Don canal.

Then there was the supply problem. The headquarters of the First Byelorussians was here because this was where the roads were. The axes of any attack had to be in areas where supplies could be concentrated and moved. The problem was that the road and rail nets centered on Stalingrad. Operations south of Stalingrad were impossible unless the road net was cleared. Andrei Mikhailovich Taffkowski shook his head and kicked some mud from his boots, the roads had been sprayed with water to keep dust clouds down.

That British moron Fuller had seemed to believe that tanks were invincible, invulnerable perpetual motion machines that could float over unfavorable terrain and keep going regardless of any need for resupply. The flaws in his work were so obvious it was hard to understand how he had been taken seriously by so many for so long. Finland had taught the Russians the error in Fuller's theories and the lesson had been reinforced by years of fighting along the Volga front.

That was the final problem. The attack had to be on the widest possible front. Hard-won experience had shown that an attack on a narrow front was doomed to failure; the Germans could react faster than any other army in the world and they had an eerie ability to assemble the shattered scraps of destroyed units into effective fighting forces. A thrust that was too narrow would simply be smothered by counter-attacks into its flanks.

Theorists might speak of an avalanche of tanks descending into the enemy rear to wreak havoc but realists knew it just wasn't going to happen. They understood the attack had to be on a wide front, pushing as hard as possible on the widest front possible, to create so many crises that the Germans would be overwhelmed by them. Either they would eventually be goaded into lashing out with a counter-attack that would bring them out of their fortifications or the pressure would eventually snap their forces like an elastic band breaking.

It worked, it was the way battles were always won, Fuller and his foolish nonsense to the contrary. There was a catch, here there was no broad front. There were just the two narrow strips leading to a water obstacle. In fact the Don-Volga line was probably the strongest natural defensive position in the world.

And that, Andrei Mikhailovich Taffkowski thought, was where his secret weapon came in. The Volga was uncrossable, everybody knew that. At 800 meters, it was too wide and too deep for pontoon bridging. By the time the engineers had built their pontoon bridge, the Germans would have assembled one of their scratch battlegroups and the Volga would run red with Russian blood again. But Andrei Mikhailovich Taffkowski had a secret weapon, one that had the strange initials PMP. Pomtommo Mostovoj Park.

Quite simply, the best pontoon bridge set in the world. A truck mounted system that cut the time needed to bridge a river to a small fraction of the original and over distances users of previous bridging systems would regard as inconceivable. The PMP was going to allow the Russian Army to do the impossible. The First Byelorussian Front was going to make an assault crossing of the Volga River.

Cockpit RB-58C "Marisol" Carswell AFB

"You never take me out anywhere. "

The voice was sulky and had a pronounced Hispanic accent, one that had developed since *Marisol* had first spoken to him. Kozlowski couldn't blame her for being frustrated. She and her sisters were a new type of aircraft, and, as with all new aircraft, there had been were problems that delayed crew training. He'd been scheduled to take *Marisol* up for the first time last week but the whole fleet had been grounded while the engineers hastened to find out why the fuel balancing system had failed to work, causing another Navy PB5Y to crash.

It didn't help matters that ground crews and maintenance troops were still learning how to service and fix these strange new planes. They lacked technical manuals, special tools and support equipment, and the RB-58C was sophisticated in ways ground crews of earlier aircraft hadn't even considered. The metal panels for example, were a lightweight honeycomb. Damage one and it had to be replaced using special high-precision jigs and tools.

"Its OK *Marisol*. Take a look at your nosewheel. We're about ready to start engines and run our Power-ON checks. I'd say that things are going about right. No problems so far. That yellow tractor should be towing us out any minute now."

Sure enough, there was a jolt as the tractor hooked up and, for the first time in a week, *Marisol* was towed out of her hangar into the sunshine. Even that was no guarantee that they would fly today, her last trip out had been back to the Convair facility for upgrades. The technical problems and their fixes had meant a constant stream of those. The 305th had 36 RB-58Cs on strength now and every one of them was different. *Marisol* was one of the earlier aircraft and the accumulated number of modifications had meant it would be quicker to take her back to the factory for an upgrade to the latest standard. Hopefully, that included a fix for the fuel problem, that's what today's flight was to test. That and to get Kozlowski's crew finally into the air.

But this was a real flight, Kozlowski heard the roar of the air turbine cart added to the noise already caused by the electrical generator parked beside *Marisol*'s wingtip. A jumble of electrical cords, air hoses and interphone cables lay on the ramp. That had been another delay, it took a lot of equipment to support pre-flight and maintenance of a supersonic airplane and much of it simply wasn't available in the quantities required. "Time to button up guys" and his crew lowered their overhead canopies.

In the rear seat, Dravar started to read the checklist aloud, Kozlowski responding according to the prescribed manner as the dozens of items were called out. SAC was strong on procedure and doing things right. That was a legacy of when President LeMay had run SAC. It worked and what isn't broken doesn't need fixing.

While the checklist was being read a tall access stand had been wheeled up beside the forward fuselage and then moved away again. Soon one inboard engine started turning, as the starter cart fed high pressure air to the little turbine which in turn drove the main engine. The engine turned over faster and faster, and suddenly smoke and hot air rushed from the tail cone. In a few minutes all four engines were running. The roar was deafening. Chief Gibson chivvied the ground crew as they struggled to remove the maze of hoses, cords and equipment. Now, at long last, *Marisol* was running off internal power, for the first time she was truly alive.

Chief Gibson raised his hands and Kozlowski eased *Marisol* forward. The engines roared and she began to roll only to stop abruptly as he checked his brakes. Then, once more she began to move, with the crew chief using hand signals to guide the pilot onto the main taxiway and move toward the runway. The chief saluted smartly as he waved the plane clear of its parking spot. At the wide spot in the taxiway, just short of the active runway, the plane stopped. There, Kozlowski ran the engines to a higher power setting, his last check of all instruments, hydraulics, electrical and flight control systems before takeoff.

At that point, Kozlowski cut in the afterburners on all four engines. Flames shot out behind the plane for twenty feet or more as the extra thrust was added to accelerate the plane down the runway for takeoff. Slowly *Marisol* picked up speed and started accelerating down the runway. More than 8,000 feet would be needed before the nose began to lift. Then she climbed, up and away from the pavement, already going over 200 miles per hour at lift-off and gathering speed every second. Behind her a Convair owned F-102 chase plane slid into position to observe the test flight.

The plan was for *Marisol* to accelerate normally from subsonic cruise at Mach 0.91 to reach 600 knots and then climb to about 45,000 feet. If the ram air temperature permitted she could go to Mach 2.0. Below them, Kozlowski could see the long lines of B-36 and RB-36 bombers waiting to be scrapped; there were so many of them that the first wave of scrapping had actually caused a short-lived glut of aluminum on the metals market. Behind them the F-102 was already having problems keeping up with *Marisol*, the sluggish performance of the F-102 was a serious problem, but there was a new interceptor joining NORAD, the F-106 that was supposed to handle that.

"Boss, ram temperature OK for supersonic, we're cleared for Mach 2. Say bye-bye to our chase plane."

"Andale, lets dance." That was *Marisol's* voice in the intercom. Kozlowski rammed the throttles forward and she accelerated smoothly through the sound barrier.

"Ram air temperature only 105 degrees, cleared to take her up to full speed." Dravar reported.

Before *Marisol* got to the 115 degree limit she was indicating Mach 2.2. The next job was a high altitude Mach 2 simulated bomb run at the Matagorda Island range off the Texas coast. That was when Kozlowski felt things start to go wrong, the crew were leaning heavily to port in their seats, as if they were tilted to one side and sliding to the left. The four engines, now in full afterburner, were consuming fuel rapidly from the main fuel tank, the only one with adequate pump capacity to sustain the acceleration.

Kozlowski recognized the problem, a phenomenon called "fuel stacking", a condition where fuel in the main wing tank tended to move laterally in flight. This was an especially disturbing problem when the tank was half full or so, and most worrisome during supersonic flight. He had to struggle to keep *Marisol* on course and complete the bomb run and reach the target. It was dangerous, for such heavy fuel stacking could result in loss of control and possibly exceed limits on the aircraft's structure.

After what seemed an eternity he started deceleration and descent to subsonic cruise. As he decelerated and began descending, the remaining fuel in the tank shifted forward toward the narrow portion. That tended to improve stability and gradually Marisol's flight behavior started to recover. By the time she reached Mach 0.91 and leveled off, things had returned to normal. The crew let out a collective long sigh of relief. Kozlowski patted the instrument panel in front of him. "We'll make a deal *Marisol*, we won't bail on you and you don't bail on us. Agreed?"

"Agreed" The comments came simultaneously from Korrina and Dravac.

"OK, Agreed ." *Marisol's* voice came over the intercom.

"Hey, I heard that!" It was Korrina from the center seat.

"Of course I let you hear me. We're a team aren't we?"

Chapter Five
Early Advantage.

Admiral Soriva completed his letter and placed it to one side. It was a professional courtesy, from one of the last battleship commanders to another, expressing his sympathy for the terrible events on INS Hood. It was an insult to all true sailormen to do what that steward had done. After forty years of admirable service, the Hood would now be remembered as the ship where a crewmember assassinated an honored guest. It was more than terrible, it was dishonorable to treat her that way.

Honor settled, Soriva turned his attention to his own Navy. The task force he was supposed to be leading was still swinging around its anchors in Kagoshima Bay, waiting for the word to go. A word that had been delayed three times already and was now being delayed again.

There was no proof, and the Army wasn't talking, but there was a rumor that the operations planned by Masanobu Tsuji were not going as well as their promoters had hoped. It seemed though starting an insurgency was much easier on paper than it was when dealing with real people in real situations. It was taking more time and was less certain than the text-books suggested.

There were rumors that the Army were trying to hurry things along, the same rumors also suggested that some of the agitators had already met with an untimely end at the hands of the very villagers they were supposed to be recruiting as a result.

Well, that was all the Army's problem. They'd nailed their colors to the mast of these new ideas about "revolutionary warfare" and they could live with it. Still, the basic plan was still in place. It might be moving more slowly than originally intended, but it was still the same basic form. Once the Burmese government was being faced with widespread civilian unrest, there would be an appeal for peace-keeping troops and the Japanese would respond.

They'd put a Special Naval Landing Force ashore, seize the capital and install a new, Japanese-dominated government. It was fortunate that trouble had flared in both India and Australia to take their attention away from the problems developing for them in Indo-China. It was very fortunate, very convenient. That reflection caused an uneasy thought to stir in Soriva's mind, like a poisonous snake hidden in a bowl of salad. Soriva resolutely pushed it to one side. There were some things better left unthought.

The Navy had problems all of its own, the chief of which was shortage of ships. The Navy was showing the effects of years of under-funding and what little money there was had gone on building the missile-launching submarines currently stationed off California. Japan had tried to build a heavy bomber to match the American B-36, the G10N-1 Fugaku. The G10N-1 was meant to cruise at 10,000 meters with a maximum speed of 680 kph and be able to carry a 5,000 kilogram bomb payload for a maximum range of over 19,000 kilometers. For shorter ranged missions, the payload could be as high as 20,000 kilograms.

Overall, the G10N-1 had been a pretty impressive aircraft with capability close to and in many cases, exceeding the B-36. The problem had been that Japan just didn't have the industrial capacity to build them in large numbers and by the time the force had reached a significant level, the aircraft was becoming obsolescent.

Instead, once Japan had tested its first nuclear weapon, they had used a low-flying turbojet powered missile as a delivery system. Each of the I-400 class submarines carried six and could fire them at one per minute. A few obsolescent bombers, a handful of cruise missiles flown by heroes, an ageing and obsolescent fleet and an army that was mostly tied down trying to rule the most populous country in the world. That was Japan's claim to great power status.

Still, some progress had been made. His battleships had been refitted in the early 1950s with the twin 10 centimeter gun mounts replacing the older 12.7 centimeter guns and they'd been given a decent radar fit. Floatplanes had gone and been replaced by helicopters. That gave him better protection against submarines but his destroyer screen still dated from the 1940s. They were anti-ship destroyers, still armed with torpedoes. A good torpedo, perhaps the best, but what good were they when the threat came from the skies? The Germans had relied on guns at the Battle of the Orkneys and there had been few survivors to reflect on that mistake. There were newer destroyers in the fleet, some carrying anti-aircraft missiles, but they were with the carriers. His battleships had to rely on their guns. As they always had.

Outpost 3, Ban Rom Phuoc, Thai-Burmese Border

The eyes were hardly visible, buried underneath camouflage nets and brush. They watched as a column of men crept past on the approach path to Ban Rom Phuoc. A finger on the hand that served the eyes gently pressed a switch on a portable radio. The mouth that also served the eyes remained closed, to speak would be to attract attention. Instead the finger broke squelch on the radio three times in quick succession then again, more slowly. Once for each group of ten. Then three more quick breaks to sign off. Then the finger stopped and the eyes watched.

Village Center, Ban Rom Phuoc, Thai-Burmese Border

Back in the command center at the center of Ban Rom Phuoc, Phong Nguyen added another marker to the map. It was the third report, the number of enemy troops massing outside the village was more than 150. He nodded to the headman; the Tahan

Pran volunteers were already mobilizing and sliding silently into their defensive positions. The unarmed villagers, most of them, started moving into the bunkers underneath the small houses. Others continued loading magazines for the Tahan Pran.

He'd been expecting the attack after the killing of the Cadres and the arrival of the Army unit. Now, the Army had gone. Their last act had been to build a barbed wire entanglement around the village perimeter. Theoretically, it was there to stop the enemy infiltrating the village, in reality it was an open challenge. "If we build it, they will come" Phong Nguyen thought grimly. And they were coming in strength. A fourth observation point clicked in, another estimated 30 men moving on to the perimeter. All gathering along the North and West sides. No surprises, no aces to pull, this was going to be a straightforward infantry slugging match

The tension in the air made it feel heavy and thick, threatening to suffocate the waiting villagers. In fact the night was cool, even by local standards. It was 00:30, the heat of the day had passed and it would be a comfortable time to sleep. Only nobody would, for at that moment when the enemy started to pour mortar, rifle-grenade and machine gun fire from several positions surrounding the village. The explosions inside the village marched across the defense positions, or at least, across the old ones.

Nguyen had guessed the Cadres would have passed information on what they had seen to the Main Force fighters. So he'd changed the positions around and moved the foxholes forward. He winced as several mortar shells landed in the area of his hut and that of the headman. At least it indicated the Main force were unaware the Tahan Pran were waiting for them. The explosions were deafening even though the mortars were mostly 50 millimeter, the ones the Japanese called the "Knee Mortar". Nguyen hoped, with grim humor, that at least some of the enemy had taken that name seriously and shattered their kneecaps in the attempt.

Now his own mortars thumped. He had three of them, American 60 millimeters. They weren't firing explosives though, instead the area over the wire perimeter was bathed in brilliant white light as the Tahan Pran parachute flares ignited over wire entanglements. As he'd guessed, there were sappers in the wire, cutting paths for the infantry to follow. They were already most of the way through; the next stage would be for them to use satchel charges on the defensive positions. There would be more sappers following the main infantry attack, they would be carrying flamethrowers to burn the women and children sheltering in the bunkers. Nguyen knew the pattern well, he'd organized similar attacks himself during his days with the Viet Minh.

But the lead wave of sappers weren't going to get anywhere, they were trapped in the wire and the villagers were starting to open fire at the targets highlighted in the harsh white light. Nguyen could hear the slow rhythmic thumping of the AK-47s against the light crackle of the Japanese Arisakas. The sappers were dropping, pinned down, unable to go forward or back. One forgot himself and jumped up only to be tangled in the wire. Nguyen could see his body jerking as the 7.62mm bullets struck him.

The Tahan Pran were doing it right, each of them had multiple fire positions and they would fire a short burst from one, then roll to another before firing again. Rifle and machinegun fire was coming out of the woodline, suppressive fire intended to make his men put their heads down. Even as he thought that, he saw the streak of a rocket flash out from one of the Tahan Pran positions and explode in the trees, he thought he saw bodies thrown by the explosion but it could all have been a trick of the light.

The rocket might as well have been a signal. Enemy troops boiled out of the treeline, a quick estimate, showed at least 300. The outposts had obviously missed some of the infiltrators. Some dropped into cover position and started laying down grazing fire on the Tahan Pran positions, hoping to keep the defender's heads down while others tried to run forward to seize new positions.

The AKs continued their dull thumping, backed up by longer bursts from the two light machineguns. They forced the advancing enemy to drop into cover, made them fire their Arisaka automatic rifles at the fortified defenders. Now it was a straightforward firefight, the bogged-down attackers trying to suppress the fire that held them; the defenders trying to prevent any additional movement towards them.

The attackers had one advantage, they knew where the village was, their mortars didn't need the flares to see where to direct their fire. The Thai mortars were tied down delivering flare rounds so the riflemen could see what they were doing. On the other hand, the attackers were relying on rifle grenades to handle the Thai foxholes, while the Tahan Pran had their RPGs. Even as Nguyen watched, another rocket slashed out across the field, smacking into a small knot of enemy troops sheltering in a dip.

In the village, some of the children were running out of the bunkers, carrying fully loaded magazines to the Tahan Pran riflemen and bringing back the empties for reloading. A mortar round landed close to one and the child was thrown into the air, hit the ground and lay still, the empty magazines he had been carrying scattered around him. A girl ran out, collected them up and ran back to her shelter with them. For once, just for once, in an infantry battle, ammunition wasn't a problem for the defenders, they had plenty of it stockpiled. The problem was just getting it to the rifle pits.

Out on the wire, an enemy officer was trying to drive the riflemen forward, to get them moving against the vicious fire from the AKs. Suddenly he spun around and dropped. He hadn't really stood a chance, the automatic rifles were pumping out so much firepower that the attempt to lead men forward was almost suicidal. Automatic rifles made standing up on a battlefield a mistake that carried its own, terminal penalty. Nevertheless, the attack was moving forward. The enemy was extending the front to the sides, stretching the flanks to envelop the defense. On the left, they were almost up to the wire before the threat was seen and pinned down by the AKs.

At least the enemy mortar fire was petering out. The enemy did have a restricted ammunition supply, for their heavy weapons at least. As if to take advantage of fire support while they still had it, the troops on the left surged forward. As they did, there was a heavy thudding burst, a Japanese 13.2 millimeter machinegun that had previously been silent, opened up on a defense position.

The big machinegun was quickly silenced as another rocket tore into its position but the damage was done; the Tahan Pran defenders at that point were killed or pinned down for a crucial few seconds. The attackers were through, into the main line of resistance. At close quarters they had a slight edge, it was down to bayonets and the longer Arisaka was a better bayonet platform than the short, stubby AK-47. There was a brief fight around the rifle pits in the area of the breakthrough, then the pits were silenced.

This was critical, Nguyen knew that the militia would fight well from fixed positions and defenses but lacked the tactical skills and co-ordination for a running fight. Now, the attackers would start their next move, to roll up the positions on either side of them, opening a hole through to the center of the village. Nguyen grabbed his own AK and gathered his reserve up. Vo Nguyen Giap, in their long hours together, had hammered the lesson home, always have a reserve. No matter how stretched the line, no matter how few the resources, keep a reserve. Even if its only yourself and your best friend, keep a reserve.

Now, at this crucial moment, he had a force to meet the penetration. He and his Tahan Pran troops ran forward and dropped into the cover of the buildings. The attackers had directed their last few rounds of mortar ammunition to support their breakthrough but it was too little; one of Nguyen's reserve force went down but the rest poured automatic fire into the disorganized attackers. The Tahan Pran riflemen in the rifle pits on either side of the penetration were also firing, hosing bullets into the group in their midst. Swamped by fire from three sides, the attackers fell back.

Nguyen's men re-occupied the rifle pits, moving the bodies of their previous occupants to provide some extra cover. He left enough of them to fill the gap in the line then took the rest back. Keep a reserve, always keep a reserve. The enemy group were falling back now and the observation groups deep in the jungle were reporting that the enemy attack was breaking up.

One OP took the chance of using voice radio instead of the agreed break-squelch codes. They'd just taken out one of the Japanese 50 millimeter mortar teams and captured the mortar. The mortar had only one box of three rounds left, the OP was going to return them to their owners. A few seconds later there were three rapid explosions in the enemy troops hung up in front of the wire. That hastened the movement of the enemy back into the treelines.

They'd be disengaging now, and heading for what they thought was a sanctuary the other side of the border. What they didn't know was that there were Thai regular troops, Long Range Reconnaissance Patrol forces, out there who would follow them back to the base. They'd pursue the matter further but, for Ban Rom Phuoc, the fighting was nearly over. The rifle fire slowed down until it was a few sporadic shots then ceased.

When dawn came, the villagers could see the damage. Their wire was down in several places, some of the huts had been damaged, two had been destroyed completely. There was enough smoke to make the eyes sting and the smell of cordite saturated everything. The well had been hit, several of the animals were dead including one of the precious buffalo.

Worse there were eight bodies brought in, seven Tahan Pran and the boy who had been killed carrying ammunition. Some of the women were crying, an old man watched impassively as his son was added to the line of dead. A Monk in his orange robes was sprinkling their bodies with water quietly repeating the Bhuddist chant. A dozen more villagers were wounded, most badly. The Japanese 6.5 millimeter round did a lot of damage for a small bullet. Together, almost a quarter of the strength of the village defense unit was dead or wounded.

The good news was that all five of the two-man OPs had returned to the village safely, one triumphantly carrying its captured mortar. That wasn't the only weapon captured, there was a pile of captured rifles, all Arisakas, mostly the new automatic rifles but some the old-fashioned bolt actions. There were a couple of Type 99 light machine guns as well and some of the villagers had found the Type 93 13 millimeter machinegun. Nguyen shook his head, another rule foolishly broken. The captured weapons pointed straight at the people really behind the attack last night.

The enemy wounded would tell more, the villagers had brought them in and they had been taken to the huts to wait until they could be treated – or until they died. The villagers hadn't brought the enemy dead in yet. There were at least forty, hung up on the wire or in the rifle pits where they'd come close to breaking through. There were more in the jungle and probably more still on the way out. How many more wounded were out in the jungle they had no means of knowing.

His thoughts were broken by a choking cloud of dust, a helicopter was landing. One of the Army's Sikorsky transports. An officer got out, the same one who had been in the village earlier. Nguyen watched while he saluted the village headman and paid respects to the line of dead. The helicopter had also brought a medical team who were starting work on the wounded. There would be more troops coming and a resupply of ammunition. Nguyen saw the officer speaking with the other militia troops.

Eventually, he addressed the village as a whole. It was the usual thing, commending them on a well-fought defense, stressing the strength of the enemy, the skill and courage with which they'd been repulsed. Sympathizing with them on the loss of their friends and family. Then adding that he was writing a report on the action here at Ban Rom Phuoc and would personally make the report to the King himself, describing the courage and sacrifice of the villagers.

"Will you really be telling the King himself of what happened here?" Nguyen asked the officer later.

"You dare to suggest that I would associate His Majesty's Name with a lie?" had been the cold and hostile reply. Then the officer had relaxed, he was speaking with a Vietnamese after all, one who could not be expected to understand such things.

"Yes, His Majesty will be told in person. And the families of those who died or disabled here will receive Royal pensions as a mark of respect for their courage and loyalty. Ban Rom Phuoc will be receiving some gifts as well, so that others can see that resisting the terrorists may require courage but is the way to a better future. Now, Khun Phong what went wrong last night. And how do we fix it?"

Phong Nguyen thought carefully. "We were too light on firepower. We need more light machine guns, automatic rifles don't substitute for them. We need more mortars and we need at least one heavy one. An 82 or 120. We also need a way of lighting the perimeter so we are in darkness and the enemy lit up. The flares from the 60s did a good illumination but they tied down the firepower from those mortars. We need more and better radios. Most of all we need landmines. We must have antipersonnel mines, American Claymores for preference."

"Some of that we can fix now. There is a truck convoy coming that will replace the ammunition expended last night. It will have extra weapons we can leave here. One of the gifts that is coming is a generator for the village and a grant of diesel fuel for it. We must think of the best way of using it when the next attack comes."

Baronial Hall, Walthersburg, New Schwabia

Pre-dawn, the horizon in the east was beginning to turn grey before the sun appeared. As always, Model was up and getting to work. The Ivans were building up for the attack, there were at least seven Fronts identified now. Six on his left, in the west around Donetsk, one in the east facing Kapustin Yar. Almost 90 infantry divisions, 14 tank divisions and 12 mechanized division. And an Airborne Army of five parachute divisions. There would be more, much more, the Ivans held most of their heavy assets at Front level. Especially artillery. Russians called the Artillery the God of War. There was a cruder version. "Infantry is the queen of the battlefield, artillery is the king of war, And we all know what the King does to the Queen." Truly, the Russian artillery was a hammer to be feared.

Then there was the other side of the equation. His own forces, six panzer divisions, two panzergrenadier, nine infantry and one parachute division. Plus his strategic reserve, the SS-Wiking Division. He had his own high-level assets as well of course, but nowhere near the resources the Russians could call on.

That was the real problem of course, the Russians were American allies and could call on American support. Almost superstitiously Model looked up as if he expected to see American bombers about to rain Hellburners on his little country. The Americans didn't fight their enemies, the Americans just destroyed them. Ruthlessly and without conscience. Model didn't think the Americans could fight. They'd done well enough when the First and Second U.S. Army Groups had been in Russia but that was more than a decade ago. Now, they just relied on their bombers.

It didn't matter though, what did matter was that the Russians could call on American funding and had used it to equip their armies. His own forces were ill-equipped and threadbare. Even his supplies of Japanese equipment were only a partial solution to that problem. His units might have proud German names, but the bulk of their strength was Arab trainees and Russian feudal conscripts. The Arabs could fight, sometimes, if they felt like it, but the Russians? He doubted it. Not for him, not for the Germans. They'd have to be driven into action and driven to fight.

So it would come down to his fortifications. A thick belt of them covering his left flank. It was a strange irony that the French were criticized for building the Maginot line yet the Germans had spent more on steel and concrete fortifications before the War than the French had – and the French had done a better engineering job. Model's own fortresses were modeled on the Maginot line, deep bunkers in a mutually supporting web. Most of New Schwabia's concrete production had gone into those bunkers.

There was a deep opening belt, dense enough to require a major attack, thin enough to conserve manpower. That would blunt an attack, define its axes and buy him time. Then there were the serious fortifications, the anti-tank guns and artillery and the new anti-tank missiles, all in massively built bunkers on the reverse bank of the Don River. Backing the whole system was the mobile reserve of the panzer divisions, ready to counter-attack and fill any holes in the system. If they could just hold out long enough, it might be enough. Russia was tired, desperately tired after almost 20 years of war. If he could hold them and break their attack, they might give up, accept that they were not going to get back this last piece of what had been their territory and offer terms.

There was a quiet knock on the door and one of Model's Russian women brought in his breakfast tray. Tea and black bread and cold meat and some fresh fruit. The woman placed the meal on the table and backed away. Like any good officer, Model was adept at reading body language and he could sense her fear and then her relief when she made it to the door. That was good, it was fine to have one's people love their ruler but it was much better to have them afraid. Frightened people didn't change their minds.

It would be decades before New Schwabia would be properly established as a new German country. An entirely new generation of new children had to be born, fathered by Germans and brought up as Germans. A new society had to be created for them to grow up in. Model had taken the first step there, in the selection of his title. He liked the rolling sound of Baron, Rittmeister sounded like something out of a circus and Graf was a title best used for engineers. But Baron Model had sounded good, impressive. In New Schwabia, there was no higher authority than Baron. The SS had got the message early. A Priest had posted a list of the Ten Commandments and an anonymous SS officer had added had added "The above only valid when approved by Baron Model."

Model poured a cup of tea and placed it on the window ledge beside him. Then looked out again, in the east the sun was just rising, its leading edge just showing above the hills. And, as it came into sight in the east, from the west Model heard a long, quiet sustained thunder. It could have been a far-off storm except the weather was good and no roll of thunder was ever sustained like that. Model looked at the cup of tea beside him. The surface was rippling with concentric waves forming on the surface. It wasn't thunder then.

The God of War was speaking.

Belaya Kalitva, Primary Objective, 69th Guards Rifle Division, Second Ukrainian Front

A few minutes to go and everybody had their mouths open. Not from shock or surprise but to equalize pressure and save their eardrums from the hell that was passing over their heads. The numbers were awesome. The total strength for 2nd Ukrainian Front was 550,000 soldiers, 336 tanks, 1270 of the deadly JSU-152 assault guns, 7136 artillery pieces and heavy mortars, 777 multi-barrelled rocket launchers and 500 aircraft. The thrust on Konstanthovsk was taking place on a 160 km wide front with a first wave of 30 Rifle Divisions. The main attacking Rifle Divisions had attack sectors that were only 1.5 km wide on the primary threat axis. That mean there was one gun or rocket launcher for every 20 meters of front. They were all firing, as fast as the gunners could thrust rounds into the breech or stack rockets on the rails.

Further to the east, the First Ukrainians were attacking towards Kalachna Don and driving towards the Don-Volga Canal. In 24 hours time, even further east, the First Kazakh Front would launch its assault towards the Volga River at Kapustin Yar and Akhtubinsk. That left the First Byelorussians, but Nikolai Fedorovich Lukinov didn't know where they were going. Head on into Stalingrad he supposed. That would make sense but it would be the devil's own battle. It still made as much sense as anything, if anything could make sense in this hell of noise and shock. The ground underneath him wasn't just shaking, it was moving in waves as the sheets of shells and rockets poured into the German positions in front of them.

Lukinov would have liked to have lifted his head to look at the earthquake enveloping the German fortifications but he knew better than that. Three years fighting the Germans, clearing their gangs of bandits off the soil of Mother Russia had taught him never to lift his head until he had to. And, if he forgot that lesson, Klavdia Efremovna Kalugina was laying down just a few meters away to remind him. She and her spotter, Marusia Chikhvintseva, were one of five sniper teams attached to his battalion. Even now, in the middle of the artillery storm, her rifle was rock-steady.

A few days earlier she'd dropped a German message-runner at a range of 1,200 meters. Lukinov knew that the Germans had snipers also and there was no reason to believe they were any less capable than Kalugina. Well, that wasn't true. There was the greatest reason all to believe that Kalugina was one of the best. She was still alive.

They'd need every edge they could get to take the fortress in front of them. It was called a "block" and was shaped like a hand spread on a table. The fingertips were the front bunkers. Three were anti-personnel with two turrets each housing a pair of machine guns. The other two were anti-tank with a single turret housing an 88 millimeter gun and a single co-axial machinegun. The palm was the artillery bunker, with two turrets each holding a single 105 millimeter howitzer. Intelligence said the turrets were taken from old tanks, that might be so but it made little difference.

The weak point in any fortress was the entry point, here the only one was at the rear of the artillery bunker. The infantry would have to overrun the fortress before they could get to an access point. Of course, the whole ground area of the block was thoroughly infested with landmines, anti-tank and anti-personnel. As a final touch, the block wasn't isolated, there were other blocks either side and behind it that could sweep it with machinegun and tank-killing fire.

This was the front edge of the battle zone, the fortifications at the main line of resistance along the Don would be much heavier.

The raving of the artillery barrage doubled in intensity and a new sound was added, the howl of fighter-bombers streaking across the sky to dump their loads onto the defenses. The ground-attack pilots were taking a terrible risk, diving through the artillery barrage to dump their loads on the enemy.

The screaming, sky-ripping noise of air-to-ground rockets terminating in the vicious flat crack of their explosions, the dull roar and wave of evil-smelling heat from napalm.

Nikolai Fedorovich Lukinov silently blessed the Americans who'd supplied their Russian allies with napalm, the one weapon that terrified the Germans beyond sanity. Jellygas, the fascists called it. If the bunkers had been old-style with firing slits instead of turrets, the napalm would have eliminated them by sucking out all the air but that didn't work against the ones they faced today. Still, napalm would burn off all the cover, let the attacking Frontniki see what they faced. And now the last act of the fighter-bombers, the heavy dull boom of the big bombs with fuze extenders, the plan was that they would detonate or destroy the landmines. Most of them The rest, the Frontniki would find the hard way. Then – silence. Sudden, eerie and complete.

"Follow Me! Urrah! Urrah!"

The cheer was answered along the jump-off line as the Frontniki surged forward. Their mortars, the 82 millimeter ones that went everywhere with them, started yapping, dropping smoke rounds all around the Block that was Nikolai Fedorovich Lukinov's target. Isolate it, try to deprive it of support from the other blocks. Also, try to deprive the artillery observers of lines of sight so the Germans couldn't call in their own artillery support.

The Frontniki were running forward as fast as they could, trying to close as much of the gap as possible before the stunned defenders could recover and start hosing the ground in front of them. Priority target was the two anti-tank guns, if they could be knocked out, the JSU-152s could close up and destroy the machinegun positions with relative safety. Overhead, but not by much, there was a scream of high-velocity shot, somebody was firing at something.

The ground was hot and crumbling now, shaken to powder by the artillery and scorched by napalm. At least the wire was down, blown up and ripped apart by the artillery barrage. Nikolai Fedorovich Lukinov heard cracks and saw some of the infantry start to go down as they tripped off the mines. The little schu-mines were designed to wound, to blow off limbs and remove genitals rather than kill, the idea was that a wounded man would need three or four others to take him back to a casualty station.

The Frontniki had come up with their own solution to that approach. Get wounded and you were on your own until the sweep unit behind them got to you. Ruthless but fewer died that way. Long, vicious sawing bursts of machinegun fire. The Germans were coming back to life. The machinegun turrets were firing continuously, raking fire backwards and forwards across the lines of advancing Frontniki. The drill was well-known, one gun in the turret was firing while the other cooled and was reloaded. That way, the stream of fire could be maintained almost indefinitely.

Behind the Frontniki, a JSU-152 broke cover and lurched forward, its big gun firing on the bunker that had opened up on the infantry. Its first shell missed, overshooting. Before it could reload, the long-barrelled 88 in one of the anti-tank bunkers had swung to engage and fired a shot. The hit resounded across the battlefield, a screaming clang that blended with all the other noise of the attack. The thick armor on the JSU had taken the hit and its 152 millimeter fired again, this time landing its hit squarely between the two machinegun turrets in the central bunker.

The Frontniki had gone to ground when the sawing bursts had started to cut them down, since then they had been trying to synchronize short runs forward with the swinging streams of fire from the machine guns. With the central bunker temporarily silenced, they made a bit more ground. Nikolai Fedorovich Lukinov saw the hatch on one of the 88 millimeter turrets open and one of the crew, probably the commander, very carefully and cautiously looked out.

As he did so, his head distorted and snapped back. Klavdia Efremovna Kalugina had scored again. Only about 300 meters, she wouldn't be boasting of that one. Behind them the JSU-152 had taken more hits and was silent, smoke coming from its open hatches. Lukinov hoped the crew had gotten out safely, at least they were far enough back to escape being machine-gunned as they bailed out.

Over to his right, there were three smoke trails, smacking into the side of the turret of an 88, the one whose commander was still draped over the side of the steel cupola. One must have penetrated because smoke started to rise from the turret and its barrel drooped slightly. Nikolai Fedorovich Lukinov started another short run forward, one of the anti-tank guns down, one to go. Suddenly, something, perhaps a glimpse below open perception, warned him and he changed his foot placement at the last instant. A schu-mine had been where his stride would have landed. Still shaking from the near miss, he took a short red wand out of his belt and stuck it in the ground by the mine. Somebody from a penal battalion could deal with it later. Another shot from an RPG hit a machinegun turret on the center bunker, it vanished in a burst of flame. Much thinner armor than on the 88 turrets.

The defense in this block was beginning to come apart, one of the 88s was down and the central machinegun bunker was damaged. That left the machinegun bunker on the extreme right isolated. If they could take that out, the remaining anti-tank gun could be eliminated and the JSU-152s could deal with the rest of the machine guns. He angled his advance over, the bunker was firing long bursts, but its coverage was spotty. More Frontniki went down as they closed in but soon the RPG-7 rounds flew across the space and the turrets were destroyed. There was a sound like a train going overhead.

Looking behind him Lukinov saw the other two JSU-152s in the support platoon had broken cover and started firing as they lumbered forward. As they did so, five figures got up from the ground by their disabled vehicle and ran back for cover. The crew had survived, good. Their tank could be recovered, it would be repaired and could be back in the battle again in a day or two.

From their position well back, the JSUs had seen something Lukinov had been too close to spot. A blind zone caused by a dip in the ground. It would have been covered by the destroyed 88, now it was a path forward. The central machingun bunker took a flurry of hits from the 152s and ceased to function.

That cleared a path for the Frontniki to swing around and take the other 88 from the rear. There were more vicious cracks as schumines claimed victims but they were beside and behind the 88. Again, the RPG-7 gunners scored their hits and the gun went down. Freed from its threat, the JSU-152s barged their way forward again, firing on the remaining machinegun position. It didn't last long and now the Frontniki had their last job to do

The artillery bunker, it hadn't fired yet. It was supposed to support the forward bunkers but it had remained silent. It was visible now, through the smoke and carnage but the Frontniki drew no fire from it. Its guns were intact, apparently, but one sign as to what may have happened was lying outside. A German soldier, his head shattered by a rifle bullet. Score two for Klavdia Efremovna Kalugina. Must have been a difficult shot and her second for the day. The girls in the sniper teams believed they got one good shot per day, a second was a bonus. A third was an occasion for a party. All the girls knew what the Germans had done to the women they had captured and the sniper teams took grim satisfaction in the retribution they exacted. Their only regret was the sniper code – one bullet, one kill - didn't allow them to cause the Germans some of the suffering they had inflicted on others.

Come to think of it, the dead "German" looked odd. Nikolai Fedorovich Lukinov knew it was a myth that all Germans were fair-haired and blue eyed but this one had black hair, brown eyes and an olive-colored skin. And his nose was unduly prominent, even allowing for the fact that most of the head behind it had ceased to exist. Looking around, he could see what had happened, the crew of the artillery bunker had abandoned the position. Kalugina had been caught by surprise and only managed to drop the last one out. The others had been machine-gunned as they ran away. By the Frontniki? By their own comrades in the other blocks? Nobody would ever know.

Nikolai Fedorovich Lukinov cautiously approached the entrance. It was open but it could be booby-trapped or there could be hold-outs inside. Still this was why Mother Russia paid him such a generous salary and gave him no less than 900 grams of black bread a day.

"Follow me!"

He jumped in and looked around. The entry passage had a pair of right-angle bends as a grenade and gas trap and then opened out the fighting room. There was a portrait on the wall. Not Model or Hitler, but some unkempt looking man with a black turban and a disheveled beard. Nikolai Fedorovich Lukinov knew he had stumbled onto something important here, something that shouldn't be touched until experts got to look.

Outside, the two surviving JSU-152s had pulled up next to the captured artillery bunker. They had positioned themselves carefully so they were shielded from the anti-tank guns in the block behind this one. Lukinov saw his infantry had spread out also and gone to ground. A quick head count, he almost sighed with relief. Of the 50 men he had started with, no less than 12 had made it this far alive. Probably a few more wounded in the ground behind them.

He went over to the command JSU, he needed to radio back quickly, the GRU battlefield intelligence people needed to look at this bunker as soon as they could get here. Meanwhile there was another block to be attacked and counter attacks to be driven off. The work of a Frontniki never ended.

Parliament House, Canberra ACT, Australia

The staff were good, quiet and discreet. They'd brought a buffet meal in without disturbing the meeting and made sure everything was in order. Drinks had been served, the food was suitable – there was even a cheesecake for the Thai Ambassador. But even the staff were being distracted by the television news showing the Russian assault on Kalmykia – or New Schwabia as the German occupiers called it. It was a mark of how the world was changing as well; the newsreel footage was barely 12 hours old. The Russians had flown it straight from the front for distribution to the rest of the world, to show that the liberation of the last stretch of their homeland was in progress. Also to show them the price Russians were prepared to pay for the defense of their homeland.

Being able to watch a battle while it was still in progress was a new experience. Sir Martyn Sharpe didn't fully grasp what he was seeing, he was a politician and an economist, not a soldier. Prime Minister Joe Frye was better placed, he'd served as a ranker in the Australian Army and he was appalled by the way the Russians were paying with flesh and blood to chew through the concrete and steel of the German defense line. The Ambassador was watching with the calculating interest of a professional soldier evaluating the military of another country.

"How do they do it Ma'am?" Sir Martyn was almost afraid to ask, as if the answer would transfer him into the images on the screen. "How does anybody do it? How did you do it?"

"This is why it is wise to have men as soldiers Sir Martyn. One day, there comes a time when we have to run straight at a machine gun, and it is best to have those around who think that is a good idea."

"Oh." Then a long pause "Ohhhhh." As the meaning sank in. The Ambassador's eccentric ideas on feminism sometimes took a little getting used to.

"How would I do this? Much the same way I think. There are not so many options in trying to break through defenses like this. The Americans would, of course, drop a number of their atomic bombs on such a line and remove it from the earth but we do not have that choice. The Germans have had twelve years to build that defense line and breaking it will be costly no matter how it is done. A more interesting question is what Model plans to do about this. He has many options and none of them are very good."

The television news ceased showing the film from the Russian battles and switched to domestic news. The lead was, of course the funeral of Sir Gregory Locock and the other victims of the Hood bombing. The Ambassador briefly wondered what was really in Sir Gregory's coffin then indulged herself in the self-centered luxury of trying to spot herself in the news film. Prime

Minister Frye and Sir Martyn were doing the same; television was still enough of a novelty to make the game exciting.

Behind them, the serving staff grinned at the sight of the high and mighty behaving like normal people. The film switched to shots of the three Indian warships in Melbourne. They had their foremast yards slanted to port, the mainmast yards sloped to starboard and lines hanging from them and over the sides. The newsreader explained that this was called "Scandalizing the Rig" a mark of the deepest mourning and respect. He noted the last time this had been done was when the death of Queen Victoria had been announced almost sixty years earlier.

With the novelty of the television news over, the meeting resumed. The funeral of Prime Minister Locock had provided an admirable excuse for a quiet, low-key meeting of the three. There was due to be a public conference of the heads of state; President Nehru of India, General Sarit of Thailand and the Australian President in a few days time which promised to be a complex and difficult period of negotiations. Therefore, it was wise for the three people present today to decide on the eventual outcome before it all started. The Ambassador elegantly licked crumbs of cheesecake off her fingers.

"I have some good news I think. Over the last few days there have been a series of attacks on our border villages near Burma. None of the attacks were successful, although the villagers have taken casualties defending themselves. In passing, Prime Minister, we would like to buy some more of the excellent water-buffalo you are now breeding here. Those villages lost heavily in the attacks and their water buffalo are an important part of village life. Sadly they were very vulnerable to mortar fire."

"There will be no need to buy them Ma'am. Your villagers lost their friends, family and possessions fighting on behalf of us all. The least Australia can do in return is to donate the livestock needed to replace their losses."

The Ambassador nodded in grateful acknowledgement "We learned many things from these incidents. Almost all the weapons we captured are Japanese supplied and are quite modern.

Although the attackers claim to be the Shan States Army, we have inspected the dead and have reason to believe many are Japanese regular troops. We have taken prisoners and their interrogation leads us to think that some are Burmese nationalists, others are Chinese. Our LLRP forces tracked the retreating enemy units across the Border in Burma and then, sometimes, as far back as China. So, we have a positive identification on our enemy now.

"More good news is that the Japanese themselves appear to have an insurgency problem. Their attempt to take over Vietnam and Laos has not met with local support and attacks on Japanese possessions and personnel are growing. An organization called the Vietnamese People's Liberation Army is claiming responsibility for these attacks."

All three were smiling, they were well aware that the VPLA was a Thai-run counter-guerilla operation.

"The Japanese have made matters worse by installing a brainless dolt named Nguyen Tat Thanh as their puppet ruler there. The man is a doctrinaire communist and is determined to force his ideology on the local population. I believe he is very unpopular."

Idly Sir Martyn wondered if that meant Nguyen Tat Thanh, whoever he was, had already met with a regrettable accident or was about to depart the world in some other manner. Then he remembered his first lesson in the ghastly business of revolutionary warfare, kill the competent, allow the incompetent to live. Nguyen Tat Thanh would be safe.

"The bad news is that the insurgency effort in Burma has been much more successful than in our country. There are areas of the North where the SSA is in virtual control. We believe the time is approaching when they will ask the Japanese for assistance in maintaining peace and security. And that will, of course, lead to a Japanese occupation."

The Ambassador reached out and helped herself to another slice of cheesecake while Sir Martyn rolled the thought around in his mind. "The best option would be for us to get in first would it not? To have our own peacekeeping force there so that there is no excuse for Japanese intervention."

Frye picked up the idea and ran with it. "Sir Martyn, Madam Ambassador, may I make a suggestion? It would be foolish to deny that the assassination of Prime Minister Locock was intended to cause a rift between Australia and the rest of the Triple Alliance. What better way to show the world, and those who planned that appalling crime, that they have failed by sending an Australian peace-keeping force to Burma? Say, a division of troops, maybe two.

"That would provide a telling demonstration that we will not bend the knee to terrorists nor allow them to dictate our national policy. Madam Ambassador, how urgent is this matter? How much time do we have."

The Ambassador's eyes defocused for a few minutes. "We have at least three months, no more than six. If the VPLA score a few successes in the next few days perhaps a little longer. Plan on three months Prime Minister."

Sir Martyn tried to get the initiative back. Triple Alliance meetings always tended to be like this. "Prime Minister, I have a further suggestion. If the troop convoy will leave from Australia in three months time, may I request that our squadron presently here, *Hood, Rana* and *Rajput* be allowed to form part of the escort for the convoy? You have few heavy ships of your own, your two ex-British carriers serve as troop transports while the two Essex class you bought from the Americans are hardly in service yet. An Indian escort for the convoy would also be a telling demonstration to our enemies that their plans and machinations have failed."

"A very good suggestion Sir Martyn, thank you. Your ships will return here after their current cruise?"

"I think the timing would work well. Madam Ambassador, what are your thoughts?"

"Sadly my country does not have any great ability to fight at sea. But we will be very pleased to see your troop convoy arrive safely. But my guess must be that the Japanese will be displeased in equal measure.

"There is one other thing I would suggest. Before moving troops around the world it would be wise for us to speak with the Americans. When unusual things happen, the Americans get worried and when they get worried they bomb people. Keeping their government briefed would be a wise thing.

"Also, I have had word from them, they have learned some things from the Russians in the last few hours that they think we should know. Sir Martyn, perhaps Sir Eric should accompany me on a trip to the United States?"

Chapter Six
Blocking Actions.

Office of President Cherniakhovskii, New Kremlin, Moscow, Russia

There was no doubt about it, the New Kremlin building was a great improvement on the old one. The Germans had helped of course, during their occupation of Moscow, the original Kremlin had been destroyed so thoroughly that even the foundations had been dug up and dismantled. It must have been a temptation to try and rebuild the structure but any plans to reconstruct the old building had been vetoed by President Cherniakhovskii. There was no need to go back to the bad old days of Tsars and Commissars, he'd said. Russia needed to look forward, not backwards.

So the New Kremlin was designed from the start as a Government headquarters building with all the latest facilities a government could need. The building was also pleasant and airy with large windows and wide corridors, giving it an open and relaxed feel. Of course the windows were bullet- and blast-proof and the corridors meant guards could move quickly from one point to the next. The walls weren't quite what they appeared to be either. Steel reinforcement webs and the best fireproofing money could buy were just two of the secrets hidden within them.

Doctor Wijnand followed his escort into the waiting room outside President Cherniakhovskii's office. The red light over the door was on but it switched to green almost immediately. Wijnand's escort spoke into the intercom then ushered him through the door. At 53, President Cherniakhovskii was the youngest Marshal of the Russian Army in many, many years and the abilities that had gained him military success had also made him Zhukov's designated heir. On becoming President, he'd summarized Russian policy in a single sentence. "There are two groups of people a good Russian never forgets: his friends and his enemies." He didn't rise as Wijnand entered his office but he did wave his visitor to one of the seats in front of his desk.

"It is always a pleasure to see the Head of the International Commission of the Red Cross, Doctor Wijnand. How are things in Europe?"

Wijnand grasped the implication of the greeting immediately. President Cherniakhovskii had the time and inclination to speak with the Head of the ICRC, he had neither the time nor the desire to speak with a European politician. He was expected to frame his words accordingly.

"Good Morning Mr President. It is always a pleasure to visit Russia and see the speed with which your country is recovering from the devastation of war. I only wish that the recovery of Europe could take place at the same speed. Although the Great Famine is a thing of the past now, our farmers still have far to go before their productivity reaches pre-war levels. It is thought that there are long-term effects from the American bombing of Germany that nobody fully understands."

"I doubt that Doctor Wijnand. I doubt that very much. I believe instead that God has withdrawn His Grace from Europe and turned His Face against Europeans. I believe that Hitler was an Antichrist and Europe failed to oppose him when he was weak and powerless. In that failure of will, the countries of Europe betrayed both God and the rest of humanity. Now Europe, having failed in its duties as a great power, is given just enough to survive but not enough to be of any great consequence in the scheme of things. Russia also failed in those years but our struggle, aided by God and our American allies, redeemed us and God smiles upon us again. For you, now your privations must redeem you. But that is past now and we must look to the future."

Wijnand listened to the rebuke impassively. Since the disappearance of communism, there had been a void in Russian life that the Eastern Orthodox Church had returned to fill. In its new form, it was a taciturn and gloomy religion, given to the presumption of a strict and demanding deity that rewarded good and punished sin with the same merciless diligence. The concept of hating sin but not the sinner didn't figure in this equation; both were due the same pitiless retribution just as virtues and those who practiced them gained abundant rewards. Sinners had to earn redemption for their sins by suffering both in this life and the next, those who were redeemed gained earthly success as well as rewards in the hereafter.

Viewed in that context, President Cherniakhovskii's comments could be understood – and Wijnand had an uneasy feeling he could be right. And the pointed remark about European insignificance was correct as well. Wijnand had seen the film from the battlefield north of the Don; the Second Ukrainians were deploying more military force than the whole of Europe put together and they were just one of the five (or was it eight, the numbers were confused and contradictory) Fronts involved. Then again, Europe didn't have American Marshall Aid dollars bankrolling its military or its industrial recovery.

"This is so and it is the future that the Red Cross wishes to discuss with you and the rest of the Russian Government."

That was a polite fiction, Wijnand was speaking to the only part of the Russian Government that was of any significance. "The attack on New Schwabia…" It was a mistake and Wijnand knew it as soon as the words were out of his mouth. President Cherniakhovskii voice was a lash that cut across the room.

"I think you mean our liberation of Kalmykia, the Kuban and Georgia presently occupied by Nazis?"

Wijnand cursed himself. It was easy to forget that the President was also the toughest, most ruthless General Russia had produced in a generation of senior officers noted for their toughness and ruthlessness. And he was a Russian patriot.

"My apologies President Cherniakhovskii, I merely used the name as a general term for the area occupied by fascists. It is, of course, certain that the areas in question will indeed be liberated by the Russian Army. May I ask what you intend to do with the surviving Germans who are in the area after liberation."

"Certainly you may ask Doctor. We intend to kill them. Every man, every woman, every child."

The stark, uncompromising statement hit Wijnand in the pit of his stomach. This was what he and the rest of the ICRC had guessed but hearing it spoken so coldly and with such certainty was vastly different. This was what they had feared and what he had come to Moscow to prevent. Somehow.

"President Cherniakhovskii, there is another way. Europe is prepared to take these people in, to absorb them, to help resettle them. Germany is a shattered wreck, a mere shadow of itself and one that will never threaten anybody again. Even so, President Herrick will take these people in, allow them to try and rebuild what, if anything, can be rebuilt in Germany. All we ask is to be given the chance. Mr. President, if you do this terrible thing how are you different from the Fascists? How will history look back on you?"

Wijnand braced himself for the explosion. It didn't come. Instead, Cherniakhovskii spoke quietly.

"We did not go to other countries and massacre their civilians Doctor. We did not launch a Europe-wide witch-hunt aimed at exterminating entire races of people. We kill our enemies, those invade our country and who fight against us. We do not kill people because we think they have the wrong shape to their nose or the wrong color in their eyes.

"Do you know what has been happening in the occupied territory since it was occupied by the fascists? Of the slave labor camps and the extermination of anybody the Germans regard as inferior? Did you know that Russian men have been massacred so that Germans can take their women? That Russian sons are castrated at birth or slaughtered but daughters spared to become brood-mares for Germans? What, exactly, is the ICRC position on forced pregnancy, Doctor Wijnand? Perhaps before pleading the cause of such people, you should read a little on who they are. Perhaps you may want such people as your neighbors, we do not."

He deposited a thick file onto the desk in front of Wijnand. The Doctor started reading it, then started to go white. By the time he was a few pages in, he was sweating and his stomach heaving. Cherniakhovskii was watching impassively. When he judged the time was right, he simply said "Door on the left"

Wijnand made a run for the Presidential private bathroom and just made it to the toilet before he lost control of his stomach contents. President Cherniakhovskii listened to the sounds and thought carefully. The German question had been tormenting him and his advisors. How could they slaughter people without becoming what they detested, but how could they not slaughter such people? Surely they were beyond redemption, their sins were so great there could be no way they would find their way back into grace.

Suddenly a great light dawned on him, an inspiration he attributed to his stern and judgmental God. This could be turned to Russian advantage, to Russia's very great advantage. It could even save the lives of his poor Frontniki. Some of them, anyway. He made a quick telephone call to his chief assistant. A small but important matter to be arranged quickly.

Doctor Wijnand was back now. He'd washed his face and recovered his composure. Knowing about such things, reading about them was one thing, seeing pictures was another. Still he had to keep trying, whatever these people were, whatever they had done, he had to try and save lives whenever he could. "My apologies Mr. President, I have tried to clean up the mess. But you cannot blame a whole people for the crimes of their leaders. Please, at least let us take in the women and children."

"There is something to what you say Doctor, perhaps you may be right." Cherniakhovskii spoke thoughtfully "Perhaps there is room for redemption in the Germans. Perhaps they should be given the chance to show there is some hope for their humanity. Listen well Doctor. Our offensive on the Don Front is proceeding according to plan. Soon we will be reaching the Don River itself. There, we face the main line of German resistance. We believe that the Germans will use chemical weapons against our troops when they start the assault crossing of the Don. If they do so, we will strike back with chemical weapons of our own, and our biologicals.

"We will ask our American allies to drop some of their nuclear weapons as well. Military casualties on both sides will be dreadful but the sufferings of the civilians will be terrible beyond description. We will liberate our territory but what we retake will be a burned and poisoned wasteland. Better a burned and poisoned wasteland than our land occupied by fascists. Better yet for neither to happen.

"We will allow the Germans to judge themselves. We will let them pass verdict upon themselves. The fate of the Germans in Kalmykia, in the Kuban and in Georgia will be decided by their own actions. If they use chemical weapons or any other weapons of mass destruction against our troops then we will see there is no hope for them and we will exterminate them, root and branch. But, if they refrain from doing so, if they fail to use such weapons against us then we will know that there is hope of redemption for at least some of them. The men we will hold for trial as war criminals but their women and children we will release to you. For deportation of course."

President Cherniakhovskii leaned back in his seat. Holding the German women and children hostage against the German use of chemical weapons was the best way out of an awkward situation. The attack had been planned so that the left hook over the Volga would break through into the German rear and cause a situation where enemy units could be overrun before chemical weapons could be used.

But, breakthroughs were chimeras; often sought, rarely achieved. This gambit might help prevent the chemical holocaust he and his commanders feared. If it didn't, killing the hostages would divert and absorb the explosion of rage and hatred that would follow the devastation. It was now down to Dr Wijnand and his ICRC. If he could get word that the German women and children were being held hostage against the use of chemical weapons, if he could persuade Model to refrain from using such weapons then that would be good. Even if he could not, it was one more bit of maskirovka, one more item of deception to persuade the Germans that an assault crossing of the Don was coming.

After Doctor Wijnand left, Cherniakhovskii took off his uniform before going into his private bathroom. There were no mirrors in his office but there were in his bathroom and he would not stand in front of a mirror wearing his uniform. In uniform he was Cherniakhovskii the president, without it he was Cherniakhovskii the man. And Cherniakhovskii the man hated Cherniakhovskii the president to the point where he couldn't stand to look at him.

National Security Council Building, Washington D.C.

The entrances to government buildings, Sir Eric Hoahao reflected, represented the character and mind-set of their occupants. The Viceregal palace in New Delhi was an economist's dream, lean, aseptic and cost-effective yet lacking humanity. Supreme Command Headquarters in Bangkok had an opulent and hedonistic face masking a modern and efficient interior. The Elysee Palace was rich in pomposity and arrogance but short on signs of real power. He'd never been in the new German government building but he assumed whatever was there glowed in the dark.

Even allowing for that, the NSC building was unusual. The centerpiece of the reception lobby was a 15 foot tall statue of Death, complete with cowl and scythe, and mounted on a skeletal horse. It was modeled and positioned so as visitors entered through the glass doors, the lighting made the eyes of the statue appear to glow and be fastened on them. Visitors inevitably felt a chill when entering the reception area, partly from the statue, partly from the fact the area was kept cool enough to induce that effect. It helped to emphasize the point. This building was the Headquarters of the National Security Council, it was where the Targeteers planned their nuclear wars.

Sir Eric and the Ambassador had arrived by limousine from their respective Embassies. They'd been met by representatives and conducted through security and into the offices. Now, they were being taken up to the top floor, where they would meet with the National Security Advisor. The Ambassador hadn't said much on the trip over and was still keeping her own counsel. That did not bode well for somebody.

'Sir Eric Hoahao, thank you for coming. Please take a seat." The NSA rose from behind his desk and shook Sir Eric's hand. Then he turned to the Ambassador, his voice notably softer. "Hi, Snake, its been a long time. How are you?"

"Good Morning Seer, it has indeed been too long. One day you must come to Bangkok again. You would be surprised by how the city has changed. Few of our old favorites are left now."

"You two know each other?" Somehow, Sir Eric was perturbed by the discovery, it was like discovering a trusted guard-dog was friends with the local contract assassin.

"Certainly Sir Eric, Snake and I have been friends for years. From long before The Big One. May I offer you a cup of coffee? It would have to be black I'm afraid, milk goes sour almost immediately in this building. I have some Johnny Walker Blue Label for you, Snake. Now tell me what brings you both to our fair city?"

"I would prefer a small glass of that excellent whisky if I may sir. For some months now, the senior leadership of the Triple Alliance has been increasingly concerned by the spread of lawlessness and insurgency in some of our territories. The problem is most serious in Burma, Northern Thailand, and the

Northern Provinces of India. However, we also have a lesser level of difficulty in the Philippines and Indonesia. You will notice the pattern of course. There are some strange aspects to this situation, some of the insurgent movements appear to be highly trained in a tactical sense, others are not. The Ambassador will be able to give you more professional assessments of that side of things. Returning to the political background….."

For the next hour, Sir Eric outlined the developing situation in the Far East and the activities facing the Triple Alliance. He'd had a long briefing document prepared that covered the same ground, when The Seer picked it up, it seemed to Sir Eric that the paper yellowed and aged. Probably just his imagination, he thought. The Seer had a habit of looking straight at the person speaking, one that made concentration slightly difficult. By the time he got to the end he was feeling uneasy and uncertain, what seemed to be hard certainties once now appeared less convincing.

"So we intend to move at least one division of Australian troops by sea to Burma in about three months time for peacekeeping duties."

"Thank you Sir Eric. Now, can you tell me why that should be of interest to the Government of the United States? The Sea is an open highway, free for the use of all. As long as you do not threaten others using that highway we have little interest in what you move where. As far as I am aware, Burma remains an Indian protectorate and how the Triple Alliance deploys its forces is an internal matter for you alone. If you chose to move them by sea, then that is your decision. The United States of America puts great importance on the freedom of the seas, indeed our navy is deployed to guarantee just that. America is a trading country and maintaining free access for all to the trade routes is a vital national interest of ours.

"On another matter, we have received intelligence from our Russian allies that may directly concern you. It may also explain some of the military problems that Snake has described. As you are doubtless aware, for almost a week now, the Russians have been crushing German defenses North of the Don River and

East of the Volga. In doing so they have taken a number of prisoners, many of whom have come from Middle Eastern and other Islamic countries.

"Upon, ahhh, vigorous interrogation they have revealed that they are only the latest groups of what has been a continuous stream of such people through the ranks of German forces in the area. In effect, it appears that, for some years at least, the German forces in occupied Russia have been acting as a training school for a variety of the elements whose activities concern you. This may well explain the tactical skills that you refer to in your briefing.

"The Russians have also captured significant amounts of Japanese-produced war materials, much of it quite recent origin. It therefore appears that there are strong linkages between the Islamic terrorism that you face in the Triple Alliance and the German forces in Occupied Russia. It also appears there are links between Japan, China and those forces. How everything fits together is something we would wish to determine. However, I would also point out that insurgencies are your internal affair also; the United States only involves itself in situations where its vital national interests and those of its close allies are directly affected.

"I have a small request though. As you know, the Philippines was once a US trust territory and, although it is now an independent country, we still feel great affection for the people. We would like to send some aircraft on a goodwill visit to Luzon, I believe the Navy would like to send a PB5Y unit, VPB-33, to Clark Field on such a visit."

"VPB-33?" The Ambassador's eyes opened wide "That patrol group has 72 aircraft on strength, that's a lot of aircraft for a goodwill visit."

"What can I say Snake? We have a lot of goodwill to show the Philippines. We'd also like to send a small detachment to U-Thapao for a visit. About a dozen B-60s and a few RB-58Cs. I do hope that such a visit would be acceptable to your country?"

"Certainly Seer, we would be happy to extend some true hospitality to your pilots and their crews."

"Good, that's settled then. I'm sure the movement orders will be in place when the units are ready. Sir Eric, I think it would be advisable if the current commander of SAC, General Dedmon, was to visit India. We fly bombers worldwide and we always like to have access to divert fields in case of technical problems. Perhaps we could arrange an agreement with India for such facilities. Snake, you going straight back to Bangkok?"

"No, I have been asked to stay on here for a while; there are some problems my Government wishes me to resolve. Perhaps we can have dinner one evening? Tomorrow?" The Ambassador nodded. The Seer pressed a button on his desk set "Lillith, honey, book me a table for two for tomorrow night, find somewhere that has really good cheesecake. Charge it to Uncle Sam."

A few minutes later, Sir Eric and the Ambassador were on their way out. "Well, Sir Eric that went very well indeed."

"How so ma'am? I was under the impression that apart from some pleasantries and a gesture of friendship, the Americans promised nothing."

"Sir Eric, you must listen to what people say. Freedom of the seas was defined as a vital American interest and our right to move troops by sea were described as an example of that interest. The Seer told us that America would not get involved unless its vital interests were involved – which says that they would get involved if they were. So if anybody interferes with our troop movement, the Americans will intervene – and they are moving one of their maritime attack bomber groups to allow them the option of doing so. Furthermore, they have moved nuclear-capable bombers to act as a deterrent against an invasion of our territory. Although I do not think they have nuclear strikes in mind yet. They are sending B-60s rather than B-52s."

"I'm sorry Ma'am, my Oxford Degree was in the classics. I know they are both big bombers but the significance you allude to escapes me."

"The B-52 is a much more modern aircraft than the B-60, it is much faster, flies higher and has much better electronic warfare capability. The B-60 is a dated design, it is just a jet version of the old B-36, but it has one great advantage, it was designed in the days when the mark of a bomber was its ability to carry very large loads. The B-60 carries more than three times the bombload of a B-52.

"The Americans call using their strategic bombers to support ground troops an ARC – Army Reinforcement Capability – operation. When those bombers drop atomic bombs on ground forces it is called ARC-Heavy. When they drop conventional bombs, it is called ARC-Light. I think The Seer has just offered us an ARC-Light capability in case of a Japanese invasion. And a strategic reconnaissance detachment to find out what is going on and open the way for the B-60s. Yes, Sir Eric, it was a most satisfactory meeting."

Chapter Seven
Breaking Through

Chernyy Yan, River Volga. Forward Headquarters, First Byelorussian Front

Early morning, just before the light of pre-dawn was a fine time, a great time. The darkness still almost absolute but just beginning to purple with the coming day. The sounds of the night had faded but those of the day had yet to be born. The result was a strange tranquility that rested the soul and revived the spirit. Soon, as the east began to lighten, the birds would start to sing their chorus to the dawn and the day would begin on a note of beauty.

Yes, thought Colonel-General Andrei Mikhailovich Taffkowski, a fine time. But this was better, the sky slashed apart by a howling gale of multi-colored tracers as eight divisions and six independent brigades of anti-aircraft guns started pouring fire into the German defenses across the Volga. The guns were mostly twin 37 millimeter guns with a number of the single-barrel 57 millimeters that had started to arrive and some 85s. Every round a tracer, ripping at the sky in a blinding array of light and the ground shaking and the ears shattering with the roaring scream as the massed guns raved at the enemy. The whole anti-aircraft firepower of two Fronts was firing flat trajectory across the river that was the spiritual heart of the Russian people.

Flat trajectory, that was the secret. The big guns, the 122s, 130s and 152s were silent. When they fired, their shells were tossed at the enemy, high in the air and, in doing so, they would endanger what was already happening. Also they wouldn't do the job that the anti-aircraft guns were doing now. The First and Second Ukrainians had learned that heavy artillery was almost ineffective against the German bunkers; they were too small to be hit except by blind chance. The hail of smaller-caliber fire from the anti-aircraft would help keep the bunkers suppressed but those guns had another role, one not obvious from the ground. From the air, though, it was different.

From above, the streams of tracer fire formed giant arrows pointing at the landing zones for the first wave of the assault crossing of the Volga. The Fifth Guards Airborne Division would be making its approach now. In the slowly lightening sky, Taffkowski saw the silent dark shapes winging overhead. Gliders. Paratroopers were all very well but try to do a night drop and they ended up too dispersed to do much against an organized defense. But gliders landed their troops in organized formations with their equipment and weapons. Using gliders in daylight was only slightly short of murder, they stood so little chance of survival, but at night, and supported by this mass of fire they could still get in. Oh, some would go down from German fire, others would be hit by the Russian barrage but most would get in. Fifth Guards Airborne here, Sixth Guards Airborne to the north at Verkniyh Baskunchak, Ninth Guards Airborne to the south at Nikolskoye.

The radar fire control on the anti-aircraft guns would be tracking the gliders in. At the last possible moment they would order the guns to cease fire so they could drop into their landing zones. That was when some guns didn't get the message or the crews elected to unload via the barrel and Russians would die from Russian fire. The chop when it came was sudden and brutal; after the vicious snarls of the guns, the silence was positively painful. Then, across the Volga, Taffkowski could hear the crackle of small-arms fire as the paratroopers started to engage the defenses.

Behind him, the sky was gray now as the sun edged nearer the horizon. Then, the leading edge peaked over the hills and the second assault wave started. A Regiment of Russian Marines had been brought down from Petrograd and they were crossing the river in their amphibious vehicles. Some of them were old lend-lease American DUKWs, others were GMTs, the Russian version of the DUKW obtained under MSDAP. Other were PT-76 amphibious tanks.

It would take them at least eight minutes to cross the river and, under normal circumstances, they would be wiped out by the German gunners. But, two things gave them a chance. The German defenses were under attack from the paratroopers and the German gunners were having to stare directly into the rising sun. It bought some chance but it was still going to be bad for the Marines in their thin-skinned vehicles. Even as Taffkowski watched, fountains rose around them, the drops of water sparkling and forming vivid rainbows in the dawn sunlight. In the midst of them, a GMT burst into flames and started to sink.

The Airborne and the Marines were buying time for the third wave, the assault crossing itself. At two selected areas of river bank a line of Kraz cross-country trucks backed up to waterline and stopped sharply. The pontoons slid from the back of the vehicles and splashed into the water, automatically unfolding as they did so. The locking catches slammed shut and the pioneers ran forward, boarding each pontoon, turning them around and bringing them into position. Sledgehammers swung, slamming the connecting clamps into place.

Taffkowski couldn't see it but he knew that fingers were already being lost and hands crushed in the desperate struggle to get the bridge ready. The Pioneers had been told the truth, that the Paratroopers were fighting steel and concrete fortifications with light infantry weapons and Marines were burning and drowning in the river to buy the time the Pioneers needed to get the bridges built. Every minute that was wasted meant more of their lives were lost.

36 sections of pontoon bridge had to be assembled to give the first 225-meter span that was already taking shape along the shore. Further down, a second unit was assembling their pontoons into a square powered raft. That would act as the first waypoint on the bridge over the Volga.

Eighteen minutes in, two minutes ahead of schedule. What was left of the Marine Regiment had long since made it to the other side now, leaving the river surface scarred with its wrecks. The first span of bridge was ready and the BMK bridging boats got to work. One end of the bridge was cast loose and the current took it, swinging it out into the river. The BMKs took control and brought it into position, vertically out from the bank. By the time it was in properly in position, the shoreside end was already secured and the shore access panels laid.

Out on the river, Taffkowski could see smoke rising from the diesels on the BMKs as they fought the current in order to hold the bridge steady. The big raft was already on its way out, its own engines and the BMKs trying to keep it aligned properly. They had it roughly into place but through his binoculars Taffkowski could see the Pioneers fighting to get the connecting bolts into place. Minutes were racking up and couldn't be recovered, if the defenses opposite overwhelmed the Paratroopers and Marines assaulting them, the Germans could concentrate their fire on the bridge and wipe it out. . Already the second span and second raft were being assembled on the river bank and the first raft had to be secured by then. Then, he heard the "Urrah" from the raft, the connecters were driven home at last.

Not before time, the second span was almost ready and the BMK bridging boats were racing back to collect it. They had to ferry it out from the shore then pivot it in mid-river. They had to get it out parallel to the shore, if they swung it so the river current struck the 225 meter length of the span rather than its 3.25 meter width too early, that current would carry it away. It was on its way now, he saw the BMKs fussing around, pushing it out while more prevented the current from taking it downstream. 36

minutes in, the second span was starting its pivot, its upstream end swinging down to match with the first raft while the downstream end was held steady. Then the BMKs pushed and the whole bridge shook as the span slammed into place. The Pioneers swarmed over it, hammering the connectors home.

Meanwhile the second raft was already making its way out while a third group of trucks had dumped its pontoons into the river. The bank was chewed up now and a few of the trucks had bogged down. Didn't matter, this was the last span. "Urrah" came floating across the river, the second span had locked into place and the raft to match up with it was arriving. Closer into shore the Pioneers from the first span were threading cables through their pontoons, powerful winches would put them under tension and help to take the load on the bridge.

40 minutes now, the Pioneers were linking the second raft to the central span of the bridge. Looked like it was going easier than the first one. Obviously a solution had been found to whatever had caused the problem when linking the first raft. The sounds of the infantry assault on the fortifications the other side of the river were still floating across, if only the Paratroopers and Marines could hold on for a few more minutes. Just a few. Fifty five minutes and the last span started its way out and across.

Taffkowski watched as the BMKs herded it across and spun it into alignment. It was too far away now to see details but on the third span Pioneers were surging around the connectors while more ran to the shoreside end. They were under fire from the shore now, through his binoculars, Taffkowski could see men falling as they worked on unfolding the shore ramps.

At long, long last, 62 minutes after the first trucks had started to unload, there was an "Urrah!" that echoed up and down the Volga and a red flare shot into the sky from the left bank. More cheers from both banks, from the waiting troops, from the exhausted Pioneers, from the brutally hurt Paratrooper and Marine units.

As the cheers subsided, the first of the waiting T-55s edged into the bridge and started its way across, tankriders crouched behind its turret. Behind it followed the rest of its platoon, then its company, then its regiment. The heavy tanks, the T-10s and JS-3s would follow, the SU-130 tank destroyers, the JSU-152 assault guns. The mechanized infantry in their carriers, Taffkowski felt a message being pressed into his hand, it confirmed that the unit he had been watching had beaten the next fastest division by a clear five minutes in completing its bridge.

His jeep pulled up at the bridge. Some of the Pioneers were extracting the bogged-down vehicles, others were getting the tensioning cable system into place. Others were just too exhausted to move, As Taffkowski had feared, medics were treating men with crushed hands and feet. Wounded were being brought back from the left bank; the dead were left where they had fallen. In the middle, the divisional commander was supervising the clear-up of the worksite. He saw Colonel-General Taffkowski and sprang to attention.

"Major General Vladimir Ivanovich Surov. You are no longer commander of the 254th Engineer Division." Taffkowski saw his shock, Ok so the first bridge junction hadn't gone well, but they'd picked up the time. Surely the days when minor setbacks sent men to the Gulag had gone? "The 254th Engineer Division will now be renamed the First Guards Engineer Division with the Honorific "Volga" and, Lieutenant General Surov, you are its commander."

There was a surge of pride in the exhausted men, and a ragged series of cheers, there would be other Guards Engineer Divisions but there would never be another First Guards Engineers. They would have bragging rights for as long as there was a Russian Army.

Taffkowski swung his finger along the line of bridging boats, watching Surov out of the corner of his eyes. When his finger reached a BMK commanded by a grizzled Sergeant, Surov nodded slightly. "You, Sergeant. I was watching you. What is your name?"

"Boris Alexandrovich Dick, Gospodin Colonel-General"

"You handled your boat with great skill. You are a Hero of the Russian People and I have that medal here for you. Remember you hold it in trust for all your crew. Bratischka, I have something else you may appreciate even more." Taffkowski's driver handed him a bottle of vodka. Taffkowski read the label then gave the bottle to the Sergeant. "Good vodka for a good man. Russia thanks you, Boris Alexandrovich."

Behind them, Russian armor of the 57th Mechanized Army, First Byelorussian Front, was pouring across the bridge over the Volga.

Baronial Hall, Walthersburg, New Schwabia

The fortifications had done their job, Model could see that. The Russian assault had been ferocious and three of his nine infantry divisions had been destroyed but he'd expected that. He'd positioned his weakest three divisions north of the Don and east of the Volga. The divisions north of the Don had taken the full force of the First and Second Ukrainian Fronts. The first day, some of the defenders had abandoned their bunkers and run but there had been a cure for that. Behind the German lines were the Einsatzgruppen, waiting for deserters. Those they'd caught had been hanged from the nearest convenient object. After that, the infantry in the bunkers had got the message, it was safer to stay where they were and fight.

It had taken the Russians a week to chew through the defenses north of the Don, and that was the easy part. The Don Line itself was defended by three of his better infantry divisions in heavy fortifications, ones that made the bunkers north of the Don look feeble. His three best infantry divisions were north of Walthersburg, that was the one sector not protected by a serious water obstacle. Instead it was solid concrete, minefields and wire.

A messenger came in, bearing a sealed envelope. Model glanced at it, it was from the International Committee of the Red Cross. They were probably whining again about the treatment of Russian civilians in New Schwabia. Spineless old women, complaining about a few hardships on peasants while he was trying to build a country. He waved the message away, it was put in his in-tray with the rest of the mail.

So the next stage would be the assault over the Don. The Ivans would try to break through there and swing around to take Walthersburg from the south while the three fronts massed north of the city, the Second Byelorussian and the First and Second Moldovian Fronts tried to crush the defenses. He could hold them, he was sure of it. Crossing the Don would be a nightmare under the best of circumstances and he had Sarin and Tabun shells moved up to make sure it was far, far worse than that.

He'd also moved XXXXVIIth Panzer Corps with the 3rd Panzer, 11th Panzer, 14th Panzer and the 10th Panzer Grenadier divisions up behind the Don to counter-attack any break-throughs. He had a second Panzer Corps behind Walthersburg, ready to counterattack there. That left him stretched very thin, he only had the SS Wiking Division left in reserve. The 2nd Fallschirmjaeger division was spread out along the hills on the left bank of the Volga. The Ivans had tried a feint there, the First Khazak Front had driven in the defenses east of the river but Model wasn't biting. The parachutists were the best infantry he had, they would contain any minor raids the Russians launched across the river. The Volga itself was the best defense.

A messenger came in, dirty, his uniform torn and stained. Model reflected that if he'd been in a war film, he would have berated the man for his condition but this was reality not drama. Any man who came into a military headquarters in that condition had a very good reason for doing so. The man was weaving on his feet, he'd come far and fast.

"Sit down, son. Gather yourself, a few seconds more won't matter. Orderlies, get this man some coffee and schnapps. And some food. What unit are you from?"

"Fallschirmjaeger sir, from the Volga. The Russians have crossed in strength. In great strength here." The courier pushed a dispatch bag to Model. The seal was broken and Model raised an eyebrow. "Einsatzgruppen sir. They thought I was deserting, they were going to hang me, they broke open the case to see what was inside. When they saw it was for you they let me go. It wasted half an hour sir I'm sorry."

Model wondered briefly how many more vital messages were hanging by a roadside. He opened the message bag and started to read. As he did so, he went white. The report had obviously been written by the commander of a unit in the last stages of destruction. Three bridges over the Volga. More being built. Heavy armor over. Units identified, First Byelorussian Front., 57th Mechanized Army, 5th Guards Tank Army, 1st Mechanized Corps, 2nd Mechanized Corps, 20th Tank Corps. All units that were supposed to be North of Walthersburg. The defenses on the left bank of the Volga overrun. 2nd Fallschirmjaeger Division overrun and destroyed. What was left was falling back to Sadovoye. Where was Sadovoye?

Model went over to the map and looked. "SCHEISSE."

The exclamation made everybody look up. Model took a breath. There was no need to panic, panic was a worse enemy than the Russians. The Ivans hadn't got that far, it was just the German survivors of the Volga defense line were falling back to there. Keep calm, he ordered himself. Disasters happen in wars, that is why they are called wars. Armies get routed in wars and the art is to put the pieces back together again. He heard his old instructor from Staff College talking. "Always remember the feint you ignore is the enemy's main thrust." It sounded like a joke or something a cynic would say but it was true. And he'd forgotten the lesson and fallen into the trap.

So it was time to plan. Another memory from his old instructor "If you can keep your head when all about you are losing theirs, victory will be yours."

The Russians were across the Volga. How had they done it? An assault crossing of the Volga was impossible, it was too wide. It would take days to build bridges over the river and even his this screen of paratroopers would be able to hold them off. It had to be the Americans. Had to be. They weren't satisfied with their damned Hellburners and loathsome jellygas, they'd invented a way of letting their troops walk on water. No, that was absurd.

The Americans weren't gods, although it was about time somebody made them aware of that.

The answer was obvious, it had to be their Marines. They'd built a six-division Marine Corps for the invasion of Europe but never used it. Postwar, they'd kept it and now they'd used it. They'd done the crossing of the Volga and opened the way up for the Russians. The Russians would be advancing, the American's ridiculous Pentomic Divisions couldn't fight their way through a paper bag.

Now, what to do? The Ivans were over the river on a what was it, a 30 kilometer front? Say 30 kilometers. They must be planning to race across New Schwabia behind his lines and take his Don fortifications from the rear. They'd cut Walthersburg off from the rest of the country as well. Then they could mop the south of the country up at their leisure while besieging the fortresses along Northern edge. But, the way to eliminate a bridgehead was to hit the flanks. Pinch it off from the river, surround it and destroy it.

By sheer blind luck LII Panzer Corps was in the right place. It had 2nd, 12th and 13th Panzer divisions and the 8th Panzer Grenadier Division. They were almost in the right place anyway and they would have to change their facing but that was routine staff work. The SS Wiking Division was at Volgodonsk, most certainly not the right place. It would have to move fast. To Sadovoye. To link up with the other troops there. And a division from Walthersburg itself, he would have to strip one from the city defenses. They were the three best divisions he had and the 106th Infantry, well, it was the best of the best. They, and the survivors of 2nd Fallschirmjaeger could form a stop line.

Now to beef it up a bit. There had to be troops around there. Service unit, truck units, fuel depots. Get to work, get the officers to sweep up anybody wearing a uniform. And anybody who wasn't but looked like he should be. Or could be. There was a penal battalion not far away, at Malyye Derbetyy. They'd do as well. He would issue the orders but in truth it wasn't necessary. Every officer would already be gathering up whatever men he could find and forming them into combat units. They'd be holding out where they could, pulling back and trying to link up where they couldn't.

This was one thing the German Army had down to a fine art; making defenses out of nothing. Time and again, the Russians had learned that what appeared to be a gaping hole in the German lines was nothing of the sort. There would always be something there, tenuous, thin, ill-supplied but they'd hold until reinforcements arrived. Now, they would have to do it again.

One thing was obvious, he couldn't command from here. He'd have to go south, to join the forces there. He's co-locate with the SS Wiking Division, he could rely on his Wehrmacht units to keep a calm head on their shoulders but the SS tended to get distracted by irrelevancies and target fixated. And, truth be told, they may have the best equipment and the best manpower but their officers weren't Wehrmacht standard. He'd have to keep a closer eye on them. Talking about keeping an eye on things. The courier who'd arrived was drinking coffee now and picking at some black bread and jam. He was probably in shock, coming within seconds of being hanged as a deserter tended to do that.

"What is your name Leutenant?" The courier looked up nervously.

"Martin Sir. Willi Martin."

"You did a good job getting here Leutenant Martin, I can use men like you on my staff. A good courier is hard to find." Model reached out, an aide had anticipated the request and put a badge in his hand. "You got here without one of these, but in future, this will make your work much easier. If the Einsatzgruppen stop you again, show them this then they will apologize for delaying you while polishing your boots with their tongues."

Model started rapping out a string of orders, moving some units, getting word out to others. Getting his own staff to prepare a shift to the new forward headquarters. He reflected that, with a gaping hole in his front, a Russian tank army or two loose in his rear areas, no reserves left, nowhere to retreat to, it was quite like old times. Reassuringly familiar in fact. The Russians had pulled a coup, a superb stroke that had cracked the whole situation wide open. Now, it was up to him to glue the pieces back together. In the organized chaos of his headquarters, the urgent letter from the International Committee of the Red Cross sat in the in-tray, unread and forgotten.

Primary Debriefing Room, United States Air Force Air Warfare Center, Nellis AFB, Nevada

The glaring wave of resentment hit Captain Kozlowski as soon as he stepped into the debriefing theater. A montage of images involving a rioting mob, being ridden out of the base on a rail, tarring and feathering, lynching and some enthusiastic application of chainsaws flooded his mind. There was no doubt about it, the Fighter Mafia were taking what had happened very badly.

It was a relief to join the ranks of the Bomber Barons. The B-52 crews were on their feet applauding the crews of *Marisol* and *Tiger Lily,* slapping their backs and cheering. General Montana, commander of the 100th Bomb Group actually rose to his feet to salute the RB-58 pilots. The RB-58C had made its first appearance at Red Sun and this the results threatened to reduce the debriefing session to utter chaos.

Captain John Paul Martin walked up on the Podium and banged his gavel. There was almost instant silence. Amongst his many responsibilities, Martin had to organize the search and rescue exercises, the SAREXs that paralleled Red Sun. Crews would be assigned the roles of shot-down airmen while the Combat Search and Rescue, CSAR, teams tried to find and extract them. Of course, the crews got to practice their desert survival skills while waiting for the rescue.

Any pilot who argued with Martin's judgments as range officer had their objections carefully evaluated, the relevant range tapes called up for inspection and the situation explained in detail. His objections answered, next day, the pilot in question would find himself sitting in the desert, waiting to be rescued and watching the Rattlesnakes, Sidewinders and Gila Monsters edging closer. It was not for nothing that Captain Martin was also known as Captain Sarex and old-timers at Red Sun did not argue with him.

"Gentlemen, welcome to the first debriefing session of the 1959 Red Sun National Air Warfare Evaluation Exercises. After the events of this morning I am sure you will all agree that we all have much to learn. I would like to start by welcoming the crews of *Marisol* and *Tiger Lily* from the 305th Strategic Reconnaissance Group following their – explosive – entry to Red Sun. To recap, this morning's exercise was a small-scale operation that was intended as a warming up and systems check mission prior to the start of the main sessions tomorrow. However, as you all well know, that wasn't how it ended.

Earlier That Day, Range Administration Hut, United States Air Force Air Warfare Center, Nellis AFB, Nevada

It wasn't a hut of course, the description of the buildings as "huts" stemmed from the early days of Red Sun when the range had been thrown together using whatever could be found. Now, the "Hut" was the center of an elaborate network of visual, radar and other sensors that provided the range administration officers with complete coverage of everything that was going on. Not only that, it recorded them so that the track charts, conversations and events could be played back and examined to determine exactly what had happened and when. Sometimes, when aircraft had crashed, that had been of more than operational importance. The purpose of the morning exercise was primarily to test that network.

The basic plan was simple, there was a target on the ground, representing an enemy force that had allegedly invaded the United States and it was to be attacked by a cell of SACs heavy bombers. The target was defended by three Ajax missile batteries, 12 F-101B Voodoo interceptors from the 60th Interceptor Squadron at Otis AFB in Massachusetts and four F-104A Starfighters from the 83rd Fighter Interceptor Squadron at Hamilton AFB in California.

From the range data, Martin could see they'd set up a fairly standard defense. The Ajax batteries were positioned to provide an initial salvo at the attacking formations, the B-52s would probably be able to evade them but their formation would be broken up by the effort and that would degrade their bombing and leave them open to the fighters. The long-range F-101s were already up, orbiting behind and to either side of the target area. Once the bomber formation started to break up they would close in and pick off the bombers. Finally, the four F-104s were waiting on the ground, as soon as the bomber formation they'd take off, climb to altitude and pick off any bombers that had leaked through.

It was the US defense system in miniature. Missiles providing long-range defense and breaking up the attacking formations, long-range fighters to destroy the bulk of the attackers and short-range point defense interceptors to finish off the survivors. It was beginning to work now, the bombers were finding it harder and harder to get to their targets and were taking increasing losses in the process.

This year, the defending fighters had a few wrinkles added, including the MB-1 rocket. Martin was wondering how the SAC bombers would cope with that. He'd find out soon. The leading edge of the SAC formation was appearing on the radar scope now. A main formation of four B-52Ds, and way out in front a pair of RB-52Bs. That was standard, the RB-52s would use their electronic suites to find the SAM batteries and jam them then try to snarl up the fighter operations by jamming and deception. That would open the way for the bombers. Fundamentally, it was the same way SAC had breached German defenses in The Big One and it was getting old. The attack pattern here seemed almost the same as in the comparable operation the year before, the only difference was that the RB-52 element was a bit further out in front – perhaps that was because of the MB-1s.

The defensive forces were already beginning to react to the approaching attack force. The search radars on the Ajax batteries were lighting up and the F-101s were adjusting their position, at this time they were hanging back to clear the field for the Ajax missiles. The F-104s on hot-pad alert were spooling up ready for take-off. The F-104 was a controversial aircraft, Martin had heard that the Thai Air Force had taken delivery of a batch and wondered if they'd found all the things that were wrong with it yet.

"Ye Gods what is THAT". The monitor terminals in the Range Instrumentation section had two sections. The big one was from the range instrumentation sets, the small overhead ones were the repeater sets from the defense air search radars. The latter could be – and usually were - jammed as part of the exercises. The range instrumentation radars operated on rigidly defined frequencies that were prohibited to everybody else and could not be. There were seven defensive radars in use, the three volume search and three target tracking radars for the Ajax missiles and the fighter control radar. They'd all exploded into jagged pinwheels and masses of drifting electronic fuss. However, the range instrumentation was still clear. The two "RB-52" aircraft had accelerated and were now doing over 1,600 mph – and had started to climb. This, thought Captain Martin, had every promise of turning into an interesting day. He mentally wrestled with the picture of a B-52 doing 1,600 miles per hour, then asked himself the critical question. Just what was going on up there?

Defense Systems Operator's Position, RB-58C "Marisol"

"Time to go guys. Get ready for defended area penetration"

"Air-to-air and Air to ground modes engaged."

"Defensive Systems up running and ready."

"Andale, let's dance."

Xavier Dravar checked the defense systems in front of him. The ALR-12 display was showing seven threat radars operating. There'd be more but the Red Sun range instrumentation radars were filtered out. For the last hour he'd had the ALQ-6 blip enhancer working, modifying the radar image of the RB-58C so that it resembled the larger and slower RB-52B. That bluff wasn't going to hold any longer. As *Marisol* had said, it was time to dance. He flipped the ALQ-16 from "stand-by" to "barrage transmit".

Now, the system was picking up the radar frequency energy from the threat radars and using it to generate a mass of contradictory and deceptive signals, giving the receiving radars the electronic equivalent of a hissy fit. And the same time he felt the punch in his back as The Boss up front firewalled the throttles and the afterburners cut in. Out of the tiny window in the side of his position he saw the other RB-58, *Tiger Lily* fall back a fraction and then accelerate with *Marisol*. Her pilot, Captain Joel Mitchell, had worked with them before. That cut down on communications, at these speeds, there was no time for all that. His rudimentary flight instrumentation gave him speed and altitude only, all he needed for his job. 1,620 miles per hour, 66,500 feet up.

On the ALR-12 display, he could see the icons for the Ajax missile batteries flickering. The operators would have seen the jamming, they couldn't help but see it, their screens must be glowing white-hot with all the energy he was pumping out. They were flipping frequencies, trying to get through the jamming. They were also rippling their transmissions from one to the next, hoping to hide their positions. Too late, he thought, far, far too late. We had you before the dance even began. Now all that was left was to finish them, he flipped another switch and transferred the information from his emitter location system to the navigator/bombardier station in front of him.

Range Administration Hut, United States Air Force Air Warfare Center, Nellis AFB, Nevada

Martin watched the maneuver with fascination. They had to be SACs new RB-58Cs, nothing else in the inventory performed like that. They'd soared straight through the Ajax battery's engagement zone while the radar operators were still trying to cope with the jamming and then peeled over.

"Papa-November, Papa-November." That was Lieutenant Wu from *Tiger Lily*. The message was accompanied by the burst transmission of the target co-ordinates. "Papa-November." That was Korrina in *Marisol*, also with his target co-ordinates. Three

GAM-83B missiles were arcing downwards towards their targets. Now, it was range instrumentation's job to work out the impact points of the missiles. Although given the "November" bit of the launch code, it didn't matter very much.

The range operators were flipping slide rules to calculate the real impact points, the GAM-83 had a known CEP so it was just straightforward maths. Sure enough, all three radars were within the radius of total destruction for the warheads. Martin cut the transmissions to the Ajax radar operators and watched them jump as their screens went black.

"Ajax sites 19/78, 17/25 and 18/03 you may stand down now. You have been destroyed."

Then Martin did a double take at the display screens. There really were dragons, the check really was in the mail and politicians spoke the truth. Or, in the crazy universe that had obviously crept up on them, they would from now on. Because, in the sky over the Red Sun test range, the bombers were attacking the fighters.

Bombardier-Navigator's Position, RB-58C "Marisol"

Display management was another art that had been introduced with the RB-58C. Eddie Korrina was playing his displays like a master. He'd had the input from the ASQ-42 radar bombing system on his main scope with the repeat from Xav's emitter location system on the left-hand secondary screen and the air-to-air input from the ASG-18 on the right hand secondary. That had allowed him to keep an eye on the Voodoos but they were too far back and out of position. It looked like the sheer speed of the attack had completely thrown the defenses.

Now to deal with the fighters, he toggled the displays so the air-to-air picture took center stage. The F-101s were heading in and the distance was closing fast but he had them locked. The ASG-18 was track-while-scan and could paint two targets simultaneously whole continuing to search for more. He had the Voodoo formations on the left and ahead dialed in, *Tiger Lily* would be taking the formation over on the right.

"Fox-November, Fox-November"

Now, if this was for real, two GAR-9s would be streaking out in front of *Marisol* accelerating up to Mach 6 and climbing up to top out at over 150,000 feet. Then, they would plunge on the formation beneath and initiate their nuclear warhead in its middle. The data package attached to the GAR-9 launch rail was transmitting target and course data to the range instrumentation center that was simulating the missile launch. Korrina looked, the right hand Voodoo was flying straight and level – that made them dead meat but..." Break left, break left. MB-1 inbound."

Marisol did a barrel roll, changing altitude by 15,000 feet and breaking left by 90 degrees. *Tiger Lily* did the same breaking right. Now, they'd hear from Range Instrumentation if it was enough.

Range Administration Hut, United States Air Force Air Warfare Center, Nellis AFB, Nevada

"Jeez, will you look at that." The range observer's voice was hushed with awe, fighters maneuvered radically in these exercises but nobody had ever seen a double-sonic barrel roll before let alone one performed by a bomber. "Won't that break their radar lock's sir?"

"Doesn't matter." Martin's voice was awed also, even after five years at Red Sun, he'd never seen anything like this before. SAC had sprung a major strategic surprise on the defending forces. Certainly, the missile crews and fighter pilots knew the performance details of the RB-58 and were aware the aircraft were coming this year but it was one thing to read figures, another to see what they meant in the sky. Another demonstration of the old military maxim "surprise exists in the mind of the enemy."

It wasn't as if *Marisol* and *Tiger Lily* were maneuvering hard or were exceptionally agile, Martin would have to inspect the tapes later but he doubted if either aircraft had exceeded one g. It was the sheer blinding speed with which they were shifting from one maneuver to another and flipping between targets and weapons that were decisive. They were way inside the decision-making curve of the defenses, to the point where it seemed that the defensive aircraft and missiles were co-operating in their own destruction.

"The GAR-9 is an active radar homing missile, its got its own guidance radar. The MB-1s are unguided. Have we got results on them?"

The analysis team were frantically working to get the results of the launches calculated. There were rumors that computers were being developed that would take over this role but it seemed unlikely, Computers were big, expensive and unwieldy, even now, there were engineers going around with baskets of spares replacing blown valves. Until that happened, the analysis team would make do with slip-sticks and pie-cutters.

"MB-1s clean miss. Not even close. GAR-9s direct hits on formation centers. Wipe out, small chance of some of the fighters surviving but not much – and if they did, they aren't gonna be doing anything useful."

"*Marisol, Tiger Lily*, nuclear explosions behind you. No threat. Vampire One, Vampire Two and Vampire Three return to base. You have been shot down. Say again, you are nuclear fission products, return to base."

Martin looked at the situation display again. The four F-104s, Sierra-One, were climbing towards the battle area but they were already late. The RB-58s were above and on either side of them and were already swooping down for the kill. Looking at the screen, Martin was reminded of the days he'd watched hawks hunting for prey. Same devastating precision.

Pilot's Position, RB-58C "Marisol"

Captain Mike Kozlowski focused on the F-104s below him and to his left. His inlets were cooling off now, the barrel role had taken them to 102 percent of safe operating temperatures. That meant the ground crews would have to check the panels overnight for distortion. If he'd gone over 105 percent, *Marisol* would have been grounded for a thorough inspection. Now, he was diving on the F-104s at just over 1,620 miles per hour. He'd be going behind and below them any second now. "*Tiger Lily*, extend."

The second RB-58 leveled off and accelerated away from the F-104s. The Starfighter was a point defense interceptor, very fast, with a superb rate of climb but its radar had a very narrow tracking scan while the pilot had poor vision aft. Their radar warner would pick up a lock-on but Korrina would be scanning only. He wouldn't lock until the last second. The situation now was a sandwich with the F-104s in the middle. *Marisol* was closing in below and behind them while *Tiger Lily* was ahead and climbing away. Kozlowski grinned and selected his GAR-8s. He framed the central F-104 and waiting until the annunciator growled. It would be a perfect GAR-8 shot, point-blank range against a target perfectly framed. "Fox-One."

It took only a second for range instrumentation to get back. "Kill confirmed. Sierra one-one, break off, return to base. You have been killed."

"Sheee-it." It was Sierra One-two who, very correctly, believed that a second GAR-8 was already locking onto his tailpipe. The F-104 formation broke up, the leader diving away to return to Nellis, Sierra one-two trying to turn and climb into the sun to duck the inevitable missile. Sierra one-three and one-four were breaking left, hoping to scissors and sandwich the RB-58 between them, the way the RB-58s had trapped them a few seconds earlier. The problem was that while their radars had a narrow scan cone, the ASG-18 did not. *Tiger Lily* was already turning and bringing her missile armament to bear. All she needed was enough separation to fire safely.

"Fox-One" From *Marisol* "Miss" from Range Instrumentation. Kozlowski swore and started to lock his third GAR-8 on. He'd been afraid of that, the sun was too strong an IR source. In the rear seat, Dravar was locking his 20 millimeter cannon onto one of the two F-104s now behind them. A long, long way behind them

"Fox-November" from *Tiger Lily*. A pause then "Sierra one-three and Sierra one-four. Break off and return to base, You're history."

Ahead of Marisol the last F-104 was running out of energy; the long climb up to the battle area had left the little fighter short to start with and the climb into the sun had bled off what was left. In contrast, *Marisol* had dived into action and her weight gave her an energy reserve that was still undepleted. The F-104 ran out first and rolled out of its climb. In doing so, its afterburner made a perfect target

"Fox-One"

"That's a hit, Sierra One-two, go home, its all over." The two RB-58s formed up and, still on full afterburner, exited the target area leaving the defenses a (simulated) smoking shambles. Behind them, the B-52s split up for their own bombing runs.

Primary Debriefing Room, United States Air Force Air Warfare Center, Nellis AFB, Nevada

"Gentlemen, that concludes the mission review. *Marisol* is credited with one Ajax site, eight F-101 Voodoos and two F-104s. *Tiger Lily* is credited with two Ajax sites, four F-101s and two F-104s. Much more importantly, the B-52s were able to make their bombing runs unmolested. Captain Kozlowski, would you take the podium first please to answer any questions?"

Kozlowski looked down on the audience. During the account and video trackfilms of the wild furball over the exercise area, the resentment of the fighter pilots and triumphalism of the bomber crews had gone, to be replaced by hard professional interest in the mechanics of the fight. The implications of what had happened were quite clear, the bombers had taken the fight to the interceptor and missile defenses and won decisively. That meant somebody else who had the same equipment could have done the same and an American city could pay the price.

"Captain Kozlowski." It was the pilot of Vampire One-one "How close to the envelope edge were you pushing your aircraft. Did you have much performance in hand?"

"We went slightly over the edge ducking your MB-1 shots. By the way, its very obvious when you are lining up for those, the radar picture shows it clearly. Frankly, I don't think you should rely on MB-1s, they are fine against B-52s but we're fast and agile enough to see them coming and get clear.

"We went to 102 percent on inlet temperature and 99.8 on leading edge and canopy. That means the aircraft have to go in for a check-up. It was a transient, not sustained so no harm done. We're getting new inlets and cockpit canopy materials that will ease the limitations a bit. We're told we'll be cleared to 1,700 mph when they arrive. We're limited to 1,660 tops at the moment."

The Voodoo pilot nodded. What he was about to say would get him ridiculed but professionalism demanded he ask. "Captain, I'll be honest, you wiped the floor with us. How did you do it, and from your perspective what could we have done to stop you?"

Kozlowski thought carefully "Our big edge is that we have three people in the crew. Lieutenant Dravar was defending us jamming your radars and the ground sets, leaving Lieutenant Korrina to concentrate on attacking the defenses. That left me clear to fly. Another big edge is fuel. We can fly on full afterburner an hour or more." That caused an intake of breath from the Fighter Mafia.

"If all else fails we can just run you out of fuel and energy. Or, if that fails, just run. You can't catch us and, to be honest, in a tail chase, I don't think your missiles can. We're scheduled to fly against the new F-106 a little later. That may be different. As for what would have made our lives harder?" There was laughter and a stir of interest.

"Get in close, we rely on nuclear weapons to take you out. We can't use them if you're right beside us. Don't forget our tail gun though. And spread out so we don't take whole formations out with single shots."

Other pilots, fighter and bomber were rising with questions. Kozlowski realized that it was going to be a long, long session. Ruefully he thought that if he'd wanted an early night he should have lost the battle, But there were lessons to be learned and learning lessons was what Red Sun was all about.

Ban Rom Phuoc, Thai-Burmese Border

Name of a name, they were all crying again. Who would believe that a creaky drama series could have this effect? It was called Path of Virtue and was centered around a rich family living in Bangkok. The hero was their son who had fallen in love with the heroine, a girl from a poor family. His parents had opposed the match and done everything possible to break the couple up – even to the extent of making false accusations against the heroine. Then, the wealthy wife had been in a serious accident and been taken to hospital. There, her husband had seen the girl they had condemned was a nurse and was working her hardest to save his wife, even though they'd done so much to harm her.

Stricken with guilt at their cruelty and injustice, the rich parents had approved the son's marriage and the father had become a Monk to make amends for all his wrongdoings. But now an evil Japanese company man also had designs on the heroine and, deciding if he couldn't have her, nobody would, had poisoned her wedding meal. The heroine was just to eat when the black-and-white image had faded and the credits had rolled. Tune in again next week.

Phong Nguyen reflected on the power that box had. It was incredible, it could manipulate peoples feelings and their whole outlook. Path of Virtue was brilliant propaganda, entertaining and enjoyable with its messages carefully presented so they didn't jar. No matter how hard the trials, no matter how great the injustices, the young hero and heroine always overcame them by their honesty and integrity. The guilty were always found and punished, those who behaved bravely and decently were rewarded.

Suddenly he realized something very profound. This one box could revolutionize the whole art of insurgency. The riskiest part of running an insurgency was the initial stages, sending cadres out to spread the word. As the Chipanese were finding out, this was a hard, hard task and the risks were great. But use this box, and the whole thing could be done centrally, Work the revolutionary message into the scripts and an insurgency could be started without sending the cadres in. The groundwork could be done without risking those valuable assets. That box, sitting in the corner of the communal hut, could do it all.

Even here it had done so much already. After the night of the attack, Army engineers had arrived and installed a diesel-powered electricity generator. It powered lights in the village hut, ran a radio and operated a few simple machines. Then, the box had arrived. It was said that a wealthy man, who owned the factory that made them, had heard of the courageous fight put up by the village and sent them the box to show his respect. The television set head been set up in the hut and a couple of men from the Army had helped tune it into the television transmitter. First night they'd switched it on and their whole world had changed.

It wasn't just the drama shows. There was a program for farmers just before dawn that gave them a weather forecast and advice on crops and livestock. The same program also gave the prices that were being paid in Bangkok for rice and eggs and meat, all the products that earned the village its money. With that information, they'd been able to make the merchant who bought their crops pay the village farmers a much better price for their produce.

So the television was made to work for an hour in the morning for the farmers and for another hour in the evening so the women could watch their drama and the men the news. That was another astonishing thing. There was a world out there, different countries, different people and so much was happening. The national news was on now, followed by the world news. The first international item was from Australia. Everybody in the hut chorused "G'Day Nudge". Nudge had been the Australian who had brought some young water buffalo to replace the one killed during the night of the attack. He'd stayed for a few days to get the animals established and taught people a few words of English. Now, whenever Australia was on the news, everybody would greet him, as if the box would take their picture to him.

Fighting, a lot of it. From a place called Russia. Phong Nguyen watched with the eyes of a professional. This wasn't insurgency, this was regular war. And, by what these films showed, this one was a bloodbath. Grim, he could see the steel tanks forcing their way forward through what appeared to be a heavily-fortified position. Apparently the Russians, had done something quite remarkable and now some sort of great battle was expected. If the great battle was expected, what was this? He noted a lot of the Tahan Pran were watching with the same interested professionalism. They were coming on well.

They'd stopped being a defensive force now and were taking the battle to the Chipanese over the border. Their main attack defeated, the Chipanese had started sniping at villagers while they worked. A couple of villagers had been hit, none killed mercifully, so Phong Nguyen had taken some of the most skilled Tahan Pran volunteers out and set up an ambush. They'd picked up a sniper and left his head on a stake as warning.

From then on, the patrols and ambushes had become more ambitious. The villagers had learned they couldn't just sit behind barbed wire, they had to control the countryside around them. So they'd started patrolling and sending out night ambush groups. Then some Army specialists had come and given a little expert advice. Now the village was becoming a center for offensive operations against the Chipanese insurgents in Burma next door.

It was becoming a center in another way as well. About a third of the people in the room were from surrounding villages, come to enjoy the electric light and marvel at the wonder of the television set. They would go back home tonight and ask why it was that their village couldn't have such things. And the answer would be that if they supported the government as bravely as Ban Rom Phuoc had, they would have them. Loyalty and bravery were virtues and virtues were rewarded.

There was another incentive as well. Some of the visitors were men who'd come here hoping to catch a girl they could take home as a wife, But many of the girls here wore the black overalls of the Tahan Pran and carried their AKs slung over their shoulders. Their attitude was simple. If their suitor was not Tahan Pran, he was wasting his time. The hopeful suitors had been given an unambiguous message,

"Go home, boy. If you wish me consider you a man, you must prove it. Join the Tahan Pran." It was the same for visiting women, hoping to catch husbands they saw that eligible men looked first to the Tahan Pran women when courting.

That was reasonable, for it was the wife's duty to protect the family home – and what better way was there to prove they could do that than to join the militia? And so other villages were forming their own militia units – and when they did so, they committed themselves to the government. It was a classic insurgency but turned on its head, the techniques used to subvert and bring down a government instead serving to support and defend it.

The television had a picture of the Bangkok skyline – that meant a Government message coming. The spokesman was a young man who gave out a grave warning to the villagers. There were men around who were going to villages, offering to give young women well-paid jobs in the city. But they were a fraud for the women would be taken to Chipan to act as comfort women for Chipanese soldiers. Any women who went with those men would not be seen again. So if such men come to your village, seize them and hand them over to the Authorities for punishment. And send your Tahan Pran to other villages that cannot hear this warning, tell them too of this danger. And that was another thing that was happening, the village militias were becoming a communication system, spreading word and messages through the countryside.

He felt a touch on his arm, it was Lin bringing him a bowl of her Pad Thai noodles. He thanked her gracefully and started in on his dinner, feeling the other men in the room envy him. He and Lin were accepted as a couple now, it was assumed they would soon be married. And that would mean nobody else would get to try her superb Pad Thai.

Later that evening he was taking a patrol out, the Tahan Pran had been asked if they could take a Chipanese insurgent prisoner and bring him in alive. It was the sort of thing the Tahan Pran did well, they knew the area so intimately, in the ways no regular army could, that they could find the insurgents no matter how well they'd thought they'd hidden themselves. He'd be back by dawn, just in time to check the prices on eggs and chickens.

Flag Bridge, HIJMS Musashi, South China Sea

Armed forces never changed. Their operating principles had remained constant for centuries. Hurry up and wait then get the job done by yesterday. After months of swinging around their anchors, getting one set of movement orders after another issued then cancelled, they'd suddenly got the word, make maximum speed for Burma and screen the transport group that carried the Special Naval Landing Force. Now, his bows were heaving and his ships had bones between their teeth as they hurried to make up lost time.

It was raining, quite badly as it happened but the visibility was still good enough to see the rest of his task group around him. Behind was the *Yamato*, and there were two cruisers, one on each flank. *Tone* and *Chikuma*. Old ships now but they had their sterns cleared for aircraft operations. Once they had carried floatplanes, now Kayaba Ka-5 ASW helicopters. Japan had been the first country ever to deploy ASW helicopters, Soriva remembered the little Ka-1 with affection, and it was one of the few areas where Japan's Navy was still supreme.

Good question he asked himself, how could the Ka-5s cope with the American's new nuclear-powered submarines? He'd heard their latest boats, the Skipjacks, could do 35 knots underwater and hold that speed for months if necessary. If true, that was a terrifying threat. Down there, underwater, the submarines wouldn't be affected by weather, they could run at full speed undisturbed. In the old days, keeping speed high was a sure defense against submarine attack. The slow boats would probably be in the wrong position to launch and, even if they were in luck, they got one shot and no more.

But if the rumors about the Skipjack were true, then they had more than seven knots on his battleships. That made them deadly threats. They could run ahead, get a firing position, shoot, then run again and reload. In fact, they could simply outrun the destroyers, in this weather none of his ships could get close to 35 knots.

That was a scaring thought, his four destroyers were virtually useless against such submarines. In truth, they'd be hard-pushed to deal with a diesel-electric submarine. They were the Akitsuki class, built as anti-aircraft destroyers in the 1940s. They'd been good ships for their day with four twin high-velocity 100 millimeter guns and four torpedo tubes. Now, though, their guns were virtually useless against aircraft. The destroyers screening the transport group were from a different class, Kageros, but were equally old and their capabilities equally dubious. They'd been rebuilt as submarine hunters but the changes were minimal, a turret and four torpedo tubes removed, depth charge throwers added.

The only really good destroyers were with the carrier group. Agano class destroyers, built in the late 1940s and early 1950s. Originally they had been designed as light cruisers but the class had been remodelled and rearmed. Now they had two twin 100 millimeter guns forward and anti-aircraft missiles aft. They could carry Ka-5 helicopters as well. It was well they were around. That carrier group was vital. In a very real sense, the whole operation depended on two carriers with 108 aircraft between them and their screen of six Aganos.

Of course, it didn't matter if the Americans took a hand. Not only did they have more aircraft, they had better ones and they had nuclear weapons with no inhibitions about using them. An American task group would throw more than 500 aircraft, Crusaders, Skyhawks and Skywarriors.

Individually the aircraft had an edge over anything on the Japanese decks, well, perhaps that was too pessimistic, they could match the old F2J Dragon. The Japanese Navy was still struggling to get supersonics to sea and their current fighter, the A7W-2 was, at best, transonic. Their strike aircraft, the turboprop powered B8A Ryuseis was an impressive load-lifter, most people believed it superior to the US Navy's Skyraiders. But they were slow compared with the jets.

If, however, the Americans didn't take a hand, then things were different. Both the Australians and the Indians had bought a US Navy lightweight fighter for their carriers, the Grumman Tiger, and Skyhawks for strike but, like the carriers, they were taking their time about getting them operational. Neither the carriers nor the air groups had been cleared for service yet. Even some mediocre aircraft were better than none and so the Japanese carriers had things their own way.

They might need it as well. The reason for the haste was on his signals desk. Intelligence had reported that an Australian troop convoy was forming up and it was reported they were heading for Burma. Admiral Soriva had his orders. Get the SNLF to Rangoon first by whatever means necessary, the only restriction being the obvious one. Don't get us destroyed by the Americans. Projecting time, course and speed, assuming that the Australian Convoy would set sail as soon as *Hood* and her escorts had refueled, it was going to be very, very tight.

So, he had his fleet arranged. His own battle group out in front, clearing the way. Behind him was the troop convoy with its merchant ships. Then, bringing up the rear, the carrier group. The problem was that troop convoy, merchant ships were faster now than they'd been when Admiral Soriva had been a youngster but they were still painfully slow. His fleet could hold the speed of the slowest ships and the merchies could do 12 knots sustained at best.

He'd routed his formations so that they would keep clear of land based aircraft, assuming that the Australians deployed their carrier groups from land bases. But his eyes kept going to Clark Field in the Philippines. If anybody had long-range bombers there, it would put him in a critical position. It was fortunate nobody in the Triple Alliance had them.

Captain's Bridge, INS Hood, Perth, Australia

The crew had turned to with a vengeance. *Hood* had pulled into Perth almost out of fuel and supplies after her high-speed run across the Pacific. She'd finished her tour and got back on schedule but it had been tight. Her tired engines shouldn't have been capable of holding that speed so long but they had and they were still in good condition. There was something ominous in the way her engines had been making the ship tremble and in the way her bows cut the water. Captain Jim Ladone could feel that the old ship was furious at the insult to her honor and wanted her chance to get back at those responsible.

The crew certainly were. There was suppressed rage at the cowardly bombing on her quarterdeck. The stern area itself was now sacred ground, the teak planking still ripped and scarred from the bomb, memorial tablets placed to honor the dead. Well, all but one of the dead. The rage and humiliation of the crew hadn't, thank God, resulted in deaths on board *Hood* but there had been a mysterious spate of "accidents" on board the two destroyers. All the victims had been Moslem crew members. All the deaths had been investigated as far as the law and the circumstances allowed but nothing had come up to show that they were anything other than accidents.

It wouldn't. The crews of the ships, Moslem and Hindu, had kept their mouths welded firmly shut. The trouble was that, following an "accident" on *Rana*, the locker of the victim had been searched. And there had been bomb-making equipment inside. Equipment that hadn't been there when the ship was searched after the bombing on *Hood*. Had it been on the ship and moved ready for another attack? Or brought on board at one of the many port stays? Or even planted by other crew members to justify a killing or stir up more trouble? Nobody knew, everybody had a theory, everybody worried.

Now, the primary task in hand was getting the ships to sea. With a little luck, everybody was working to hard and getting too tired to worry over such things. There was so much to be done before the ship was ready to put to sea again. Stores were being replenished, magazines topped off. Somehow, the Australian Navy had even managed to find some 15 inch shells for her guns. The oil hoses were throbbing as *Hood* sucked in the bunker oil that was her life blood. It was a crash job to get her ready for sea again, the Australian troop convoy was almost ready to leave.

Across the way, the two old carriers, *Sydney* and *Melbourne* had loaded up with vehicles and heavy equipment. Like Captain Ladone, they'd been Royal Navy once, *Illustrious* and *Victorious*, but it would have been too costly to convert them for modern aircraft. They made excellent heavy transports though, fast and their flight and hangar decks allowed even the heaviest vehicles to be stowed.

Beyond them, there were the liners that had been requisitioned as troop transports. It was going to be a fast convoy, they should be able to hold 20 knots all the way to Rangoon. One day, they would be able to airbridge formations like this. In fact on paper they already could, Quantas had a fleet of Cloudliners that could transport the personnel, it was carrying the heavy equipment that was impossible, One day there would be aircraft that would lift tanks and self-propelled artillery but until then, the big stuff would have to go by sea.

It was going to have to be a fast run. The Chipanese already had a troop convoy at sea and it was reported to be heading for Rangoon also. If they got there first, they'd be able to install a new government that favored the demands of the insurgents in the north of the country. On the other hand, if the Australian division got there first, they could support the existing government. The Chipanese squadron was nearer but the Australian squadron was faster.

There was one problem, at the moment a small one but one that could only grow. When Ladone projected the Japanese Fleet's course and speed then superimposed the Triple Alliance fleet's equivalent plans, the two plot's coincided. In fact, not only did they cross, but the two groups of ships would be in the same area at the same time. And that did not bode well.

The Australian troopships had an escort of course, the three Indian ships, two Australian cruisers and four more destroyers but that was barely adequate. In addition to the surface ships, they had air cover from an Australian Navy air group based at Darwin, 36 Grumman F11F-2 Tigers and 24 A4D-7 Skyhawks and another group had been moved up to Java.

Once they were close to Thailand, they'd have land-based air support from there. That was good, the Thai Air Force was small but it had the latest aircraft money could buy. Perhaps too recent, there were stories that the new aircraft were proving hard to keep operational. It wouldn't matter though, the problem was, in the most likely area of confrontation, all the available aircraft would be operating at the edge of their range. If there was going to be a confrontation, the ships would be on their own, without air support.

Ladone fingered his orders. They were very clear, very explicit. The Australian troop convoy had to get to Rangoon. No if, buts or maybes. If it cost the entire escort to get the troopships through, then so be it. It was one of those last man and last bullet type situations. The problem was that, as usual, the people who gave the orders were neither the last men nor did they have the last bullet in their possession.

Chapter Eight
Gaining Ground

Cockpit of Su-7 "For Maria Chermatova" over Malyye Derbety

It was quite like old times and it was nothing like old times. Charging through the tree-tops on his way for a ground attack strike at the Germans, it was almost like being back in his old F2G over France. Until he looked out of the cockpit of course. Then, instead of seeing Scott Brim's dark blue *Dominatrix* on his right there was a green and brown splotched Su-7, *For Ivan Fedeev* flown by his wing man Mikhail Boroda. The Su-7 was nothing like the F2G, in fact Colonel Tony Evans would have preferred his old mount over the new Russian aircraft. The old F2G had long legs by comparison with the fuel-guzzling jet.

But, the Su-7 had virtues all of its own, It was fast, even low down, and as solid as a rock. It kept going, and it fought hard for its pilot. He'd seen other Su-7s come back with damage that would have downed less solid aircraft and the ground crews had fixed them and sent them back to battle the next day. It could lift loads as well, he had two 2200 pound capacity hard points under the belly, and four 1100 pound hard points, two under each wing. Total theoretical load almost 9,000 pounds. Of course, if he carried that much, his tactical radius would equal his take-off run.

Still, he had napalm tanks under his belly and four 20-round S-8 rocket packs under his wings. And his two 30 millimeter cannon. His aircraft's name said it all. He was carrying the load *For Maria Chermatova*.

After The Big One, he'd flown F2H Banshees, then been sent to Russian language school for a while, then back to ground attack units. He'd flown the North American F2J-4 Dragon from carriers for a while, working his way up the command chain. Then, a little over a year ago, he'd been offered a 3-year tour of duty flying as an exchange officer with Russian Frontal Aviation. Bored with peacetime flying, he'd jumped at the chance. He'd done the three-month conversion course for the Su-7 then joined the 16th Guards Fighter Division. A proud unit that had been fighting the Germans since 1941. They'd made their names flying American aircraft, P-39 Airacobras, now they were back where they'd started, in the skies of the Kuban. It had been a long, long journey and the price paid had been frightful.

One thing had puzzled him when he came to Russia. Go down a street in any American town, and soon you'd see a house with a gold star hanging in one window, indicating a son or husband killed in the Second World War. He'd never seen anything like that in Russia. At first he'd wondered why, then as he knew more Russians, he'd found out. Every family in Russia had lost not one but many members during the long war. In fact, during his stay he hadn't found a single family that didn't have a long list of the dead to remember. Nobody knew what the total casualties were, some figures suggested more than a third of the population had died.

One sign was the shortage of men. Women were everywhere in the armed forces, maintaining aircraft and vehicles, when the pilots slept, the women were refueling and repairing their birds, taking oil samples for analysis, reloading guns and hanging ordnance from the racks. Those women were quietly desperate to find husbands and, in their hearts, most knew they would not. The best they could hope for was a temporary relationship, a "Campaign Wife" as the Russians called it. Prior to being sent to Russia, the American exchange officers had been given a quiet, private briefing.

"Because of the situation and the shortage of men, there are a lot of Russian women seeking partners. That means you. If you choose to enter such a relationship, you may do so but expect your assignment to Russia to be made permanent. We're in their country help them rebuild, to give, not to take."

When Evans had met his ground crew, he'd learned that Maria Chermatova had been the grandmother of the armorer responsible for maintaining his cannon and loading the proper ordnance for the strikes. During the occupation of Nizhny Novgorod, the Germans had murdered the old woman and her entire family. His armorer was the only survivor; Evans didn't have any Russian relations so, when he had heard the story, he'd asked if he could name his aircraft for the old lady. The gesture had gone down well with the unit, it had marked the acceptance of the American Marine into the Russian Fighter Division. Ever since then, he'd fired his rockets and dropped his napalm "for Maria Chermatova".

Now he was off to do it again. The Germans were moving a heavy armored force south on the Volzhskiy Road. It was threatening the northern flank of the Volga breakthrough that was taking back the last piece of Russian ground occupied by the Germans. Overhead, he could see MiG-19s were flying top cover for the heavily-laden Su-7s skimming through the treetops. The Germans had started the battle with few aircraft and most of what they'd had were gone now. Still, there was no need to take chances. He nestled the Su-7 closer to the ground, the old lessons still held good. Low and fast meant life. He'd shared those lessons with the Russian pilots and listened to theirs in his turn. One good thing about the Su-7 was its speed low down, he was holding just over 600 miles per hour. With a tactical radius of 200 miles, that meant each mission lasted less than an hour. Of course the down side was that they all flew two or three missions per day.

The Su-7 was bumping and jolting, something he'd noted in the old F2G days but the extra speed was making it worse. Some of the jolts were almost bad enough to tear the stick out of his hands. He spent every evening trying to ease the bruises out of his back but nothing much worked. Speed had another effect as well, he had a harder job staying ahead of the aircraft. The trees flashing underneath him gave precious little warning of sudden rises in the ground or obstructions lost in the haze. Tracers floated past his cockpit, he'd had even less warning of that. The two aircraft following behind him would deal with the gunner whoever he was.

There were clouds of smoke off to his left, that would be other fighters striking at the German movement. Evans had something different in mind. He'd noticed that the Russian pilots tended to strike at the head of a convoy. It was sensible, hit the leading vehicles, stop them moving and the rest of the convoy would pile up. Trouble was, they did it too often, so Evans was taking his section parallel to the German movement, he'd swing in and hit the rear of the convoy. With luck all the soft skins and command vehicles would be back there and the anti-aircraft guns up front.

More bumping and pounding, there was the wreckage of an old railway line under him now. Getting close to the time to swing around and in. The F2G had been no ballet dancer but the ponderous Sukhoi made his memories of trying to maneuver the vicious Super-Corsair a pleasant thought. The Sukhoi also had spanwise drift problems on its sharply-swept wings. They'd been fitted with wing fences but it was barely a partial solution. It meant that in a turn, a wrong move could cause the outer section of the wing to stall. That threw the aircraft into a flat spin and, down here, recovering from that just didn't happen. He was keeping the columns of smoke on his left roughly level with his shoulder, assuming the troop convoy was the standard length, the swing should bring them around just behind its tail.

Just over to the right, a column of black smoke interlaced with red flame shot into the sky. A ground attack bird, probably an Su-7 had gone in. The Germans didn't have an air force to speak of anymore but they'd never been short of flak. Further to his right he could see the road approaching, the swing in was working perfectly. Glory be he had been right, there were a mass of soft-skins stationary in front of him. He could see the figures running backwards and forwards as they saw the ground attack aircraft boring in. drivers were diving out of the cabs of the trucks.

Another thing from the past, Evans wasn't aware he'd pressed the firing button but his cannon were thumping, sending tracers arcing down to the traffic jam beneath. More chaos underneath now, trucks backing, trying to get away. Wouldn't do them any good. Evans lined his sight up with the rearmost trucks and squeezed the firing button. The packs were set to ripple off the rockets so salvos of four would land at closely-spaced intervals along the flight path. Air-to-ground rockets had come a long way since the old days,

Evans' particular favorite was the huge 450 millimeter S-20s, he could only carry six of them but each had the hitting power of a thousand pound bomb. But the little S-8s he was carrying today were doing their job. They were a mix of explosive, fragmentation and incendiaries, turning the target into a sea of flames and explosions. *For Ivan Fedeev* was adding the fury of its rockets to the hell developing underneath the racing jets. Evans punched the centerline racks release, dropping his two napalm tanks to bounce across the stalled trucks in front of him, then curved away. That was it, back home.

Only it wasn't it. As his Su-7 arced away from the inferno, Evans felt a heavy thump in the belly of *For Maria Chermatova* and the instrument panel erupted into a kaleidoscope of warning lights. The controls, always heavy on the Sukhoi, felt like they'd been set in concrete and a thick trail of black smoke erupted behind his aircraft. He'd been hit by something heavy, perhaps even an 88. "Comrade, you have a flame" It was Boroda, radioing over the bad news. There was a time when being called "Comrade" by a Russian would have set Evans teeth on edge but not now. Now, Russians had reverted to the traditional Grazhdanin as a form of address and Comrade meant again what it should.

Boroda hadn't mentioned bailing out when they had been swapping lessons. Both Russians and Americans had agreed on one thing at least, you don't bail out near troops you've just bombed and strafed. They tend to be resentful. Anyway *For Maria Chermatova* was still flying even if she was one very sick aircraft. Evans had some limited control and he knew where he was. It was about 70 kilometers to the Volga and safety. He just had to keep flying east, towards the sun. Those were the good things, the bad news was he was running out of speed, running out of altitude, running out of energy , running out of fuel and running out of ideas.

The Lyulka turbojet was banging and thumping, grumbling, spitting and coughing but it wouldn't quit. The vibration was getting worse as well, whatever was wrong under there was getting worse. The fuel gauge was slumping down much too quickly, his fuel tanks had been punctured. Just another addition, in fact losing his fuel may even work for him. He was only five minutes out from the Volga, if the aircraft would just hold together long enough. It was crabbing, trying to turn into its wounds, if he let it continue spanwise drift would spin her in. He fought the controls, sweat trickling into his eyes so at first he didn't see the streak of blue in front of him.

There were two bridges, one of the original assault bridges and a new heavy capacity pontoon. Tanks were using the latter one now, the lighter assault bridge had been devoted to trucks and their cargoes. *For Maria Chermatova* skimmed over the left bank of the Volga and kissed the water between the two bridges. Evans slammed into his harness, banging his forehead on the sharp screws that held the Perspex of the cockpit to the metal frame. They were supposed to be covered by rubber washers but the Russian rubber hardened and fell off.

The Su-7 was skimming across the river towards the right bank, huge arcs of water spraying into the air.. Across the river, he could see men were running towards the anticipated crash site. Evans braced himself and there was a sickening crash as his aircraft hit the right bank of the river, caught one wing on a tree spun and smashed through a stone wall. A group of pioneers were running up to the aircraft and started hacking the cockpit open with their pick-axes. Evans felt himself being grabbed and hauled through the shattered Perspex and metal to the grass outside. *For Maria Chermatova* was already starting to burn and there was enough explosives still on board to create a small scale disaster. Everybody was getting clear now, the aircraft was gone and everybody knew it, there was going to be nothing left to save.

"Hey American!" The sergeant in charge of the pioneers who'd pulled him out of the wreckage was calling him. An old, grizzled Sergeant with a brand-new Hero of the Russian People medal pinned to his uniform. In his hand he held a bottle of expensive Vodka with one good gulp left in it. Better yet, he was offering it to Evans. There were, Evans reflected, times when some gifts were beyond any achievable measure of gratitude.

German Forward Headquarters, Obil'noye, Kalmykia, Russia

The Russian advance was swinging further south than he'd expected, they were using the marshes of the Caspian Depression to guard their left flank. It appeared the largely infantry groups of the First Khazak Front were working their way through the marshes towards Astrakhan. The Don and Volga-Don Canal lines were still holding, in truth they weren't under that much pressure. The Russians had cleared the areas north of the defense lines, advanced to the bank of the river and then stopped. They were pounding the right bank defenses with artillery but that was it. Obviously, it was the heavy armor of the First Byelorussians that was the primary thrust.

It all came down to those bridges. He'd been trying to take those damned bridges out. He'd tried air strikes and lost his last aircraft in an attempted raid that had been a disastrous failure. They'd been shot down before even getting close. Long-range artillery had failed as well. The guns were firing a few shots then moving. So far they'd dodged the Russian fighter-bombers that were swarming over the battlefield but their luck wouldn't hold forever. And their chances of hitting the bridges were negligible.

Model shook his head, the southern swing of the Russian armor was disrupting his plans. Not disastrously but enough to make a difficult situation critical. He'd hoped the Russian advance would bring their northern flank onto LII Panzer Corps allowing them to fight as a cohesive whole. Instead LII had to move south and had been hammered by air attack all the way. The Russian aircraft had been all over them. They hadn't lost much armor but the Sturmoviks had crucified their supply vehicles and softskins. The open-topped half-tracks had suffered as well, hurt badly from the jellygas. LII Panzer wasn't out of the fight but it was hurt.

Without its supply vehicles it was going to have its work cut out staying in battle. That was another thing that British moron Fuller had forgotten about. Very fond of talking about penetrating long distances and getting into enemy rear areas and chewing up whatever they found there, but tanks burn fuel and they can only go as far as their fuel lasts. Without trucks to bring more fuel, the tanks stopped.

On the other hand, the head of the Russian advance was closing on SS Wiking's position. He'd thought it was SS-Wiking that would have to move and get pounded by the Sturmoviks but it wasn't going to be that way. The Russian advance was orientated south of Sadovoye and that would bring their lead tank army head-on into SS-Wiking's existing positions. There was going to be a tank battle there, one that would be worthy of the history books. The tanks of SS-Wiking were preparing positions, backed up by anti-tank guns.

They were using the hills for cover so the Russian armor would have to roll over open country towards them. Whatever happened, however much the battle deserved that recognition, it still wouldn't make those history books. Even if it did make it, it would be only as a footnote. His little country and its fight to survive were little more than a footnote itself, a small residue of unfinished business from World War Two. He knew well that most of the world regarded him as a little more than a bandit, a pretentious local warlord. Model knew it and resented it. Why should he be condemned so cavalierly when nobody condemned the Americans who had burned an entire country to death?

Model kept staring at the map. If SS-Wiking couldn't stop the avalanche of Russian armor, where to go? What to do? There were two options open. Most of his army was in the North, he could try and form a defense position south of the Don Line using the existing fortifications as one frontier and doing what he could with the other. But that was just buying time. He couldn't build new fortifications, his port would be gone, his oil supply gone. The Russians would pause, gather their forces and strike again. And he would be isolated, the rump he could secure in the North would be cut off from the sea, from any hope of help.

The other option would be to head south. He could take the infantry divisions out of Walthersburg and strip the Don Line. Those units could move more easily than the heavy armor, they weren't road-bound. Who knew? XXXXVIIth Panzer Corps might be able to make it out as well. Even if they couldn't, if the air attacks were too heavy, they could be the rearguard for the retreating infantry. If they could retreat south, down towards Chechnya and Georgia, they could hold out in the mountains. And his back would be towards friendly territory, Iran. When everything finally fell apart, he and the survivors could get out to there.

Or perhaps swing more towards the Black Sea? Reform behind the Kuban river, with the mountains guarding his flanks. Northern flank at Novorossisk, southern at Sokhumi. He'd have his back to the sea but he'd have two small ports for supplies and a small oil supply. Even if the Russians caved his front in again, he and his people could get out by sea to Turkey. And he had another card to play. If Walthersburg fell, no be truthful, when Walthersburg fell, he'd lose his chemical factories, the ones that supplied him with Sarin and Tabun. The supply was at Proletarsk now, along with the specialists needed to use it. That was a key card, it needed to be protected. It had to be shifted. If the supplies were shifted to Armavit, it would be easy to shift to wherever he decided to make his final stand.

Because it was going to have to be one of the two southern options. The northern option was a death sentence. The armored units would have to do what they could. Buy time for the rest of the Army to get out of the trap. But that was a move that could wait. The critical issue now was whether SS-Wiking could hold the Russians. If they could, it opened up new options.

On Board USS Skipjack SSN-585, At Sea, Pacific Ocean.

Not for the first time, Captain Donald Runken felt that he would cheerfully kill his father. It simply was not fair that parents should indulge their twisted sense of humors at the expense of their children. At school he'd been the "Drunken Student" who'd become the "Drunken Sailor" when he'd enlisted. In fact "What Shall We Do With A Drunken Sailor" had been the anthem of his

Academy class. He still winced whenever he heard it. Which seemed to be often. As a young lieutenant, his first love had been Daisy Garfield. She'd turned him down because she didn't want to spend the rest of her life as "The Drunken Wife". Now, he was technically, Captain Donald Runken, Officer Commanding USS *Skipjack*, the US Navy's latest, fastest and most deadly submarine. In reality (except to his face), he was the "Drunken Submariner". Killing his father was too quick, he ought to torture him a little first.

That would have to wait though. He had a mission to perform, one that would require skill, deviousness and total sobriety. He slipped that in just before anybody else could. As far as the world was concerned, he was taking *Skipjack* out for one more in a series of her interminable machinery and handling trials. It wasn't just that she was nuclear-powered, *Nautilus*, *Seawolf* and the Skate class had proved that technology. She did have a new reactor design, the S5W, but it was an incremental improvement on the earlier ones. It gave a bit more power and it had a lot longer core life than the ones in *Nautilus* and *Skate*.

It was her hull design that was different, the earlier SSNs had modified diesel-electric hulls but *Skipjack* had the new "body of revolution" design that made her handle underwater in ways that resembled aircraft rather than older submarines. She was truly capable of maneuvering in three dimensions. The crew were having to explore all the operational implications of that maneuverability.

That wasn't the task at hand now though. That would exploit another one of *Skipjack's* revolutionary capabilities. The same hull form that made her so agile underwater made her a pig on the surface. Capable of 16 knots in theory, more like 12 in any sort of sea. Slower than most diesel-electrics. However, there was a profound truth about the nuclear submarines that was slowly percolating through the fleet and awing those who thought about it. Nuclear-powered submarines didn't have to surface. They left port, dived and that was it until they returned home. If they returned home. How they handled on the surface was irrelevant, they were never there. What mattered was how they handled underwater. There, *Skipjack* had no equal. She'd topped out at 35 knots on her full-power trials and her nuclear powerplant meant she could hold that speed for unprecedented times. She would be doing so now, a speed run across the Pacific.

Runken flipped to his orders. There was a Chipanese task group at sea, its position was known but he had to intercept and tail it. He had to report its exact position daily to Clark Field where the information would be passed to VPB-33. The Batwings were a PB5Y group. The catch was the Chipanese task group was split into three smaller forces and he was supposed to track all three and keep the Batwings aware of what was happening. And, he wasn't to be detected in the process. That, he thought, was going to be a challenge. The Chipanese force was in three sections, a battleship group out front, a troop convoy in the middle and an aircraft carrier group bringing up the rear.

There was a second half to the orders. There was an Australian troop convoy on its way to Rangoon and the Chipanese were thought to have intentions of stopping it. His orders noted that the Freedom of the Seas and Freedom of Navigation were vital American national interests and he was required to act in defense of those interests. If the Chipanese attempted to interfere with the Australian convoy, then they were to be stopped from doing so. VPB-33 would handle the battleships, *Skipjack* would handle the carrier group. They'd co-ordinate on scene.

Interesting, combining submarine and air attacks was something quite new. Then deal with the troopships as appropriate. Another interesting thing, detailed instructions on what to do if the Chipanese interfered with the Australians (summarized as "do whatever it takes") but not a word on what to do if the Australians tried to interfere with the Chipanese. There was an unspoken message there.

OK, he'd need to get his torpedoes checked out. He had a mix of Mark 14s straight-runners and the new Mark 37 homing torpedoes up forward. *Skipjack* had no stern tubes, her new hull form didn't allow it. Runken decided to get all the Mark 14s stripped and checked over, he had an ingrained mistrust of his torpedoes, based on too many bad experiences. According to the Torpedo Factory and the NUWC, all the problems had been fixed and the torpedoes were as good as any in the world. The Mark 37s, they were another matter. If they worked, they'd be truly deadly. If. They were new and untested. That had been the next item on the original trials schedule.

Suddenly Runken had an inspiration. One of the Torpedomen was Long Tree, a full-blooded Apache Indian. It was rumored he'd joined the Navy after doing something unimaginably horrible to a man who had abused his sister. When he went down to the torpedo room, he'd consult with Long Tree, get some expert advice on a suitable fate for his father. With that satisfying thought in mind, he gave the orders for the speed run.

Nellis AFB, Nevada. Primary Operating Base of "Red Sun" Combat Training Range

The sun was setting, the cloud-streaked red globe just touching the horizon. The evening was already darkening as the F-106A interceptors flared on final approach and touched down, landing lights shining from the shadowed fighters like stars, the last of the sunlight coloring their drogue chutes a rich crimson. Originally, it had been planned that the first of the F-106 units, the 498th Fighter Interceptor Squadron based at Geiger AFB in Washington would take part on this year's Red Sun but it hadn't happened. Tension was flaring in the Pacific and the powers that be hadn't wanted to move NORADs latest and most capable interceptors from the West Coast. Instead, the second operational F-106 unit, from the Eastern USA, was taking its place.

As the interceptors landed and taxied to their revetments, the base personnel saw the tailcodes and nose art on the aircraft. Word spread like wildfire across Nellis where concessionaires anxiously compared anticipated revenues with likely damage and the base police grimly resigned themselves to a lively few days. The news didn't even hesitate at the base perimeter and howled into Las Vegas, sweeping through the Strip and its associated "entertainment" areas. Bar owners frantically contacted their wholesalers, quadrupling their orders for every alcoholic beverage known to man. The Casinos doubled their staff and put everybody on overtime. The showgirls readied themselves for long shifts and made inquiries about buying new convertibles and fur coats on the anticipated proceeds. The word surged on, spreading across the residential areas that surrounded the Strip. Anxious fathers sat by their front doors with loaded shotguns while their nubile daughters climbed out their bedroom windows and set off for Nellis. The Louisiana Air National Guard 122nd Fighter Interceptor Squadron, better known as The Bayou Militia had arrived.

Nike-Hercules Test and Evaluation Battery, "Red Sun" Combat Training Range

One of the merits of Red Sun was that things happened very fast once the exercises made their necessity clear. The lesson of the first four days of the exercise had been very clear. The old Ajax missiles were hopelessly outclassed by the new high-flying supersonic bombers. Their range was too short and their performance too low, the new RB-58s simply blasted straight through their coverage arcs. By the time the Ajax missiles were off and on their way, the bombers had fired their own weapons at the launching sites – and the projected nuclear explosions left few survivors. That left the Ajax flying ballistic and the bombers ducked them easily. As a result, word had already come down that the Ajax withdrawal was being accelerated and the batteries would all be converted to Herc by the end of next year.

Major James and his Ajax battery crews were in the Herc control battery facility gaining initial experience with the new missiles. The new missiles were a great advance on the old Ajax, faster, effective up to 100,000 feet and 100 miles range. Even better, they had a nuclear warhead. With a little luck, they would be able to cope with the new aircraft SAC had brought to the battle. Today would be their major trial, already the sky was filling up with aircraft and the cumulative electronic emissions from radar sets and jamming were causing the desert air to sizzle. It was the first of the big, no-holds-barred exercises. It was the Day of the Big Gorilla.

The Big Gorilla was the lineal descendent of the exercises that had started Red Sun. The bombers had to get through by whatever means they could, the defenses had to stop them by any means they could. Nobody was in any doubt that, by the end of the day, they would be counting crashed aircraft and mourning lost pilots and crews. Already, an F-102 had been lost; its engine had started to suffer power failure on takeoff and the pilot had realized he lacked the thrust to get over the ridge ahead. So he'd ejected. Unfortunately for his professional reputation, the reduction in weight caused by the loss of himself and his seat just allowed the F-102 to clear the ridge before progressive power loss caused it to belly in the other side. It had landed in soft sand and, although written off, was strippable for spares. The initial accident report already concluded that "on this occasion the aircraft did much better without the services of a pilot."

Now, the main action of The Big Gorilla was starting. The long range acquisition radars of the Herc battery were showing formations of SAC bombers approaching the exercise area. The main body, B-52s and a few B-60s were still far back but a number of smaller groups were racing ahead. Those would be the RB-58Cs that had been the stars of the exercise so far.

The problem they presented was, conceptually, quite simple. The RB-58 moved high and very fast. From the time the long range search radars had picked them up, it would take eight minutes for them to get overhead. That was a great improvement over the Ajax experience, there the batteries had had less than a minute to respond and they had proved incapable of meeting the challenge. Now, could the new Hercs do any better? The flight path of the Herc was an up-and-over, peaking out at 100,000 feet and diving on the formation beneath. That had an unexpected advantage, warned of a surface-to-air missile attack, pilots tended to look down to see the threat, not up. The catch was that the missile trajectory had to be such as to bring the target within the lethal radius of the warhead.

James saw that the radar screens had already exploded into a jagged mass of electronic noise and pinwheels, the effects of the Hustlers using jamming to buy time for their attack runs. The Herc operators were dancing around with frequencies, adjusting the jitter factors to try and exclude the radar energy being poured into their sets. The Nike radars were tagging their transmissions now, applying specific shifts of frequency and pulse repetition factors to make the genuine transmissions distinct from the white noise that tried to drown them out.

The screens cleared, the radar images showed that the racing RB-58s had already closed much of the gap. The operators initiated launch and James was stunned to see the big Herc missiles lifting off their rails as they hurtled downrange. For an insane moment he thought the battery was shooting live rounds and had a nightmare picture of what might be coming back the other way. Then the words "Smoky Sams" forced their way into his mind. The launches were Herc boosters with dummy second stages, designed to give the sound and visual signature of the launch without being a danger to the real aircraft overhead.

The game now was to put the missile into the right position for the intercept. That meant a limited footprint that was growing smaller by the second. Once within a set distance of the launchers, the intercept became impossible; by the time the missiles had reached the right target altitude, they would be in a tailchase and their chance of catching the fast-moving Hustlers would be remote.

As James watched he saw the pair of aircraft that had been assigned to their battery split up. One arced left and started to climb, the other dived to the right. Ajax had a problem, given a choice between two targets splitting apart like that, it would fly between them, missing both. It hadn't mattered with the old B-36s and B-60s and even the B-52s lacked the performance to exploit the flaw. The RB-58 did and that factor alone was enough to cause the Ajax to be withdrawn. Herc had solved the problem with elegant simplicity; there was a simple random choice routine built in, the guidance radar flipped an electronic coin and took whatever target chance indicated.

The simulated track of the intercepting missiles was arching up and over but the two targets had split wide and were swinging fast. As the operators watched, the targets made barrel rolls that reversed their turns and took them inside the projected course of the Hercs. They would pass outside the lethal radius of even the nuclear warheads on the Hercs. The tracks vanished from the scopes and the two targets were diving on the Herc battery.

"*Marisol* and *Tiger Lily*" grunted the Herc operator. James raised his eyebrows, there was no IFF data on the screens to identify the two aircraft. "It's that balls-to-the-wall style. Nobody else does it quite like those two."

The Hercs had scored, at least two RB-58Cs had been judged hit and were returning to base. Suddenly the radar screens blacked out; the Herc control room was judged to have been destroyed by the return shots from the two bombers. "Can we have long range surveillance feed restored please. We have trainees here and we'd like them to see the rest of the Big Gorilla?"

"Negative, we'll transmit range surveillance feed instead."

The screens lit up again. It took a few seconds for the observers to adapt to the changed situation. In those few seconds, *Marisol* and *Tiger Lily* had broken through the SAM line and taken out two more Herc sites. Other RB-58Cs had flowed through the breach and were rolling up the defenses. However, to the south, a group of fighters was streaking in to restore the situation, coming in much faster than any of the other groups that had been involved to date. James nodded to himself, the Bayou Militia had arrived.

The F-106s were spread right out, in loose pairs at staggered altitudes. That had been another change that Red Sun had brought about. After the first disastrous fight with the RB-58Cs, the fighters had abandoned the traditional tightly-spaced "finger four" and replaced it with the loose pairs of aircraft, a formation already known as "Loose deuce". It hadn't saved the fighters from the nuclear-tipped radar homing missiles but it had cut the casualties from four per shot to two.

Even as James watched, several of the pairs broke away, presumably deemed to have been killed by nuclear fire from the RB-58s. There was no nuclear counterfire in the situation reports. He guessed the Cajuns had left their nuclear-tipped MB-1s at home, the Genies had proved useless against the fast and agile Hustlers. Later waves of interceptors would carry them, to deal with the lumbering subsonic bombers. Even as he watched, *Marisol* and *Tiger Lily* waded into the Bayou Militia.

Pilot's Position, RB-58C "Marisol"

He felt like he had been beaten with baseball bats then fed, feet first, through a mangle. *Marisol* was fighting like a wildcat, taking down three Herc sites and a pair of F-106s already. That left 12 of the new fighters, out of an original 18. The Cajuns were not going to be happy with that. He was literally going head-to-head with another pair of 106s now. From a combat point of view, it was the safest thing to do, at a closing speed of over 3,000 mph, the fire control systems on the two aircraft simply didn't have time to react. The danger was collision, last year an F-101 and a B-52 had gone down in a head-to-head when neither pilot had given way.

It wasn't going to happen this time. *Marisol* ripped through the gap between the two F-106s, the concussion waves from the three aircraft blending together to give a multi-G thump that hurled him against his straps, adding more injuries to his bruised shoulders. Still, with that pair behind him, he could arch round now to two more on his left. Kozlowski was looking for *Tiger Lily* but they'd been split up evading the Hercs and had been fighting without mutual support ever since. He could see the two F-106s he'd picked swimming across his view, he'd got them cold, if they broke away, he'd get a perfect tail shot, if they broke towards him, the angles would be wrong for any shots they tried to make and they'd be wide open to *Marisol's* tail gun when they crossed.

"Fox-two, fox two." That was the lead F-106, he'd broken towards Marisol and must have fired at the edge of his envelope. "Negative, Charlie five-one, two misses." Bad angle and Dravar had been pouring radar jamming at the little Falcons. But his own GAR-8s were also hopelessly out of envelope, no shot possible. "Fox Three" That was Dravar with his tail gun. "Negative *Marisol*"

It had been a faint chance anyway, that tail gun was deadly under some circumstances but this wasn't one of them. He pulled Marisol into a steep climb and rolled out at the top, an F-106 had followed him up and tried a Fox-One but the heat-seekers had been decoyed away by flares and the sun.. Another F-106 was below him and he could hear the annunciator growl as the GAR-8 homing head locked on. Constant tone and – "Fox-one". A pause and then. "Positive hit. Charlie Five-Two, break off and return to base. She got you."

"Damn it, he's behind us." It was Korrina, Kozlowski's Bear, reporting that an F-106 had swung in behind them. Unlike the old days, it was a bad, bad angle for an attack, the high speeds involved meant that a missile hit was almost impossible and the fighter behind couldn't close that much for fear of *Marisol's* tail gun. And if the attack degenerated into a tail chase, the Hustler had more fuel and staying power to out-run and out-last the frustrated fighter jocks. But it meant that he couldn't turn without giving the fighter behind him a good shot and that set him up to be picked off by another fighter. "Got you, bitch" came over the comms system from the F-106 behind.

"You hear what he called me? Mike, beat him, kill him, torture him. Make him listen to Perry Como records" *Marisol's* voice was outraged. Suddenly there was a terrifying crash and Kozlowski was hurled against his straps again, through the blur of pain he saw his instrument panel light up into a sea of red warning indicators. Their afterburners were off and they were already subsonic, speed dropping fast. Behind him, the fighter's overtaking speed advantage became too much and a break-away turn became necessary to preclude a collision. There was not enough time for the F-106 pilot to react and score a "kill". However, as he shot past, his afterburner presented a target that even the stunned Kozlowski couldn't resist "Fox One."

"Kill confirmed. Charlie Nine-One return to base. You're gone."

"Negative on that range, request assistance from Charlie Nine-One, we've got a problem here." Kozlowski tried to get his brain working again. "We have had a major on-board explosion and multiple systems failures. Afterburners are out and we're holding only 300 miles per hour. We're losing altitude. Request damage check."

"Charlie Nine-One here. Shee-it *Marisol* what did you pull then it was like you stopped dead in mid-air. OK coming around for check underneath. *Marisol* don't know how to tell you this but your main wheels are down. Looks like you dropped your main undercarriage. Gearwell doors are gone and there's damage to the belly. Nosewheel is still up."

"Range Administration here. *Marisol*, We show you as having lowered your undercarriage at over 1,200 miles per hour. We expect severe damage and undercarriage collapse if you try to land. Eject now, we wills end helos to pick you up."

"Negative Range Administration, if we do that we won't find out what went wrong. Anyway, we have a deal up here. We're bringing *Marisol* in."

Marisol was shuddering badly as she limped back to Nellis, Charlie Nine-One hovering protectively around her. Oil pressure was sinking fast, Kozlowski had a feel something in the hydraulics had blown and started the problems off. The controls felt like they were set in concrete, there was barely enough movement to keep Marisol under control. If they had fuel stacking problems now, they'd have to eject. They didn't, although an initial effort to lower the nosewheel failed. Kozlowski deployed the Ram Air Turbine and used the backups to get it down.

The long Nellis runway was in front of him now, all he had to hope was that the undercarriage wasn't too badly damaged. There were fire trucks and crash vehicles already lined up. The problem was that the B-58, with its delta wing and unique flying characteristics, required a nose-high attitude on landing. The nose had to be about 12 degrees up on final landing approach. That made it difficult to see over the nose to keep the runway in view, something quite important when trying to land at over two hundred miles per hour with a screwed-up undercarriage.

Kozlowski guessed the sink rate was critical, too much and *Marisol*'s damaged undercarriage would collapse. He kept the nose up on the way in, using aerodynamic braking to slow the aircraft down. Then, as the main wheels touched, he gently lowered the nose for the final rollout. Drag chute out, lift the nose a little and then come to a stop.

"Thanks *Marisol.* "

"Hey we had a deal you didn't bail on me so I didn't on you." *Marisol's* voice was weak and shaking. "Oh Mike I'm hurt inside. Get me some help huh?"

The canopies were opening and crew stairs were in place. Two flight line engineers were lifting Dravar out of his seat, he seemed to have been concussed from the terrible slam when *Marisol's* undercarriage had dropped. A tow truck was already in place to get *Marisol* to the maintenance shop.

Maintenance Hangar, Nellis Air Force base, Nevada.

"Sir, we've found out what went wrong." Kozlowski thought it was time, for eight hours he'd been bouncing off the walls waiting for Chief Gibson to report back. "It was hydraulic systems failure, at some point during the battle the primary system went out, probably from shock and the backup was overloaded. It failed and dropped the undercarriage.

"We need to replace the hydraulic system aft, the main gearcovers are gone, blown off, and there is skin damage under both wings. I'm sorry sir, you're out of Red Sun as of now, *Marisol* is going to in here for at least two weeks."

General Declan patted him on the shoulder. "Don't worry son, you two have already made your mark here. By the time she's fixed, the Group will be back home, we're basing out of Bunker Hill, Indiana from now on. The 43rd is taking our place at Carswell. We've got a TDY detachment though. As soon as *Marisol* is repaired you'll be leading an element of four birds to base out of U Thapao in Thailand. Friendly visit."

General Declan started to leave, then turned. "Oh, the Bayou Militia wants to take you and your crew out for a party tonight. They seem to have been quite impressed. Try not to do too much damage to Las Vegas."

In Front Of Sadovoye Ridge, Kalmykia, Russia

"Rejoice Defenders of the Russian Land!" Major Oleg Leskowitz Ulyanov bowed his head as the prayer echoed across the long line of T-10s. The crews stood in front of the heavy tanks, their heads bowed for the battle today was a sacred duty. More than sacred, it was a day of destiny. Today his heavy tank battalion would be part of the destruction of the last SS division. Once the SS had been the scourge of Europe, the terror of all who opposed tyranny but now, they were almost part of history. Almost, that was the rub. Today they would have to be sent into history. Today, Russia would finally wake from the long nightmare. Today was the day they would destroy SS-Wiking.

Behind him, there was a reminder that it would not be easy. There was a patch of fresh moss-green paint on the glacis plate of his tank as a stark lesson of that. The previous day, his unit had been advancing when they'd come across a ruined farmhouse sitting in the rolling grassland. In front of it was a BTR-40 armored car, burning with the bodies of its crew around it. Other parts of the recon platoon were also around it, some dead or wounded, some pinned down.

As he'd taken in the scene, he'd heard the vicious clang as an armor-piercing shot had bounced off his glacis plate. He'd backed up, spread his tanks out and they'd pummeled the building with fire from their 122 millimeter guns. They'd leveled the building, reduced it to rubble and silenced the anti-tank gun but the defenders had fought on until their position was stormed and silenced. The anti-tank gun had been an ancient 50 millimeter PaK, the defenders cooks from a field kitchen unit. There was a grim joke made about that, they'd had two guns, the PaK and a Goulash-Cannon. But the joke didn't change the fact that a few cooks with an obsolete anti-tank gun had held the advance up for the best part of an hour.

Prayers over, clouds of black smoke as the T-10s started their diesel engines. That would alert the Germans to what was coming. Infantry attacks started with a massed artillery barrage that shattered the defensive positions and stunned the Germans within them but that was not the pattern today. Instead, the attack was being lead by the heavy tanks that would push forward to unmask the enemy defenses.

Already in position were the SU-130 "Battleships", so called because they were armed with a naval 130 millimeter gun coupled to a cross-hull rangefinder. The big gun had been designed for use on destroyers, but any hope of building a Russian Navy had long since faded. Instead, they'd been adapted as long-range anti-tank weapons. If German tanks appeared, the SU-130s would pick them off. But, that wasn't likely. Not at first. The front line of the German defenses would be anti-tank guns supported by dug-in infantry. The guns would be positioned so that their fields of fire interlocked, any tank turning its heavy frontal armor to face one gun would expose its weaker sides to another. Only when the Russian tanks were entangled with the net of anti-tank guns would the German tanks attack and drive the Russian armor back.

There was an answer to that. As a battalion commander, Ulyanov had two artillery batteries dedicated to him. Both his company commanders had one more each. Each battery had a designated code word to activate its fire. In the sector ahead of his battalion, Ulyanov and his commanders had a series of pre-planned impact points, sited in likely areas of German anti-tank nests. All Ulyanov had to do was give the code word for the battery then the one for the impact point and the shells would be on their way.

When he'd been a young Lieutenant, Ulyanov had seen the Americans fight and marveled at the way they could switch their artillery from target to target, massing and dispersing their fire as the situation required. The Russian system couldn't match that but it was better than nothing. And there were always the Battleships. They had explosive ammunition for their big guns as well as armor piercing bolts.

Ulyanov took a last look round before he crested the ridge and passed the jump-off line. The weather was far from ideal, there was a heavy overcast and the sun was hidden. But, his battalion was moving forward fast, the seven tanks of his first company on the left, the seven tanks of the other on the right. Other T-10 battalions were on either side of him, surging forward to engage the German positions. From above they must look like speedboats racing across the sea, the dust clouds behind the tanks resembling the plumes of spray and the waving grass and bushes, the wake on the sea surface.

Behind the T-10s, Washingtons were getting ready to move forward as well, exploiting the hole that was to be formed in the German positions. Getting them there through the first line of the German defenses was the job of the heavy tanks, it was the T-10s that would have to absorb the first fury of the German defensive fire. Both the T-10s and the T-55s were carrying tankriders, tankodesantniki, who would dismount to kill the SS infantry in their positions.

Now, though, they had a different job, the heavy tanks were surging through overgrown grassland, the tangle of weeds and plants waist-high or more. The tankriders were crouched behind the turret and the auxiliary fuel tanks for cover but their AK-47s were constantly swinging from side to side. The long grass was perfect cover for tank hunters with Panzerfaust rocket launchers.

Once the good, rich black soil had been the finest farmland in Russia, the farms here had been the wheat basket for most of Europe. Then, the Germans had come, they'd killed the farm animals, destroyed the crops and left the people here to starve. Now, the derelict fields could grow a deadlier crop. Like the one in front, a German soldier had suddenly risen from the grass, Panzerfaust aimed to fire. He never got the chance, Ulyanov's gunner cut him down with the coaxial machinegun. A split second later there was a slight, almost unnoticeable bump as the racing heavy tank ran over the body. Ulyanov though he heard a scream but it was probably just the tracks running over the steel return rollers.

Ahead, a stream of fire came from an almost invisible dip in the ground. A rocket, a big one with four large fins, Ulyanov could see a flare on each fin tip and the missile changing direction as its controller lined it up with its target. All 15 tanks in his battalion opened up with their machineguns at the source of the missile, their guns were loaded with tracer to maximize the effect of the converging cone of fire. "Alexei, Katya"

"On its way" came an emotionless voice. For a brief second, the missile flew normally, then went straight up, stalled and crashed. Before the gunners could launch another there was a roar overhead and a salvo of shells smashed into their position. The system worked then. That was good to know. Lucky the Germans had set up on one of the pre-planned points. The tank raced ahead for a few seconds then lurched as it nosed into the dip where the tank-hunter team had hidden Ulyanov couldn't hear them over the noise of the big diesel but he knew the tankriders would be spraying the position with full-automatic fire from their AKs.

The T-10 hit the other bank of the dip and climbed out, Anya fishtailing it so that the soft underbelly wouldn't be exposed. She'd been a tank driver now for two years, one of three women drivers in the battalion. She was a slightly-built woman but all those months of wrestling with the heavy controls of a T-10 had given her muscles a professional weightlifter would envy. Once, she'd punched out a rear-echelon maggot who had insulted her, breaking his jaw in five places.

Over on the left, a T-10 was staggering, black smoke boiling out of its engine hatches. Through the powerful optics built into his commander's position, Ulyanov could see beyond the damaged tank to a suspicious looking clump of shrubbery. Sure enough, close to the ground a long barrel was swinging to its next target, looking for all the world like a snake sliding through the grass. He put his cross-hairs. He felt the turret swing as Vitali lined his sight up with the indicator from Ulyanov's command sight.

"Cucumber"

"Up"

"Shoot!"

The 122 millimeter crashed, the brass cartridge case ejecting on the floor and the turret filling with acrid smoke. Sometimes it was hard to tell whether he'd fired or been hit. The green-painted high explosive round, called a cucumber by every Russian tankoviki, was already going downrange to the concealed PaK gun. Now was the dangerous moment; while he was dealing with the PaK, an unseen gun could deal with him. But, they were getting away with it, there were four explosions at the position, three other tanks must have spotted the gun and engaged. Then a big secondary and Ulyanov was able to get back watching for threats. They weren't long coming. Another tank, over on the right suddenly staggered and halted. No fires and the tankriders leapt off to form a perimeter around the stalled T-10. The crew were bailing out as well, the tankriders would protect them until the fate of their damaged tank was known. But where was the anti-tank gun that had done the deed?

Ulyanov felt his tank suddenly swerve and stop. An AP shot passed in front of them, so close that he fancied he could feel the wind of its passage through the heavy turret armor. Anya was still backing up, that shot had come from the right, where was that damned gun? Ulyanov scanned frantically, nothing. Then he slammed forward into the eyepiece of his commander's sight, if he lived he'd have a black eye tomorrow. The tank was already pivoting on its tracks, she'd slammed the transmission into neutral then pushed the tiller hard over. The left track had gone full ahead, the right track full reverse, spinning the tank to the right.

A good tank driver went by instinct, not careful thought and Anya had it. Her maneuvers dodged shots she couldn't possibly know were coming. The next had passed the T-10, a few centimeters to the left of the turret, if it hadn't been for the halt and turn it would have ploughed into their main fuel tank. But now Ulyanov had seen where the anti-tank gun was. The Germans were clever, very clever, they'd positioned the gun right back in the bushes so only its muzzle showed. But the same position meant the bushes were disturbed by the muzzle blast and he'd seen them move.

"Pickle"

"Up"

"Shoot!"

"Cucumber"

"Up"

"Shoot!"

The armor piercing bolt had torn into the shrubbery, hurling it away, the follow-up explosive round had blown the concealed gun apart. Ulyanov heard the co-axial machinegun firing as it cut the crew down, then the T-10 was rolling forward again. They were heading uphill now, towards the crest of the first ridge. He'd seen the sandtable model of the ground while the plan of attack was being explained. The Sadovoye Ridge looked as if a giant had placed two hands on the table, fingers outstretched and interlocked. The "bodies" of the "hands" were two large hills defended by the SS infantry regiments. They were being pounded by artillery now, prior to an attack by the Frontniki. But the complex mass of ridges between them were the target of the tanks. That's where the German armor was waiting. Destroy that and the mobility of SS-Wiking was gone. That meant the day would be won.

The T-10 was laboring as it climbed the hill, it was a great tank for the flat plains but its heavy weight of armor and gun meant it was underpowered. Already, Anya would be watching the temperature gauge climbing, she couldn't let the diesel overheat. They had to make it to the top of the first ridge, Phase Line Anatol, where they'd stop and let the heavy tanks cool. The Washingtons would be taking it from there, up to Phase Line Boris at least. So far, they'd only faced a skirmish line, Ulyanov estimated a company of infantry and a battery of anti-tank guns at most. But there would be German tanks on Anatol. Panzers. Or a reasonable imitation thereof.

A vicious clang on the side of the turret and the T-10 rang like a bell from the shock. Ulyanov pitied his tankriders, the spray of metal from the hit must have at least injured some. Up ahead of them, He'd had seen a flash from the ridgeline. His scope saw just the edge of the turret, the tank was hull-down, just the top of the turret and the gun showing. Boxy turret, roof front sloping up to the mid-line then back. Probably a Chipanese Chi-Te. Fast, good gun, a long-barrelled 75 same as on the Panther, but very thin armor.

"Pickle"

"Up"

"Shoot!"

The ground just to the right of the enemy tank exploded in a shower of dirt and pebbles. Ulyanov cursed "Again" then was flung against the side of the turret as his driver spun the tank on its suspension to dodge another round. That sent the T-10 shot wild . "Again." That one was short, smacking into the ridge just under the turret. If the enemy tank hadn't been hull down, it would have torn through the glacis plate. But it had sent the German gunner's aim off too. The enemy shot came nowhere close. "Again" and that one was true. The Chi-Te's turret flew into the air on top of an orange fireball as the tank's ammunition and fuel cooked off. A few tens of meters away from it, another Chi-Te exploded in an even more ferocious eruption. Ulyanov saw a roadwheel spinning into the air and bits of the engine compartment flying sideways. A battleship sitting on the ridge behind them must have seen it and picked it off with its big gun.

The laboring tanks made it up to the ridgeline, stopping hull-down. The tankriders leapt off and spread out along the ridge itself, checking for tankhunter teams and enemy tanks on the reverse slope. They waved the T-10s forward urgently, four Chi-Te tanks were destroyed on this section of the ridge but the fifth tank of the platoon was backing frantically, trying to make the next ridge. The tankriders dropped flat and a flash of lightning seemed to pass along the section of front as all the T-10s opened fire simultaneously. The enemy tank erupted under a hail of hits and near misses. If ever a tank had been killed, Ulyanov thought, it was that one.

He looked around, 13 of his 15 tanks had made it to the ridgeline and, even as he watched, another one, the T-10 stalled earlier made it up to the line and joined them. They were holding Phase Line Anatol and the Washingtons were coming up fast behind them. The T-10s would hold this position now while the T-55s moved through them to assault Phase Line Boris. With the Washingtons were resupply vehicles, carrying ammunition reloads and fuel. Plus vodka for the tank crews, although that wouldn't be on the manifest. Ulyanov threw his turret hatch back, allowing the cool air to clear some of the smoke and fumes from the tank.

Around him, the tankriders were securing the area. A couple of German tankers had survived the destruction of their vehicles and tried to surrender. If they'd worn the grey of the Wehrmacht, it might have saved them, for a while anyway, but they wore the black of the SS. The tankriders shot them down then bayoneted the bodies to make sure.

The rest of his crew threw their hatches open. Vitali had his gunner's hatch open, deep in the hull Dmitri was working his way up around the ammunition cases. Anya was already sitting on the edge of her driver's hatch, she was wearing a sleeveless man's cotton undershirt and it was transparent with sweat, her hair was plastered down by her helmet and her khaki pants were black. The white scars on her arms and shoulders, from hot steel fragments and burning oil and the jagged internal fixtures of the T-10 were highlighted by the moisture running over her. The rest of the crew would be bombing up soon, throwing out the empty brass casings and reloading fresh ammunition but Anya, along with the other drivers, was excused that duty. Driving a T-10 was physical punishment enough for anybody.

Their brief rest over, if bombing up could be called a rest, Ulyanov's battalion got back to work. Now they were providing overwatch while the Washingtons assaulted Phase Line Boris. Meanwhile, the battleships would be moving up so that the T-10s could move up themselves, ready for the assault on Phase Line Christian. That was the highest of the ridges and the main line of the German resistance. Once they'd broken that, it would, literally be downhill all the way. The sky was still overcast but the smoke from the shots, explosions and burning vehicles was forming a brownish haze across the battlefield. That was going to make overwatch difficult.

It didn't matter much, the Washingtons took Phase Line Boris without calling on the T-10s and SU-130s although they paid brutally for it. As Ulyanov brought his T-10s forward they passed the burning wrecks of a dozen T-55s, some with the bodies of their tankriders strewn around them, others with survivors sheltering by the wrecks. Some raised a cheer as the T-10s passed, others even signaled the heavy tanks to slow down so they could scramble on board and continue the fight.

Phase Line Boris itself was a charnel house, the wrecks of the T-55s and German tanks within a few meters of each other. The German tanks, a mixture of Chi-Tes and Panthers, mostly the version with the 88 but a few had the absurdly long 75 millimeter 100 caliber barrels. Smoke from the wrecks permeated everything making it difficult to breath. Still no sun, the heavy clouds were trapping the smoke and haze, creating a growing fog over the battlefield.

"Panzers!"

The alarm cry brought the tired tank crews back up to alert. The Germans were launching their long awaited counter-attack. From the ridge marking Phase Line Christian, a pack of German vehicles moved forward. Ulyanov spotted at least a dozen King Tigers, he guessed some would have 88s and a few of them the 105 the Germans had been introducing just before Germany was burned off the map.

There were half a dozen tank destroyers, Jagdpanther IIs with their 127 millimeters and some Chipanese tank destroyer he'd never seen before. More smaller, lighter tanks. And two dozen half tracks carrying infantry. The Germans didn't use tankriders the way the Russians did, they gave their infantry special armored carriers. Now, the Tankniki would show them why trying to fight from such thinly protected vehicles was a bad idea when tanks ruled the day.

"Turnip"

"Up"

"Shoot!"

It was a slaughter. The armor-piercing high explosive rounds smashed into the halftracks, sending them spiraling backwards, flying apart or just erupting into pyres of greasy black smoke. By the time they'd covered half the ground towards the Russians holding Phase Line Boris the halftracks had gone. The German tanks shot back but they were firing on the move at small targets seen only fleetingly through the fog of smoke and fire. The half-tracks destroyed, the surviving Washingtons and the T-10s started on the German tanks.

Once the half-tracks had gone, the Jagdpanthers were the top priority, they had the best guns and the best fire control. Ulyanov saw his sabot shot bounce off the glacis plate of one. Then a second and a third shot went the same way. Only with the fourth shot did the tank destroyer lurch to a halt and start to burn.

By then the lead German tanks were within a hundred meters. Ulyanov lined up on a King Tiger then saw its turret fly into the air and the hull explode. Unnoticed, a group of SU-130s had moved up to Phase Line Boris and there was no armor a tank could carry that could stop a sabot round from a 70 caliber 130 millimeter at these ranges.

"Drop back, drop back." Ulyanov shouted into his radio, he didn't have the authority but he was officer on the spot. His T-10s went into reverse backing off the ridgeline, leaving three of their number burning on the crest. Five of the Washingtons had joined them. They backed off the ridge then stopped some 30 meters down.

As the German heavies crossed, none of the lighter vehicles had survived, his command fired a salvo into their midst. Then it was utter chaos, tanks fighting at point-blank range. The tank destroyers, German and Russian, died first, their limited traverse guns being a deadly limitation in this knife-fight. Ulyanov didn't even know how long it lasted, only that he survived when the divisional commander lead his reserve tank battalion into the fight and the 45 Washingtons turned the tide.

"Driver Forward. We're in the lead and by God and Saint Aleksandr we'll lead." The survivors of Ulyanov's group, six T-10s and two T-55s swept forward, over the ridgeline of Phase Line Boris and down into the valley. Ulyanov still had three turnips, one pickle and four cucumbers on board and he was damned if they would be wasted. Again, some of the Germans tried to surrender but the Russians had no time for them. They crushed them under their tracks.

Down they swept, and up the ridge to Phase Line Christian. By the time they reached the top their T-10 was overheating badly and they'd shot their bolt. Anya maneuvered the tank into a hull-down position and her voice came defiantly over the intercom. "That's it. Overheated. Move another meter and she'll seize up." In her compartment, she doubled up in her seat, sobbing with the exhaustion that had suddenly caught up with her.

The other T-10s would be the same but it didn't matter for Ulyanov could see something he'd never believed he would. The SS-Wiking Division had broken and was running. Below Phase Line Christian was a mass of vehicles, soft-skins, towed and self-propelled artillery, heading for the ridge marked Phase Line Demeter and, they hoped, safety. Only the Washingtons were already passing through the line of stalled T-10s to hound and harry the Germans just as Cossack cavalry had once hounded and harried Napoleon's retreating Grande Armee. Ulyanov squeezed off HE round after HE round at the fleeing enemy until his rack was empty. Then it happened.

At last, at long last, the sun broke though the morning overcast. Its light interacted with the smoke of the burning vehicles to fill the battlefield with a sulphurous yet strangely comforting yellow glow, reminding him of a gas-lit window seen through an evening fog.

The sight suddenly filled Ulyanov with inspiration. Standing in the turret of his tank he drew an icon from his pocket, actually a picture of one torn from an American magazine, the National Geographic. It was folded and dog-eared now but he held it up over his head like the priceless relic that, to him, it was. As the Russian armor surged past him, his shout was, somehow, carried on the divisional radio net.

"REJOICE DEFENDERS OF THE RUSSIAN LAND!"

Chapter Nine
Scoring Points

Alekszejevka Oblast, south of the Don River, Russia

The previous night had been terrible. The German women had known "it" was coming, ever since the Russian Army had broken through the border defenses but, by an unspoken agreement, had carefully avoided discussing or even mentioning "it". The Russian women had been more forthright. 'Better raped by a Russian than loved by a German' had been one common phrase. The Russian Army had arrived the previous afternoon, first the heavy tanks and mechanized infantry had passed through Alekszejevka, setting up a defense line for the night to the south and west. Then, the infantry had followed them and they'd stayed in the village.

The actions of the German women had been varied. A few had fought desperately but they'd only succeeded in proving that even a desperate women couldn't fight trained and battle-hardened soldiers. They'd been beaten into submission, now some were dead and the rest were badly injured. Some, most, had tried to divorce themselves from what was happening, tried to isolate their minds in a private place far away and so save their sanity. They'd tried to insulate themselves from the groups of soldiers who'd come for them hour after hour throughout the night.

Elsa, Margrafin of Alekszejevka, had been one who'd tried that. She was hurt inside, bleeding and sick but she had survived. So far. A few other German women had copied the Russians, put bread and salt on the table and waited to accept the inevitable. It hadn't quite saved them but when the first group of Russians had finished, they'd left guards on the doors to make sure these women were not attacked again.

Then, in the morning, the entire population of the village had been herded out into the open. They'd been searched. Men and women with their blood groups tattooed on their arms and any who'd been foolish enough to keep their Nazi Party membership cards were taken away, pushed up against a barn wall and machine-gunned. The bodies were still over there. The Russian villagers had been told to go home but the Germans had been kept out in the open, the men and women separated from each other. Now they were waiting while their homes were looted.

The men were taking machines, clocks, valuables, even light bulbs. The female soldiers were taking the German womens' clothes and other personal things. The Margrafin saw one woman, with a rifle and telescopic sight hanging over her shoulder, struggling with boxes and a pile of clothes taken from her home. She even recognized her own wedding dress, now the property of that female sniper. Elsa, once Margrafin of Alekszejevka, hated her.

Colonel Tony Evans sat in his radio-jeep and tried not to think on what was going on around him. After he'd been shot down, he'd been assigned to forward air controller duty until a new Su-7 was delivered for him. He'd been with the infantry ever since and, although he'd arrived this morning, it was obvious what had happened the night before. Anyway, it didn't take imagination, it had been the same in every village the Russian Army had taken. The authorities even rotated units so that every one got their chance. He shook his head, the Marines had a motto, "No better friend, no worse enemy" but the Russians took both parts to the ultimate extreme.

He'd seen some of the German women appeal to the Russian female soldiers for protection, only to have the Russian girls laugh in their faces and promise to come and watch next time the men raped them. Yet he couldn't blame them, the war had gone on for seventeen - almost eighteen - years. Two generations had been butchered, their lives stolen by the invaders and the chances for any of the women to have a normal life after this were bleak. It was natural for the women to be bitter towards the invaders who'd stolen their hopes for a family and a future. Anyway, after what he'd seen of how the Germans had treated the Russians it was hard to find any sympathy for them.

"Grazhdanin Sniper-Sergeant, may I offer some assistance?" Evans had seen one of the women soldiers struggling with a bulky pile of loot, her rifle and some boxes.

The Russian Army even provided a special parcel service so that the Frontniki could send loot back to their families. The front newspapers had carried a story about a postal clerk who'd stolen from one such box and had been shot as a result. Even so, the woman was looking at him with suspicion and wariness in case he wanted to take some of her treasures. Evans smiled "Bratischka, please be reassured, I do not look my best in a bra and panties." The woman laughed and relaxed. She'd seen the American flag on the shoulder of his uniform, everybody knew the Americans were rich and didn't need to loot.

"Thank you Gospodin Colonel. I would be most grateful for some help." She unloaded the pile on the hood of the jeep and started to unfold the cardboard boxes. The wedding dress was first, obviously it was her prize catch. Another Russian girl hoping against hope that her loot would help her find a husband. Evans stopped her.

"Bratishka, the cardboard is thin and may get damaged. If so, the fabric of your dress may be harmed. Let us put some other things in first so they will pad your dress and protect it."

The girl smiled her thanks at him and smiled again as she watched the American pack her loot into the boxes, neatly and efficiently. It never occurred to Evans that decades of packing his possessions for transfers and assignments had made him an expert luggage handler. Once he'd finished, they carried the boxes over to the mail truck. Evans looked at the boxes, the address was Petrograd, the name that of a woman.

"Your mother?" he asked.

"My aunt. My mother and sisters died in the siege of the city. They were starving so they tried to make soup out of engine oil. It killed them of course but perhaps it was a quicker death than starvation. Allow me to introduce myself, Gospodin Colonel. My name is Klavdia Efremovna Kalugina, 69th infantry. I forget which part of that unit I am from now, we have been merged and reformed so often since the offensive began.

Evans whistled to himself. He was speaking to a legend. "I have heard much of your skills Klavdia Efremovna. It is an honor to meet you. My name is Tony Evans. I am a pilot with a Sturmovik regiment on exchange from the US Marines. I was shot down a few days ago and, until my new aircraft comes, I am a forward air controller. Now I call in airstrikes. Pilots serve in this role because we understand what our comrades in the air need to know if they are to hit the right targets."

"Gospodin Tony, you are Sturmoviki? Did you drop napalm on the fascists?"

Odd, thought Tony, that was the question all the Frontniki asked him. And they all glowed with satisfaction when he said that it was his favorite. "Klavdia Efremovna, I just *love* the smell of napalm in the morning." It was a corny line, one all the Marine pilots had used for years, but it worked. Sure enough, the girl laughed and looked at him admiringly.

"Gospodin Tony, perhaps you would like to share my lunch?"

Whoa, thought Tony *this could get complicated.* Still, it was a unselfish offer, Russian rations were adequate rather than generous and it was a real sacrifice to offer somebody else a portion. He had food of his own in his jeep he could offer but he'd have to be careful, if he produced too much, he'd belittle her own offer and cause offense. He did not want to offend anybody who could blow his head off at 1200 meters. They'd reached his jeep now and Klavdia Efremovna produced some black bread, cheese and some canned meat. Spam, Tony noticed.

"Perhaps I can add to our meal?" he asked. He reached into his own pack and got out more black bread, 600 grams as opposed to Klavdia's 900 and that made her beam with pride. She might be only a Sergeant but she got the Frontniki ration of 900 grams whereas the Colonel only got 600. He also produced an onion, some tomato sauce and a field heater so they could make some tea.

That's when inspiration struck "Would you like to try an American dish Klavdia Efremovna?" The girl nodded. Evans slid a metal plate onto the other burner of the field cooker. While it was heating, he cut a thin slice of bread, coated it with the tomato sauce then layered it with some slices of cheese. Finally, he topped it with some thinly-sliced spam and onion and put it on the plate. Then, he put his metal field cup over it to hold the heat in. A couple of minutes later, the cheese had melted and the bread hardened enough to form a soft but firm crust. "Klavdia Efremovna, I present you with - Pizza."

She took it and tried a tentative bite. Then a startled grin spread over her face and she wolfed down the field-substitute pizza. She licked the grease off her fingers while Evans made more slices. He kept going until all the bread and toppings had gone.

"Pizza is good, Grazhdanin Tony. Thank you for showing me."

The water was boiling and she started to make the tea. To have hot tea was a real treat. In the field, so often they had to make do with cold tea that had been in the canteens too long. They chatted on over their tea, comparing notes about the fighting and telling gallows-humor jokes. Evans showed Klavdia Efremovna pictures of his old aircraft, *"For Maria Chermatova"* then had to explain who the old lady was and why he'd named his aircraft for her.

As they talked, he couldn't help thinking that staying on in Russia might not be such a bad idea. After a twenty year hitch in the Marines, he had few ties in America, nobody to go back to and nothing much to do there. But Russia was a wrecked and smashed society that badly needed expert help if it was going to recover. With his pension for capital and a world of opportunities to pick from, he could build a good life here.

There was no need to sever ties with America, the rule was that if he started a relationship with a Russian girl, he would be expected to stay with her and make his home here. There would be no restriction against traveling back to America as often as they wished or having their children in the US, so the kids would benefit from dual American-Russian citizenship. And, he suddenly realized, even without makeup and in the baggy Russian uniform, Klavdia was a very attractive woman.

War had a beautiful symmetry to it, thought Nikolai Fedorovich Lukinov. He'd started this offensive in command of a platoon of around 50 soldiers. Then, he'd made a Captain in command of a composite company of around 50 soldiers. Now, he was a major in command of a composite composite battalion - of around 50 soldiers. He got a grim feeling that when he finally made President, it would be of a country with around 50 citizens. If that wasn't worrying enough, his best sniper, the legendary Klavdia Efremovna Kalugina was making eyes at an American pilot. Well, if anybody deserved a chance to snag an American, it was her. Lukinov decided it was time to give the gods of love a little helping hand. He went over to the American's jeep and saluted

"Gospodin Colonel Evans, welcome to the 69th. I understand you will be our forward air controller for a week or two. I am required to assign a soldier to you as an escort and bodyguard. Heroic Sniper Klavdia Efremovna Kalugina, I understand that your spotter, Marusia Chikhvintseva, is seriously injured and will not be returning to us for some time. You are therefore assigned to escort Colonel Evans for as long as he is with us. Any questions?"

She snapped to attention and saluted, spilling her tea as she did so. "No, Tovarish Major. And thank you."

Lukinov returned the salute and stalked off in a good imitation of an officer who'd just had to part with a valuable unit asset for no very good reason. As he went he sneaked a look backwards. Evans and Klavdia Efremovna were grinning broadly at each other. Well, he'd done a good thing today, a selfless thing. He'd given two people a chance to be happy. Doubtless, God would recognize that and reward him. And even if he didn't, Klavdia still deserved her chance. Now he had more important things to organize.

The German men were to be handed over to the security police, SMERSH, for interrogation before being put on trial for war crimes and executed. The women were to be sent to a detention camp where they would kept until their fate was decided. It was being rumored they were being held as hostages against something. Well, that was somebody else's problem. Trucks would be arriving in a few hours to take the women away. Then R&R would be over. His "battalion" would be moving out, keeping up the pursuit of the retreating Germans. The work of the Frontniki was never done.

German Forward Headquarters, Elista, New Schwabia

He'd heard that some animals, once they realized that the trap was sprung and escape impossible, would lie down and die. Baron Walther Model had never thought that was a particularly good or useful idea. Now, he was beginning to understand what might lead to it. The situation facing him was worse than any he had ever handled. All three of his fronts had caved in. In the east, SS-Wiking was dead. It had taken the Russians less than six hours to break through its defense position, their heavy tanks grinding the world's last SS division into history.

There would be no survivors. Oh, some men may still be alive, hiding in woods or ruined buildings but the Russians would hunt them down and kill them. LII Panzer Corps had died also, destroyed in a whirlwind of airstrikes and armored thrusts. But, LII had achieved something that SS-Wiking had not, they'd bought enough time for the three infantry divisions in Stalingrad to escape. Model grimaced, his capital of Walthersburg had fallen almost without a fight and was now Stalingrad again. Those three divisions were out and moving south along the Kotelnikovo Road. They were already south of Proletarsk, heading for the Kuban and Armavit. With them was XXXXVII Panzer Corps, by a miracle, they were out also, damaged certainly but still capable of fighting.

That was the good news, the real disaster was in the north. The blow across the Volga had threatened to take his defense line on the Don River from the rear. He'd had to abandon his painstakingly-built fortifications in an attempt to get the infantry there out and south. Only, once out of their steel and concrete, the three infantry divisions had just melted away. The Russians had realized what was happening and launched a pursuit, overrunning the retreating units and turning their rout into a catastrophe. The decision had been a bad mistake, if he'd known the units would collapse that way, he'd have left them put to fight in their bunkers and die there. But he hadn't and the divisions hadn't even made an effort at fighting. In the west, his port of Rostov had fallen, also pretty well without a fight

Now, all that was standing between the Russian northern units and what was left of his army was the creaking Russian logistics system. The Russian tanks had slowed down, waiting for their fuel convoys to catch up. He had a breathing space now, not much of one for certain but it was a breathing space. If he could reassemble his force south of Armavit, he could cut his way out to the south. It would only be a few tens of kilometers and his troops would be in the Caucasus Mountains. There, they would be safer from the murderous Russian fighter-bombers and any pursuit would be seriously slowed.

He could head through the mountains to Tbilsi in Georgia then south to Yerevan in Armenia. Finally, he could make it over the border into Iran. His friend the Ayatollah had already promised him sanctuary there, sanctuary for him and as many of his people as could make it. Looking at the map, Model knew what he envisaged would be a military epic. If the tale was ever told, it would go down as one of the greatest fighting retreats in history. The survivors of his army would have to move as a wolf pack, non-combatants and soft-skins in the middle, armor and infantry on the outside. More than 40,000 people moving as a column with a little over 300 kilometers to cover before they reached safety.

And there was another problem, the stockpile of war gasses at Proletarsk. He couldn't evacuate it now and the Russians were closing in on the town. Then, inspiration struck. If his engineers just released the gas, it would form a huge cloud. The prevailing winds would carry it north and west into the heavily-populated areas of the Donbass. It would kill thousands for certain, probably tens of thousands, perhaps hundreds of thousands.

The Russians would go berserk and chase those responsible with every asset they had. And, he'd order the engineers to make for a port on the Black Sea, Primorsko Akhtarsk would do. That would take the Russians south and west while he was planning to go south and east. The misdirection would cost him his engineers but buy him hours, perhaps a day or more. Each such hour meant his column could be further on its way before the Russians started the real pursuit.

Model wrote the orders out clearly and precisely, then called for a courier. The duty officer was Willi Martin, the paratrooper who'd brought him word of the Russian crossing of the Volga. Model repeated the written orders verbally, explaining that the gas release was to cover the retreat to the Kuban and the Black Sea coast so his army could evacuate by sea to Turkey.

The Road To Proletarsk, Kalmykia, Russia

Willi Martin left Model's headquarters a profoundly troubled man. He might be a junior officer, but he could read a map and what he had been told just didn't make sense. The gas cloud would be militarily inconsequential, oh it would snarl the Russian rear echelon and supply columns up for a while but they'd cope with that. The slaughter of civilians would be unimaginable, horrible to contemplate. And the Russians would be enraged, they'd come after the surviving Germans with everything they had and there would be no mercy for anybody.

Had Model gone mad? Or had he decided that if he was going down, he'd take as many people with him as he could? What was he thinking, why was he doing this?

As Willi Martin drove north, the question continued to plague him. The tires of his Kubelwagen, beating on the road surface seemed to be chanting *why? why? why?* He was stopped at checkpoints but Model's pass saw him though them without delays. Anyway, the checkpoints were manned by chainhounds, not SS. The Einsatzgruppen who'd been so keen on hanging "deserters" when the front was holding had evaporated now that the Russians had broken through. Perhaps they'd died, fighting heroically as a rearguard, but somehow, Martin doubted it. It was more likely they were running south as fast as their legs would carry them.

And as he drove west, the question in his head was never answered. At the last checkpoint, the chainhound read his pass but stopped him anyway. "Road forks up ahead sir. Left fork leads to Proletarsk, right fork to Orlovskiy. Make sure you take the left fork, there is a Russian mechanized recon battalion in Orlovskiy already."

The tires were still asking, he still couldn't find an answer when the fork in the road appeared. Martin suddenly realized that the fork really was the question and he had to pick the right answer. It was almost a message and he suddenly understood that the answer was, quite literally staring him in the face. He had to make the right decision. So, he took the right fork in the road.

Orlovskiy, Kalmykia, Russia

Martin had hung his shirt on his radio antenna, it was a poor enough white flag but it would do. As promised, there was indeed a Russian mechanized recon battalion in Orlovskiy, the eight-wheeled armored personnel carriers and SU-76 tank destroyers were parked but ready to move. He swerved his

Kubelwagen to a halt and got out, hands raised. Russians were surrounding him, one took his pistol, another his wristwatch.

Then, an officer with the word "SMERSH" on his collar arrived. Martin showed him the dispatch case with Model's crest on the front then broke the seal, opened it and took out the orders. The Russian didn't speak fluent German but he spoke enough and the words "Sarin" and "Tabun" were understood in any language. His eyes widened and he stared at Martin.

"It's wrong." Martin said "I can't be part of doing that. It's just wrong. It'll be two, perhaps three hours before Field Marshal Model realizes his message didn't get through. You've got that long to stop this. I didn't see much on the road as I came up, a few chainhounds - a few military police. That's all"

The intelligence officer stared at him and nodded. Another officer arrived, obviously the battalion commander. The SMERSH officer showed him the papers and spoke quickly. Martin heard the senior officer's "Borgemoi" and now everybody was staring at him.

Major Yeltsin stared at the German. Was this a trap? Was the Fritz officer luring his unit into an ambush? He looked at the German officer's eyes. Shame, despair, doubt. And anguish. No, this wasn't a trap. Anyway, there was no time to ask permission or follow procedure.

"Get the unit mounted up. We're moving out NOW. We're heading for Proletarsk as fast as we can move." He looked at the SMERSH officer. "Lieutenant Putin, get this German officer to Colonel-General Taffkowski as fast as you can. Stay with him all the way until you speak to the General yourself. We cannot afford for this man to be shot while trying to escape. We're going to try and seize Proletarsk, its only 15 kilometers down the road, but we'll need back-up and reinforcements. Get a message through to the General's staff, see the General sends anything and everything he has."

Major Yeltsin saw the intelligence officer bundle the German and his briefcase into a BTR-40 and head off. Then, he swung himself into his command vehicle, a BTR-60K.

"Right, move out. Su-76s in the lead. Don't stop for anything or anybody. If something gets in the way, crash through it and keep going."

Krasny Kut, Southern Russia. Primary Headquarters, First Byelorussian Front

Although Colonel-General Andrei Mikhailovich Taffkowski was unaware of the fact, he'd made several key decisions and issued a string of orders while his vehicle and its escort were returning from the main headquarters meeting. The situation had cracked wide open, First Ukrainian, Second Ukrainian and First Byelorussian Fronts had broken through the German defenses and were pursuing the broken remnants of the German army south. The news from the Sadovoye Ridge had been even more satisfying. The 18th Guards Tank Division had broken SS-Wiking and were mopping up its fragments. First Khazak Front was wandering off somewhere down towards Astrakhan. All in all, it had been a good meeting.

It was when he got into his command compound that he realized how hard he had been working in his absence. The place was a bustle of activity, people running around, messages being carried. More, there was the suppressed air of excitement that spoke of something major going down. By the time he got to his command caravan, he knew it was important. His staff were working frantically to get something up on running.

"What is it?" he asked testily. He was feeling happy after a good meeting and he didn't want it ruined.

"Colonel-General SIR!" His chief of staff was sagging with relief. "Thank God you're here. Sir, earlier today, a German officer surrendered to a Major Yeltsin, the commander of the 64th Reconnaissance Battalion. He was carrying a series of orders from Field Marshal Model to a number of special engineering units that were stationed in Proletarsk. We were aware of the position of the units but had them designated as motorized infantry and assigned them a relatively low priority. These orders made it clear that the units were those responsible for handling and deploying war-gasses. They had a stockpile of many tonnes of such weapons, mostly Sarin and Tabun but also something called Soman and a lot of old-fashioned mustard gas. The German officer was carrying orders for the engineers to release all that gas then retreat to a port on the Black Sea for evacuation by sea."

"Borgemoi!" Taffkowski was horrified. The thought of the carnage a cloud of gas would cause as it floated over the densely-populated Donbass was a nightmare to contemplate.

"Major Yeltsin's words, Sir. Exactly. The Major decided that there was no time to waste. Apparently The German courier knew the contents of the orders and decided that his conscience couldn't allow such an atrocity so he defected to our troops. The Major got off his ass and, on his own authority I may add, decided to try and take Proletarsk by coup-de-main before Model realized that something had gone wrong and issued replacement orders.

"Yeltsin did some sort of cavalry charge down the road from his forward positions to Proletarsk. He got through without much of a fight, but there was a brawl in the city where he lost heavily. Major Yeltsin was wounded but he and his men broke through. They found all the war-gasses had been loaded into trucks, apparently the engineers were expecting orders to move the stockpile to the south. Long column of trucks. The Germans didn't get a chance to do anything critical, Yeltsin's men seized the trucks and their cargoes intact. The survivors of the garrison in Proletarsk are their prisoners."

"What happened to that German Officer? We need to speak with him urgently."

"Major Yeltsin ordered his field intelligence officer to bring him here. In your absence, Sir, you ordered that their progress be accelerated as much as possible, that they be given every possible assistance and that the intelligence officer, a Senior Lieutenant Putin, be made personally responsible for the safety of the German officer. Your exact words Sir were 'he dies, you die'.

"Anyway, Major Yeltsin is asking for reinforcements and assistance. You have diverted a mechanized regiment of the Fifth Guards Cavalry Corps to Proletarsk. Until it arrives, you have contacted our Frontal Aviation and ordered massive air cover over the city. Several regiments of Su-7s and MiG-17s. You have also ordered the ready regiment of the 7th Guards Airborne Division to drop on Proletarsk and attach themselves to Major Yeltsin's command. The paratroopers won't have arrived as an organized unit but they'll give Yeltsin the troops he needs to hold off any counterattacks until the rest of the reinforcements get there. Oh, one last thing Sir, you also sent an urgent message to President Cherniakhovskii advising him of the capture of the gas. This may be of vital political importance and you got the message out without delay."

Taffkowski looked at his assembled staff. Suddenly he crashed his fist onto the situation table, sending the counters jumping.

"Incompetence, rank incompetence! I should have expected no better than idiocy from you motherless cretins," He roared, his face reddened. "All this work, all these orders issued, a critical situation skillfully handled and not one of you saw fit to write yourselves a commendation. Negligence! Criminal Negligence! You will all write yourselves full commendations and have them on my desk within the hour or you will all be shot!"

He let the pretence of rage fade away, his staff were grinning broadly, familiar with their General's idea of humor. With one carefully-rehearsed gesture, they each reached into their breast pockets and pulled out the recommendations Taffkowski had just demanded. The General, looked at his staff, smiling.

"First Byelorussian has always had a reputation for excellent staffwork. I see, in your hands, that reputation is safe. With your help, I continue to surprise even me."

Taffkowski left the staff room into his private office, and closed the door behind him. From a drawer in his desk, he got out two pictures. One was a normal icon but the other was much more unusual. A battle-scared, war-torn T-34 towing a plough. Many, many years before, Taffkowski had commanded a tank company. Passing through a recaptured village, they'd seen a group of women trying to plant a field, pulling the plough themselves. The Germans had destroyed the crops and killed the farm animals. He'd stopped his tanks and used them to pull the ploughs. They'd stayed in the village that night and many of his men had promised to return when the war was over. But, none ever would, they were all dead now, some buried in mass graves, others singly. Taffkowski was the only survivor of the day a T-34 had pulled a plough.

He dropped to his knees in front of the pictures and started to pray. It was a miracle and he knew it, a militarily impossible miracle. Model had picked the one courier in his army with a conscience, that courier had defected to the one unit in the Russian Army commanded by an officer with the initiative to react fast. That unit had somehow driven through the German lines without running into one of the scratch defenses the Germans were so good at forming. A lightly-armed recon battalion had won a firefight in a major town and captured a deadly threat that only needed one man to press one button to turn into a catastrophe.

It was a miracle and it was not the only one. At his meeting, Taffkowski had been told the story of the Miracle of Sadovoye Ridge. The Germans had counter-attacked and their heavy armor had broken through the center of the Russian line. Only a single T-10 stood between the Germans and Victory. Instead of firing, the tank commander had stood on his turret and held up an Icon, praying to God for help. And God had filled the battlefield with His light and His arm had struck terror into the hearts of the Germans. Above the battlefield, standing on the clouds were the great heroes of Russian history, Zhukov, Stalin, Peter the Great, Ivan, Prince Vladimir, the Saint Prince Aleksandre Nevski. They'd lead the Russian Army forward with prayers and blessings and singing hymns. The Germans had fled and everywhere they had fled to, the yellow light had found them and driven them out to be killed by the Frontniki.

Colonel-General Andrei Mikhailovich Taffkowski suddenly felt a great peace come over him, peace born of a revelation. These miracles could only mean one thing. At last, at long last, God had forgiven the Russian people. He had restored His grace to them. The dreadful sufferings of the last twenty years had purged the Russians of their guilt for failing to fight the Antichrist Hitler and for all the other follies of the 1930s. At last God had decided the Russians had atoned for their sins. Finally, they had paid the full measure of the terrible price that failure to stand against evil brought upon the weak and now they were forgiven at last.

MFV Snapper, Port of Ban Mab Tapud, Eastern Thailand.

Obviously, Ban Mab Tapud was going to be a lucky port. He would have to come here more often, thought Captain Park Chung-Hee of the Korean motor fishing vessel *Snapper*. He'd had the standard order from the Japanese company that owned the vessel. Go fishing, sell the catch for hard currency, fish some more and bring the fish back to Pusan. His hold loaded with fish from a catch in the East China Sea, he'd pulled into Ban Mab Tapud to sell it. There. He'd had his first stroke of luck. The local fish cannery had a rush order from America but was short of stock. Deadlines pressing, they'd paid 30 percent over market price for his catch. Even better, they'd recorded the sale at 20 percent over market price and slipped him the rest in cash under the table. And that had been a pretty sum.

Most, he'd invested in consumer goods that he would sell on the black market back in Korea but the rest he'd taken to one of the bars in the town. There, he'd bought out the most attractive of the bar girls and brought her back here. She was lying on his bunk now, sleeping off the night's work. Still it was 0730, time for a good fisherman to be getting ready for sea. Even as he watched the girl opened one eye and looked at the clock.

"Hey, where are you going? You bought me out for twelve hours, You have until ten." The girl looked slightly offended, Park realized in her line of business, being kicked out of bed two and a half hours early probably was a professional insult.

Anyway, she was very good, worth every satang of her fee. And the tide wouldn't be right until mid-afternoon.

"Nowhere Noi, I was just going to order some tea for you. Now what were we doing?"

Two and three quarter hours later, Park watched the girl skip down the gangway, flip her ponytail and wave him a cheerful goodbye. Yes, he liked Ban Mab Tapud. He would definitely be back. He went up to his bridge and stopped dead. Just across the way from him was the largest ship he had ever seen, painted gray with the American flag flying from her stern. Bridge amidships, two very heavy goalpost masts forward, one aft. Helicopter pad by the stern. Small letter E large numbers 23. Park reached into the concealed recess on the bridge and got out his recognition book. That was her, AE-23 *USS Nitro*.

"Port authority contacted us sir, they regret but due to operational necessities, we cannot leave until high tide tomorrow." Park frowned then grinned. They'd have to stay an extra night. He left the bridge and went back to main deck. He was in time, the girl was still waiting for her taxi. He walked down the gangway and called her.

"We have been delayed, are you free tonight? At eight? For twelve hours?"

The girl got out a small diary and turned to today's page. "Yes Captain, I am free then. And the American ship will not be staying for shore leave, she is due in the Philippines. Very well. I will write your appointment in. Oh Captain I love you so much. Fifty percent deposit on my fee please."

The Captain chuckled as the girl's taxi left. Then, he went back to his bridge to watch the ammunition ship. her crew were bustling around on deck, the sort of organized chaos that any seaman recognized. Then the first pallet came out of the cargo hold. Park trained his binoculars on it. The long thin shape was unmistakable, the size was a little harder to estimate. He'd guess it was 250 kilograms, that made it a Mark 82. And there were ten of them on the pallet. The big cranes swung it out and put it onto a truck. There was a big airbase just down the road from Ban Mab Tapud. That must be where the bombs were going. The truck pulled out and another took its place. Another pallet of bombs was already being readied for delivery.

"We'd better count these." The First Mate grunted and made a check mark on a pad. Then another as the second pallet went ashore. By dusk, Nitro had unloaded more than 3,000 Mark 82s and the work showed no sign of ceasing. Nitro's floodlights were on and the crew were still hard at work. At 19:55 Noi's taxi pulled up and she got some tired but appreciative whistles from the ammunition ship. Captain Park retreated to his cabin with her while Nitro continued to unload her cargo. The call girl and the crew of the ammunition ship had one thing in common, they were both working hard all night.

Office of President Cherniakhovskii, New Kremlin, Moscow, Russia

Even the thick walls of the New Kremlin couldn't quite keep out the sound of the church bells. The city was celebrating a victory, but only a few people knew that the celebration was also for the capture of the German stockpile of dreaded nerve gas. President Cherniakhovskii looked up from his file as Doctor Wijnand was ushered in. The man was nervous, he knew something was up but he had no idea quite what. That was good, let him stew for a few minutes. He waved at a seat, watching Wijnand sit down then finished reading the report.

"My apologies for my rudeness Dr Wijnand, but some things cannot wait. It is a great day is it not?" Wijnand nodded. "Doctor, you may remember that at our last meeting I said that the Germans would judge themselves, that they would determine their own fates? Well, it appears that fate has indeed rendered its verdict. Model gave orders for the nerve gas to be used against our civilian population, his orders would have caused a catastrophe of unimaginable proportions. But a single German officer refused to be part of this terrible crime and risked his life to warn us. As a result, the gas was not released and is now in safe hands. God has undoubtedly passed his verdict and told us of it. And you can see what this is of course?"

President Cherniakhovskii watched Doctor Wijnand squirming in his seat. The poor man didn't know what to say and Cherniakhovskii was thoroughly enjoying his dilemma. In the end, he took mercy on the Doctor.

"Why Doctor Wijnand, I would have thought it was obvious. We have been shown that there is goodness, even in the Germans and it is our duty to save what goodness we can find. But enough of that. I told you that if the Germans did not use their gas, we would release the German women and children into your custody. For whatever reason, the Germans did not use their gas. Therefore, we will hold our part of the bargain true and the women and children will be released. Furthermore, it was our plan to execute all German men as war criminals but God has shown us this is not just or right. We will execute all members of the SS and all members of the Nazi Party. But, for the rest, if no crimes are proved against them, then they too will be released into the custody of the Red Cross."

Wijnand felt a great load come off his mind. He had hoped that he could save the women and the children but to save some of the men as well was more than he could have expected. Whoever that German officer was, he'd done his people an immense service, much more than he probably would ever know. President Cherniakhovskii continued.

"We will release the people to you, but they take nothing out of Russia. You understand this? They will take nothing. Not a scrap of food, not a shred of clothing, not a child's toy. Nothing. They will be an object lesson that those who come to us in friendship will be welcome to share our last crust of bread in friendship. But those who come as enemies will be very lucky to leave with their lives and as naked as the day they were born. Make your plans to move the people I am entrusting to you Doctor Wijnand. They are your responsibility now."

President Cherniakhovskii leaned back as Doctor Wijnand left, with preparations to make and arrangements to complete. He picked up the report again. In one sense, he didn't believe in miracles. He'd heard the story of the Miracle of Sadovoye Ridge but he knew it was just a trick of the light and the imagination of desperately tired soldiers who had finally beaten a dreaded enemy. The Miracle of the Gas, well, recon battalions had the most independent and free-thinking officers and this one had moved across the front of the German line, not through it. Not a miracle, just the happenstance of war. But on another level, it was a miracle that two Miracle Stories had come at just the right time to rescue Russia from having to make a terrible decision.

And another thing. When Zhukov had become president, he picked a group of younger men to be groomed as his successor. Over the years, one by one, they'd been found wanting and, one by one, they'd been discarded until only he, Cherniakhovskii, had been left. Cherniakhovskii smiled to himself, on his visits to America, he'd watched television and the game shows the Americans loved. Perhaps there was a game show idea there; get a group of people, give them tests and eliminate them one by one until the last survivor gets the big prize. He shook his head, now peace was finally coming, Russia could think about television and game shows. But, he, Cherniakhovskii, had to start the process of grooming his successor. Perhaps this Major Yeltsin? No, the man deserved better, Colonel Yeltsin would be a good candidate.

Peace? Was it really at hand? The report Cherniakhovskii was reading was alarming. It was an analysis of the paperwork and documents found when Model's "Baronial Hall" had been taken. More than alarming, it was terrifying. It laid out in specific detail the arrangements made between Chipan, Model's government and a consortium of Islamic states in the Middle East. That much had been expected. What was not were the developments in the Middle East grouping. They were far advanced down the road to setting up some sort of federated state. There was a guiding council, called The Caliphate, headed by a man called Khomeini. Russian "experts" had thought that any such alignment was out of the question, that the various kinds of Moslem hated each other too much for such an arrangement.

It was now clear that assessment was wrong. They hated each other certainly, but they hated the rest of the world more. And they were prepared to ally against the rest of the world even at the expense of their own internal feuds. Cherniakhovskii read, horrified, of what the captured documents revealed of the nascent state's policies and goals. They amounted to a complete rejection of the modern world, a complete renunciation of everything humanity had achieved in a thousand years.

Except in the technology of death of course. The Caliphate wanted nuclear weapons, they wanted gas, they wanted biologicals. Nuclear was out of their reach, at least for the time being but Model had already given them the technology, knowledge and personnel to make chemicals. He'd given them something else as well, something that made Cherniakhovskii sick to his stomach. Model and the Caliphate had shared one particular hatred, one that Model's little state had been very well placed to accommodate. The report remarked that Caliphate documents were full of references to "The Final Solution of the Jewish Problem". And Model had given them that technology as well.

President Cherniakhovskii slumped into his seat. Dear God was it starting all over again? Last time it had taken the lazy, self-indulgent Americans to get themselves off their indolent butts and harness the awesome power of their country to burn evil off the map. That had been one country in Europe. What would happen if half the world had to be eliminated the same way? Could humanity survive it?

There was another consideration. Russia was redeemed at long last, it had paid the price for failing to confront evil and was redeemed. They should never make that mistake again, if evil showed its face, it had to be fought. There was an old Russian fable about guard dogs. The fable said they should always come in pairs, a big guard dog and a small guard dog. Big dogs were immensely powerful but lazy. They slept most of the time. Small dogs had to keep alert because they were weak. So if the enemy came, the small dog would bark and wake up the big dog who would then do the fighting. Cherniakhovskii thought that wasn't a bad paradigm for his relationship with America. Russia was the small, alert and dedicated dog, America the big, powerful, lazy one. When danger threatened, it would be Russia's job to wake America up.

This report put another light on the world. Everybody was worried about Chipan, the effects of a unified China and Japan on world order. But this report made it clear, Chipan wasn't the threat it appeared to be. The country was desperately short of resources, of technology, of foreign exchange and of scientific expertise. They were ringed off and contained. Whether they'd done it deliberately or by accident, the Triple Alliance had contained Chipan and, given time, it would collapse under its own weight. No, Chipan was a short-term threat, no more than that. The medium and long term threat was the emerging Caliphate. This report was the first real look at just how dangerous it was.

The report had to be circulated. The little guard dog had to start barking. Copies had to go to the Targeteers in America and to that charming and ever-so-deadly Ambassador from Thailand. Cherniakhovskii smiled affectionately at the thought. Even now, his secret service still hadn't worked out how she'd assassinated Mahatma Ghandi.

Destroying Model's "New Schwabia" had torn the mask from the Caliphate. And what lay beneath the mask was uglier than anybody had dreamed possible.

Chapter Ten
Going For Broke

Clark Field, Luzon, Philippines

Marisol's crew heaved themselves out of their cramped cockpits. It had been an almost nine hour flight from Honolulu with an aerial refueling half way and muscles were painfully locked into position. Major Mike Kozlowski was half way down his steps when he saw two things. One was the arrival of a line of armament dollies with a complete set of war-shot missiles for *Marisol* and the other was his friend Commander Paul Foreman waiting to greet him.

"Hi Mike, I see you're going up in the world. Heard about Red Sun, getting your lady back, that was a slick bit of flying. What happened?"

"Hi Paul. Went between a pair of Cajun 106s when we were all double-sonic. It was our pod that saved us, it split the airflow enough to protect the main gear when it dropped. *Marisol* is a dash-thirty now. New hydraulic systems with a better back-up, we've got two new missiles, an air-to-surface version of the GAR-9 and the AAM-N-7 Sparrow IIs. Not having a medium-range conventional air-to-air hurt us at Red Sun. You got a new toy under your bird?"

"Ain't that the truth. We just got'em. Its called an Orlan. Means Eagle. Russians developed the basic idea then Lockheed took it over and got it to work. We lock it onto a ship, shoot it from about 40,000 feet, it goes up to 80,000, flies to its target then does a vertical dive on the victim. Giving the skimmers conniptions working out how to stop it. Your GAR-9s seem the best bet. You see *Marisol* being loaded with war-shots? Us too. Our Orlans are live, 350 kiloton thermonuclear. We've got a job to do, when we get back, beers are on me Mike. I want to pick your brains on what you learned at Red Sun

Flag Bridge, HIJMS Musashi, South China Sea

Admiral Soriva sighed and took the communication pad. He shuddered, if the existing situation wasn't bad enough, now he had this to worry him. The old escort carrier *Chuyo* had been ferrying some aircraft to Danang when she'd hit a mine in the main shipping channel. The Captain had tried to beach her but the damage was too bad and she'd gone down, blocking the channel completely. A minesweeper had found another mine nearby, it was an old Japanese Navy one, the serial number suggesting it had been laid back in 1941 and never swept. They must have broken loose and drifted into the channel. Anybody who believed that would believe anything. Still, it didn't matter, the port was closed until sweeping was completed.

Soriva shook his head, then went back to his chart. While he was shackled by his twelve-knot merchant ships, the Indian-Australian convoy had got out in front of him. It was more than 50 miles ahead now and pulling further away every hour. There was no way the merchant ships with Soriva could overtake it so it had to be stopped. If he took his battleship group group to flank speed, he could close on the convoy in six to eight hours time. Then he could give an ultimatum. Either they turned back or he would eliminate them with the nuclear shells he carried for his big guns.

It was an unanswerable argument and they'd have to obey. The other option was the two carriers under Admiral Idzumo behind him. There was a problem there, *Shokaku* and *Zuikaku* carried only 28 fighters and 32 bombers each. There were two Australian carriers with the task group, reportedly they carried 36 F11F Tigers each. The Japanese carriers didn't have the power to take them on, at best they could provide cover for the existing Japanese formations and a limited strike capability to mop up stragglers. The one good thing was that the Tigers had no strike capability, they could defend but not attack. No, the battleships were the best solution for this job. And pray that it would be over before the Americans found out. Soriva bent over the chart table again as he felt the vibration in his feet tell him *Musashi* had gone to flank speed.

Captain's Bridge, INS Hood, South China Sea

"Signal reads Good luck and God's Speed Sir" Captain Jim Ladone shuddered slightly, *Hood, Rana* and *Rajput* were swinging away from the convoy. Earlier, the Japanese battleship group heading the formation behind them had accelerated and started closing on the Australian-Indian convoy. The threat was obvious. Unable to overtake the fast troopships, the Japanese commander had decided to bring his battleships up and give an ultimatum. Turn back or we use our 18 inch guns. It was well-known the Japanese had nuclear shells for those guns.

There had been a quick conference and Ladone's suggestion had been accepted. He'd take the three Indian ships back to confront *Yamato* and *Musashi*. If they tried to blast past him, he'd hold them as long as he could while the convoy scattered. Then, the Australian cruisers and destroyers would try and buy more time. With luck, the convoy would be well-scattered by the time the enemy got through and most of the troopers would get clear.

"What can we do Sir? We're no match for one of those monsters, let alone two."

"We can challenge them Number One and they will ignore our challenge. We will fight them and they will sink us. That's all there is to it."

"Sir, there are two thousand men on this ship, We can't take them to be killed. We must save the lives of our crew."

Ladone nearly exploded with rage, then brought himself under control. His Number One was young, still learning his business. He should be taught. However hard it would be.

"Number One, there are fifty thousand men in that convoy and we are their escort, we are responsible for them. You remember what happened on our quarterdeck only a few months ago?"

Number One nodded, he was the Number One only because the officers senior to him had died in the explosion. "We were responsible for their safety as well and we failed them. We will not fail again. But that's not what's important now. There is something much more important here.

"Number One, we're a warship, we were built to fight. Not to run away, not to hide. To fight. To bring as much harm upon the enemy as we can. The Indian Navy is a young navy, our traditions are not yet set. Today, we're going to help set them. We're going to establish a precedent that Indian warships fight. Regardless of odds, regardless of chance of winning, we fight as long as we have weapons to fight with.

"After today, every enemy who faces one of our ships will know that if a fight starts, it will be a fight to the death. And, one day, an enemy facing that choice will back off even though the odds are in their favor. More than that, once our enemies know a fight with our ships means a fight to the death, they will enter the battle scared. And then our ships will win against the odds and the more they do so, the greater will be the odds they can overcome. Today we fight, not just for the troopships under our protection but for the future. For the future ship in the same position we are in today that will live because today we choose to fight, not to run. Now ring up flank speed. We have an appointment to keep."

Ladone looked out of his bridge over his forward 15 inch guns as he felt the vibration in his feet tell him *the mighty 'Ood* had gone to flank speed.

On Board USS Skipjack SSN-585, Periscope depth, South China Sea

His radio mast was up, he was in intercept position and all he needed was the position data from the Batwings. He was well away from the carriers and outside the detection arcs of their sonars. He was listening out for one minute at ten minute intervals and that was longer than he liked to have a mast up. Still, at least he wasn't emitting. That would come later. Commander Runken looked back to his plot. Two carriers in line ahead. One destroyer in the lead, one in trail, two on each side. And not one of them had the slightest idea what they were up against. Almost 90,000 tons of shipping. "Sir, burst transmission from Batwing-one." We have the position data, they want us to start in 15 minutes.."

"Very good. Dive to 300 feet then flank speed for this position here." Runken made a mark on the map. "We'll run out under the inversion layer then pop up to start." Runken relaxed as the deck angled down and *Skipjack* vibrated as she went to flank speed.

PB5Y-1 "Batwing-One" 60,000 feet over the South China Sea

Up here, the sky was dark blue and the PB5Ys were almost invisible against it. The radar horizon was more than 500 miles away and the radar bombing system was showing five groups of ship. The Australian convoy was well off to the west, in the center was *Hood* and her two destroyers with the two Japanese battleships, two cruisers and eight destroyers nearby. There was less than 30 nautical miles separating them now, the situation was about to blow wide open. Then, halfway towards the east, was the Japanese troop convoy with the Japanese carrier group on the extreme east of the screen.

If the situation did blow, Batwing-One to Batwing-Eight would take the battleship group, Batwing-Nine to Batwing-Sixteen would take the Japanese troopship convoy. The Orlans would make short work of them, that was for certain. But first....

Batwing-One accelerated as Foreman opened the throttles wide. He felt the kick in his back as Batwing-One and Batwing-Two started their long dive for the high-speed run.

Captain's Bridge, INS Hood, South China Sea

"God, they're big!"

Even at this distance. Ladone was awed by the size of the Japanese battleships. *Hood* had been the biggest battleship of her day but these two dwarfed her. "Kanali, when we open fire, take your two destroyers and go in for a torpedo attack. Make sure your engineer gives you every pound of steam you can get. You've got good fish and your magnetic exploders work, if you can get hits you can really hurt those two. You must hit the battleships."

"Roger. Wilco. Good Luck *Hood.*"

"Signalman make to Japanese battleship. 'Military operations in progress. Exclusion zone applies as advised in notices to mariners. Request you change course and allow us searoom to complete our operations.' And may God have mercy on our souls."

Flag Bridge, HIJMS Musashi, South China Sea

Soriva was furious. How dare the Indians tell him where he could take his ships. "Signalman, Make to *Hood*. 'You are instructed to clear our path. Remaining in your present position will be considered a hostile act and dealt with accordingly.' Order gun crews to close up for surface action. The Indians will attempt a torpedo attack with their destroyers when the firing starts. *Tone* will take *Akitsuki, Terutzuki, Hazuki* and *Ootzuki*, intercept the attack and eliminate the destroyers."

"Sir, high flying formation of unidentified aircraft to port. Raid count is 16 aircraft, estimated altitude, 20,000 meters. Sir, two aircraft diving at very high speed." Soriva's scowl deepened. What the devil was going on?

Captain's Bridge, INS Hood, South China Sea

Number One was the first to spot them Their air search radar had spotted the unidentified formation while it was still over a hundred miles out but it was closing fast. Now two aircraft had detached and were diving. "Dark blue sir, delta wings. My God they're moving, estimated speed over 1400 miles per hour. Must be Americans. Nobody else has aircraft like that."

PB5Y Hustlers thought Ladone, He'd never seen them but he'd heard of them. The latest long-range maritime attack bomber in the US Navy. And it had a long-range nuclear-tipped anti-ship missile. It looked like the cavalry were arriving at the traditional last minute. The only thing that worried him now was whether he was going to be clear of the blast.

There they were, they were arcing downwards, less than a dozen miles away and closing very, very fast. "Almost 800 knots" came an awed whisper from the air warfare station. The two blue bombers were less than 200 feet over the sea surface now, carving across the space between the two groups of ships. Behind them, the concussion wave from their passage was throwing up a giant wall of spray, reaching over the two aircraft themselves. As they passed *Hood* there was a deep booming crash and the scream of the bomber's jets. Even as Ladone heard it, the bombers were already pulling up, climbing for the safety of the stratosphere. Behind them, the wall of spray collapsed, leaving nothing but a long, thick white line painted on the sea surface.

"Bloody Yanks showing off again." said Ladone in deepest gratitude.

Flag Bridge, HIJMS Musashi, South China Sea

For a moment Soriva thought the noise was his own guns opening fire but it was the sonic boom of the two American bombers. They'd been so fast, he hadn't even had a chance to see them properly but he'd heard them all right. And he'd seen a wall of spray, made iridescent by the sun, forming in front of him then collapsing to form a long white line on the sea surface. It was spreading and fading now but there was no doubt what it meant. If there had been any doubt, the electronic room ended it. "Sir, we're being painted by multiple missile guidance radars, They're locked onto us. No launches yet, but very strong tracking signals, if there was tempura out there it would be deep-fried already."

"Signal Admiral Idzumo, tell him to send air cover to drive off those bombers NOW. Helmsmen swing to oh-one-oh, parallel with that white line." It was theatrical and very American. Draw a line in the sea and send a message. Cross it and we shoot. "Get those fighters here!"

On Board USS Skipjack SSN-585, Periscope depth, South China Sea

"Showtime folks. Up radar, illuminate the nearest destroyer with radar, full power, as many blasts as it takes to wake them up." Runken looked at the map, if anybody had his plot they'd see that his radar emissions were on a direct bearing from his target to the Japanese transport group.

Flag Bridge, HIJMS Shokaku, South China Sea

"Sir, enemy radar transmissions bearing two-seven-zero. No visible source, sir this is a submarine attack."

"Ready helicopters on *Yahagi* and *Sakawa* to take off and localize contact. Engage if hostile. *Agano* and *Noshiro* to detach to contact and pursue. Keep it pinned down until we're clear."

On Board USS Skipjack SSN-585, Periscope depth, South China Sea

"Flank speed, full emergency power, maximum emergency turn to port, take her down maximum rate."

The violent high speed turn and dive would leave an unmissable knuckle in the water but, just to make sure, they'd pop a noisemaker right into the middle of it. By the time the Chipanese helicopters got to it, *Skipjack* would be 3,500 yards away, under the inversion layer and moving underneath the two approaching destroyers, perpendicular to their course. This needed careful timing. Runken closed his eyes, visualizing the tactical picture above him. The helicopters, one, possibly two, would be closing on his decoy target now – yes, there were the sounds of the first pair of depth charges. They weren't trying to kill or they would have used torpedoes. That would come later. But he should be the other side of the destroyers about now... OK. Time for act two.

"Bring her up, periscope depth."

As soon as he was there Runken surfaced the scope, high speed and too much exposure causing a spray of water that could be seen for hundreds of yards. The Japanese had seen it all right, they might be outclassed but they weren't dumb.

"Take her down, 400 feet, then round to course oh-oh oh." Time to give the carrier commanders a nervous breakdown.

Flag Bridge, HIJMS Shokaku, South China Sea

"*Noshiro* reports periscope sighting sir. Off to their port." Idzumo looked at the chart, damn, it was a second submarine, it had to be, more than 4000 meters away from the first sighting and the helicopters still had that one pinned down..

"Order *Noshiro* to divert and engage the new contact. What's out there?"

Admiral Idzumo paced his deck then something clicked in his mind. He took a horrified look at the chart and "Belay that order to *Noshiro*."

It was too late

Bridge, HIJMS Noshiro, South China Sea

The Captain assumed that *Agano* had received the same order and started his turn to port to engage the new submarine contact. By the time he realized his mistake, he was across *Agano*'s bows. The other destroyer didn't have a chance, she was half way through her evasive turn when her bows ploughed into *Noshiro*'s side just aft of the boiler room. The captain saw the side buckle and heard the scream of tortured metal, then the gout of black smoke. Locked together, the two stricken destroyers suddenly had more to worry about than their submarine contacts.

On Board USS Skipjack SSN-585, South China Sea

The control room erupted into cheers and high-fives as the sounds of the collision were picked up on the passive sonar. Then, *Skipjack* charged forward again, her speed eating up the distance between the outer screen and the carriers. But first, the task was to freak out the commander of the lead destroyer. "OK boys. Get ready for periscope depth again."

Flag Bridge, HIJMS Shokaku, South China Sea

Admiral Idzumo looked at the chart in horror. His screen was a complete shambles, two destroyers disabled off to port, the trailing and one starboard destroyer working to ready their replacement helicopter. "Sir, *Oyodo* reporting periscope contact sir dead ahead."

Idzumo scanned his tactical plot, what was happening out there? There were three submarine contacts now, all widely separated and this last one was in a perfect position to rake his carriers with torpedoes. Somehow, the enemy had worked out exactly where he would be and set up a perfect ambush. There would be more submarines he was sure of it. He had no choice, no choice at all.

"All air operations to cease. Carriers to execute maximum evasive action, maintain highest possible speed. Detach *Agano* and *Noshiro* to proceed to base on their own. What was that!" A vicious jar had just shaken the ship.

On Board USS Skipjack SSN-585, South China Sea

After giving the lead Japanese destroyer a periscope flash, *Skipjack* had gone deep, then swung up, heading at the bows of the approaching lead carrier at an up angle of around 40 degrees. At the last minute Runken reversed the ascent, taking the submarine back down but leaving a massive wake surge in the water. It was that wake surge that hit *Shokaku* in the bows, giving quite convincing but inexplicable imitation of a serious collision.

"OK boys, games over, get below the inversion layer and clear. We'll shadow from a distance."

Flag Bridge, HIJMS Shokaku, South China Sea

"Admiral Soriva Sir. He's threatened by maritime attack bombers, he needs air cover to drive them off now. "

Idzumo looked out at the scene. His ships were zigzagging violently, trying to evade any torpedoes that might be coming for them. If he stopped the evasive action to launch aircraft, he'd be wide open to torpedo attack – that crash might have been a hit already, and he'd lucked out by catching a dud. He couldn't take the risk..

"Make to Admiral Soriva. Regret under heavy attack by estimated three to six enemy submarines. Two destroyers damaged one possible hit on a carrier. No flight operations possible due to evasive action."

Flag Bridge, HIJMS Musashi, South China Sea.

Admiral Soriva re-read the message and felt his blood pressure climb another couple of notches. Just what was 'Regret under heavy attack by estimated three to six enemy submarines. Two destroyers damaged one possible hit on a carrier. No flight operations possible due to evasive action,' supposed to mean? How could there be a "possible hit" on a carrier, either she was hit or she wasn't. Soriva wanted to pound his head on a bulkhead, or more precisely, wanted to pound Admiral Idzumo's head on a bulkhead. His chest started to hurt so he took a deep breath and told himself to calm down. The situation was stressful enough as it was.

Yamato and *Musashi* were running parallel with the three Indian ships, distance just under 20 nautical miles. Just out of gun range. The line the American bombers had drawn on the sea surface had long since dispersed and faded but he knew where it was and they knew he knew. They were lashing his ships with their fire control radars just to remind him. He couldn't close with the Indian ships until the bombers were driven off and he couldn't do that until Idzumo got his fighters up. Then he gets this.

Whatever was happening back there was serious. Two destroyers torpedoed, fortunately it seemed both were still afloat. The message must be corrupted, the original must be 'carrier hit, damage possible'. Since Idzumo would know very well what was the situation if his flagship, *Shokaku* had been hit, the stricken carrier must be *Zuikaku*. Things were making a bit more sense, he'd probably seen the tower of water from a hit but also seen *Zuikaku* was apparently undamaged. So the hit was a dud or had only done superficial damage.

This was beginning to make a lot more sense. What he didn't know was whether Idzumo had actually successfully counter-attacked the enemy submarines. And he needed those fighters desperately. Every minute he was held up here would mean it would take him three minutes longer to catch the Australian convoy - and that meant it was a nautical mile closer to friendly air cover.

"Signalman, send following to Admiral Idzumo. Air threat of utmost seriousness. Launch air cover soonest. Have you engaged the enemy?"

Flag Bridge, HIJMS Shokaku, South China Sea.

Admiral Idzumo paced the bridge anxiously. After the flurry of contacts, there had been no more and the pause was deeply worrying him. There were four helicopters now trying to localize and destroy the original contact but they were losing it. They'd dropped depth charges and torpedoes but the crafty submarine crew had evaded them all. They were still there though and dropping behind the group, submarines just didn't have the speed to catch up with a fast carrier group once they'd fallen behind.   That meant the task group had probably outrun the ambush.   It was time to get a final damage report off to Admiral Soriva. Then he could see about getting his aircraft up.

"Take this to the signals room. 'Damage to fleet, two destroyers collided while prosecuting submarine contact. *Shokaku* hit by an unidentified object possibly a dud torpedo.'"

The signals officer was gone only a few minutes, barely more than enough to get to the radio cabin and back. When he returned, Idzumo could see his face was forced into impassiveness. He handed the message flimsy over to the Admiral. Idzumo read it, and was first outraged. 'Air threat of utmost seriousness. Launch air cover soonest. Have you engaged the enemy?' Surely this was an insult, an implication that he was evading his responsibilities. Then he thought more carefully. Admiral Soriva was a respected, indeed admired, officer with a reputation for skill and ability. A handful of point defense fighters couldn't possibly be an air threat of utmost seriousness.

Then it clicked. Idzumo realized what Soriva was telling him and he mentally flayed himself for not spotting it earlier. Both the Indian and Australian Navies were British trained and the British always had two groups escorting a convoy. A close-in group of cruisers and destroyers and a screening group of carriers, some distance from the main body but ready to engage an attacker.

Soriva must have located that second carrier group, the screening group. Idzumo remembered the Indians and Australians had purchased two Essex class carriers each. They were supposed to be working up, six months or a year from commissioning but perhaps they'd been thrown in early. Admiral Soriva must be expecting an air attack from their combined groups, no wonder he was describing the threat as utmost seriousness. Well, carrier warfare doctrine was clear. Do unto them before they do it unto you.

"What is the news from the helicopters? Have they got that sub yet?"

"Helicopters say they have her sir. Contact disappeared after last torpedo attack. There was an explosion and she can't have broken clear. They got her."

"Make to Admiral Soriva. 'Have outrun enemy ambush. One enemy submarine sunk. Am readying air strike. What is position of second enemy carrier group?' Then cease our evasive maneuvers and prepare a strike for launch. Anti-ship. Rocket torpedoes on the bombers, fighters to carry air-to-air missiles. We'll be getting the target co-ordinates from Admiral Soriva."

Flag Bridge, HIJMS Musashi, South China Sea.

Admiral Idzumo's follow-up message hit Admiral Soriva like a kidney punch. Two destroyers collided, *Shokaku* torpedoed. That meant that four of Idzumo's six destroyers were out of action and both carriers had been hit. What sort of battle was going on back there? The submarines he'd run into had taken out more than two thirds of his screen and it was only by the luck of the Gods that the carriers weren't sinking. This action wasn't a happenstance convoy skirmish, this was turning into a full-blooded naval battle. But that raised another question. Why hadn't the Americans simply blown him out of the water? Without fighter cover he was helpless against those bombers. There was something he was missing, something very important.

"Sir another message from Admiral Idzumo."

Soriva took the flimsy and read it. Suddenly, light burst into his head and he felt the deepest shame and mortification of his career. He'd been mentally savaging Idzumo for his conduct with the carriers and now Idzumo sends this message. 'Have outrun enemy ambush. One enemy submarine sunk. Am readying air strike. What is position of second enemy carrier group?' This was the missing piece of the puzzle.

Idzumo had detected a second carrier group waiting in ambush. Instead of playing it safe and leaving Soriva to save himself, he'd bulled his way through the ambush so he could get clear and launch a strike to protect the battleships. He'd risked his life and career, not to mention his command, to save the battleships. Mentally Soriva apologized to his fellow Admiral for the injustices he'd been thinking. The man had acted like a true warrior and Soriva had cursed him for it.

Then another light came on and Soriva at last understood the situation. The battleships weren't the target of the second carrier group. He'd made the traditional mistake, he'd assumed that he was the enemy's main target. Of course he wasn't, the transports were. The enemy plan was to pin down the Japanese carriers with the submarine ambush while the second carrier group took down the transport group. That explained the Americans with their threats but their strange refusal to open fire. Everybody knew that *Yamato* and *Musashi* had nuclear shells for their 46 centimeter guns. The Triple Alliance didn't have nuclear weapons, not as far as anybody knew. So the Americans, with their disgusting sense of fair play had evened the odds by checkmating the Japanese nuclear platforms with their own.

Of course the Americans had defined fair play in this case. How many Triple Alliance carriers were out there. Two at least with the convoy but how many in the second group Idzumo had spotted? Two? Four? If two, then Idzumo could have taken them on even terms. But now he had two thirds of his screen gone and his ships had been hit. And, he had to calculate on enemy capabilities. If they were committing their carriers while still half-trained he had to assume all four Triple Alliance Essex class were around. They could overwhelm Idzumo's carriers then eradicate the troop convoy. Soriva realized his battleships simply didn't matter in this equation. Idzumo must have realized that as well, that was why he had acted the way he had, prevaricating on the air cover Soriva had been demanding. He knew he had to give priority to protecting the transports.

"Signals, make to Admiral Idzumo. 'Four enemy carriers waiting in ambush. Make protection of troop convoy your topmost priority. Provide air cover to transports at earliest possible moment.' Get that message out fast."

Soriva stared at the chart. The message was obvious, it was all over. He couldn't catch the Australian convoy without getting nuked. His transports couldn't get to Rangoon and if they continued on course, they'd be subject to air attack. It would be pointless. The game was over. Time to fold.

"Signals, make to Admiral Iwate. 'Operation abandoned due to overwhelming enemy strength. Come to course oh-four-five then make for Danang.'" The signals officer cleared his throat and absent-mindedly tapped the earlier signal about *Chuyo*. "Correction make that Haiphong. Signal Admiral Idzumo and order him to make for Haiphong as well. Helm, come to course oh-six-oh."

Flag Bridge, INS Hood, South China Sea

Captain Ladone felt the tension screwing his nerves tighter and tighter. He'd felt the same way the time he'd been on the *Prince of Wales* when she'd made her run across the Atlantic during The Great Escape. His older brother Jack had been on *Barham*, one of the six old battleships that hadn't made it. A U-boat had nailed *Barham* with four torpedoes. The Germans had triumphantly released film of her rolling over and exploding. He'd always wondered what Jack had felt as his ship exploded under him, now he would know.

He had accepted he was going to die. It was only a question how. The Chipanese wouldn't back down, they'd call the American bluff. If it was a bluff. It was a logic tree. There were two possibilities, the Americans were bluffing or they were not. There were two more, the Chipanese would fire nuclear shells or they would not. First case, the Americans were bluffing, the Chipanese fired non-nuclear shells. Then, there would be a gunnery duel that would last until an 18 inch shell crashed into his magazines and his ship exploded. Second case, the Americans were bluffing and the Japanese used nuclear shells. Then, *Hood* would be incinerated instantly. Third case, the Americans were not bluffing and the Chipanese fired non-nuclear shells. Then the Americans would return fire with their nuclear missiles and it would be the Japanese who would be incinerated instantly and *Hood* would survive. Fourth case, the Americans were not bluffing and the Chipanese fired nuclear shells. Then, *Hood* would be incinerated and the Chipanese would follow them to Valhalla a split second later. But the Chipanese knew the same four cases and the logic conclusion was that they would open fire with nuclear shells as a result.

So Ladone was waiting for the lookout to report that one of the Chipanese battleships had fired a single shell at *Hood*. He'd have time to make a quick prayer and that would be it. If he was lucky, the report of the American bombers firing their missiles would arrive before that shell struck. It was the waiting for that lookout's report that was grinding his nerves down. He looked forward, over his forward turrets. Would the old girl get a final chance to get a blow at the enemy? His guns were swung out, trained on the lead enemy battleship. At this range, he could probably get off one broadside, perhaps two. If the Gods of War were just, they'd let the old girl score a single hit, for the sake of honor if nothing else.

"They're turning away."

Ladone couldn't believe it. "Confirm that."

"The enemy ships sir, they're turning away from us. All of them. Estimated course between oh-four-five and oh-seven-five. They're breaking off."

"Oh Dear God Thank You." The words broke from Ladone's lips quite unintentionally. He felt almost like bursting into hysterical laughter so great was the relief. "Hold present course, oh-oh-oh. We'll stay between them and the convoy, just to keep them honest. But, he could see the Chipanese were indeed being honest. The two enemy battleships settled to course oh-six-oh and, as the minutes lengthened, they vanished over the horizon. Soon, even their faint smudge of smoke had gone. All that was left of the confrontation was the faint contrails of the American bombers high overhead.

"Number One. Plot a course to rejoin the Australians then make flank speed. And invite *Rana* and *Rajput* to join *Hood* in splicing the mainbrace."

Admiral's Conference Room, HIJMS Shokaku, South China Sea.

Admiral Idzumo tapped the staff table. "Admiral Soriva has ordered us to produce a full account of the action fought with the enemy submarines. There will undoubtedly be an inquiry into the events today and we must have our reports ready. It is my understanding that we were engaged by a minimum of three enemy submarines, that we sank one while sustaining no significant damage ourselves. While *Agano* has been damaged in collision and *Noshiro* crippled, those are the risks of the sea and we must accept that accidents occur when handling high speed ships in close formation. Any additional comments before we reconstruct our own and enemy movements?"

Each captain, and each helicopter pilot started to add their details of the action. From the confused and contradictory data, a cohesive picture started to emerge, three possibly four submarines had taken part, two off to one side, one, perhaps two dead ahead. The enemy plan had undoubtedly been to make the fleet turn so that it would be caught in a classical hammerhead torpedo attack. The only great mystery was the strange bump that had affected *Shokaku*, was it possible she had collided with one of the enemy submarines? If so they could claim two certain kills and that would be a great achievement. After an hour, they had talked themselves into accepting that *Shokaku* had indeed rammed and sunk an enemy submarine. Nobody noticed that the Captain Iraya of *Niyodo* had failed to join in the conversation. Indeed, his face was growing steadily more worried. Eventually, Idzumo noticed his silence.

"Come Captain Iraya, have you nothing to say?"

Iraya looked at the chart. Honor demanded he speak even if it ended his career. "Sir, I have to raise an unwelcome possibility. I do this reluctantly and with the greatest respect but I must say this. Sir, we have no solid proof whatsoever that we faced any enemy submarines at all."

There was an eruption of anger around the room, shouted challenges and abuse. Idzumo banged a gavel hard on the table, over and over again. Eventually the room quieted. "Captain Iraya, you have said either too much or not enough. Please elaborate on your comment and give us your explanation of what all the rest of us are confident is the case. Perhaps you would like to start with the enemy radar transmission that was intercepted by every one of our ships?"

"Sir, it is that transmission that concerns me the most. We are agreed on its bearing are we not?" Iraya went to the plot and marked the bearing of the transmission. "But Sir, if we extrapolate the bearing backwards, we see the following." He added the extended bearing to the large strategic plot. It intercepted the position of the Japanese transport fleet exactly. Once done, the correspondence was obvious.

"Sir we are in the South China Sea, and the weather is very humid. Under these conditions, a layer of air, saturated with salt spray, forms above the sea. This acts as a duct and traps radar emissions, allowing them to propagate far beyond normal limits. This phenomena is called anomalous propagation or anaprop and the South China Sea is notorious for it. Sir, our helicopters followed that radar bearing using their dipping sonars until they came upon a water disturbance. I ask our pilots, if it had not been for that radar intercept, would they have assumed that water disturbance was a real signal?" The two helicopters pilots looked uncomfortable, itself an answer.

"As for the rest sir, sightings of periscopes, never confirmed. We never detected a sonar transmission, we never picked up another radar transmission, we never heard a torpedo being fired or a torpedo in the water. We never saw a single torpedo wake. Sir. We have nothing except an ambiguous radar detection and some sightings. And how often have our lookouts mistaken whales for periscopes this voyage alone? There may have been submarines down there sir, there may not, But I say we cannot state with certainty that there were."

The room was silent. Too many people knew in their hearts that Captain Iraya had made a strong case - and that any inquiry into this debacle would do the same.

Flag Bridge, INS Hood, South China Sea

It had taken them twelve hours to catch up with the troop convoy. As the three Indian ships started to take up their previous positions, a message lamp started flash from the force flagship

"Message from *Sydney* Sir. Reads 'Request you honor us by leading the fleet to Rangoon.'"

"Acknowledge and accept. Order *Rana* and *Rajput* to form up on our port and starboard beam. Set course for Rangoon."

More signals lamps were flashing. "Message from *Canberra* Sir. Reads 'More proof it is the size of the fight in the dog that matters not the size of the dog in the fight.'

"From *Western Star*, 'You big bully.'

"From *Warramuga*. 'The Indian Navy walks tall today.'

"From *Hobart* 'The beer is on us.'

"From *Arunta* 'Request recipe for your ship's curry. It is obviously a man's meal.'

"From *Melbourne* 'Dammit *Hood*, you let them get away.'"

Jim Ladone relaxed in his Captain's chair. His ship's honor was restored at last.

Chapter Eleven
Changing The Plays

Chipanese Naval Headquarters, South East Asian Fleet, Hanoi, Indochina

The senior Admirals filed back into the conference room, their faces impassive. On the other side of the table Admiral Soriva, Admiral Idzumo, Admiral Iwate and the ship captains awaited the results of the deliberations. Even though the room was cool, all were sweating.

"This committee of enquiry was formed to make an emergency investigation of the fiasco surrounding Operation A-Go, the transport of a naval attack force to seize control of Rangoon and, by implication, Burma. Operation A-Go was part of a much larger strategic plan which has now been compromised by this failure. It is particularly disturbing to this Committee that the collapse of Operation A-Go took place without a shot being fired by the enemy.

"It is our finding that the collapse of Operation A-Go was initiated by the arrival of American land-based maritime attack bombers that threatened the Surface Action Force with destruction unless it ceased its effort to close on the Australian/Indian troop convoy. This caused Admiral Soriva to call for air support to drive off the bombers in question. When such air support was not forthcoming, he was forced to comply with the American demands or face immediate nuclear destruction without having any opportunity to reply to the threat or to defend himself against the attack. Unable to prevent the Australian convoy from reaching Rangoon and faced with certain destruction if he tried to continue, Admiral Soriva aborted the operation and set course for Hanoi.

"At this point the Committee finds that no blame can be attached to Admiral Iwate, commander of the troop transport force. His ships were handled professionally throughout and the withdrawal of the covering forces left him with no option other than to comply with the orders to abort the operation. The Committee does, however, find that the force assigned to him was inadequate in quality and quantity. The troopships used were too slow and their escort was inadequate for close-in protection.

"The Committee also expresses its doubts as to the adequacy of the landing force assigned to this mission. However, none of these concerns affect our favorable judgment on the conduct of Admiral Iwate who is excused form further attendance at these proceedings.

"The Committee has concluded that the key question is why the Carrier Screening Force failed to provide the Surface Attack Force with the necessary air cover. Admiral Idzumo had stated that his force was under heavy attack by a coordinated force of enemy submarines that forced him to take violent evasive action and thus prevented him from launching aircraft.

"However, we can find no evidence of any such attack nor can we find any reason to believe enemy submarines were in the area. It is our belief that a series of natural events were misinterpreted and, together, mislead Admiral Idzumo into assuming a serious threat where none existed.

"It is apparent that the training standards of the Carrier Screening Force left much to be desired. Lookouts were unable to distinguish between spray, marine animal activity and submarine periscopes. Sighting reports were taken at face value without proper evaluation. Ship handling was inept and communication procedures were so poorly conceived and executed as to be totally ineffective.

"As a result, it is our conclusion that Admiral Idzumo was negligent in applying and enforcing proper training standards on the force under his command. It is also our finding that he was incompetent in using proper communication procedures. It was these failings that were the direct cause of the collapse of Operation A-Go.

"The failure to establish proper communications discipline, enforce signaling standards and train signals personnel in the proper execution of their duties was shared by Admiral Soriva. To all intents and purposes, communications between the various elements of the fleet deployed for Operation A-Go collapsed completely. This lead to false appreciations of the situation, inadequate analysis of impending threats and a gross misunderstanding of the tactical situation.

"However, the Committee also notes that the decisions taken by Admiral Soriva were fundamentally correct and prevented a serious situation from becoming critical. It is the recommendation of this Committee that Admiral Idzumo retire from active service with immediate effect. However, Admiral Soriva's sound judgment under difficult service conditions is an asset that the Navy cannot afford to sacrifice.

"The Committee also notes that the forces allocated to Operation A-Go were inadequate for the tasks demanded of them. The larger environment within which Operation A-Go existed was planned by personnel of the Army who did not allow for the difficulties of conducting maritime operations.........."

The voices droned on and on, a long menu of recommendations, observations and criticisms. More aircraft, better aircraft, better communications equipment, better training, more sea time for the fleet. New ships, built for modern warfare, replacing conversions of old designs. Viewed objectively, Soriva thought, they had done a fine job of disentangling the vital lessons from the nightmarish confusion that had doomed A-Go. Poor Idzumo was the sacrificial goat then, doubtless he was already deciding who to select as his second. His own position was better, but his career was over, he'd go no higher in the fleet.

How much of the Committee's work would see the fleet? Soriva thought very little. The money wasn't available and the humiliating fiasco in the South China Sea would seriously affect future programs. Every year, the Army was demanding more and more resources to control China and to counter the insurgencies that were springing up in the more remote provinces. No, he'd go no further in the fleet but, in a few years time, there wouldn't be much of a fleet to go further in. The Japanese Navy was a World War Two fleet in a modern era, its ships and procedures obsolete in the face of the new environment around them. Its day was done.

Listening to the Committee make its report. Soriva had a disquieting thought. If the Navy was obsolete and of only marginal usefulness and the resources to support it were lacking, then why have it at all? Why not just decide what the Navy could do given the resources available and concentrate on that, scrap everything else?

Refugee Evacuation Train, Between Russia and Germany.

Elsa, once Margrafin of Alekszejevka, sat in a carriage of the train, relieved to be out of Russia at last. A truck convoy had picked them up from Alekszejevka and taken them to a refugee camp in the forests north of the Donbass. It had been much better than they had expected, many of the women had believed they would be driven out into the woods and executed. The huts had been solid wood, they had basic beds and each had a furnace for winter. The food had been enough although nobody would have become overweight on the diet. But the camp had been surrounded by barbed wire and the wire was guarded by machine gun towers. It was a prison even though nobody called it that.

Then the man from the Red Cross had come and said the women and children would be returned to Germany. Most of the women had wept, knowing that meant they would never see their men again. Then more trucks had come and taken them to the railhead and the old steam train that was waiting for them.

The Russian-Polish crossing point was well organized. The train stopped, the women were herded off into an area in front of a long line of cubicles. One by one they stepped into a cubicle, undressed and put their clothes and personal possessions into a basket then stepped over a white line on the floor that marked the division between Russia and Poland. There, workers from the Red Cross gave them a new set of clothes and a small package of personal necessities. A few of the women had tried to persuade the Red Cross people to let them keep their wedding rings, some of the children wanted to keep a treasured toy but the workers were firm. Russian policy was that Russian women didn't have wedding rings because of Germans, Russian children didn't have toys because of Germans and it was now Russians who were giving the orders and it was Germans who would do without.

Once the border transition was complete, the train set off again, across Poland to the German/Polish border. They'd been given a meal on the train, a piece of chicken, an apple and some sauerkraut. They'd reached the German border at Gorlitz, or, rather, where Gorlitz had been. Just before the train would have reached the border, it pulled sharply to one side, off the original tracks onto a spur line. A hastily-built and poorly maintained spur line.

The line ended in something that looked like a combination of refugee camp, office block and train station. The train stopped at one set of platforms, the line it was on went no further. The women were herded off the train again, to another series of desks staffed by tired-looking workers. One of the refugees asked why they were having to change trains here. "Fallout" was the reply but nobody understood it. Whatever it was, Polish trains didn't go on into German territory.

Then the women were lined up before the desks. Soon, she found herself standing before a desk. "Name?" asked the woman behind the desk.

"Elsa, Margrafin of Alekszejevka." The woman behind the desk stared contemptuously at her. "Name?"

"Elsa Schultz."

"Thank you. Was that your name in 1947? And what town did you live in during that year.

"It was. My family come from Gladbeck."

The woman pulled a file, a simple folder containing a single sheet of letter-size paper with a double column of typed names on it. She shook her head. "There are no Schultzes surviving from Gladbeck, Do you have any other family?"

"My maiden name was Heilsen but..."

The woman behind the desk checked again. "I am sorry, there are no Heilsens surviving either. As you can see we don't list casualties, we list survivors. There are so many fewer to list." She showed the paper with the two columns of typed names. "Do you know any of these names?" Elsa Schultz staggered.

"No, but there were almost 80,000 people in Gladbeck."

"And fewer than 100 survive. Before The Burning there were 67 million Germans living in the country. Now, there are fewer than eight million. Many died when the Americans dropped their Hellburners on our cities. More died because their injuries couldn't be treated, more still from starvation and the disease epidemics. Our population continues to fall, even now. That is why President Herrick tries so hard to bring back as many of those Germans still in other lands as he can. Now, Frau Schultz, please move on so I can try to help another."

"Please, tell me one last thing. Have you ever found a refugee who has surviving family?" The woman shook her head.

The refugees were herded into a waiting area. One by one, they were taken away and given a brief medical examination, photographed and fingerprinted. Then, they were given a peculiar looking badge.

"Pin this to your dress Frau Schultz and never leave it anywhere. It is your radiation dosimeter. Once each month you must take it to a registered doctor. Your dosimeter must be with you at all times. This is the law. Here is your identity card and your food ration card. You are fortunate, as a young and healthy woman you are entitled to the B ration. When you become pregnant you will be upgraded to the A ration. But if you exceed the permitted monthly radiation dose you will be downgraded to the C or D ration."

Elsa Schultz waited as the day wore on. The last of the women were given their identity cards and radiation badges and they joined the waiting crowd. Eventually, the loudspeaker system started calling names. Elsa Schultz was one of the earliest called and she was taken to another train, one that would take her to the community that would be her new home. Once the last of the selected refugees was on board, the train pulled out. The refugee center had been surrounded by trees and behind a ridge, when it pulled clear of the center, it also left that cover. What the trees had covered and the ridge had screened made the women on the train scream.

Gorlitz had been a town of 87,100 people. Now, it was gone, completely. It was a blackened, charred ruin, the outer areas skeletons of destroyed buildings, the city center completely leveled. Right in the center of the blackness and destruction was an incongruous, perfectly circular cobalt-blue lake. The refugees stared, horrified by the sight and the knowledge that the fate of Gorlitz was that of every significant town and city in Germany. Until this moment, they'd known that Germany had been destroyed but it had been words, seeing a town that had been destroyed by nuclear attack brought home the terrible reality.

The refugees had been given a booklet that introduced them to their new world. Elsa opened it to a page with a picture of the strange circular lake. "Crater Lake" it read "a lake formed at the detonation point of the Hellburner used to destroy a city. After the explosion, the ground underneath slowly subsided and the crater filled with a mixture of ground water and rain. The water in a crater lake is both radioactive and poisonous. There are more than 200 crater lakes in Germany, all are prohibited areas."

She shuddered and looked up the word used at the border, fallout. There was an entry on that as well "Fallout. Highly radioactive waste produced by the explosion of a Hellburner. Most fallout has now faded to insignificant levels and is not considered to be a danger under normal circumstances. However, some areas are still heavily contaminated and must be avoided. The Ruhr Valley is one of these, this area is considered uninhabitable for the foreseeable future. See Hot-Spots."

Elsa turned to the entry "Hot Spots. Although radiation levels have now, in general, fallen to levels that do not pose any significant hazard, there are still areas that have radiation levels far above the norm. In most cases, these are an order of magnitude or less above average but some are much greater than this. The most dangerous known hot-spots have a level of radioactivity five orders of magnitude greater than average and exposure to these will be fatal within a few minutes. Hot spots very in size from less than a meter across to more than a kilometer. They are more common in the ruins of cities than in the countryside and are particularly common near targets where Hellburners exploded on the ground rather than in the air above the target. Cities destroyed by multiple Hellburners are particularly likely to be associated with the presence of hot-spots. However, hot-spots can occur anywhere and there is no visible evidence of their presence. People walking outside cleared areas must carry radiation detection equipment. Women with A and B ration cards are not permitted to leave cleared areas due to the danger of encountering hot-spots."

Cleared areas? What did the book have to say on those? "Cleared areas These are areas that have been thoroughly explored and are known to be safe from radiological hazards. Their perimeters are indicated by yellow-and-black striped barriers. Citizens should remain inside cleared areas unless accompanied by guides who are familiar with the uncleared area and are properly equipped to detect radiological hazards. See also Cities and Prohibited areas."

What did the book have to say on those? "Cities. All cities and major towns are considered uninhabitable and are uncleared areas due to the presence of extensive hot-spots and other hazards.

Even apparently undamaged buildings may be dangerous. Entry to these areas is prohibited unless wearing protective clothing and accompanied by a qualified guide equipped with radiological detection equipment."

And "Prohibited Areas. These areas are dangerously contaminated and must not be entered under any circumstances. Prohibited areas are indicated by orange-and-black barriers."

So this was to be her new home then. A country where the ground could be killing you even while you walked over it, one where towns and cities were unapproachable death-traps. As the train rattled over the damaged and hastily-repaired tracks, Elsa Schultz settled down to read her booklet from cover to cover.

Government Building, Rangoon, Burma.

Sir Martyn Sharpe wished The Ambassador was at this meeting but she was still in Washington. He desperately needed her assistance and advice as a soldier. There was a serious flaw in what he was hearing from General Charles Moses but he didn't have the specialized knowledge to put his finger on what was wrong. He was certain that if the Ambassador had been attending this meeting, she would have spotted it and corrected the situation.

"The situation around Rangoon and in southern Burma is reasonably stable and, due to our prompt intervention, the Government of the country is now secure. The areas to the east are also secured by forces based in Thailand. However, our problem lies here, in the North, in the areas adjacent to the Chipanese border. This long finger of land that stretches North has Chipanese territory on two sides of it. It is in this area that the Shan States Army appears to have achieved its greatest success and here that the Chipanese have established their strongest position.

"The heart of the area is here, the Hukawng Valley, between the Mangin and Kumon Mountains. Access to this area from Chipanese territory must pass through this area here, called The Triangle. As you can see, the road network in this area is extremely limited. While there are several reasonable roads in The

Triangle, they all converge here, at Myitkyina, before spreading out to service the Hukawng Valley. Furthermore, there is an airfield at Myitkyina.

"We are planning to move a full regiment of the Australian Division to occupy Myitkyina. This will fulfill three roles. Firstly, we will be in a position to control the road access to and from the Hukawng Valley and this separates the Shan States Army from their Chipanese sponsors. This will reduce their ability to operate in the valley and thus reduce the problems the insurgency there causes us.

"Secondly, we can use the base at Myitkyina as a focal point for offensive patrols into both the Hukawng Valley and the Triangle. This will allow us to take the offensive against the Chipanese-backed forces and drive them out of the areas in question. Our actions with regard to this insurgency to date have been regrettably passive and defensive in nature and this operation will allow us to change that. The Chipanese insurgents have had the initiative to date and have established their presence in too many areas. This must be reversed. It is time they were made to pay a measurable cost for their activities.

"Thirdly, the strategically vital position of Myitkyina means that the enemy cannot allow us to hold it indefinitely. They will be forced to contest our hold on the base and thus expose themselves to our firepower. We will have artillery in the base itself and we can use airpower based in Assam and southern Burma. It will be impossible for the enemy to bring artillery or anti-aircraft guns of his own to contest our control of the area so we will be able to fight on our terms and with every advantage.

"Our base at Myitkyina will be resupplied by this road here from Mandalay and by means of the river Namyin. We can also bring in supplies by air if necessary, again from the airbase at Mandalay. We propose to start moving troops into this base area within a few days, hoping to have the new base established and operational before the Monsoon starts.

"Thank you."

General Moses sat down. Sir Martyn felt his unease grow. The Monsoon was coming, and with it weather that could ground Triple Alliance aircraft for days at a time. Even the new Thai F-105Bs would be incapable of flying when the rains really started, as for the Indian Air Force's older jets and piston-engined aircraft, they would be out of the game completely.

And, when the rains started, the roads would be turning to mud. He remembered how The Ambassador had told him the importance of good roads in fighting insurgencies and his unease increased. This Myitkyina operation simply wasn't the way she'd taught him about fighting insurgencies. He spoke quietly to the Indian Cabinet Secretary

"Sir Eric, please will you organize a top secret encrypted and scrambled telephone call to Washington as soon as possible. I need expert advice."

Indian Embassy, Rangoon, Burma

Sir Eric knocked on the door of Sir Martyn's room. "Your call to Washington Sir Martyn. Its ready in the Communications Room."

They went down to the secure communications facility in the Embassy Basement. Sir Martyn picked up the telephone attached to the facility and waited while the call was connected. Soon he heard the familiar contralto, unmistakable despite the distance and cryptography. "Sir Martyn, it is a pleasure to hear from you. How may I be of assistance to you?"

Sir Eric watched him explain the Australian plan. Then there was a pause for a few seconds then Sir Martyn started to go white, holding the telephone a little further away from his ear. He started writing down notes on a pad beside the communications console. At the end of the monologue he heard Sir Martyn add.

"Madam Ambassador, I can only say how pleased I am that you confirm my gravest reservations over this operation even though I lack the professional knowledge and standing to express them so forcefully. I will take your advice immediately and thank

- - -

you for agreeing to inform the Americans of what is happening. Good afternoon Ma'am and thank you."

Sir Martyn got up shakily and poured himself a very large drink. "She wasn't very pleased." He looked at Sir Eric ruefully. "In fact her mildest comment was 'I cannot leave men alone for five minutes without them wandering off and getting into trouble' and I got the feeling she meant it. I don't think she believes the Myitkyina operation will be successful."

INS Cicala, On The Nanyin River, Burma

"By the old Moulmein Pagoda, lookin' lazy at the sea,
 There's a Burma girl a-settin', and I know she thinks o' me."

The singing came from the messdecks. Kipling's words were probably the most evocative ever written and always caused those who had served East of Suez to stop for a moment with a dreamy expression on their face. Commodore Nathan was no exception, when he heard the song, he stopped what he was doing and looked out of the bridge at the convoy heading upriver to the new base at Myitkyina.

The two gunboats, *Cicala* and *Dragonfly* were ancient by all standards except those of river warfare where fresh water and a lack of strenuous demands on the engines made for a long life. They were thumping along, escorting a group of freighters. Actually, the ships were LSTs, officially Landing Ship Tank, but universally known as Large Slow Targets. These weren't even real LSTs, they were a small cousin of the American-built ones, but up here large was still the right word. The ships were a long way upriver of their normal haunts and a bit too big to maneuver in the river, but needs must when the devil drives. The combination of supply demands and the beginning of the monsoon rains had made the road up to Myitkyina a nightmare of traffic jams.

"On the road to Mandalay, Where the flyin'-fishes play,
An' the dawn comes up like thunder outer China 'crost the Bay!"

Nathan wondered how many people in the convoy knew that the road from Myitkyina to Mandalay really was the one Kipling had written about. Different war, different era of course but the same road. And dawn really was coming up like thunder out of China. Every day now, the heavy black clouds to the North were gathering, denser, blacker, more threatening. One day, one day soon, they'd burst out and sweep south and the Monsoon would have started in earnest. All they'd had so far were the precursor rains. A mere smattering compared with what was to come. Reading about it was one thing, experiencing it was something else.

"We us'ter watch the steamers an' the hathis pilin' teak.
Elephants a-piling teak, In the sludgy, squidgy creek,
Where the silence 'ung that 'eavy you was 'arf afraid to speak!"

That was true enough also, the heavy humid air seemed to damp out sound, to stifle words in the speaker's mouth. Even the thumping diesels seemed muted as the ships ploughed on. The gunboats, the freighters, the silent jungle either side of them, the sludgy brown water flowing gently against them. Wide river too, wide and shallow, its bottom a hideous gluey mud.

Looking at his little convoy, Nathan saw there was nothing to indicate that Kipling himself wasn't on board and this could still the time when the British Empire stretched across the world and the Royal Navy was the undisputed master of the seas. Only now, Nathan knew, the British Empire was gone, fragmented, and with it the Royal Navy had gone also. Some of it still served on in the Canadian and Indian and Australian navies and there was a tiny fragment in Great Britain, little more than a reminder of a name that had once been the synonym for naval power.

Then the silence erupted in a demented howl. Low overhead, two Thai F-105s crashed through the oppressive quiet, streaking above the gunboats as they headed upriver. Nathan swung his binoculars onto them, they were loaded for bear, droptanks on the inner wing pylons, a six-pack of bombs on the centerline and four more on each outer wing pylon. Well, Nathan thought, it was back to 1959 with 1960 just a few days away.

Number One was watching the jets shrinking as they howled upriver. "How do they do it Sir? Twenty years ago, they were just another obscure little country nobody could quite find on a map. Now our air force pilots fly F-84s if they are lucky or F-72s if they are not. While they fly those."

"Money Number One, back when The Triple Alliance was being formed, the Thais signed trade deals with everybody. Good honest deals, ones that profited everybody. Only those deals put them in the center of everything financial. Then, there were a flood of businesses, banks, trading companies, all leaving Hong Kong before the Japanese could take over. They all went to Bangkok. You have a bank account Number One?"

"Of course Sir. Bank of Gujarat."

"Which is 30 percent owned by the Thai Farmer's Bank. So when you pay your bank charges every month, a third of them go to Thailand. The problem is, Number One, that we and the Australians are thinking about now and the next five years. We have to, we've got problems that have to be solved if we're going to be around beyond five years. They're thinking about the next decade and the next century. Oh, they've got the short-term problems too but they're able to look at those in the long-term context. Thank God they're on our side."

The silence returned, and with it the illusion of a world that had gone forever. It even seemed that the hot, heavy silence had hushed the explosion because, for a brief second, the sight of the tall column of water alongside *Dragonfly* seemed to be without noise. Then, of course, the sound of the explosion rolled across the river. *Dragonfly* was already far down by the bows, rolling over and going fast. As she went down, Captain Nathan heard another rolling explosion but this scene was worse. The LST had been loaded with gasoline and the explosion had set the cargo on fire. The ship was sinking in the center of a pool of blazing gasoline and the screams of her crew defeated even the heavy humid air.

Then Nathan saw the cause, a horned black sphere bobbing in the water, heading towards *Cicala*. There was no point in trying to turn, the gunboat couldn't make it and, anyway, the effort would create suction that would draw the floating mine in. He couldn't tear his eyes off the approaching object until one of the Australian troops on board acted. Sergeant Shane dropped flat on the deck, racked the bolt on his Lee-Enfield and fired a shot. The mine exploded, still well over fifty yards away. Shane held his rifle over his head. "Rule .303! Let's see the Teas do that with their Crapnikovs!"

"Get a Bren Gun team onto the bows. Pick those damned mines off. Tell the other LSTs to do the same.

There was a ragged staccato of shots and three more explosions. Then silence. The last of the floating mines had gone. After a few minutes, the convoy started to move forward again, now with the riflemen and Bren gunners in the bows scanning for the mines. They'd only been moving for a few minutes when another shattering explosion tore the silence of the river apart. Only this one was different, the previous two mine explosions had been columns of water beside the victim, this time the LST was surrounded by the blast, then a tall jet of water smashed through her bottom and broke her apart. She sank instantly.

"Sir, why are those logs moving towards the explosion?"

"Oh God, crocs. Riflemen, pick those logs off, they're crocs going after the survivors." There was a blast of rifle fire and a deeper thud as one of *Cicala's* two pounder's opened fire. It was the right weapon for a job its designers had never considered, the crocodile exploded in a spray of blood. The gunner switched fire to another "log" near to the swimmers around the sinking LST and was rewarded with another eruption and spray.

"Number One, get us over to that LST now and pick those men up."

Captain Nathan felt *Cicala* thumping forward. He wanted to shake, the LST had hit a bottom mine, probably a pressure mine, and another one could finish *Cicala* before they even knew it was there. The sensible thing was to stay clear, but just a couple of weeks earlier Jim Ladone in *Hood* had faced down the two largest battleships in the world because he had a convoy to protect. He'd set the bar high and Nathan wasn't about to let him down by taking the easy way out.

Like *Hood, Cicala* got away with it. The survivors were picked up, even some of the terribly burned crew from the first LST to be hit and some Dragonflies. Then, the convoy started backing up, returning to Mandalay. Floating mines, they could deal with but they stood no chance against pressure mines. Until they were cleared, the Nanyin River was closed to shipping. Looking at the wounded on the deck aft, Nathan was reminded of the last verse of Kipling's poem, the one few people repeated

"On the road to Mandalay, where the old Flotilla lay,
With our sick beneath the awnings when we went to Mandalay!"

Twinnge, On The Mandalay - Myitkyina Road, Burma

"Mud, mud, glorious mud.
Nothing quite like it for cooling the blood!"

His little daughter loved the Happy Hippopotamus song. He could sing it for hours and she would listen, her eyes entranced. But, she was in Australia and he was here in Burma. Wallowing in mud. And, the Hippos were wrong, mud wasn't glorious, it was horrible. A thick orange-red gloop that got everywhere and choked everything up. It got into suspensions and drive trains and exhaust systems. The American six-by-sixes were handling it without too much trouble but there weren't enough of them. Most of the truck transport was old British equipment and it lacked the all-wheel drive and powerful engines of the American trucks. All too often, the older trucks were getting stuck and the six-by-sixes would have to turn back and tow them out. Some stretches were so bad that the only way the older trucks could get through at all was with the help of a tow from the sixes.

It was the trucks themselves that were doing it. They were combining with the rain to churn the road surface into this thick, horrible mud. The first convoys had got up to Myitkyina without too many problems but each one that followed was having a harder time. Each truck convoy made the roads worse, each day that passed the rains got heavier. The Australian troops had thought the Monsoon had started but they'd been wrong. There had been a Tea unit in Rangoon, a Long Range Recon Patrol or Lurp, the Teas had called it, and they and the Australian unit had had a friendly exchange of prejudices. One that had taken up 150 yards of the High Street and wrecked three bars.

Afterwards the units had become firm friends and the Teas had told the Australians what the real Monsoon was like and when it would come. In about ten days time they'd said, two days ago. They spoken of rain so heavy that nobody could see more than a few feet, of torrents of water that appeared from nowhere and swept away anything in their path. And they'd spoken of the dreaded cloudbursts that would drop inches of rain in a few minutes and anybody caught in the open would drown while standing on their feet.

They'd given a lot of other advice as well, which could all be summarized as "in the Monsoon - don't" . Yet, it was obvious that they loved the monsoon as well as feared it because it was the rains that made their crops grow and brought richness to their farmland. Only, the Australians didn't love the rains they were seeing and now they feared the monsoon. Nobody had told them that the dirt roads turned into mud wallows before the monsoon started. Behind them, far behind them, engineers were black-topping the road, turning it into an all-weather highway but that wouldn't help the trucks now. Captain Golconda knew his truck column was way behind schedule and saw no way of making the time up.

Then, a miracle. A stretch of the road ahead had been smoothed out. It was still muddy, but it wasn't churned up. Some engineers had improved it a bit, probably put stone gravel down to stabilize the soil. Perhaps they could make up some time after all. One of the lead six-by-sixes stopped at the edge of the improved section, dropped the Bedford it was towing, and set off down the road. It had made about a hundred feet when there was an explosion that wrapped it in flame and smoke. As the dust cleared, the six-by-six was on its side and burning, wrecked beyond hope of redemption. Anti-tank mine, Golconda thought, he should have known.

"Down, everybody down! Ambush!"

He didn't know it was, but better safe than sorry and, anyway, the doubt only lasted for a second or two. There was a staccato crackle of rifle fire, the rapid, light snap of the Chipanese Arisaka assault rifles and the slower, painfully slower, thuds of the Australian's Lee-Enfields. The Brens cut in as well, they evened things up. Nobody argued when the Bren was described as the best light machine gun in the world. The firefight was desultory, as if the Chipanese guerrillas weren't really trying too hard, just going through the motions. In fact, the Australian troops seemed to be gaining the upper hand if anything. Then there was a new sound, explosions. Golconda recognized them, the Chipanese 50 millimeter mortar. That was the reason, the Chipanese were just keeping the trucks held on the road so the mortars could get at them. He ducked into his Dingo scout car and got on the radio.

"This is Digger 17, we've been ambushed, trapped on the road near Twinnge. Enemy forces infantry with some light mortars. We need support."

"Digger 17, this is Ayala-One. We have your position and are three minutes out. We are F-105s with Mark 82s and 20 mike-mike. Tell your boys to keep their mouths open, this is going to be noisy." Golconda grinned, like all Tea pilots, this one had trained in America and the English had a Texan twang to it.

He saw the jets coming in, their silver skins gleaming in the sunlight, highlighted against the dark black clouds to the North. They were diving down towards them and closing fast. Golconda had heard that the F-105 was the fastest aircraft low down ever built, faster even than the Yank's much-vaunted B-58s. These ones certainly came in fast but he guessed the Tea pilot had been pulling his leg about noise, as the jets streaked overhead, they were silent. Then, he realized it hadn't been a joke, there was an ear-splitting boom and a mind-cracking scream.

In the little Dingo, glass instrument covers cracked and Golconda felt his ears burst inwards. The noise was so intense that he didn't even hear the bombs go off. Only when he looked up and saw the hill overlooking the road covered in smoke did he realize that it had been a bomb-run. Already, the jets were coming back and Golconda heard another strange sound, a vicious rattling rasp. Another area of hill vanished in a rolling sea of small explosions.

"Digger 17, this is Ayala One, that's it for us, we were running river cover for a convoy and are short of gas. Ayala three and four are on their way in to cover you. Good luck diggers."

"Thank you Ayala One. The beers are on us when we get a chance."

It was as Golconda had feared. The Chipanese had concentrated their fire on the precious six-by-sixes and destroyed at least half of them. He sighed, it didn't matter anyway. The infantry would have to go ahead now, probing for mines with bayonets. That slowed the convoy speed to less than walking pace anyway.

Four hours later he realized the loss of the six-by-sixes was even less important than he'd thought. The bridge over the Irawaddy was a smoldering mass of burned timber and blown stone abutments. If they'd had the wonderful Russian bridging gear they'd seen on television, they could be across in an hour or less. But they didn't and couldn't. They had old-fashioned Bailey Bridges and the nearest unit was twelve or fourteen convoys back. The only thing he could do was stay where he was until help came. The Road To Myitkyina was closed until further notice.

Myitkyina Airfield, Burma

Four aircraft on the ground at once, that was probably a record for this airfield. Major Ranjit thought. He doubted it would stand long though. The message in his pocket was grim. The convoy coming up the river had run into minefields and lost heavily. They were stopped until divers could get the navigation way cleared of bottom mines. The road situation was even worse. Convoys up and down the road had been ambushed and what had been a supply line was now a series of small besieged outposts defending themselves from the guerrillas, not moving. That meant Myitkyina was going to have to rely on an airbridge for supply. So, four would be a small number of aircraft to have on the field at once.

That meant they'd have to brush up on their aircraft handling practices. One of the Australian C-119s was taxiing out onto the runway, ready to take off. As he watched, it powered up its engines and took off, receding into the south while the other C-119 took its place. Beside it, two Indian C-47s were also unloading. The big cargo doors on the C-119 made it a much more practical cargo hauler than the elderly Dak. It would be unloaded before the C-47s. Then Major Ranjit frowned, what was that......

"INBOUND!"

The artillery fire exploded all over the parking area, an almost perfect time-on target salvo. The C-119 took at least three direct hits and vanished in a ball of flame. Fragments lashed one of the C-47s, the salvo had been a little short to get all the aircraft first time but it had still been a damned fine piece of gunnery. The shells were coming in fast now, the enemy gunners obviously pouring fire as quickly as they could serve their pieces. Ranjit looked in awe at the shell bursts, they were 150s, no doubt about it. This wasn't just light mortars and jungle guns. Myitkyina base was facing real heavy artillery.

One of the two C-47s was running up its engines, even as Ranjit watched, it turned onto the taxiway and accelerated towards the runway. The other one was already burning, the gunners must have corrected their aim for the follow-up shots. The escaping C-47 was moving fast, far too fast for the taxiway but it didn't matter. It turned onto the runway and started to make its take-off run. Shell-bursts were all around it, level with the wings and tail, correct for deflection but not range, others were correct for range but not deflection. The C-47 was running down the runway, tail up, shell bursts all around it.

It was a deadly horse race, the aircraft leading the shell explosions by a few yards, looking for all the world like the favorite leading the pack into the final straight. Ranjit caught his breath, one shell explosion was in front of the C-47, the enemy gunner must have tried to lead the aircraft, no mean feat with a 150. He'd almost made it but the transport was already lifting off, through the smoke of the explosion, turning and pulling up its undercarriage.

Ranjit saw it was clear of the artillery, the pilot climbing to gain height and firewalling the engines to get speed. Even as he watched, tracers erupted from the hillside and coned in on the C-47. One engine trailed black, then the whole left side erupted into flame. It struggled for a few more second then flipped on its back and spun in. A cloud of oily black smoke marked its grave.

Ignoring the artillery fire pounding the runway and parking area, Major Ranjit came to attention and saluted. After that take-off run, the crew had deserved to make it. Even as he did so, the artillery fire slackened and stopped. The gunners had made their point. The Siege of Myitkyina had started.

Mawchi Village, Thai-Burmese Border

"The old man came up to the border post pushing a wheelbarrow full of straw. He was obviously too poor to be worth shaking down for a bribe and they guessed he must also be a little simple-minded for everybody knew it was impossible to make a living selling straw. So they waved him through. Every day, he did the same and soon the guards noticed he was getting a little more prosperous each week. Then it dawned on them, he was smuggling. So they started searching him, but found nothing. They searched the straw in his wheelbarrow and found nothing. They took the wheelbarrow apart and found nothing. Every day they searched more and more thoroughly, they inspected the straw to see if it had been soaked in anything but no. They searched him, they searched his clothes but still they found nothing. And every trip, the old man got richer and richer."

Phong Nguyen stopped. The silence hung for a moment then one of his audience couldn't resist feeding him the line. "So what was the old man smuggling?"

"Wheelbarrows." Phong Nguyen replied innocently. The village men howled with laughter, slapping the ground with their hands. One filled Phong Nguyen's beer mug and clapped him on the back. They knew him as "Khun Chom, a teak dealer from Chiang Rai touring with his wife Noi to find fine timber".

To them he was an honest merchant who paid fair prices and did so in gold, not worthless paper. What is more, when he arrived, he always brought the villagers a small present to mark his gratitude for their hospitality and, much more importantly always came with new jokes and saucy stories from the outside world. Phong glanced over to where his wife, Lin, was sitting with the village women. She was retelling the stories from the latest episodes of "Path of Virtue". Phong had taught her carefully, stay away from politics, stay away from anything controversial. Talk about inconsequential things and listen, listen, listen.

"Oh No" the gasp came from several of the women. Phong and the men rolled their eyes. Phong knew this was the bit where the evil Japanese businessman had poisoned the wife's wedding meal and she had eaten it. After a dramatic pause, she would carry on eating as if nothing was wrong and the evil businessman would give himself away by his reaction. Then, it would transpire the old lady who lived in the next apartment to the bride had seen him hanging around her room and called for help from her son who was an Army officer. He'd come to investigate and saved the day. He'd found the poisoned food and thrown it away, then tasted the replacement meal for the bride himself to make sure it was safe. Then his men placed the villain under arrest and dragged him away to face justice. End of story until the next visit.

"Khun Chom, does everybody in Chiang Rai have television?" It was the Headman asking.

"No, Honored Sir only a few. But it is the custom that those who have sets invite all their neighbors in to watch the programs. That has a great advantage." Phong leaned forward confidentially. "For one hour every night the women watch their dramas and we can drink beer undisturbed." His audience laughed again. That was an arrangement they could approve of. "But we watch the news together of course. So much is happening in the world."

The headman looked solemn. "Here too. Did you hear of the great battle on the border?" Phong shook his head. "It was at the village of Ban Rom Phuoc. The Shan soldiers tried to take some village women but the villagers would not let them and drove them out."

Phong sat back and listened to the Headman tell the story of how a vast Shan force had attacked the village, wave after wave of the enemy had charged the wire fence surrounding the huts but every charge was forced back by the brave villagers. Even the village spirits had joined in the battle, throwing balls of magic light into the sky, exposing the enemy to the defenders. When the ammunition started to run short, the village children ran through the hail of fire to bring fresh magazines to the villagers on the defense lines.

He heard how the great hero Phong Nguyen had stood on top of a pile of dead enemy soldiers and shouted defiant insults at the enemy as he hosed them down with his AK-47 rifle and when two cowardly enemies tried to shoot the great hero in the back, his wife Lin had protected her husband by killing them with her carving knife.

The battle had gone on for three days and three nights the headman said and when the enemy finally retreated, they left so many dead on the field that a man could walk five times around the village without stepping on the ground or on the same enemy body twice. But the villagers had defended their homes so successfully and so bravely that people came from all over the world to honor them. Why one man had even come all the way from Australia, a place far over the mountains, to give them his own water buffalo, so respectful was he of their brave fight.

Interesting thought Phong. *They're* proud of that firefight and they call the Shan States Army "the enemy". More importantly, he had the opening he needed to ask the one question that this whole visit was intended to allow.

"Do you see much of the Shan States Army these days?" he asked. "Do they have good teak to sell?"

The headman shook his head. "They only sell what they take from others. But they are gone now. They all left for the west."

Next day, Phong and Lin Nguyen were back in Ban Rom Phuoc. Lin confirmed the women had said the same things to her. The Shan States Army units had pulled out of the area and headed west. One of the soldiers had boasted to the village women that there was a big battle going on up there, that troops from far away were surrounded at a place called Myitkyina and that every soldier the Shan States Army had was concentrating to overrun them. That was the information the people in Bangkok had asked them to get and the message would be going down max priority. It was also the last time he and Lin would be going over the border. She was expecting her first baby now, and it was time for her to take it easy.

Phong stretched out happily. A fine wife, a baby on the way and a comfortable home in a prosperous village full of good friends who were armed with automatic weapons. What more could a man possibly want?

Main Runway, U-Thapao Airfield, Thailand

"*Marisol* awaiting take-off clearance. Tower be advised our tires will blow if we stay too long here."

"Understood, *Marisol* we are just awaiting foreign object clearance report on the runway. Wait one, thank you. *Marisol* runway is clear. For your information obstruction was a baby elephant. He's been returned to his momma who was last seen whaling on him with her trunk. You are clear to go."

Major Mike Kozlowski eased *Marisol* forward. Then, he spooled the engines up to maximum power, and cut in the afterburners on all four engines. Slowly *Marisol* picked up speed and started accelerating down the runway. Her normal take-off run was 8,000 feet before the aircraft started to rotate but the heat here extended that. It didn't matter though, the runway here was a stunning 36,000 feet long and wide enough for all four B-58s to take off side-by-side.

Nobody had been able to explain why this huge airfield had been built out here. Rumor had it that the field had been designed by engineers who had specified the dimensions in feet and the Thai engineering company had read them as being in meters. Whatever the reason, the SAC crews appreciated it and were getting into bad habits. Barely a quarter of the way down the massive runway, *Marisol's* nose began to lift. Then she climbed, up and away from the concrete, already going over 200 miles per hour at lift-off and gathering speed every second.

Mission profile was to climb to 62,000 feet and head for Myitkyina in Northern Burma. The Australians had bitten off more than they could chew up there and a detached brigade was surrounded by a large and still-growing enemy force. The weather had closed down on them and, just to make life truly difficult, it turned out the maps of the area were inaccurate. Before the weather stopped them altogether, the Thais had lost two F-105s flying close support for the besieged garrison. Not from anti-aircraft fire but from flying into cloud-covered mountains that weren't where they were supposed to be. So this mission was to get the information for accurate charts of the area.

Marisol and *Tiger Lily*, the two RB-58C-30s in the formation were cover for the mission. They were fully loaded, two Sparrow IIs on the forward shoulder pylons, two conventional anti-radar missiles on the aft ones. Their belly pods contained eight nuclear-tipped GAR-9s and the usual four Sidewinders. As always, SAC policy was that its bombers flew where they wanted, when they wanted and they were armed to enforce that policy. If they didn't fly over somebody's territory, that was a courtesy from SAC, not a requirement of the airspace owner.

The other two aircraft were different. For this mission, the two dash-twenties, *Sweet Caroline* and *Coral Queen*, were designated ERB-58Cs for this mission and carried a new pod, fitted with a system called Monticello. As far as Kozlowski could put together it was some sort of sideways looking radar that produced a picture-like map of the ground, even through the black clouds of the monsoon. It was combined with a battery of cameras and a very precise emitter location system that could track radio messages as well as radar emissions.

What made the whole system work was something very special. Right in the center of the pod was a shoe-box sized unit that held an array of metal donuts. Depending on whether the individual donuts were charged or uncharged, that shoebox could remember a "word" of no less that 4,096 "letters". Of course, there were only two letters 1 and 0. The scientists had explained it to Kozlowski but it was all over his head. Something about digital information. He'd written it off as magic and left it there.

"Remember the briefing guys. This is for real. If there is an attempt to illuminate any of the aircraft we take out the radar. We don't use the nukes unless we have an air-to-air threat that Sparrows and Winders can't handle. We've got two ARMS and the two recon birds have four each - but they haven't anything else. So its down to us. But keep in mind, this isn't Red Sun. This is NOT simulated. If we screw up, we go down. So lets try and avoid that. *Marisol*, there is a very good chance you will lose your virginity on this one."

"Promises, promises." The sultry hispanic-accented voice came over the intercom. "Speaking of promises, did you remember to thank your girls for me?"

Kozlowski, Korrina and Dravar had all acquired Thai girlfriends during their stay at U-Thapao and, on one date, they'd told their girls that their aircraft talked to them. They'd been surprised to see the girls took that for granted; one of the women had explained that everything, plants, trees, hills, lakes, bits of machinery, had a spirit that lived in it. Some spirits were lazy and barely awake, others took a keen interest in what was going on around them. Some spirits were friendly and helpful, others malicious and spiteful. But humans who were friendly to the spirits could win over even the most malicious while those who were hostile could alienate even the most friendly.

Marisol's crew looked sharply at each other on hearing that. One of the B-60 crews had spent all their time cursing their aircraft and damning her by comparison with the B-52. Now, their aircraft was known as a jinx ship. She kept developing faults and system failures and her crew kept having minor injuries. One had gashed his hand open on a screw head that was left standing proud, another had broken his foot when the trolly jammed in the long tunnel through the bomb-bay. Anyway, next date, the girls had brought Buddhist rosaries for *Marisol* and explained that hanging these in the cockpits would please her and bring good luck. It had been a job finding a place to put them in the cramped crew stations, but they'd managed. They'd told *Marisol* about the gifts and she'd been delighted.

It used to take the old B-36s more than two hours to climb to their cruise altitude of 45,000 feet plus. It took the B-58s barely ten minutes to reach 62,000 and that wasn't pushing the aircraft hard. They had plenty of time to get up to the safety of high altitude before they crossed the border into Burma. In fact, there wasn't even much danger then, there was no anti-aircraft fire of note until they got to the Parrot's Beak, an area near Namkhan where Chipan jutted into Burma.

The Chipanese had fighters based at Tengchan in the heart of the Parrot's Beak and at least some surface-to-air missiles along the border. In theory, the missiles were a threat to the B-58s, in reality it would take incredible luck for the Chipanese to score a hit. Their missiles were similar to the US Ajax, suspiciously similar some said, but Ajax had failed against the B-58s despite being used by the best crews NORAD could find.

They punched clear of the monsoon clouds at 35,000 feet and were in bright sunshine from that point onwards. That meant, of course, that they couldn't see the ground under the dense black cloud cover but that was no problem. They had their inertial navigation systems running and were also being tracked by ground stations that would report any deviations from course. By the time they lost ground station cover, the inertial system would have been checked out thoroughly and they'd rely on it from there. In addition, they had their navigation radar and that gave them a crude picture of the ground underneath the clouds. That gave another check on the running accuracy of the INS system. One of the underlying purposes of this mission was to determine just how accurate the inertial navigation equipment really was, a lot of things depended on that.

By the time the aircraft crossed the Burmese border, they were spread out in a long line. This was another lesson from Red Sun, air-to-air nuclear weapons made old ideas about formations and formation-keeping obsolete. Grouping aircraft now just increased casualties from single shots. The present generation of bombers would be the last ones where formation flying would even be considered; when the B-70 entered service, it would fly to its targets alone. In some ways, the RB-58 wasn't just a strategic penetrator, opening the way for other aircraft, it was the prototype of a whole new concept of bomber.

However, this time there was another reason for the spread out formation. The two aircraft with Monticello pods were on the outside of the formation, where their scans overlapped, special equipment could turn their radar imagery into a three-dimensional picture of the ground. They'd do their run over the target, then come back on an exact reciprocal. The result would be a large box of countryside imaged in three dimensions, allowing accurate maps to be made. For most of Northern Burma, this would be the first time the area had been accurately mapped.

They were heading on 350 degrees now, waiting for the big search radar at Tengchan to be detected. They'd be using it as a navigation aid as they flew north and would keep its signal at constant strength. That would swing them in a wide arc south and west of the Parrot's Beak before they headed North to Myitkyina. As they approached the spur of Chinese territory, Korrina picked up airborne radar transmissions as well as the expected search radar.

Two, no four, fighters. The Kawasaki heavy fighter American intelligence had named "Brandi". Delta wings, two jet engines with a rocket booster mounted between them. The Chipanese Army Air Force had gone heavily for jet/rocket hybrid fighters in recent years. On its jets, the Brandi was no threat to the RB-58s, but as long as its rocket fuel lasted it could get up high enough to intercept them. Armament was four 30 millimeter cannon and four heat-seeking missiles, reputed to be very similar to the GAR-8 Sidewinders. Like their anti-aircraft missiles, the similarity was suspicious. Perhaps it was time for another inquiry into the leakage of American military secrets to Japan, like the Atom Bomb Secret hearings a few years ago. Senator Macarthy had died of cirrhosis of the liver a few months back so he wasn't around to head this one but there would be somebody else.

The four Brandis were keeping their distance, paralleling the B-58 formation but about 20,000 feet below them. They were still in the tight formation the USAF had used until Red Sun had shown them the dangers of keeping aircraft close together. Korrina had a GAR-9 locked on them just in case but it wouldn't be necessary, he could sense it.

As *Marisol* and her sisters swung clear of the Parrot's Beak, the four Chipanese fighters broke away and returned home. There was less than a 100 miles to go to Myitkyina. Apart from the Chipanese radars in the Parrot's Beak, there was no hostile activity. Monticello required very specific speed and altitude settings to give the most accurate results and it was up to *Marisol* and *Tiger Lily* to make sure *Sweet Caroline* and *Coral Queen* could do their work undisturbed. But, as the two Monticello aircraft started their flight runs, hostile radars flicked into action. Obviously cued by the Chipanese radar over the border

"Mike, we're getting two Fire Can gun control radars. Probably controlling twin 37s but its possible there's bigger stuff down there."

"Take one out Eddie." The air in Marisol was tense now. Korrina made his final adjustments, locked one of the two ASM-10s on then stroked the fire button. After all the simulated shots, it was shocking to see the smoke trail streaking out in front of them. The ASM-10s had been tuned to the Fire Can frequency before take-off and the attack profile pre-selected. The missiles angled up and climbed to over 80,000 feet before rolling over and diving on the radar set underneath. The radar was blind in the arc directly over the set and the crew never saw the missile coming. In a powered dive, the anti-radar missile streaked into the clouds underneath. A few second later, the target radar blinked out.

"Radar transmission ceased at predicted time of impact *Marisol*. There are radio transmissions all over down there. You got it."

"Thanks *Sweet Caroline. Marisol*, you aren't a virgin anymore."

The familiar voice came over the intercom system, now throaty and lazily accented. "Well boys, was it as good for you as it was for me?"

Hill Kumon 541, West of Myitkyina, Burma.

The radar on top of Hill 541 controlled six twin 37 millimeter cannon on the eastern slope of the hill. The guns overlooked Myitkyina airfield and had already accounted for three transport aircraft. The radar wasn't working now though, the duty set was a little further to the north on Kumon 525. Lieutenant Wu Si Bo was looking at its position when there was a streak of light from the black monsoon clouds overhead, followed by a shattering explosion. The radar had gone, blasted into a blackened ruins. Behind the Lieutenant, the gun and radar crews were muttering anxiously.

"You see that sir, the stories are true." For weeks now, stories had been circulating about their radar fire control sets. Nobody knew where they had come from, they were all of "my cousin's friend's sister's boyfriend" type. But the stories all agreed on one thing. If one operated a radar set in a thunderstorm, the antenna attracted lightning and the explosion destroyed the set. And its crew. It was time to do something about morale, the situation could not be allowed to continue.

"Men, the stories you have heard are absolute nonsense. Of course our antenna does not attract lightning." Lieutenant Wu Si Bo hooked his foot around a power supply cable and yanked it firmly out of its socket. "And even if those stories were true, it wouldn't matter, Our radar isn't working."

Viceregal Palace, New Delhi, India

There was something about India that drew its visitors in, that got a hold on their hearts despite all the obvious problems, difficulties and discomforts of a country that was hot and swarming with people many of whom lived barely at the edge of subsistence. A grandeur, a vision of what this country had once been and could become again. A richness of spirit that offset the physical poverty that was everywhere. General Dedmon looked out of the windows of his limousine at the crowds of people that thronged the street and marveled that so many could live in such a small area. Whole families lived on the street, handing their rights to sleep on a specific stretch of sidewalk down through the generations.

The limousine was met by two attendants, tall Sikhs in white uniforms. There was a great debate over who made the better soldiers, the big Sikhs with their beards and turbans or the small wiry Ghurkas. One thing professionals agreed on, it was a bad day when one had to tangle with either. One of the Sikhs held the door of the car open while General Dedmon climbed out. On the steps above the car, Sir Martyn and Lady Sharpe had come out to meet him.

"Welcome, General. May I introduce my wife, Rebecca. Rebecca, this is our friend from America, General Bob Dedmon."

"I'm delighted to meet you Lady Sharpe. I've been looking forward to this evening ever since Sir Martyn made the invitation. Its not often that an American gets to be a guest in a real honest-to-God Royal Palace"

Sir Martyn laughed warmly while mentally complimenting himself. For rabid republicans, the Americans were suckers for anything that had a Royal connection. "Come on in, General. I'll show you around although, to be honest, this place hasn't been a Royal Palace for over a century. We've plenty of time. Dinner will be served at 20:30. I hope you like Anglo-Indian food?"

"Anglo-Indian Sir Martyn?"

"Anglo-Indian started as a mixture of English and Indian food, originally an attempt to make English traditional dishes with the ingredients that were available in local Indian markets. As the confidence of the Indian cooks grew, they started to experiment with the recipes, adding here, subtracting there, changing a little this, a little that.

"Soon, they had developed an entirely different style of food, neither English nor Indian but something unique to itself. A meal that could be eaten by Englishmen and Indian alike, both feeling that they were at home, with meals that were comfortable and familiar.

"In many ways, it is a microcosm of what we are trying to do here in India today. To take the best that both India and England have to offer and use them to create something new and unique that we can all share and that will benefit everybody."

Sir Martyn turned out to be an excellent tour guide, able to describe the history of the building and the artwork it contained. In fact, he seemed to know an amusing anecdote about events that had taken place in every room. Dedmon was stunned by the residence. He'd heard about the opulence of the Indian princes and the almost unimaginable luxury in which they lived but this was beyond anything he dreamed.

It made a stark contrast with the poverty and squalor he'd seen in the streets outside. It was a contrast he found hard to accept as being part of the middle of the 20th century. How did anybody manage to live surrounded by either extreme?

"Lady Sharpe, I must confess, if I lived here I would be too terrified to move in case I broke something priceless."

"Call me Becky, please. All my friends do. Martyn and I do not live in this part of the Residence, we have apartments on the top floor with our own furniture from England." She seemed sad for a second, probably remembering a way of life that had gone forever. It must have been hard for her to leave behind everything she knew and loved for a strange country. And then to be trapped there when her whole world fell apart in 1940. Dedmon wondered whether Sir Martyn had ever really understood the sacrifices his wife had made. "But, General..."

"Bob, Becky."

"Why thank you Bob, you have something equally precious to care for. Did you bring *Texan Lady* over with you?"

"No Ma'am, she's in our Air Force museum now. I go and see her regularly though." A gong rang, summoning the party to dinner.

Dedmon didn't know what impressed him the most, the dining room or the food. The dining room was exquisite, the table richly polished teak, decorated with superb silver ornaments and laid with starched white linens. They'd been joined by Sir Eric and Lady Haohoa. Sir Eric was the Indian Cabinet Secretary and the couple were long-time friends of Sir Martyn. Dedmon sternly reminded himself that being the Cabinet Secretary also made Sir Eric the head of the Indian intelligence services. He gave the impression of a traditional, self-effacing British civil servant yet all the reports made it clear he was very far from being that. He was a man it was very foolish to underestimate.

The food was as Sir Martyn had promised, a magnificent blend of English and Indian styles that contrived to be both yet neither. What appeared to be a familiar English dish would have nuances of seasoning and cooking that turned it into something exotic yet there would also be something strangely familiar and reassuring about even the most mysterious. About half way through the meal, a servant came in with an urgent message. Sir Martyn read it and his eyes widened.

"Bob, I must ask your apologies but we need to turn our television on. There is news that we both need to see." The set was wheeled out of its cupboard and turned on. It took a couple of minutes to warm up, then a newsreader, a woman in an elegant evening sari took the screen.

"And now we must repeat the main item of news tonight. The American presidential election has been thrown into turmoil following the tragic death of Democrat Candidate John F Kennedy. News reports from Boston say that the Presidential Candidate had been badly delayed at a series of electioneering engagements and was late for a Democrat Party strategy party meeting near the family home in Massachusetts. In order to save time, John F Kennedy accepted an offer from his brother Edward to drive him in a family car to the meeting.

"At a place called Chappaquiddick Island, near Martha's Vineyard, their car apparently spun off the road into the water. Presidential Candidate Kennedy was trapped in the wreckage, apparently due to the effects of an old back injury suffered while commanding a river gunboat in 1943. His brother Edward made a valiant effort to get help for the trapped victim but, by the time he got back, John F Kennedy had drowned. Police are investigating the incident and have not stated whether any charges will be made."

The broadcast was mostly library footage of JFKs life and his campaign against President LeMay. Sir Martyn spoke to a servant who left the room and returned with the week's issue of the Washington Diplomatic list. Sir Martyn turned to a page, raised an eyebrow and showed the page to Sir Eric. Both men were trying hard not to smile out of courtesy to their American guest. "Not a Japanese chauffeur this time." Sir Eric said in a slightly strangled voice. Then the elegant newsreader cut in again.

"In a late development from Washington, the Vice Presidential candidate, Lyndon Baines Johnson, has resigned from the candidacy, quoting his shock and distress at the sudden death of his old friend John F Kennedy. In an emergency meeting, the Democrat National Committee has elected an almost unknown automobile company executive, Robert Strange McNamara, as their new candidate."

"Bob, can you give us an insight as to what is going on here? Why did Johnson stand down? I'd have thought he would have stood a very good chance of being elected. And who is this McNamara person?"

Dedmon shook his head, his mind still absorbing the news. "LBJ is probably the wiliest politician in Washington. He knows very well that the Democrats changing candidates this late into the campaign makes his chance of being elected slender. It's not as if the Democrats were doing well, they were level-pegging the Republicans in the early stages of the campaign but that didn't last. It didn't help them that LeMay is the 'man who brought our boys home' and that Kennedy was a comparative nonentity.

"Kennedy had a lot of charisma and did well in the conventions and on whistle-stop tours but the radio debates with President LeMay went very badly for him. One thing the President has always been good at is making sure his staff work is up to scratch. I'd guess he had his aides burning the midnight oil for weeks thinking of every possible question that could be thrown at him, and he had all the answers waiting. Kennedy kept getting caught out by details and came off sounding like a lightweight. His poll figures never recovered.

"So, combining the change in candidates and the poor starting position, LBJ has worked out that he doesn't stand much of a chance. The Democrats will be down to depending on a sympathy vote and that's no way to win an election. He's betting that if he runs and looses, he'll be damaged goods for the 1964 election and somebody else would get the nod for that. So he bows out now, and sets up that fool McNamara get hammered this time around. This way, he's set to scoop the pool in '64.

"McNamara did the one unforgivable thing somebody can do in America. He designed a dreadful automobile. That'll be thrown at him over and over again. 'How can we trust the man who came up with the Edsel?'

"It is a hard thing to say about a man's death, but JFK served his country better by dying now than he could have done as President; his advisors had some pretty foolish and damaging ideas. Replacing bombers by missiles for example, and not maintaining the national air and missile defense system. Using the resources to rebuild the Army, another thing that will send him to the political graveyard. To American families, a large army means sending our boys back to the Russian Front. Ruthless as it may sound, God has looked after America here."

"I don't think God had much to do with it," said Sir Eric Haohoa levelly.

Chapter Twelve
Touchdown.

Supreme Command Headquarters Building, Ayuthia Road, Bangkok, Thailand

They'd flown over in General Dedmon's personal aircraft, the prototype XC-144 Superstream. A derivative of the B-58 with seats for six passengers, it was cramped and uncomfortable but its speed took hours off long-haul flights. Full production had been postponed while the Fort Worth production line turned out RB-58s and PB5Ys as fast as triple shifts could manage. The delay was being used to wring the design out as thoroughly as possible. The speed of the trip had allowed them to arrive the previous evening and sleep before the meeting scheduled for early this morning. It was early too, by Bangkok standards there was still a chill in the air.

"Sir Martyn, Sir Eric, General Dedmon, welcome back to Bangkok. It is so good to see you again."

The Ambassador had come out to meet their car. Sir Martyn noted she was wearing civilian clothes, not her military uniform. The bulge under her silk jacket indicated she was still carrying a handgun of formidable proportions.

"Madame Ambassador, it is indeed a great pleasure to have your company again. I trust your stay in Washington was productive?"

"Indeed so, Sir Eric. In fact you will be seeing one of our achievements a little later." Sir Eric gulped and had a quick mental picture of John F Kennedy's head mounted on the wall of her apartment. "It is essential that we find a quick and effective solution to this Myitkyina debacle. To that end we have hired some consultants who will provide us with their advice and opinions. Their first action was to evict us from our own conference room so we are as interested to hear what they have to say as anybody else. If you will come with me."

The Conference Room was guarded by soldiers, fully armed and alert. They opened the doors for the Ambassador and she lead her party in. The room was already filled with a mixture of military personnel and civilians. By some strange trick of the light, no matter where they stood, the civilians seemed to be in the shadows. The Ambassador looked around then went over to them. "Seer, I am very pleased you could make it over. Now perhaps I can repay some of your hospitality."

"Thank you Snake. I wouldn't have missed this one for anything. You were right though, the city has changed out of all recognition since I was last here. Is the Galaxy still open? If everybody is present I think we'd better get started."

The cover was pulled off the table that occupied most of the center of the room. When it was fully removed there was a collective gasp. The entire area was covered by a three-dimensional model of Myitkyina and the surrounding countryside. Even the coloring was correct, the artists had caught the languid menace of the jungle perfectly. The Triple Alliance positions were outlined in blue, those of the surrounding forces in red. The gasp was not of admiration though. Even in a roomful of people who were skilled map-readers, the model showed something that wasn't apparent from a two-dimensional map. The position of the besieged garrison was critical.

"When we start a consultancy contract like this, our first question is always the same yet our principals never have a well-thought answer. So we started this one the same way, with the same question. 'What is the objective of this operation?' As usual, we didn't get a straight answer. Or, more to the point, the answers that we did get were not consistent with the operational environment and the demands of counter-insurgency warfare. Nor, may I add, were they consistent with the forces committed to the operation.

"The objectives, we were advised, were to block Chipanese supply lines, to act as a base for offensive operations and to act as bait, drawing Chipanese forces into a kill zone where they could be destroyed. Unfortunately, the supply line question is irrelevant under the circumstances prevailing, the forces committed were not adequate to both defend the Myitkyina base and conduct offensive patrolling. Indeed, the forces committed to this operation are inadequate to defend the base area itself, let alone conduct any offensives.

"This is, I must regretfully report, a common factor throughout this entire operation. On a strategic, operational and tactical level, there has been an unfortunate compromise between the forces required to achieve a stated tactical aim and those that were available. As a result, the planner's grasp has fallen far short of their reach. If we look at the configuration of the Myitkyina base itself, we can see this very clearly. We have the central base area here, with the airfield and the town, surrounded by eight defensive positions. Anne-Marie, here in the north, then Beatrice, Claudine, Dominique, Eliane, Francoise, Gabrielle and Isabel."

"Seer, how did you get this map? These positions are classified?"

"We've been running radar reconnaissance missions over the area, Snake. There are no reliable maps of this area, a good enough reason why this operation should never have been launched. There are now. We'll give them to you. As for your dispositions? Don't kid yourself. They are common knowledge; why do you think we didn't ask for them? But the dire effects of compromise are clearly visible.

- --

"These defensive positions are too far out from the central area to be mutually supporting yet not far enough out to protect the central area from artillery bombardment. Note how they are all dominated by higher ground further out. Their garrisons are not large enough for each position to be self-sustaining yet are large enough to drain off so many troops that inadequate numbers are left to defend the central area. In short, anytime the enemy wish to, they can pick these outlying fortifications off and, once that's done, the central area will collapse. The only reason why they haven't done so already is that they're bleeding your air transport units dry keeping the place going."

General Moses couldn't restrain himself any longer "Why are we listening to a bunch of mercenaries?"

"We are not mercenaries General. We are a private company that has been hired jointly by the three governments of the Triple Alliance to provide an analysis of this situation and suggest solutions. We work for the United States government on the same basis, providing State Department and National Security Council services under contract."

The Ambassador's voice cut quietly across the room. "General Moses, if you have a life, return to it. If you do not I suggest you find one. Either way, *get the hell off my sub-continent.*"

General Moses face went deep red, his body shaking with rage. "Madam, if you were not a woman, I would strike you for that remark."

"General, I have never claimed immunity because of my sex and do not do so now."

He voice was a low hiss and suddenly Sir Martyn realized where her nickname came from. He also realized that General Moses was a split second from death. His had was over his baton and he was on the verge of grabbing it and lashing out. If he did, he would die before he'd moved more than a few inches. The Ambassador was staring at him with an expression of polite interest on her face, Sir Martyn saw the Seer's expression was that of quizzical amusement and he'd had stepped back out of the line of fire. He guessed he'd seen similar scenes before and asked himself just how far the relationship between these two went back. No matter, it was time to do something.

"General, the Indian Government endorses the opinion expressed by the Ambassador."

"As does the Australian Government. General Moses, your request for retirement will be approved."

Prime Minister Joe Frye hadn't said anything so far, but when he did speak the effects were immediate. General Moses stormed out of the room, trying to slam the heavy teak doors behind him. They were on shock absorbers so he didn't even get that right.

"Seer, our first priority must be to solve this mess."

"Not so Sir Martyn. This mess can be cleared up. Your first priority is to make sure it doesn't happen again. You need to establish a command structure, this whole Myitkyina business started because your alliance conducted military operations without clearly defined lines of command and authority. One of our recommendations is that you establish a permanent military command structure. We have some ideas on how you can best organize that. In the meantime, you need to appoint a new commander for this operation.

Sir Martyn looked at Prime Minister Frye who nodded at the Ambassador. "Madam, would you take command of this operation please?" She nodded and her eyes defocused. Sir Martyn knew she was lost now, in calculating forces, movements and distances. Suddenly, he felt sympathy for the Japanese forces she had defeated in the past.

"We can't do it, not by the book." She said after a few minutes. "We'll do it backwards. Break the siege from the inside first, then relieve the garrison from the outside. That means we have to get reinforcements in and that means we have to break the Chipanese forces surrounding the base. One thing works for us.

Our intelligence sources tell us that the Chipanese have concentrated nearly all the Shan States Army around Myitkyina. Also that the so-called SSA units are, in reality, Japanese Army. Please note that, Japanese, not Chipanese. Break them and we do grave damage to Chipan. Seer?"

"The enemy are in three main concentrations, north east, north west and south. Take them out and we take the artillery with them. General Dedmon, have we concluded satisfactory agreements on emergency basing rights in India and elsewhere in the Triple Alliance?" Sir Martyn took the bull by the horns and nodded. The agreement hadn't been signed but would be. Immediately.

"Then I think we can demonstrate to the Shan States Army that SAC's bombers can do more than just drop nuclear weapons. A whole world of hell more."

Cockpit RB-58C "Marisol", Main Runway, U-Thapao, Thailand

The four RB-58s were going first. Unlike the B-60s, they wouldn't be flying straight to their assigned targets, their flightpath was a series of loops that would cover the bombers against any attack. Their orders were quite simple "Defend the bombers against any threat using all necessary means." After the months of training and the reconnaissance milk-runs, the Hustlers would be doing what they had been built for. Flying into enemy defenses and destroying them. With a little luck, after today, *Marisol* would be a little less egotistical. She'd been unbearable for the last few days, flaunting the lightning flash painted under her cockpit that denoted a radar system destroyed. It was most unlikely that, after today, she'd be only one in the B-58 fleet to have a kill to her name.

"*Marisol, Tiger Lily, Sweet Caroline, Coral Queen.* You are clear for takeoff. Good luck ladies."

"OK boys and girl its party time."

"Andale, lets dance!"

Main Tower, U-Thapao, Thailand

The glass shook as the four RB-58s went off the runway on full afterburner. Behind them, the long line of B-60s were taxiing forward, the glare of the tropical sun reflected from their silver skins almost unbearable. Most of the American ground staff at U-Thapao were gray with exhaustion, eight more B-60s had arrived overnight along with a clutch of C-133 Cargomaster transports. Some of those had been carrying extra weapons and equipment, others were simply stopping to refuel before heading off to, somewhere?

The new arrivals had to be refueled and checked over prior to today's mission. The munitions crews had been working all night, stuffing 500 pound bombs into the bellies of the bombers. 176 per aircraft, all fitted with fuse-extenders so they would go off above the ground, not buried in it. Radar pictures taken by the RB-58s had been loaded into the bombing systems of the aircraft. There were three formations going out, six aircraft per formation. Two spares, just in case one of the scheduled aircraft didn't make it.

Cockpit, B-60E "Flying Fiasco" U-Thapao, Thailand

"Cleared for take-off, lets get this apology for an aircraft rolling." Throttles firewalled, the B-60 started its run down the huge runway. Ahead of them *Miss Tressmine* was already halfway down the runway, her nose lifting as she started rotation. *Flying Fiasco* followed her, picking up speed smoothly as the eight jets pushed her down the runway.

"Hey guys, look on the bright side. This one goes well and we could get hauled out of this rust-bucket and given a decent aircraft. Ohhh sheee-it."

Suddenly, *Flying Fiasco* was slowing, not picking up speed. Engineering station confirmed it "Loosing power on one, two five and seven sir. And hydraulics loosing power as well, I don't think we can get the gear up even if we rotate. We have to abort sir."

"Tower, This is *Flying Fiasco* power loss on four engines, hydraulic pressure going. We are aborting take-off."

"Understood *Flying Fiasco*. Keep going to the end of the runway and wait there."

Main Tower, U-Thapao, Thailand

"We have an abort General Dedmon. Captain Zipster's *Flying Fiasco*. Engine and hydraulic failures. *Lady Lace* is taking her place. Sir, Zipster's crew are swearing at their aircraft something terrible."

Dedmon shook his head. "I've had it with that bunch of whining losers. Colonel, find whatever the lowest rank in the US Armed Forces is, invent a lower one, and bust the whole load of them to it. Then kick them out of SAC and assign them to ground duty somewhere else in the Air Force. Preferably in Alaska. Its time we made an example of somebody. When the mission is launched, tow that bird in, get her thoroughly inspected and I'll put a new crew in her. We've got some good kids who'd welcome the challenge of getting Captain's bars by bringing a hard-luck bird around."

"Take offs are still on schedule sir. God knows why the Thai Air Force built this runway so big but its paying dividends now. The last two aircraft went either side of *Flying Fiasco*." Dedmon laughed, that was a new way of giving the finger to a thoroughly disliked crew.

Lek's Farm, Ban Mab Tapud, Thailand

Chong reached out and scratched the water buffalo's left ear with his toe. Obediently, Bok turned left, pulling the plow around and starting the next furrow. The Monsoon rains were ending and it was planting time. This year, it was good, the price for last year's harvest had been high, they'd been able to buy the seed for this year's crops without borrowing money. There had even been some left over. They'd made a generous offering to the Monks and Father had bought Mother cloth for a new dress. He'd also bought her a gold chain she could wear as a necklace. If times got hard, they'd have to sell that of course but not her new dress.

Father was walking behind Bok now, making sure the plow turned the wet soil over properly while the other children planted the rice. Soon, the field would be flooded and the rice crop would grow.

The new furrow was taking them towards the airfield at U-Thapao. Approaching them was an aircraft, one of the giants that came from America. It wasn't the first to pass this morning but the earliest had been the fast ones with triangular wings. Then, some of the giants had passed further inland but this one was going to pass directly overhead. The giants were behaving differently from usual, trailing clouds of black smoke from their engines. Even to the farmer and his family, it was obvious those engines were straining hard to lift whatever it was the giants carried. Sitting on Bok's neck, Chong reached up and waved to the giant. To his stupefied delight the giant rocked its wings in acknowledgment then swept overhead.

Chong jumped off Bok's neck, grabbed a small handful of rice seed and climbed the bank to the road. A few yards away was a simple shrine, one of tens of thousands that stood beside the roads all over Thailand. Chong made a deep wai in front of the cracked and peeling Bhudda statue then put the rice seed in the shrine. An offering on behalf of the crew of the giant who had returned his wave and a quick prayer for their safety.

Cockpit RB-58C "Marisol", 65,000 feet over Eastern Burma

From this altitude, the ASG-18 radar was giving a panoramic view for hundreds of miles in every direction. The four RB-58s were flying racetrack patterns. *Marisol* and *Tiger Lily* formed one pair, they were heading southwest, towards the three formations of B-60s far behind them. They were weaving, their paths interlocking as the turns widened their search scans. To the south, flying northeast, were *Sweet Caroline* and *Coral Queen*, also weaving to maximize their search scans and confuse the watching radars. For watching radars there were. They'd already picked up the big, long-range search set at Tengchan. There were others now, ones they hadn't seen before. Fighter control radars.

The northeast portions of the racetracks were longer than the southwest ones; that meant the RB-58s were steadily moving towards Myitkyina. *Marisol* reached the end of her southwest leg and turned northeast again, the turn pointing her nose straight at the Parrot's Beak.

"Contacts Mike, Hostiles. Three formations. Designated Bandit-One and Bandit-Two coming towards us, Bandit-Three heading south of us. Estimated speed Mach 1.2. Tentative identification, three groups of four Kawasaki Brandis. Range 180 miles closing fast, intercept course for the B-60 formations. If they aren't over the border yet, they will be in a few seconds. Whoa, they just went to Mach 2.1 must have cut in their rockets."

"They must be hoping to do a speed run past us and get to the bombers before we can catch up. Flight Control, this is *Marisol* we have twelve enemy aircraft closing fast, intercepting the bombers. We're taking them down."

"*Marisol* understood. For your information, enemy aircraft are already at least twenty miles inside Burmese territory."

"*Tiger Lily*, take the formation on the right, we'll take the left. Take'em out Bear"

In the Bear's Den, Eddie Korrina already had a GAR-9 locked on each of the formations. He selected the left-hand one and stroked the firing button of the GAR-9 system. He could feel the whirr and thump as the belly pod launcher operated, then the lurch as the GAR-9 dropped clear. That was something they'd never felt before, the simulated launches and practice shots didn't have anything like the same feel.

There was a stream of brownish-white smoke in front of them, curving up, far out of sight. It would climb up to over 100,000 feet before slashing down in a glide - if anything moving at over Mach 6 could be called gliding. Korrina and Dravar had already drawn their steel blinds, Kozlowski flipped down his black visor. Any second now....

A new star suddenly appeared in the sky, white, painful, glaring white even through the black protective visor. In the rear cockpits, even through the shields and filters, the stations turned white from the thermonuclear explosion fifty miles away. A split second later, even before the first new star had reached its full power, there was a second flash and another new star lit up the sky over Burma. There was a gap, a couple of seconds no more than that, then a third, much dimmer star, one that was marginally less painful to see, appeared. Marisol shook and rolled from the blasts, another thing they hadn't expected.

Yet, the strange thing was, 45,000 feet below the place where the fighters had died, under the black clouds of the Monsoon, nobody would know that the RB-58s had captured little pieces of the sun and unleashed them on their enemies. It showed on the radar though, there were ugly splotches where the weird electronic effects of a nuclear initiation had blanked out the radar transmissions. Under those leprous patches, twelve enemy fighters had been blotted from the sky in less than five seconds. Tengchan and the other radars would be seeing the same thing and they would know what had happened.

"Control, this is *Marisol*. Four enemy fighters destroyed with one GAR-9. One more kill and we're aces."

"Negative *Marisol*. Word from the top. Multiple kills with GAR-9s count as a single kill towards ace status. You've got four more to go. Good hunting."

A nice sentiment, but it didn't look like it. Xavier was reporting the Tengchan radar was still working but all the others were down. Kozlowski turned *Marisol* towards Tengchan then grinned as it hurriedly went off the air. It stayed off, even when *Marisol* turned away, back on her racetrack.

A few minutes later Tengchan came on again, only to shut down as soon as *Marisol* turned towards it once more. That time, it stayed shut down. The first stage of today's lesson had been delivered; challenging SAC was a very, very bad mistake. A mistake that carried a nuclear penalty.

Cockpit, B-60E "Miss Tressmine" 47,000 feet over Haipaw, Burma

"Whoa, the Ladies are throwing a Hissy Fit. Three nuclear explosions, 45,000 feet. GAR-9s. *Marisol. Tiger Lily* and *Sweet Caroline* are all claiming kills. They're reporting the Chipanese shut down air activity on the spot. Don't want their airbase nuked I assume. I'd suggest we alert Guns to get his new toy ready, just in case."

The B-60E carried the six-barreled Vulcan cannon in place of the old twin 20mm mount. Even the B-52s hadn't got those yet, they still had quadruple .50s.

General Cameron relaxed in the commander's seat. This was the second time he'd done something like this, the first one had been twelve years earlier in Paris. Then, he'd incurred the lasting hatred of every shopaholic in Europe by devastating the Champes Elysee. What his B-60s were about to do today built on that experience. Already the formation was splitting into its three sub-groups, each targeting an enemy concentration

"Bring the group around to zero-zero-five. Load up the radar picture, drop a reference bomb. Now let's hope the Ladies clear a way in for us."

Cockpit RB-58C "Marisol", 65,000 feet over Myitkyina, Northern Burma

"We have enemy radars sir, Fire Cans, nine of them. Positions dialing in now."

The number made sense, electronic reconnaissance had isolated twelve hostile fire control radars, four per enemy concentration. Three had been picked off during the reconnaissance runs. That left nine. And the RB-58s had a total of 12 AAM-N-10s. It was time to make a demonstration. This time, the anti-aircraft gunners would be in no doubt about what was killing them.

"Take 'em down. We'll hit from under the cloud cover."

Central Command Post, Triple Alliance Base, Myitkyina, Northern Burma

There was something wrong with the clouds, Major Ranjit noticed suddenly, they seemed to be boiling and spreading as if giant stones were being thrown into them. Then, four shapes burst through, big delta-winged aircraft surrounded in a ball of shimmering, shining silver. They were silent, silent as the grave, even as rockets streaked from under their bellies and curved into targets far out in the enemy hills. Then, the roar of their jets and the supersonic bangs drowned out the explosions of the missiles but the delta winged jets were already gone, climbing through the clouds, leaving eight oily smoke tracks boiling up into the sky from the enemy-held hills. The anti-aircraft guns that had remained obstinately out of reach of the Australian 25 pounders were blind.

Hill Kumon 541, West of Myitkyina, Burma.

They hadn't stood a chance. Lieutenant Wu Si Bo had guessed the bombers were doing around Mach Two when they'd blown up the other radars, way too fast for any of the guns to get a shot in. He'd yanked the power cable from his radar and shut it down as soon as he'd seen something was about to happen so his crews were alive, none of the others were so lucky. Or were they the lucky ones? One thing they were clear, they were fighting Americans now and Americans didn't fight, they destroyed. But the Shan States positions were too close to the Australian base for the Americans to drop nuclear bombs without destroying their allies as well. And they weren't that ruthless. Were they?

Cockpit, B-60E "Miss Tressmine" 47,000 feet over Myitkyina, Burma

Everything was in the hands of the K-11 radar bombsight. They had the radar pictures, they'd identified the aim points, the reference bombs had provided the corrections. Lost in all the noises of the B-60, the crews didn't hear the bomb bay doors open, but they felt the thump-thump-thump-thump as all four sets of snap-action doors opened. More than half the length of the bombers was their bomb bay. The B-60s were adjusting their positions, delicately, elegantly, their grace deceitfully denying the deadliness of what they were about to do. The intervalometers had been set, when the K-11s gave the order, they'd start to spew 500 pound bombs out of that cavernous pit. 176 per aircraft, 1,056 in total on each enemy concentration. The big bombers didn't even lurch as the stream of bombs left the bays.

Hill Kumon 541, West of Myitkyina, Burma.

Lieutenant Wu Si Bo saw something very strange. Six long black lines had emerged from the clouds and were heading steadily for him. Far over to the north he could see six more. The lines seemed to go on forever, and now they were matched by a soft, gentle but all-enveloping howl. As if a dragon was wailing defiance at them. A dragon above them.

The Dragon had been born in Paris, on the Champes Elysee. What had started out as a warning to the French not to start any opportunistic wars of conquest or revenge had turned into something else. When the targeteers had inspected the devastation, they'd quickly understood that something quite unexpected had happened. What was supposed to have been a long, snake-like path of destruction had actually been an extended egg-shape, the destruction going far beyond that anybody had expected. What was even more curious, the Arc de Triomphe had been destroyed before the last salvo of bombs had hit it.

The explanation had taken some finding, but once found it had been obvious. Each of the thousand pound bombs had landed just behind the blast and shock wave front of the one that preceded it. So, as the explosions had marched down the Champes Elysee, they'd multiplied their effects over and over again. Each bomb had built on those before it to create a piston that shattered everything in its path.

An even stranger effect had taken place behind the leading front of the piston. The consuming inferno of the explosions sucked in air from the surroundings to feed their fires. For tens of yards on either side of the blast-piston, everything was sucked towards the explosion, only to be met and hurled back again by the deadly blast waves. As the targeteers had said, it was the perfect suck-and-blow. This time, suck-and-blow would blend the six lines of bombs into a single whirling phalanx of shockwaves, fire and fragments.

The leading end of the long black line landed just over a mile away from Lieutenant Wu Si Bo, the first of over a thousand five hundred pound bombs marching westward across the jagged mountains that surrounded Myitkyina. At first, they looked like a normal series of explosions, no different from the clouds of fire and smoke that had risen over the Australian base at Myitkyina during the artillery bombardments but, as the bombs started their cavalcade of devastation across the mountains, a shining silvery-blue wall of energy, the blast piston, formed in front, hiding the horrifying carnage that was following it.

As the blast piston tore through the Chipanese position, the exquisitely beautiful shockwave smashed through everything in its path. The few things that survived the concussion wave were shredded by the whirling hailstorm of fragments and debris or burned in the roaring mass of explosions. It took only a minute for the blue-silver wall to reach Lieutenant Wu Si Bo and, to him, it seemed to approach slowly. As it neared his position, he reached out to touch it then the world burst and turned into fire.

Central Command Post, Triple Alliance Base, Myitkyina, Northern Burma

Major Ranjit was stunned beyond words. What had once been the lush, menacing green of the jungle-covered hills was now brown and bare. The trees, even the grass and bushes had been destroyed in the roaring cascade of bombs. Nothing, neither animal nor plant, could have survived.

Even as he watched, he heard a drone of engines. A transport aircraft, one with four engines, had dropped through the clouds on final approach. As it lined up with the runway, another came through the clouds, then another. Almost at the same time, there was a scream of jets, the four delta-winged bombers flew overhead, speed reduced to subsonic, goading any surviving guns into firing at them. Ranjit doubted there were any left to take up the challenge.

As they patrolled, the big transports started landing and started to disgorge the troops they were carrying. Troops, and food, and ammunition and artillery. At first Ranjit thought the troops were Ghurkas but through his binoculars he saw the short, stubby rifles with curved magazines. Thais. No matter, after 57 days, the siege of Myitkyina was over.

Chipanese Naval Headquarters, Imperial Fleet, Tokyo, Japan

Admiral Soriva knew something had happened as soon as he entered the building. The summons had been short and to the point. He was to report directly to Admiral Tameichi Hara immediately. He'd been on leave ever since he'd been relieved from command of his battleship division, and, in truth he'd never expected to be given another position in the Navy. He reminded himself, he didn't know he was receiving a posting now, he could simply being informed of his retirement. But surely, the Commander-in-Chief of the Imperial Navy wouldn't concern himself directly with that? And what was going on?

As he entered Admiral Hara's office, The CinC was reading a report. He looked up at Soriva standing before him. "You have heard what has happened?"

Soriva shook his head. For three months, he'd carefully avoided reading anything or seeing anything. He'd been trying to regain some sort of inner peace after the fiasco of his last mission. Poor Idzumo might have had a better deal after all. He was at peace now.

"After the Americans forced us to abort your naval movement, Masanobu Tsuji put a back-up plan into action. Tsuji took three divisions of the Imperial Army, including the Imperial Guard, and deployed them in Northern Burma as a purported insurgency force. There was a ragtag of local tribes with them as local color but the force was Japanese. His authority to make such a deployment was highly questionable, that is one thing that is being investigated now. One thing is not questionable. The Triple Alliance asked the Americans for help and produced proof that the so-called Shan States Army was really Japanese regulars. As a result, the Americans obliged, in return for some substantial political and economic concessions of course. The Australians had precipitated the situation, by placing a full regiment of their division where it was vulnerable to a concentration of our forces in Northern Burma. The Americans obliterated our forces with their bombers.

Soriva shuddered, his mind filled with the pictures of orange-red mushroom clouds rising over the troops. Would the same be happening to Japan? "They used nuclear weapons?"

"Not against our troops, no. As you know, the whole crux of Tsuji's plan was to create a situation where we would fight the enemy on their territory and intermingled amongst them. Under those circumstances, the Americans would not be able to use nuclear weapons on what amounted to their own territory and their own people. Tsuji was convinced that Americans would be unable to fight without using their nuclear bombers and so this strategy offered a way of beating them without risking destruction. However, it appears he fundamentally miscalculated.

"The Americans hit our troops with conventional bombs but in such numbers and with such violence that they might as well have nuked us. Few of our troops survived, those that did will never be of any use to anybody. They are all deaf, some are insane, others have had their sense of balance destroyed. The Americans did use nuclear weapons against our fighters though; a squadron of Army Kawasakis that tried to intercept the American bombers was incinerated in mid-air.

"Admiral Soriva, I can think of no set of circumstances that could do more to thoroughly vindicate the actions you took when faced by American bombers. Tsuji's rashness and arrogance throw your own judgment and good sense into sharp relief.

"His Imperial Majesty was most perturbed by news of the destruction of our forces and wrote an Imperial Rescript expressing his deep concern to Colonel Tsuji."

"Ah so that pest is dead then?" Any officer receiving such a Rescript would commit suicide on the spot.

"Not that one. Reportedly, he denounced it as a forgery and has disappeared somewhere into Western China. In the meantime, The Triple Alliance had consolidated its hold on Northern Burma and is undoing his work there. To make matters worse, the insurgency in Vietnam and Laos grows worse by the day. Admiral Soriva, Japan is being stretched on the rack.

"Which brings us to the subject of this meeting today. I am assigning you to a newly-created post within Imperial Naval Headquarters. The post is Head of the Navy Strategic Planning Directorate. You will report directly to me. Your duties will be to examine, in great detail, the strategic position of Japan, establish our naval priorities and determine what assets will be required to meet those requirements.

"The Army is establishing a similar position to examine Army priorities and the two of you will be required to work together. Failure by either of you will be considered to be a failure of you both. The future structure of the fleet will be based upon your decisions just as the future of the Army will be based on those of your counterpart. Whatever is superfluous to our needs will be scrapped to fund our real requirements.

"I am giving you a very heavy responsibility Admiral. Do not let me down. And please, do not delay in starting this task."

Cockpit, B-60E "Flying Fiasco" U-Thapao, Thailand

Lieutenant C.J. O'Seven looked at the cockpit of the aircraft, his stomach sinking. Had his family's fabled luck deserted him? It had all started when his grandparents had come ashore at Ellis Island. Their family name, Ossenvierneira, had been beyond the spelling ability of the Irish-American immigration officer who'd shortened it to O'Seven. As immigrants they'd done well and prospered.

Charles John O'Seven had made it into the Air Force, trained on B-60s and his crew been picked as a reserve for this deployment. Then, he'd been given a shot at *Flying Fiasco*. The Colonel had been honest, she was a hard-luck ship with a history of minor accidents, aborts and generally sub-standard performance. She was a challenge, turn her around and O'Seven would get Captain's Bars years earlier than otherwise. Fail and it would be a black mark that would really hurt.

He'd jumped at the challenge, grabbed the chance and now regretted it. *Flying Fiasco* was a B-60E, only three years old, yet she looked like an aircraft that had seen a decade of hard service. The paint was battered and scraped, the seats and worktables chipped and stained. Worse, not all the damage was wear and tear, some was deliberate, there was graffiti scratched into the paint and cigarette burns that looked intentional rather than careless. Hell, nobody was supposed to smoke on the flight deck anyway. But it wasn't just the mess. There was a sullen, resentful attitude in the cockpit. It had been there since he'd climbed in.

"OK guys, everybody find your station and we'll start to clean her up. Make notes of any damage and we'll try to patch it up. Chief, how did she get this way?"

"Ground crews tried to keep her neat Sir, but they gave up in the end. They can only do so much. They kept her running mechanically well, you know even after the abort yesterday, we couldn't find anything wrong with her. But her crew just didn't care. I'll get some cleaning stuff, Sir and a couple of men to start work on your station."

"Chief, I think you misheard me. I said 'everybody find their station and start cleaning,' not 'everybody except me find their station and start cleaning.'"

The Chief grinned and O'Seven realized he'd just passed a little test.

"The cleaning supplies are good idea, can we also get the right paint so we can touch up all this damage? Another thing, that name outside, it isn't fitting for an aircraft. Can you remove it? That we would appreciate some help with."

"Yes sir, that paint's hard to get off, but we'll strip it. Have you selected a new name for her?"

O'Seven thought for a moment. "How about *Honey Pot*? With some artwork of a sexy blonde rolling dice, five and two showing?" He reached into his wallet and took out a twenty "I understand that's the standing fee for nose art."

The Chief was marveling. A young officer who didn't mind getting his hands dirty. One for the books. "No Sir, this one's on the house. And, Sir, I think I know something else that might help. If you'll excuse me."

O'Seven got on his knees and crawled under the seat, there was debris under there, papers and just plain dirt and junk. Obviously, the previous crew, now on their way to Alaska, or so he'd heard, had just tossed trash around. That could explain some of the malfunctions. Silver foil from a cigarette package could play hell with electronics if it got to the wrong place. He heard steps behind him.

"Get me a bag for all this garbage and tell the guys to be on the look-out for debris that's found its way to places it shouldn't."

"Yes Sir" said General Dedmon dryly.

"General, Sir, I'm sorry, I didn't, I thought you we, I mean, oh hell, sir. Please be merciful and kill me quickly."

"At ease Lieutenant. Status?"

"Sir you wanted us to take her out in 24 hours. I request we stay for at least another 24 beyond that. I want to have a blitz on cleaning her and fixing her up. You know how it is Sir, once started, if we have to stop, we never quite get back in the swing again. Can we have 48 hours?"

"We're clearing the base in 72 hours. You'll have to be gone by then. You'll have to bring the ground crew back with you as well. I see they're scraping the old nose art off?"

"Yes Sir. Change the name, change the luck."

Dedmon nodded. "Wise move. Good luck Lieutenant. After what happened yesterday, the B-60 is going to be around for quite a bit longer than we'd thought. And may be working a lot harder than we'd thought. Fly High Lieutenant."

O'Seven had just started to relax when the Chief returned with four Thai girls, wearing coveralls, their hair tied back under scarves. "Lieutenant, these ladies have been helping keep the base and hangars clean, they've been cleared for working here. They'll clean the decks and bulkheads and the other traffic areas for you. They're paid from base funds, per diem and meals."

"Meals Chief? Proper portions I hope, not left-overs."

"Sir!" The chief appeared genuinely offended. "The ladies eat as guests of the Sergeant's Mess, Sir."

Privately, the Chief gave O'Seven another tick of approval, most young officers wouldn't have thought to check that point.

"Buckets of hot water, soap, bleach and brushes coming up Sir. If your people lower the dirty water out of the nosewheel bay, we'll dump and refill for you. My people will be cleaning up the outside. Paint will be here this afternoon. Also, sir, we have some leather coming up, you can buy real good leather here. Once it arrives, the ladies will try and repair the seats as best they can for you. Oh yes, and sir? I got some coveralls for you and your crew to wear. This is going to be a long, dirty job."

Lieutenant C.J. O'Seven started stuffing debris from around the aircraft commander's seat into a trash bag. Then he stopped and ran his hand along the instrument panel. "Don't worry *Honey Pot*," he whispered "We'll get you looking real nice again."

Twinnge, On The Mandalay - Myitkyina Road, Burma

After almost two months of smelling rotting jungle and foul mud, the odor of freshly-laid tar was a blessed relief. The Indian Engineer battalion had reached them the night before, now they were just finishing putting blacktop on the reconstructed road to Mandalay. Two more companies of the battalion were hard at work building a new bridge over the Irawaddy.

Captain Golconda wouldn't be taking what was left of his convoy up to Myitkyina though, there wasn't enough of it to make the effort worthwhile. Two months of mortar fire and probing attacks had seen to that. Instead, his unit would become a guard detachment for the bridge that was now going up and would start to secure the area.

General Moses would have apoplexy if he read the operational guidance for that. He'd been a great one for taking the fight to the enemy, for offensive patrolling of the jungle to search for and destroy enemy units. All that had gone.

Now, the orders were, go to the villages, make friends with the local population, guard them against the guerrillas. Cut the guerrillas off from the villages, leave them in the jungle. If we control the people, the guerrillas can have the jungle, given time it will kill them all. Remember the golden rule. Fifteen percent of the people support you, 15 percent support the enemy, seventy percent just want to live in peace. So if your presence means that they will live in peace, those seventy percent will be your supporters.

His men had done well, Golconda thought, few could have done better. They'd held here for two months until relieved. Just like dozens of small outposts up and down the road. The Australian Expeditionary Force had won laurels in this campaign, even if the strategic concepts had been a bit misdirected.

There were lessons to be learned certainly, and faults to be put right. A new infantry rifle was one of them, it hadn't escaped his notice that as many of his men as had the chance had dumped their Lee-Enfields in favor of Chipanese Arisakas. But, there was much to be proud of as well. Much to be proud of.

Captain's Bridge, INS Hood, Mumbai

Every so often, a Captain got orders that were a real pleasure to obey. This was one of them. A string of signals had arrived over the last few hours, all of them good. The first had told him that the orders to decommission and scrap *Hood* had been reversed. Then, a second set had instructed him to prepare his ship for sea, he was to take *Hood* to the United Kingdom and return her to the Royal Navy.

Apparently, the British were setting up a naval history center in Portsmouth and had requested that *Hood* be sold to them as the centerpiece. She'd be joining some other famous ships there, including *Victory* and *Warrior*. The request had come with a note from the Americans attached, stating that they would consider the donation of *Hood* to the new Naval History Center 'a friendly act'. They'd even offered one of their decommissioned battleships to India for breaking up so Indian industry wouldn't suffer from the loss of scrap steel.

Even better, he'd got permission to bring his wife Indira and their children along on the trip. He'd left Great Britain almost 20 year ago and had never been back since. It would be interesting to see what had become of the old country. By all accounts, Britain was recovering fast, the long years of privation following the war were fading away as prosperity returned. Idly, Ladone wondered what had happened to the family properties in England. He was the only surviving child, his brother and sister had both died in the war and he had heard nothing from the rest of the clan.

Still, he'd be able to show his wife his original country and give his children some idea of where the rest of their roots lay. They'd have a chance for good tour before they came back home. He had the money saved, Indian Navy salaries were far from princely but Indira came from a wealthy family and they had always had that to fall back on. He could go to a British pub again, see Trafalgar Square and the Tower of London where Halifax had been executed. And, he'd get a chance to have some sausages, the one thing he truly missed in India. Sometimes, Captain Jim Ladone had thought he would kill for a decent British sausage.

Petrograd, Russia

Brides always looked beautiful, they couldn't help it. The wedding dress had arrived safely and been altered to fit Klavdia Efremovna Kalugina. Now, she was standing next to Tony Evans in it. Tonight, a seamstress would adjust it again, and tomorrow, another bride would get to wear a proper wedding dress on her marriage day. Tony was in Marine Dress Blues and there was an honor guard for the couple. The decision to stay in Russia had been both hard and easy. Hard because he would be living in a strange country, easy because he'd be living there with Klavdia.

He'd already started a prospering business in Petrograd, it turned out that pizza was the perfect restaurant meal for a country that lacked money yet sought something exotic to take away the memory of two decades of privation. His restaurants in Petrograd were crowded and he'd be opening one in Moscow soon. To get the raw materials in from the countryside, he'd started a road transport business using surplus army trucks and that was prospering as well.

And he would be going home soon, for a visit, to introduce Klavdia to his home town and his family. Their children would be brought up as Kaluginas because there was nobody else in her family left to carry on the name but there were plenty of other Evans family members in South Carolina.

Their visit would coincide with the start of the deer-hunting season. In a state where the first day of deer-hunting season was a universal holiday, anybody who could shoot like Klavdia would be a local heroine within hours. Evans listened to the Eastern Orthodox wedding ceremony going on around him and decided he was a very fortunate man.

Ossetia, Georgia, Russia

A hundred kilometers to go, perhaps a little more. His column was still moving, his surviving army units on the outside, fighting off the attacks of Russian Army units, bandits and anything else that threatened, the civilians and supplies and everything that couldn't fight in the center. A whole country on the move, looking for sanctuary, looking for a place they could survive. Right in the middle of his column were his precious technicians, the ones with the expertise to design and build biological and chemical warfare production plants. They were his passport to sanctuary.

When he'd started, Model had found himself with a column of more than 70,000 people, twice as many as he'd expected. He had about half that number now, and that included some more that had joined him on the march out. The first hundred kilometers had been the worst, his attempt to divert Russian attention away from his break-out had failed. The Russian sturmoviks, the Sukhois and the twin-engined Ilyushins, had slashed at his column day and night, ripping at it with their rockets and burning it with jellygas.

They'd made it to the mountains though, and in doing so traded one source of misery for another. The mountains had killed almost as many people as the Sturmoviks. Cold, rock falls, the impossibility of keeping the column properly screened on the narrow, twisting paths through the mountains. They'd made it through though, and debouched from the mountains just north of Tbilsi. Now, it was a straight march to the border with Iran.

The ground was smooth, the land rich and there was plenty of food. The Russian Frontal Aviation was the wrong side of the mountains and their sturmoviks were out of range. Even better, word had spread from Iran, the column was protected by The Caliphate. As a result, the local people were helping them on their way south. They brought food, and medical attention and guides to show the best routes and avoid the worst traps. More importantly, they warned Model of any threats.

They were over the worst now. His people would survive. Despite the best efforts of the Russians, his people had survived. As he walked south, picking them up and laying them down, the age-old infantryman's step, Model laughed. He'd beaten the Russians again.

EPILOGUE

Ayuthia Road, Bangkok, Thailand - Six Months Later

Even at mid-day the roads were jammed and travel by car was a time-consuming process. Then again, there wasn't much choice. Still, the limousine had finally pulled away from the Palace, the agreements that had resolved the crisis, at last signed and in place. In the back, Sir Martyn Sharpe, Sir Eric Haohoa and the Ambassador relaxed, the strains of the last year lifted. The Ambassador opened the bar in the car and poured out drinks. Sir Martyn was looking out the window, enjoying the bustle of the city but Sir Eric was troubled. Eventually, he broke the companionable silence.

"What did it all mean Ambassador? What did we achieve? It seems so much effort, so much work, so many people killed and for what? A few small adjustments on a map? A few changes in the ways we do things?"

The Ambassador looked thoughtful. "On one level perhaps you are right. What we have achieved seems little perhaps. But things never are solved with a great flash and a magnificent stroke of genius. Only in novels does a wonderful achievement by the hero solve the problem and change everything for ever. It is rarely the case that a situation like this ends with an absolute victory. If we think on the implications of this, we can see why. If every such crisis was continued to an absolute end then they would be fought using absolute methods. We all have Germany to remind us of the terrible end that lies on that path.

"Instead, we resolve situations like this by increments. We agree that we can end a situation in a way that everybody can live with. We recognize a change in the balance of power by adjusting the outward appearance of that power. Changes are small, a little is achieved here, a little there. Some ground is lost here, a deadlock is the result there. And over the years, small things add up to a surge that cannot be stopped. History is bigger than any of us Sir Eric, the momentum of history is so great that one person can rarely make a great difference.

"That is why we call it The Great Game. At most we who play The Great Game can make only a small ripple in the passage of time, a minor deviation in the great river of events. We play our hands in The Great Game and in doing so we give the flow of history a nudge here, a small prod there and herd things a little in the direction we want to go. And that is what has happened now.

"Today, the Triple Alliance is a little stronger than it was. We have shed blood, our own and that of others, together, we have shed blood for each other. We have had our mettle tested and we have each seen we can depend upon the others. A potentially serious weakness in our organization and procedures has been revealed and dealt with. Our new Permanent Military Council will ensure that operations are properly planned and evaluated before our forces are committed. The Seer was right, our attempts to conduct military operations without clearly defined command authority was a recipe for disaster. We made a mistake and it has cost us dearly. We must make certain we do not repeat it.

"More good news is that a shaky part of our territory has been shored up and supported. Burma is more stable now as a result of our actions. Burma is now independent yet has become a member of ASEAN so is still a part of our alliance. That is the best of both worlds. Also, we have tied the Americans a little more to us. This crisis saw the Americans commit their military in our support. In doing so they forced the Chipanese to take a step back. The American B-60s broke the back of the Shan States Army and that buys us time to rebuild the country and bring it under a firm rule.

"As a result, Chipan is a little weaker than it was. There is more dissent between the Army and the Navy and they are having more trouble with the insurgencies in their country. The insurgency they face in Indo-China is growing with every month that passes and their pre-occupation with Burma means they have done little to counter it. The Vietnamese People's Liberation Army is well established now and rooting it out will be a major undertaking. Frankly, I doubt that Chipan can do it, their resources are more stretched and their commitments are greater then ever before.

"Most importantly, Masanobu Tsuji's plots have been exposed and he has lost face. Not for the first time I might add. His influence is weakened and that means that more reasonable people have a chance to make their voices heard. It is our understanding that more and more officers in the Chipanese armed forces are protesting against Masanobu Tsuji's grand designs and extravagant plots. They suggest it is time for Chipan to take stock of their capabilities and resources and scale their ambitions down to match their real abilities.

"But all of these developments are double-sided. The insurgency war in Burma has not ended, the Shan States Army was a reflection of real problems and real desires. They have been pushed back certainly, crippled, probably but not destroyed. They will have to go back to the initial stages of an insurgency and start over. Having learned lessons, they will do better next time.

"On our part, we now owe the Americans a serious debt and they will collect on it. Sooner I hope, rather than later, I do not wish to have that indebtedness hanging over our heads. The Chipanese have benefited from their failure also; if they listen to their voices that call for a cut-back of commitments and a reduction of imperial overstretch, they may yet come out of this stronger than they went in.

"The Americans have benefited also, they have shown once again that their bombers can go where they wish and do what they want. If anybody doubted that they could do so, such doubts have been dispelled. They have tested out some of their new doctrines and evaluated their new technologies. I tried to get The Seer to admit that was why they helped us but failed in that. It is a pity because admitting they had interests beyond supporting us would have reduced the debt we owe them.

"They have benefited politically as well. The tragic accident, and it really was an accident, there is no doubt of that, which befell John F Kennedy has given President LeMay a second term in office." She paused slightly, she know Sir Eric believed she had been responsible for Kennedy's death even though she had not, it really had been a genuine accident, driving too fast on a wet road. "By the time of the next American election, the momentum of American policy will be so set that no radical changes will be possible. That is to the benefit of us all, of course. The one thing the world does not need now is a weak-willed or unstable America.

"America has done something else that is also very important for them. There were those who believed that America would only fight with nuclear weapons so if they could create a situation where such weapons could not be used, then America would be helpless. That was the calculation that lay at the heart of Masanobu Tsuji's planning. He attempted to use an insurgency to create a situation where we could be attacked without inviting American reprisals.

"For as long as the situation remained an insurgency, the Americans stayed uninvolved but when the Chipanese escalated the situation to involve their regular forces, the Americans acted. First they warned off the Chipanese Navy, then they destroyed the Chipanese regular units around Myitkyina. By using conventional rather than nuclear weapons on the Shan States Army, they demonstrated to the world that, while destroying enemies with nuclear weapons was their preferred option, they would use other solutions if the situation demanded. But their use of nuclear air-to-air missiles demonstrated that attacking SAC always brings about a nuclear response and that when SAC is around, nuclear weapons are always on the table as a viable threat.

"The big winner over the last year has been Russia of course. They have peace now for the first time in almost twenty years. They now have their territory back under their own control yet their victory is also a matter of shading and degree. Their economy is wrecked, their country needs decades to rebuild and their casualties are beyond counting. Life will be hard in Russia for decades yet that too is a matter of degree. For where there is such hardship and such great tasks, there are also great opportunities for those with the wisdom to see them and the strength to take them. I think Russia will be the stronger for this ordeal but that strength will not be seen in your lifetimes.

"Even the military results are shaded. Field Marshal Model is leading his people out to the south, it is a military achievement that few other commanders could equal. Model may be a most hateful person but he is one hell of a fighting soldier. And he has left the Russians with the problem of southern provinces bubbling over with war and rebellion.

"Our real enemy has been exposed also. The Russians releasing their report on the rise of The Caliphate have done us all a great service and we owe them a debt of honor that we must repay. The view The Caliphate has of the world, the kind of society they wish to introduce and their attitude to everybody who does not share their beliefs are all deeply disturbing. It is indeed most fortunate that we have been warned of the danger The Caliphate poses years before their emergence causes a situation that will be critical.

"So now we have time to plan, to make our first moves and to start the long process of deflecting history in our favor. The extra time the Russians have given us means we can plan properly and we can make small changes now that will bear great fruit in years to come. These will have more time to bring about their effects and will remove the need to make larger and more dangerous changes later. This must be our priority for the next few years, The Caliphate must not be allowed to grow in strength. They are being dealt their hand in The Great Game now and our part of the Game is to guess what cards they hold and work out how they will play them.

"Sir Eric, we have gained much this year. A shade here, a shade there, but adding up to a significant gain for us. One that will be apparent when the histories are written. This time, we have played our hand in The Great Game well and the balance of forces in the world has shifted in our favor. But in truth nobody has finally won or finally lost. Another hand in The Great Game is being dealt and we must wait to see what the cards will hold for us. The Great Game never ends, my friends, it existed before we were ever born and will go on long after you are dead.

"Sir Eric, Sir Martyn, may I make a suggestion? We are in the courtyard of the Supreme Command Headquarters Building now. Although being appointed Chairman of our Permanent Military Council is a great honor, it means I have work that cannot wait. May I suggest you visit our National Museum? It has many treasures and exhibits of life in the past here. Few visitors to our country go there so the material on the exhibits is in our language only but the guides will be happy to help you and speak about what you see."

"Why thank you Ma'am, that sounds a delightful way to spend the afternoon."

The Ambassador got out of the car and spoke quickly to the driver before vanishing into the building. The official limousine drove a few yards and stopped outside the Museum. Inside, it was cool and peaceful, the air filled with the slight yet unmistakable odor of very old things carefully preserved. The two visitors lost track of time wandering around looking at the range of displays.

Unlike most museums, it didn't concentrate on the lives of the wealthy and powerful but also contained exhibits of the life of commoners, of the tools the craftsmen used, the clothes they wore and how they passed the time when their labors were completed. At each point, somebody would step forward and quietly explain what was being shown and fill them in on the background to the exhibit. The guides were students who were doing research work at the museum and helping out visitors was a secondary role for them. As a result, they lacked the smooth patter of professional guides but made up for it by being genuinely interested in their subjects and pleased to share knowledge with other people who shared that interest.

As the visitors went around the building they were absorbed by a richness of a history they had hardly known existed. The museum was laid out in a grid so that, walking around one way, visitors were gently lead through all the different aspects of life at varying points in the country's history. By changing direction they could follow the development of a single aspect of society as it changed through the centuries. They ended in an art gallery, full of paintings of Kings and Queens and courtiers. They varied in quality but some were extraordinarily lifelike, so much so that the figures seemed to leap off the canvas and take possession of the room.

"Eric, look at this." Sir Martyn's voice was urgent. Sir Eric joined him in front of a large painting, one of the largest in the display. In common with all the others, it was centered around the King and Queen, sitting in the middle, the noblemen and noblewomen of the court gathered beneath them. This painting was different though, for standing behind the King's Throne was a woman, her hand on the back of the throne itself. The symbology of the picture was overpowering, clearly showing the importance and status of the woman.

As Sir Eric looked closely he realized it was the Ambassador. The painter had caught her appearance perfectly, somehow even managing to suggest that, despite the expression on her face, nobody could possibly know what she was thinking. The hands, the stance, the painter had caught everything. The picture was almost frighteningly lifelike, so much so that Sir Eric felt if he spoke to the picture, he would hear a reply from the familiar contralto voice.

"I don't recognize the King, it must be King Ananda. He died in 1946. What a beautiful painting."

"Can I help you sirs?" One of the guides had seen their interest in the picture and come to speak with them.

"We were just admiring this superb painting, and the lady in the background."

"Ah sir, that is the King's Personal Ambassador, a very famous person in our country. Many are the tales told of her brilliant achievements as a soldier and as a diplomat. She is an inspiration to all the women of our country."

"Excuse my ignorance but I do not recognize His Most Gracious Majesty in this picture. Is it King Ananda?"

The girl broke out laughing, the sound echoing the notes of wind-chimes in a gentle evening breeze. "Excuse me sir, but no. That is King Ramkhamhaeng. This painting is more than three hundred years old."

THE END

Printed in the United States
105944LV00005B/36/P

9 781435 704428